A Time-Travel Romance

Spellbound

Patricia Simpson

Lucky Publishing
United States of America

Other Books by Patricia Simpson

Whisper of Midnight
The Legacy
Raven in Amber
Lord of Forever
The Haunting of Brier Rose
The Night Orchid
Lord of the Nile (Purrfect Love Anthology)
The Lost Goddess
Mystic Moon
Just Before Midnight
Jade
The Dark Lord
The Dark Horse

Visit Patricia Simpson's Website

www.patriciasimpson.com

Note: This is a work of fiction. All the characters and events portrayed in this book are either products of the author's imagination or are used fictitiously.

Spellbound

ISBN 0-9823442-4-4
EAN 978-0-9823442-4-8

To Beth and Kay,

who hung on through the many iterations of this book,

to my mother, June, who has a keen eye for detail,

and to my daughter, Camille, who encouraged me.

Chapter 1

Scotland, October 2008

"David!" Tara clutched the armrest of the Jaguar sedan as they roared into oncoming traffic outside Glasgow Airport. She was unaccustomed to seeing cars approach on the right, and the sight unnerved her. But she was even more unnerved by David's brusque manner. They'd been apart for more than a week, and he'd given her only a brief kiss and hug after she'd cleared customs. "Do you have to drive so fast?"

"I'm not driving that fast!"

She glanced at his profile. "Is there something wrong?"

He gave her a terse smile. "Of course not. Just stressed. Sorry if I snapped, Tare."

Tara sat back and tried to relax, but her shoulders felt as tight as stone. Maybe David was experiencing the same doubts she was and just didn't want to admit it.

He'd asked her to marry him in the heat of the moment a month ago—and facing her thirty-fifth birthday in December—she'd said yes. So here she was, racing through the Ayrshire rain to Corbin Hall, the Scottish family estate of her fiancé, the place where she would become David Corbin's wife.

Every time she thought about becoming his wife, Tara felt a rush of claustrophobia. It wasn't just the idea of marrying David that made her panic. It was marrying anyone. She couldn't imagine vowing to stay with someone until death did them part. She hadn't met a man yet who'd inspired such loyalty in her. Not even David.

Tara looked over at David as he answered his cell phone for the fourth time in the last half hour. She glanced at his thinning chestnut hair that he'd soon have to buzz cut instead of spike. She let her gaze wander over his slight frame and narrow face. He wasn't the most handsome man in the world, and he didn't make her heart go pitter pat with happiness, but that was all right with her. She wasn't the type of woman to get swept off her feet by a man's appearance anyway.

She knew she had trust issues, especially with men. But David had entered her world from the sidelines, which had allowed her to lower her guard with him. When he'd been hired as her cohost on *Fact or Fiction*, they'd both been in relationships. Over the seven months she'd known him, she'd grown to enjoy his outgoing personality on the show, never expecting their banter to morph into anything more serious. But when their relationships both failed, they turned to each other for solace. And six months later, he'd proposed.

She had come to believe that for her, David was as good as it was going to get.

"Good," David said into the phone, his Scottish accent barely noticeable. "We'll do the episode shots as soon as you get here, and then the wedding on Saturday. Hire a local with tons of lights. The place is like a cave!"

Tara jerked to attention. Shots? Wedding? Tons of lights? She stared at David, demanding that he look at her.

"What's going on?" she asked. As far as she was concerned, the wedding was to be a private affair. No paparazzi and no fans. David had agreed to a quiet ceremony.

David winked at her and looked away. "The future Mrs. Corbin is asking for details," he said into the phone, most likely to Chris Gable, their director. "You know how she is." He gave the dry chuckle she'd come to recognize as his way of masking his innate nervousness.

Tara came to full attention at his words. No, how *was* she? Was her behavior part of an inside joke with the crew? Apparently Chris was in on the joke, because David laughed again. His small, gray eyes crinkled at their corners.

"You've got that right," David said, rolling his eyes.

"David!" Tara exclaimed. "What's going on?"

"I'll have to get back to you, Chris," David began, and then paused to listen to the voice on the other end of the phone.

"Hang up!" Tara mouthed, pointing at the phone and glaring at him.

He glanced at her, grimacing.

"Hang up!"

They'd promised each other to leave their jobs behind until after the honeymoon, but David had only stuck to the agreement for a few minutes. Finally, he jabbed the call off, but kept the phone in his hand, always at the ready.

"David, what in the world is going on?"

Still holding the phone, he grabbed her wrist with two of his fingers and gave her a squeeze. "I've come up with a killer idea, Tara."

"Really? Like turning your phone off for a week—and I mean really off?"

"Funny." He smirked at her and then switched his attention back to the rainy road. "No, when I say killer idea, I mean *killer*."

"So what is it?"

"Well, first off, you remember how I told you about my uncle's property?"

"That it's been in the family for centuries?"

"Yes. But more to the point, there's an old castle on the estate. One of the oldest in Scotland. Nothing more than a ruin, actually."

"I take it this is the dark place?"

"Yes. But here's the cool thing, Tara. Castle Corbin is supposedly haunted. By a ghost. By the Lady in Green."

"You never mentioned that."

"I know. I'd completely forgotten until an old friend of mine reminded me when I got here the other day. And the even cooler thing is, this Lady in Green shows up at a certain time of year—every year—like clockwork."

"And when is that?"

"October 11th."

"The day of our wedding."

David raised his eyebrows at her. "Exactly!"

"You're telling me, David Corbin," Tara said, trying to keep her voice level, "that you want to turn our wedding into a *Fact or Fiction* episode?"

"Exactly!" He slapped the steering wheel with his free hand. "It's genius! I'm a frickin' genius, Tare!"

He squeezed her wrist again and grinned, his enthusiasm filling up his side of the car. Obviously he hadn't noticed the icy cloud that had descended upon the passenger side. He was like that when obsessed by an idea—totally self-absorbed.

"You're going to turn our wedding ceremony into a television show," she added. "A circus."

"I knew you would say that!"

"But you went ahead and made arrangements anyway?"

"Hell, yes! Most of the crew is coming to the wedding anyway. We can kill two birds with one stone, Tare. And once the episode airs, Castle Corbin will be famous—which will bring in some tourist bucks for my uncle."

"No," Tara said.

"No to what?"

"No to the whole idea. You promised we'd have a quiet wedding, David, and that's what I want. Only a few people. Me in a white dress. And you in a church."

"Fine. Castle Corbin has a chapel."

"I thought you said it was a ruin."

"It is, but its chapel will make a great backdrop. You'll see." He glanced at her. "Besides that, there's one other thing."

"What?"

"I didn't want to tell you and ruin the trip."

"Tell me." She crossed her arms. "You know how I hate being in the dark."

"Our ratings have slipped again. I had a conference call with the producers yesterday. They think we need more woo-woo and less science."

"More spectacle, you mean."

"They said it, not me." He took both hands off the wheel for a moment and shrugged.

Tara frowned. "So not only do we make the show more of a spectacle, we make a spectacle of ourselves, too."

He shot her a smile. "You have to admit a televised version of you and me getting married will snag a ton of viewers."

"No!"

"It could save the show, Tara. Save our careers!"

"David, are you listening to me?" Tara clutched his arm. "I don't want our wedding aired on national television!"

David jerked away just as the car hit a particularly nasty curve. Taken off guard, he slammed on the brakes. Without so much as a squeal of tires, the Jaguar slid sideways. David dropped his phone and grabbed the wheel with both hands while Tara jammed down an imaginary brake on the floorboard. But neither of them could keep the sedan from hydroplaning off the wet asphalt. Tara screamed David's name as the car sailed over the edge of the road and plunged down an embankment. The

Jag hit the rocky slope, crushing the grill and shattering the windows, and then rolled end-over-end and crashed into something hard a hundred feet down a glen. She felt a sharp sensation in her leg, a rush of cold air, and then everything went black.

Chapter 2

Tara awoke to pain glowing in her ankle and David's worried face hovering over her. She lay on a hard surface, her senses swirling, her face and hands stinging.

"Tara, thank God!" he exclaimed, brushing away wet tendrils of hair that were plastered to her cheek. "You're alive!"

"Just," she gasped. She glanced at his slender face. He looked pale, but then his fair Gaelic skin always looked pale to her. "Are you okay?"

"Yeah, but Jesus, Tara, you could have gotten us killed! What were you trying to do, for Christ's sake?"

"I was trying to get your attention," she retorted, amazed that David had just accused her of causing the accident.

"Well you certainly got it all right." He clenched his jaw and bent to assess her physical condition.

Tara bit back the outrage she felt at being blamed for the wreck. Had David been more careful—if he hadn't been speeding and self-absorbed—she wouldn't be lying half-dead at the bottom of a ravine. But if she allowed herself to blow up, she might say more than she meant to, things she could never retract. She took a deep breath, knowing how close she was to using David's recklessness as a reason to ditch him and their life together, just as she had found a reason to ditch every relationship she'd ever had when the old claustrophobia set in.

She held her breath and remained silent until the flames of her anger subsided. She was determined that her relationship with David would be successful. She was thirty-five years old. Her biological clock was ticking—faster every year—and the older she got the fewer eligible men crossed her path. It wasn't every day she was going to meet a man as well suited to her as David Corbin, and she knew it. In fact, one day, should David's uncle remain childless, David would become Lord Corbin, and she would be his lady.

Lady Corbin. Heady stuff for a girl who had grown up in the backwoods of Tennessee. And she did love David in her own stunted way. She was sure of it.

Tara ran a dry tongue across her lips while David checked out her leg. Her body ached all over. Her clothes were soaked. How long had she lain unconscious in the rain? The ground beneath her hips felt unusually hard, and then she realized she must be in a cave of some kind, protected from the torrent of rain and wind outside. When David lifted her right leg, she cried out.

"Looks like your ankle is swollen," he commented, staring down at her. "But it isn't black and blue. That's a good sign."

She struggled to raise her shoulders so she could look down the length of her body, but David pressed her back.

"Don't move. You might have internal injuries." He urged her back down. "Where's your phone? Mine's not working. And I've got to call for help."

"It's in my purse."

David glanced around. Then he swore under his breath. "I'll see if I can find it. You wait here. Don't move."

Move? She had no intention of moving. She doubted she could even stand up.

Gently he placed her leg back on the stone floor, scrambled to his feet, and limped out of the cave. Within seconds, his dark shape was engulfed by the storm. Tara fought back a surge of frustration. She wasn't accustomed to being the weak one or being left behind.

She sat up. Maybe there was something she could use for a crutch. She looked around, surprised to discover she wasn't in a cave after all. David had carried her just inside the entry of a small stone chamber, no more than twelve by twelve feet. The structure was old, its walls spotted with lichen, its corners draped in cobwebs.

She squinted, allowing her eyes to adjust to the gloom behind her, and was startled to see the outlines of what looked to be a sarcophagus against the far wall, with a stone effigy of a knight on top. She could just make out two stone feet crossed at the ankles, the edge of a long sword, the rise of a shoulder, and the studded curve of a medieval helm.

"David!" she cried, not all that crazy about lying next to a dead person.

David came running, her too-flat purse hanging from one hand and something else in his other. "What's wrong?" he asked.

"This place is a tomb! I'm in a crypt!"

David shot a quick glance around the chamber, as if seeing it for the first time. "It's a crypt all right, but at least it's dry."

"Get me out of here, David. Please!"

"I will, I will. Don't panic!"

"Call 9-9-9!"

"I can't. I couldn't find your god damn phone in this shitty rain."

"It's in my purse." She nodded at the bag he held out. "There, in the outside pocket."

"No, it isn't. Stuff went everywhere when the car rolled, including your phone." He plopped the empty purse on the floor beside her shoulder. "And it's a fucking jungle out there. The place is covered with brambles!"

That explained her scratched hands and face. David must have carried her through a patch of briers.

"What about the Psalter?"

"I did find that." He held out a small box clutched in his other hand.

"Thank goodness!" She took the sandalwood box from him and carefully brushed away the dirt that smudged one corner. Just touching the Psalter's protective box settled her jangled nerves. Gently, she nestled it in her purse.

"But I'll never find your phone out there, Tara."

"So what do we do?"

"I'll have to go for help." When he saw the look of protest on her face, he held up both hands. "Don't worry. It's not far. Only a couple of miles, at most."

Alarm flared through her. "David, don't even think about leaving me here." It took every shred of her self-control to keep from grabbing his pant leg. "This place has a creep factor of ten out of ten."

"Don't tell me you're afraid of the dark," David chided, straightening. "Not Tara Lewis."

"Of course I'm not." She swallowed more fear back, determined not to let it show. "But there might be wild animals around."

"Maybe a highland cow. That's about as wild an animal as you'll get. Don't worry. You'll be safe here." David dropped to one knee. "And you simply can't come with me, Tare. You can't walk. And it's too far to carry you." His tone softened as he brushed a warm thumb across her forehead. It was the most intimate gesture he'd offered since picking her up at the Glasgow airport. "I won't be long. Corbin Hall is right down the road. I'll be back before you know it."

"Before it gets dark?"

"Long before that."

Tara studied his eyes, trying to discern if he was telling the truth or just saying words to appease her. For all she knew, Corbin Hall was twenty miles away. And sure, it was only mid-afternoon, but the storm would banish the sun much sooner than usual. The shadows at the back of the crypt were already deepening.

Still she had to trust him. In her condition, she had no choice. Besides, what could hurt her in the dark? Darkness never killed anyone. Humans in the dark could be a threat, certainly. But from the looks of it, no human being had stepped foot in this tomb for years—probably even centuries. She sighed.

"That's my brave girl," David said, bending down to peck her on the lips. Even in her agitated state, she noticed the terseness of his kiss. He had thin lips, almost as if they had been painted on his skin instead of sculpted out of warm, masculine flesh. His kisses always left her wanting just a little bit more. Even now.

She touched his arm. "Hurry back, David."

"I will, darling. I will."

In only moments, all signs of David had vanished. The storm raged outside, isolating her in the small stone chamber, shrinking her world to the perimeter of the ancient grave. For a moment, she wondered what type of man rested beneath the stone image and what had happened to him—until a sudden roaring noise and the sensation of agonizing pain flashed through her mind, shaking her to her core.

Where had that come from?

She cut off the thought. Better not to let her imagination wander in a place like this.

She turned her attention to her own physical state instead. Her damp hair hung over her shoulders and in her left eye. Deftly, she drew back her light brown hair and knotted it over itself at the nape of her neck. Then joint-by-joint, she tested her ability to move, and soon discovered she was not as badly hurt as she had first believed. Only her right ankle seemed injured. She sat up and inspected her leg by delicately probing it with her fingers. The flesh around her ankle was swelling, but she had full movement. Her layman diagnosis was a sprain, nothing more. When the accident had occurred, she'd been pressing an imaginary brake. Her right foot had likely taken the brunt of the crash. In fact, her right hip was sore as well.

The storm turned suddenly, sweeping across the opening of the tomb with a barrage of rain that drenched her all over again.

"Dammit!" Tara exclaimed. She dragged herself further into the tomb, as the iron gate banged in the wind and the brambles twining around the bars fluttered like tattered banners. All she could see beyond the gate were the canes and leaves of a massive brier patch. She prayed that David would be able to locate this brier-buried tomb again.

At the thought of being left in the crypt, especially through the night, Tara flushed with panic.

"Get a grip!" she said to herself.

She was her own worst enemy when it came to getting swept away by wild imagining. Though she had made a career of debunking the paranormal and now had her own television show, *Fact or Fiction*, where she got to disprove mysteries every week, she could still wake up in the middle of the night, convinced her bad dreams were real. She was looking forward to having sensible David Corbin sleeping at her side, keeping her imagination in check. He'd be the voice of reason when the nightmares got the best of her. His gentle touch would calm her better than any sleeping tablet. Not being alone at night was going to be the best part of marriage to David.

But one thing she had learned from her stint with *Fact or Fiction* was that there was always a reasonable explanation for things that went bump in the night. *Always.*

Tara struggled to her feet so she could get a good look at the stone effigy atop the sarcophagus. The sculptor had been no Michelangelo, that's for sure. In fact, the work seemed rushed, with chisel marks left unfinished, and details only hinted at—more a stone sketch than a true image of a man. Still, she got the impression that the knight whose bones lay buried here was broad-shouldered, clean-shaven, and had a prominent nose, from what she could see beneath the lines of his helmet anyway. She glanced down at the sculpture, which indicated that in life he'd worn chain mail covered by a flowing garment belted at the hips and emblazoned with a cross on his left breast. A distant memory niggled at her. She recognized his outfit from something she had read recently.

"You were a Templar," she said, pleased with herself. "You were a Knight Templar, weren't you?"

Tara felt a strange wave of disquiet pass through the tomb, like a whisper of wings. She shut it off. She was not going to allow herself to get swept into the dark corners of her mind. Not here, not anywhere.

Tara glanced over her shoulder at the banging gate and tried to judge how long David had been gone. It seemed like hours since he had left her in the crypt, but she had no way to know for sure. She didn't wear a watch, as she depended upon her cell phone to tell her the time of day. But her cell phone was out in the storm somewhere, hidden in the brambles. She couldn't think about time, anyway. She would drive herself crazy. She had to distract herself, keep up the chatter. Uncontrollable shivering set in.

She turned back to the stone effigy, hugging her trembling arms around her chest. There was no more to look at in the simple sculpture, so she switched her attention to the sides of the box. It was then she noticed the text chiseled into one side of the box. Maybe she could find out what the warrior's name was.

Carefully, Tara crouched down on one knee, gingerly extending her right leg. She traced the sculpted letters with the tips of her shaking fingers, squinting to make out the words.

Shadows made her task difficult. She bent to allow the dying light to illuminate the angular letters. And then she slowly read the text out loud, straining to make sense of the cryptic words and their crude rendering.

O knight, so dark, so quiet and true,
With face so fair and fine,
Find refuge from the craven crow,
Until I call thee to be mine.

On Michaelmas shalt thou rise anew,
A mortal man, again to face the fire.
Together we shall change our fates,
And thou shalt be mine heart's desire.

Craven crow? What a weird turn of phrase. And Michaelmas? What was that? Tara frowned, frustrated by her inability to comprehend the mysterious text. She still hadn't discovered the knight's name, either. Surely his name was written somewhere.

Tara rose and limped around the sarcophagus, searching for clues. As she came around the end of the box, she found a name sculpted in the shadows below the knight's booted feet.

Hugh Lachlan
1188 –

The missing date unnerved her. Strange, that someone would bury a knight but not indicate the year of his death. She forced herself to concentrate on the warrior's name instead.

She said the name under her breath. "Hugh. Your name was Hugh Lachlan." She glanced at the helmeted head of the knight. "That's a nice name. Hugh. You must have been strong and dependable with a name like that. I'm Tara, by the way."

A sudden gust of wind burst down the glen and clanked the gate, as if to chastise her for acting so familiar in the presence of the long-dead knight. A shudder coursed through her that had nothing to do with her damp clothing. She bent to the sarcophagus, determined to occupy her mind before she completely freaked out. There was a band of writing around the entire box, serving as a decorative border. The letters were interspersed with stone bullets of leaves and flowers. Tara began at Hugh's feet and made her way around the box, reading the words in a soft murmur.

"Heal, fair knight," she read, shifting to the next phrase. "Heal, fair knight." She moved up the backside of the box. The phrase repeated up the long side, across the short end where his head would be, and down the long side that bore the mysterious text she'd read earlier. She kept going, mumbling the words, grateful to be preoccupied by yet another mystery.

"Heal, fair knight," she chanted as she traced the border with her finger. And then at the very end of the line, the phrase changed. She read it without a second thought.

"Now rise, my knight."

The air stilled. She felt a drastic shift in the atmosphere, as if a preternatural force had muted the storm outside, as if the air were being sucked from her lungs and she would never take another breath, as if the whole world had taken on an unearthly bluish glow.

And then she heard a scraping noise in front of her, of stone grating upon stone. An acrid smell hit her nostrils, the smell of something burnt, something that should never be burnt. Against every shred of good sense, she glanced down.

The lid of the sarcophagus had moved. Tendrils of smoke wafted upward. Every horror movie she'd ever watched fast-forwarded through her mind.

Terrified, Tara fell back, accidentally putting her full weight on her injured ankle. Crying out in pain, she crumpled to the floor, clutching her leg as she saw the lid inch farther to the side.

Her mouth went dry with fright as she scrambled backward on the palms of her hands, propelling herself with her good foot, desperate to reach the iron gate.

"Tara!" Someone called from the tangle of briers beyond.

"David!" she screamed in answer. She pulled herself up by the iron bars. She glanced behind her, over her shoulder. The lid of the sarcophagus was halfway off now. She dared not look inside the box, afraid that she would never be able to wipe the image from her mind, once she saw what lay in the shadows there. She had enough trouble sleeping at night. She couldn't afford to add another dark tableau to her dreamscape.

"Tara!"

David appeared at the gate with a flashlight and a woman holding an umbrella. She'd never been so relieved to see a couple of human beings in her entire life.

"David!" She flung herself into his arms, nearly knocking him down. Then she grabbed the sodden sleeve of his suit and urged him away from the tomb. "Get me the hell out of here!"

"My God," she heard the other woman say as David swept Tara into his arms, "The poor thing's rather in a state, isn't she?"

"We need to get out of here!" Tara cried. "Now!" She kicked the gate shut with her good foot and refused to look back.

Chapter 3

By the time they made it to the car at the top of the ravine, the howling wind had died down. The rain didn't let up, however, and pelted them sideways as David helped Tara duck into the back seat.

"You'll have more room here to stretch out that leg," he explained, positioning her injured limb on the bench seat. "Buckle up. I'll be right back."

"You're not going back down there!" Tara warned. "Not to that tomb."

David paused. "Why not?"

"There's something down there. Something alive!"

"There can't be," the woman gave a musical laugh. "Come, David, let's get this over with before we get completely soaked."

"David, no!" Tara cried. "I saw the lid on that tomb move. I smelled smoke—like something burned. I know there was something coming to life down there!"

"Tara, get a hold of yourself," David touched her arm. "You're raving!"

"But I saw something!"

"You just had a bump on the head." He gave her forearm a squeeze. "Don't worry. I'll be right back."

"David!" She called after him. But in her injured state, there was nothing she could do to stop him. Worried sick, she watched David and the woman scramble back down the ravine for the suitcases. She kept her stare glued on the glen, barely taking a breath, until she spotted David coming back up the slope, one hand at the blond woman's elbow, sharing her umbrella. Nothing seemed to be following them. Perhaps she had only imagined the tomb lid opening.

Tara sat back, angry with herself. Who was she trying to kid? She'd seen the lid moving with her own eyes. There had been no imagining involved. She couldn't explain how or why the lid had moved, but it had definitely shifted to one side.

As soon as David stowed the bags in the trunk and jumped into the front seat of the car, his companion started up the engine and pulled onto the road.

"You didn't see anything down there?" Tara asked.

"No." David glanced at her over his shoulder, his eyes full of doubt. "What did *you* see?"

"The lid on that coffin opening. Like Dracula coming to life. I swear, it moved."

"We've got lots of fairies and the like in Scotland," the woman put in. "But vampires? I don't believe so."

Tara couldn't tell if the woman was trying to be funny or was out and out mocking her. She glanced at the blonde sitting next to her fiancé. The woman's words still burned in her memory. She had referred to Tara as a "poor thing." Tara flushed. She was not about to be anyone's *poor thing*, especially this woman's. Besides, anyone who had been in a car accident and left in a tomb in the middle of nowhere as darkness descended was entitled to be a little keyed up.

She found David's acquaintance studying her in the rear view mirror. The woman's large, clear eyes narrowed as she smiled.

"Morag Smithbank," she said.

Tara didn't break the stare. "Tara Lewis. And thanks for the lift."

"Glad to be of help." The woman tipped her head and smiled. "I was on my way to Corbin Hall anyway."

"Morag's one of my childhood chums," David put in.

Morag's glance slanted away from the mirror as she patted his arm. "David and I have known each other forever. Since birth. But I haven't seen him in absolute ages!"

As Morag talked, Tara peered out the window at the blurred shapes whizzing by. She half-expected to spot a figure lumbering through the heather, dragging a ragged burial shroud behind him. But all she saw were shrubs drooping with rain and low hills hanging with mist.

"Morag's a psychologist," David continued over his shoulder, his tone brighter than Tara had ever heard in his voice. "She has a practice in Edinburgh."

"Lucky for us, the 'doctor wasn't in' this afternoon."

"Well, I simply *had* to come home." Morag smiled into the mirror again. "When David told me he was getting married, I felt it my duty as a fellow female to make sure you knew what you were getting into."

"You'll have to dish all the dirt on David sometime."

"Yes, but will it be *Fact or Fiction*?" David turned to wiggle his eyebrows at her.

Not amused by his reference to the show, Tara turned her attention back to the scenery. She couldn't shake the feeling that something was out there—something that was following her to Corbin Hall. She clenched her jaw and told herself to stop thinking such crazy thoughts. There were no such things as vampires or creatures that crawled out of tombs, just as she doubted any Lady in Green existed.

Of all people, she should know there had to be a rational explanation for what she'd experienced in the tomb. When she recovered, she would go back and find out just what had caused the grating sound and produced the acrid smell. Until then, she had to get a grip.

Tara smoothed back her shoulder-length brown hair and wiped the soft flesh beneath her eyes, in case her mascara had smudged in the rain. She wasn't about to let David's psychologist friend think she was some kind of head case.

The car purred up a long lane bordered by trees, whose smooth gray trunks looked like sentinels in the downpour. Morag turned the car into a gravel parking lot in front of an imposing stone structure and turned off the engine and lights.

They had arrived at Corbin Hall.

Tara felt another wave of disappointment pass over her as the wedding trip continued its downward spiral. She had planned to make a good first impression on David's family, but in her present drowned-rat condition, topped by her scrapes and bruises, impressing anyone was out of the question. Instead of making the grand entrance she'd imagined, she was going to have to limp into Corbin Hall.

As David helped her out of the car, Tara glanced up at the manor house. Its symmetrical wings were laid out on either side of a central hall, giving the appearance of three tidy boxes attached by a single roof. Judging by the practical architecture and elegant but unadorned façade, she guessed the manse had been built in the Georgian era, the late 1700s, and probably for a lord who spent more time in London than he did in the country.

Castle Corbin was nowhere to be seen—at least not in this rain. Tara wondered where the old ruin was. Though she pooh-poohed the paranormal, she had a keen interest in historical buildings, and was anxious to see the old place.

David insisted on carrying Tara into the house, and she let him. Better to arrive like a bride being transported over the threshold than to hobble across it. A light came on as they approached the door, and the large portal opened. An older female servant with snowy white hair, cardigan and pleated skirt stood aside as David strode into the house.

"Good Lord!" the woman exclaimed. "What happened?"

"We were in a car accident, Mrs. MacMillan. Nothing serious."

"Oh, you poor dear. Are you all right, Miss Lewis?"

"Yes, thank you. Just a sprained ankle, I think."

"Call the doctor, would you?" David said. "And where can I put Miss Lewis?"

"In the lady's chamber upstairs." Mrs. MacMillan pointed upward.

Tara knew how heavy she would be on such a trek, especially for David. He wasn't into bodybuilding or sports. In fact, his slight frame was not much larger than hers. "David, I can walk."

"No, you can't." He headed for the stairs. "You're not walking on that foot of yours until the doctor examines it."

"Hear, hear," Morag added.

"If you insist." Tara linked her arms around his neck, glad that no other members of the Corbin family seemed to be home.

David put his foot on the first stair and turned slightly. "Don't leave, M," he said. "I'll be right down. Make yourself at home."

"Thanks, D," she called back.

D and M. What cozy pet names. Over David's shoulder, Tara got her first real look at Morag Smithbank while Mrs. MacMillan drew off the blond woman's raincoat.

Morag was stunning, from her upswept blond hair to her slender figure and long shapely legs. She wore a conservative suit made of a nubby turquoise and navy fabric cut in a short Chanel style. A fluffy scarf that looked like a cloud softened the neckline and accentuated the swan like lines of her throat. But the most amazing thing about Morag Smithbank was that she was wearing spike heels and nylons, and her stockings had remained unsnagged during her trips up and down the ravine. She looked deliciously feminine but at the same time wholly in control of her universe—exactly the way Tara had wanted to appear upon entering the house.

Glumly, Tara gazed at Morag's disappearing perfection as David carried her to the second floor. By the time he got to the top of the stairs, he was puffing and sweating.

"David, really, you can put me down now," she commented.

"Not yet. We're just about there." He pushed a door open with his foot and carried her into a huge room paneled in mahogany and decorated in melon-colored velvet and silk. A marble fireplace dominated one wall and complimented the even larger four-poster bed opposite it. Oil paintings of women and their dogs and children graced the walls. Mrs. MacMillan bustled into the room after them.

"It's lovely!" Tara exclaimed. The bedroom was as big as her entire condo.

"'Tis the chamber of the lady of the house," Mrs. MacMillan motioned David to a sofa in front of the fireplace. "When there is one."

David deposited her on the soft cushions and stood up, and planted his hands on his hips while he tried to catch his breath.

"David told me that Lord Corbin's wife died young."

"Yes. A riding accident. 'Twas a tragic day." Mrs. MacMillan retrieved a bulky plaid dressing gown from a nearby wardrobe. "But a wedding is no time for such talk, is it now, Miss Lewis?"

"You're right." Chastened by the older woman, Tara let the rest of her questions die on her lips.

Mrs. MacMillan turned to David. "Master David, why don't you see to Miss Smithbank while I help Miss Lewis out of her wet things?"

"I can't leave Tara alone, not in her state."

"I'll be all right," Tara countered. Truthfully, she would appreciate a few moments alone, now that she was safe. "Go see to your chum."

David seemed anxious to leave. "Are you sure you'll be all right, darling?"

"I'm sure. Go."

"Okay, then. Morag and I'll wait for the doctor in the parlor, and I'll bring him up first thing." He pecked her on the cheek, and then paused. "This is Mrs. MacMillan, by the way. John's treasured housekeeper."

"It's nice to meet you, Mrs. MacMillan."

"Ma'am." The older woman gave a small curtsey.

"I'll be right downstairs, Tara. If you need anything, don't be afraid to ask." He gave a small wave and hurried out of the room, obviously worried about keeping his guest waiting.

Mrs. MacMillan was gentler than Tara would have expected of the brusque, heavy-set woman. The housekeeper helped her off with her shoes and socks, careful not to jar her right foot, slipped off her sodden trousers, and pulled off her damp sweater. She held out the robe, avoiding the sight of Tara's nearly naked body.

"Put this on, Miss Lewis, until the doctor can see to your leg."

"Thank you." Tara managed to wrap the robe around her. She settled back down into the warmth of the sofa.

"Robbie will bring up your bag." Mrs. MacMillan marched to the fireplace. "And feed the fire for ye. 'Tis fairly warm now, but the frost will be drawing in th' night."

"Thank you."

"The bath is behind those doors." She bustled to a ribbon hanging by the bathroom door. "Should you need anything, just ring this bell."

"All right."

She crossed the room. "The *tele* is behind the doors of this wardrobe." She opened the doors of a large piece of furniture to the right of the fireplace. "Tea is at five. Lord Corbin should be home by then. Dinner is at eight."

"Do the Corbins dress for dinner?"

"Aye." Mrs. MacMillan raised her chin. "The Corbin family keeps to the old ways—not like some of the other houses roundabout." She clasped her hands under her ample bosom. "To my mind, Miss Lewis, if you live in a grand old place like Corbin Hall, you don't behave like a heathen and dress like a pauper—tattered jeans and the like—as so many of these folk with new money do."

Tara marveled at the fierce pride in the housekeeper's voice. "You've worked here a long time?"

"Fifty odd years," she replied. "Started when I was a lass of ten, working in the kitchen."

"That's a long time." Tara smiled.

"Aye. I've known no other home since then." Mrs. MacMillan continued. "And I hope to breathe my last here, God willing."

Tara had no idea what it would be like to put down fifty-year-old roots. She changed jobs and living quarters as often as some people changed their hairstyles.

"I'll leave you to rest now, Miss Lewis. The doctor should be here soon. And I'll bring up some nice hot tea in a few minutes."

"Thank you, Mrs. MacMillan."

Robbie arrived moments later with her bags. He was a short slight boy whose smooth face was just beginning to show the coarsening effects of puberty. He dropped her bags inside an antechamber that served as a walk-in closet and turned to go, his every muscle and sinew intent upon leaving.

"Thank you, Robbie," Tara said from her place near the fire.

"Ma'am." He ducked his head and glanced her way. His face was pale, and his blue eyes darted around the room as if he were frightened of something. He edged backward toward the door.

"Can you do me a favor?" Tara asked.

The boy froze, his expression dark. "Aye?"

"Put more coal on the fire, please?"

Robbie glanced over his shoulder to the dark hallway behind him and then back to the fire.

"Right, miss." He scurried forward, pulled back the fire screen, poured coal from the scuttle onto the glowing fire, and replaced the fire screen, banging and swearing in his haste.

"Is there something wrong?" Tara asked, smiling at him. "I don't bite, you know."

"Oh, it isn't you, miss!"

"Then what is it?"

He threw another glance behind him. "'Tis the room, Miss. My mum—she's the cook here? She told me to make quick work of this room, so she did, and clear out as soon as possible."

"Why is that?"

He shrugged one shoulder, and the corners of his mouth turned down. He was withholding the truth. She could tell. Perhaps he'd got in trouble here with the head of the house and didn't want to admit it.

"Is there something special about this room? Something bad?"

"I canna say, miss!"

Robbie stood near the end of the sofa, poised for flight, his scrawny figure outlined by the firelight, his eyes imploring her to release him.

At that moment Mrs. MacMillan bustled in with a tea tray and took a quick survey of the room. "Thank you, Robbie." She placed the tray on the coffee table. "That will be all for now."

"Aye, ma'am!" He dashed from the room.

Tara watched him go, perplexed by his strange behavior. Then she glanced up at the housekeeper. "He certainly acted strange. Like he was frightened of something."

Mrs. MacMillan clucked her tongue. "Don't mind the lad. His head's full o' stories."

"What kind o' stories?"

"Tales that were better left untold. To speak of the dead only disturbs what's better left alone."

"The dead are dead, Mrs. MacMillan. No one needs to be frightened of them."

"So you may say in America, Miss Lewis. But you are in Scotland now."

The housekeeper's words plunged Tara into thoughtful silence. She could argue all day about the lack of proof that a spirit world existed, but somehow she doubted the white-haired old woman would be interested in her views.

Mrs. MacMillan poured tea into a cup and handed it to her. "Drink up now, Miss Lewis, and turn your thoughts to sunlight. There's been enough darkness at Corbin Hall to last us all a lifetime."

Tara heard shouting and padded toward the door at the end of the dark hallway as her nightgown tangled around her legs. Vicious yelling had awakened her, frightening her. Why would the people be so angry at each other? And now someone was sobbing hysterically. She couldn't make out the words, but it sounded like a woman pleading for her life. It sounded like her mother! Her heart pounded with dread. Something bad was happening behind that door. Something really bad. She had to open the door and help the woman. She had to get to the door and open it...

With a cry, Tara ripped her consciousness from the all-to-familiar nightmare and jerked up. Her heart pounded and her hair was damp with sweat. For a moment, she didn't recognize where she was and thought she might still be trapped in the dream. Then she realized she was in bed, and the bed she sat sweating in belonged to Corbin Hall. She was halfway around the world in Scotland.

Her heart was still thudding heavily as she threw back the sheet and blanket and dropped her legs over the side of the bed. She glanced at the clock on the night stand. 3:33 am. One of her guests on *Fact or Fiction*—a supposed psychic she had easily debunked—had claimed that the real witching hour did not arrive at midnight like everyone thought, but began at 3:00 am, just before the new day broke, when stillness lay over the world and even the most restless person had finally fallen asleep.

Tara shook her head and frowned. *Witching hour. Right.* Maybe everyone else in the world was dead to the world at 3:00 am, but not her. Inevitably she awoke at this time of night and could not get back to sleep. And judging by the amount of adrenaline shooting through her veins, she was going to be up for a good long while.

She eased off the mattress and down to the floor, testing her foot. The doctor had confirmed her sprain diagnosis, and had merely wrapped her ankle in an athletic bandage and given her some pain pills. She stood up and put some of her weight on the injured ankle. Pain radiated up her leg, but it wasn't bad. She could hobble to the bathroom and back.

By the time she had returned to bed, she was wide-awake. She glanced around the shadowy room, searching for a bookshelf, but couldn't see any. She needed something to read if she was going to be waiting around for the rest of the house to wake up. Her stomach growled, reminding her that she had fallen asleep and missed dinner the night before. The Corbins had let her sleep through her first evening in the house.

Not an auspicious start to her plan of forging a solid relationship with the clan.

Tara pulled on the unflattering plaid robe, hobbled to her door, and opened it. Maybe David was suffering from early onset jet lag and was finding it difficult to sleep. She poked her head out the doorway and glanced down the long hallway. She didn't know which bedroom David had retired to, and all the doors were shut, with no bands of light showing beneath to let her know that someone was up.

She had spent countless nights like this: alone in the dark, unable to sleep, while the world rested in complete oblivion. Being alone in the dark only compounded her feelings of isolation. But her loneliness would soon come to an end. She would be married in seven days, and with any luck, would have a baby within the year. She'd timed the wedding to coincide with her female cycle, intent on getting pregnant as soon as possible. And that would be the start of her family.

With David, she would make the kind of family she never had. She would cherish her family, nurture it, and help it grow. And once she held a child of her own in her arms, she would never be alone again.

Sighing, Tara glanced in the opposite direction. Her head was hot and her eyes burned—a sure sign that she would be awake for hours. Perhaps she could find something to read downstairs.

It was then she noticed light dancing on the floor outside a room on the ground level. Maybe David was up after all.

Heartened, Tara limped to the stairs and slowly descended. If David was up, he might be persuaded to make her a sandwich. She leaned on the banister as she turned at the landing and hobbled down the final flight of stairs. Then she limped silently across the main hall to the lighted room. She could see through the open door that it was the library. She might not score a sandwich, but she would definitely find something to read here.

As she approached the open door, Tara smoothed back her hair and tightened the bulky ties of her unfeminine robe. Then she stepped into the doorway with a smile.

A fire crackled in the grate, throwing leaping shadows around the room and over the enormous desk at the far end. At first she thought the room was empty, but then she noticed a tall, dark-haired man standing with his back to the door, searching for something in the bookshelves that covered the far wall. From the back, his shoulders looked massive and his hips lean. His dark hair, uncut and shaggy, brushed the nape of his neck. He was dressed in a dark blue robe that was belted at his slender waist and fell almost to his ankles. Metallic thread glinted at the neckline of the robe and at his wrists. He wore boots made of velvet or suede over his long narrow feet and held a candle in his hand while he moved along, intently searching for something on the shelves.

For a moment, she watched him, hoping he would turn around and notice her, but he didn't seem aware of her presence.

"Excuse me," she finally said. "Lord Corbin?"

Chapter 4

The man spun around to face her, obviously shocked that someone had come into the room. He stared at Tara, while the hand holding the candle slowly lowered to reveal sharp features eerily distorted by the flame. Judging by the glower in his expression, she surmised he didn't like being taken by surprise.

She waited on the threshold for a greeting, an invitation to come into the library—anything. But he just stood there watching her, his chin tilted upward, his stare guarded. When he didn't say another word, she resorted to humor, which she often used to diffuse difficult situations on the show. "Can't find that murder mystery you never finished?" She gave a slight chuckle.

His dark eyes glinted, or perhaps light from the fire made his expression shift.

"As a matter o' fact," his voice was deep, remote. "Nay."

"Tara Lewis," she said, hobbling forward with her hand extended. At his unfriendly expression, she brightened her smile, determined to charm him.

The man glanced at her outstretched hand and then at her face. His black brows knitted together at the top of his sharp, prominent nose. He seemed confused or troubled. Still, he remained silent and made no move to shake her hand.

"I'm David's fiancée—the one with the sprained ankle?"

"Aye. I recall." His voice was dry, his words measured, and his accent was unlike anything she'd heard in Scotland so far. There was less lilt to his voice, and certainly less friendliness in his manner. But as with David, his Scottish burr stirred something deep inside her, like a song evoking an aching memory.

When he didn't step forward to shake her hand, she lowered her arm, feeling slightly insulted.

"Sorry to have slept through dinner."

"Such fatigue often occurs when one suffers an injury."

"But I'm wide awake now." She smiled. "And I'm hoping you'll let me borrow a book or two."

His glance slanted over her. She noticed there was something wrong with the left side of his face, but in the dim light she couldn't make out what it was, only that his skin had an odd texture and sheen.

"I was actually looking for something about art history—preferably modern," she continued. "That always puts me to sleep. Do you have something on the Cubists?"

"There is an impressive number of books here. I'm sure you will find one t' your liking." He didn't move. He kept standing in the same spot, studying her. David had mentioned that his uncle was old-fashioned. But he hadn't mentioned how eccentric he was.

"Do you mind if I turn on the lights?" Tara asked.

"Lights?"

"The lights." Tara motioned toward the switch near the door.

The man followed the motion of her hand but didn't say yes or no. He was too busy looking at the switch.

Tara flipped it upward. With a gasp, Lord Corbin stepped back. He stared up at the chandeliers suspended from the ceiling and then back at her, his eyes squinting.

"Sorry!" she exclaimed. "I didn't mean to hurt your eyes."

"What magic is this?" He took a few steps forward and peered up at the nearest light. Then he strode past her to the switch and turned it off.

"Holy Virgin!" he whispered, as if he'd never used a light switch before. Then he turned the switch back on. "'Tis like the sun!" He strode back into the room and stared up at the light above his head. "Where is the flame?"

"There is no flame," she caught herself explaining, "It's done with a glowing wire. Resistance. Volts. Watts. That kind of thing. But surely, you know—"

"You are the witch." He glanced over his broad shoulder at her, his eyes cold. "You do not look like her overmuch, but I am not fooled by the illusion."

"Witch?" A short laugh escaped her. "I'm no witch!"

"You are. First the tomb. Now the light magic."

"The tomb?" She gaped at him.

"Aye, the tomb." He turned to face her, his eyes flashing. "What game do you play at now, witch? You know I have no more valuables t' steal!"

What was he raving about? Tara stared up at him, seeing him clearly for the first time. Lord Corbin was tall, much taller than David. He was probably six and a half feet tall. His hair was darker than David's, too—almost black—with glossy waves at his ears and neck. His eyes were navy blue, unlike any color she'd seen before in the human eye. His face was comprised of sharp angles bordered by a flaring jaw line atop a massive neck. And except for what appeared to be a burn scar running down the left side of his face, he was an unusually good-looking man—far more attractive than David. If this man was related to her fiancé, she could see no family resemblance whatsoever. She'd also assumed that John Corbin was much older, seeing how he was David's uncle. But the man in front of her looked to be in his thirties.

Just whom was she talking to?

As she studied the man, the strangest thing happened. Tara felt a wave of longing well up inside her—a longing to be held against this man's broad chest. Somehow she knew what it would feel like to be embraced by him, and she ached for it, as she had never ached for anything in her life. A flush swept through her, as if she had fallen backward into a warm, bottomless pool.

Shocked, Tara shook herself back to reality.

"What do you mean, steal?" she stammered, her ears still burning from her unusual reaction to him. "What are you talking about?"

"Did you not speak the words that began the unraveling?"

She felt a chill. The smile faded from her lips. "The unraveling?"

"Of the spell."

"What spell?"

"The one your voice had the power to break." When she didn't reply, he added, "In the tomb."

"What?" Tara took a step backward, suddenly uncertain of the man's identity as well as her own safety. She hadn't told David what she'd done in the tomb while he'd trudged to Corbin Hall, so there was no way his uncle could know what had gone on there. "How do you know about the tomb?"

"I am right, then. You are the witch! The one who solicits a man's trust and then betrays him!"

"Listen, Lord Corbin. I'm not who you think I am." She backed through the doorway. "And you're freaking me out, I don't mind saying."

A light blinked on behind her. Tara glanced over her shoulder, relieved to see the ample form of Mrs. MacMillan bustling into the main hall. Her white hair was set in pin curls around her face, and she wore a plaid robe similar to the one Tara sported.

"Mrs. MacMillan!" Tara called, immensely glad to see the housekeeper's sleepy face.

"I heard voices." Mrs. MacMillan hurried forward. "Is everything all right, Miss Lewis?"

"Yes, I just came down to get a book and ran into someone who I thought was Lord Corbin."

"Lord Corbin is up at this hour?" She walked past Tara, into the library. Tara trailed after her, hoping to discover that the master of the house wasn't as strange as she thought, and that they'd only started off on the wrong foot, which they could set straight.

"He's here?" Mrs. MacMillan glanced around the room. Tara followed her inspection with one of her own. The library was deserted.

"He was," Tara replied, baffled. She pointed to the wall by the window. "He was right there, standing there talking to me."

"If he was, I can't imagine where he would have gone so quickly."

"There's no other entry?"

"No, just this one."

Mrs. MacMillan surveyed the room in silence while Tara felt a cloud of dismay descend. She could just imagine what Mrs. MacMillan was thinking. *Crazy American.* A crazy American woman with no pedigree or family money was going to marry into the Corbin clan. Lord save them all.

"He was here," Tara insisted, hobbling around the perimeter of the room in search of proof of Lord Corbin's presence. "I swear."

"Maybe you just had a dream," the housekeeper suggested. "Lord knows you've had a stressful day, dear."

"I wasn't dreaming!"

"Maybe it was the medication the doctor gave you. Maybe you had an hallucination."

Tara hobbled to a stop in the center of the room. There was no explanation for what she'd seen. She might as well stop trying to defend herself to the housekeeper. She'd only appear more irrational than she already seemed.

"It was no hallucination." She sighed, exasperated. "But whoever it was, he's gone now."

"May I get you something?" Mrs. MacMillan inquired, ducking her head to peer up at Tara's face. "A glass of milk, perhaps? Or something to steady your nerves?"

"No, thank you, Mrs. MacMillan." Her hunger had vanished as inexplicably as Lord Corbin. "I'll just grab a book and go back to bed."

"Are you sure? Will you be all right?"

"I'll be fine," she lied. "Thank you."

She glanced out the window to the darkness beyond and clasped her arms around her chest. Dawn was a long way off. It would be hours before David woke up. But when he did, he had some explaining to do—about Robbie and the room upstairs and about his exceedingly strange uncle.

Much to Tara's surprise, she fell asleep just before dawn and didn't awaken until someone rapped on her door.

"You awake in there?" David called. He entered the room before she could answer. Tara opened her eyes to find herself slumped up in bed with a book on Spanish surrealism still open in her lap.

"Good morning!" David strode across the room, smiling. He was a morning person, always fired up by the start of a new day. Tara was just the opposite, due to her often-troubled sleep. David's sunny disposition in the morning usually annoyed her, but today she was happy to see a familiar face. She accepted his quick peck and brushed back her tousled bangs.

"What time is it?"

"Eight. I've been out for a walk already and read the paper, waiting for you sleepy heads. Are you interested in breakfast? Everyone's downstairs."

"I'll be ready in a few minutes." She threw back the covers. "I'm starving."

"What about your ankle? Do you need some help there?"

"Actually, it's not that bad." She slipped out of bed, but grimaced as soon as her feet hit the floor. "Oh, my gosh!" she exclaimed. "I am so stiff!"

"From the accident. I was too, when I got up. I have a nasty bruise on my ribs as well."

"I guess we're lucky to be alive. We shouldn't complain."

"That we shouldn't." He helped her hobble to the bathroom.

"I'll leave you to take a shower," he said. "Come downstairs when you're done?"

"All right." Her questions for David could wait until she fortified herself with a minimum of two cups of black coffee and a plate of eggs.

After a quick shower and an even quicker application of cosmetics, Tara pawed through her luggage for a pair of black slacks and a lime-green silk top with a V-neck that would flatter her not-so-swan like neck.

She glanced at herself in the mirror that stood between the massive closets and studied the scratches on her cheeks and forehead, wondering if they'd heal before the wedding at the end of the week. Then she glanced at her hair. David and the producers wanted her to go blond. They'd been at her for months to at least put in some highlights.

Tara ran a hand over her dark brown hair. She'd always thought her shining hair was her best feature. She'd never colored it. Never had a permanent. She didn't want to do a thing to her hair. Dye would dry it out and set her on the road to monthly treatments. Besides that, everyone on TV was blonde. Even the sensible news anchors dyed their hair now. And for sure Morag Smithbank bleached hers to its platinum perfection.

Tara had done a lot of things to claw to the top of her profession. It was silly of her to draw the line at something so insignificant as her hair, and she knew if the producers insisted, she would comply. But at least in the wedding pictures, she'd still be a brunette.

After running a brush over her hair, Tara threw on the same diamond studs she'd worn the day before, slipped her feet into a pair of low-healed sandals so she wouldn't have to wear hose over the athletic bandage, and headed downstairs for breakfast. She had no idea where everyone was in the house or what the floor plan was, not having seen anything but the library and her bedroom, so she followed the aroma of food. The fragrance guided her down the long central hall to the back of the house.

A hum of voices and the clink of silverware drifted from the morning room, which was comprised of a bank of palladian windows and two sets of French doors that stretched the length of the room. A buffet breakfast had been set out along one wall, and a table with a yellow and red chintz tablecloth and white and yellow china sat in the center of the room.

Smiling faces looked up at her as she entered the room. Morag, David, and an older man who looked a lot like David were sitting at the table already, eating their breakfasts. The two men rose, napkins in hand.

"There you are," David greeted.

"Good morning, Miss Lewis," Morag said, smiling broadly.

"Hi, Miss Smithbank."

"Do call me Morag. And may I call you Tara?"

"Of course."

"I thought I'd come over and see how you were getting on."

"I'm doing surprisingly well. Thank you."

"Morag lives quite close." David put in. "Her father's the reverend of the Presbyterian church."

"I see." Tara smiled down at her, aware of the second man still standing across the table from her.

"And this is my uncle, John Corbin." David motioned toward the man hovering nearby.

Stunned, Tara studied the man. He was nothing like the person in the library. His thinning hair was the same reddish shade as David's. His frame was slight and spare, just like his nephew. In fact, the two men could have been brothers, they were so similar in appearance. The only difference was the small moustache that John sported, which softened the tight, thin-lipped expression he shared with his nephew, the chilly look in his small gray eyes, and their ages. Tara guessed John was in his sixties, while David was only thirty-seven. "Your uncle?" she repeated.

"Surely the old boy told you about me," John said, coming around to meet her. He held out his hand.

"Yes, but I'm confused." Tara allowed him to pump her hand. "I thought I met you last night."

"Met me?"

"Yes, last night, in the library."

"Me in the library?" John gave a curt laugh. "That would be the day! I'm an outdoors sort of man, Miss Lewis. Hunting, fishing, that sort of thing! No dusty old books for me."

Tara stared at him, searching for an explanation for what she had seen and finding none. "Not that I'm not very glad to meet you, Lord Corbin—"

"John, I insist!" A smile fled across his lips and disappeared as his eyes coldly surveyed her.

"John," she repeated. She forced herself to stand straighter than ever, even though she knew she had the posture of a ballerina. What could the man possibly find wrong with her appearance? She had the best hair stylist in Hollywood, went to the gym every other day, and knew how to dress. But Lord Corbin seemed to find something lacking. She could see it in the hard expression in his eyes.

Slightly unnerved, Tara continued with her explanation. "But there was a man in the library last night. I thought he was you. He never said he wasn't you. So I just assumed—"

"I assure you, it wasn't me."

Silence fell over the once merry table.

"He was dressed kind of funny, now that I think about it," Tara continued, her voice tapering off. She pictured the man in her mind—his long robe, his suede boots. "Like he was wearing a costume."

"Costume?" David snorted. He stirred his tea. "What kind of costume?"

"Like a nobleman or something. From the Middle Ages. With gold trim around his robe. He was really tall, too."

"Who could he have been?" Morag asked, turning to the master of the house.

"I couldn't say," John answered. "Not from that description."

"One of the servants, most likely." David sipped his tea. "You never know what kinds of things people wear to bed."

"Preferably nothing," Morag drawled. "I never do."

David laughed while John shook his head and frowned.

He motioned toward the sideboard. "Help yourself, Tara. Don't let these deviants get in the way of your breakfast."

"Thank you." Tara poured coffee into a china cup and carried it to the table. Maybe a strong jolt of caffeine would clear her confusion. She sat down, still troubled by the events of the previous night.

Morag reached out and patted the top of Tara's left hand. "Don't be upset, Tara. You had quite a day yesterday. Your poor system is probably still recovering."

"Meaning what?" Tara countered. She didn't appreciate Morag's soothing tone, as if she were placating one of her patients.

"Meaning nothing." Morag withdrew her hand. She shrugged. "Only that perhaps you were suffering from a delusion last night."

"I wasn't. I saw a man in the library." Tara picked up her coffee cup and was mortified to discover her hand shaking.

Morag studied her, a small lift to her lip that Tara interpreted as a knowing smile. "Maybe you think you saw someone. Maybe your mind played a little trick on you. The human brain is a delicate organ. It can be injured so easily."

"She should see a doctor, Davy," John stated, stabbing his blood sausage. "Get a CAT scan. See what's up. No sense taking any chances if Tara suffered a head injury."

Tara put down her coffee cup with a clatter. "My head's just fine."

"You're right." David leaned over and kissed her on the cheek. "In fact, your head is wonderful. I think you've got the most wonderful, prettiest head in Scotland. Maybe the world."

Tara glanced at him and couldn't help but grin. A ripple of laughter circled around the table.

"As for people in libraries," John picked up his glass of orange juice.

"Davy tells me *you're* the one who likes old books."

"He did?"

"Aye. He says you carry one around with you wherever you go."

The Psalter. Tara felt her heart lurch in her chest.

"Oh, my God," she gasped.

"What?" David glanced at her. "What now?"

"The Psalter," Tara gasped. "It's in my purse—in the tomb!"

"The Psalter?" Morag asked, looking from one to the other in confusion. "You mean a Psalm book?"

"Yes. A family heirloom. I can't believe I left it." Since the moment she'd set foot on Scottish soil, her well-orchestrated world seemed to be unraveling out of control.

Unraveling. The same word used by the man in blue. A shudder passed through her.

Tara jumped to her feet.

"I've got to go back," she exclaimed. "I've got to get my Psalter out of that tomb."

Chapter 5

Much to Tara's frustration, David and John wouldn't let her leave Corbin Hall. She was stressed enough as it was, they told her. And she couldn't go on her own, not in her injured condition.

After breakfast, the others returned to the scene of the accident to retrieve Tara's Psalter and whatever else they could find in the brambles. Alone, Tara hobbled up the stairs, determined to prove she wasn't suffering from a head injury. She'd laughed at David's comment about her head being the prettiest in the world, but she hadn't been all that amused by the other things that were said. She was known for her razor-sharp mind and cutting wit, not her hairdo and dimples. To have the others doubt the state of her faculties was something she couldn't abide. She'd seen what she'd seen, and it wasn't because of a bump on the head. She intended to research Hugh Lachlan on the web and dish up proof of his existence to her doubters.

Once in the bedroom, Tara started up the web browser on her laptop and glanced at the stories of the day on her portal. Sure enough, there was her picture with a glaring headline that read: "T-Lew to Tie the Knot in Scotland." So much for a quiet family wedding. Someone had leaked the news. Probably David. He loved any and all attention he could get for the show.

Tara frowned as she stared down at the story. They hadn't even used her real name in the headline, assuming that everyone knew who she was by now. She glanced at the unflattering photo of her walking to her car, and her frown deepened. She hadn't realized those pocket flaps on her khaki slacks made her butt look a lot wider than it really was. Or was it just the angle of the shot? The members of the paparazzi must take a vow to catch their prey at their worst possible moment.

"And I hate that nickname," she murmured under her breath as she logged into her mail program. "If anyone cares."

Still burning with indignation, she left the headlines to do a quick web search on the medieval knight. Maybe she could find something on the guy if he'd been important enough to be buried in a stone tomb. She paused, trying to remember the correct spelling of his name.

"Hugh," Tara said aloud as she typed in the letters. "Hugh Lachlan." She pressed the search button. But before she had a chance to scan the resulting links, she noticed movement on the periphery of her laptop screen. She glanced up, shocked to see a figure materializing in front of the fireplace.

For a moment, she froze as the figure transformed from a cloud of silvery glitter to the imposing outline of a man.

She blinked, disbelieving her own eyes. A person was materializing out of thin air in front of her. A person she recognized: the man from the library. Every fiber of her being told her this could not be happening.

People didn't just appear out of thin air. Though her brain refused to acknowledge the presence of the man, her heart paid no attention to the laws of physics. It hammered hard against her ribs, pumping a surge of adrenaline through her.

"You!" she gasped, leaping to her feet.

The man held up a hand, as if to stop her from fleeing, while he continued to come into full focus, his dark blue eyes fixed upon her, the scars on his face glinting in the light that streamed through the window.

Tara bolted sideways, and was punished by pain shooting to her knee. "Ouch!" she cried, hobbling backward. She glanced over her shoulder at the door, which seemed miles away. She would crawl if she had to, if it meant getting away from the thing by the fireplace—whatever it was.

Just when she was about to drop to her hands and knees, she realized what she would look like through the distorted lens of the paparazzi: her hair askew, her eyes wild, her mouth open, hobbling frantically to the door like the hunchback in a Frankenstein movie. Is this the Tara Lewis she wished to display to the world? No. And what was she running from, anyway? Someone was obviously trying to scare her, and she was falling for the ploy—hook, line, and sinker.

Maybe this was the way the clan tested the mettle of future brides. Well, she might have injured her ankle, but her brain and her courage were still intact. She would prove to the Corbins that she could pass any fright fest they threw at her.

Tara paused to regroup. She straightened and took a deep breath. Then she pushed back her shoulders and faced the man at the fireplace. She gave a short, forced laugh.

"You had me going there, mister," she said, fully in control now. "That's some trick."

"I surprise even myself," the man replied. He looked down at his velvet gown and then around the room, as if amazed at his own transformation.

"How did you do that?" Tara kept a healthy distance from the stranger, in case he posed a threat after all. "Is there a hidden door behind the fireplace?"

"That is for you to tell me." He glowered down at her. "Surely 'tis your bidding that brings me here."

"My bidding?" Tara planted her fists on her hips.

"Ye called my name."

"Really? I called you?" She curled her lip. "Does it look like I wanted someone to barge in here and bug me?"

"Bug?"

"And just who are you, anyway?"

"Enough!" Impatient, he swept a hand through the air. "Your games dinna amuse me." He broke from his stance and strode toward the window. His legs were long, his stride determined, and in just a few steps, he'd crossed the room. She watched him yank the lace panel to the side.

"The property has changed," he commented, scanning the landscape with his hard gaze. "And this manse shouldna be here. 'Tis all wrong. Where's the castle?"

"What castle?"

"Castle Corbin."

"I wouldn't know. I only just got here." Tara regarded the tall man at the window. "And if you don't tell me who you are this instant, I'm going to have the real Lord Corbin toss you out the door."

"By himself?" The man turned to face her and crossed his huge forearms over his chest. "I'd like t' see him try."

"So you know him?"

"Assuredly not as intimately as you."

His insinuation hung in the air for a moment until Tara realized what he had just said. The twisted bastard thought she had an unsavory relationship with the master of the house.

"Okay, I've had it!" Tara turned for the door. "I don't know who you are, but you're out of here!" She limped toward the large paneled door. Before she'd taken only a few steps, however, she felt his hand grasp her upper arm. She glanced back at him in amazement. For a man of his size, he'd moved with incredible speed and stealth.

"Not so fast!" he growled. His grip was firm but not tight enough to hurt her. Still, she flushed with indignation that the stranger thought he could manhandle her. No one manhandled Tara Lewis.

"Get your mitts off me!" she demanded.

His navy eyes bore into hers. "Tell me where my book is, and I shall."

She tried to yank free, but he held her fast, glaring down at her with an expression that would have pinned her in place regardless of his grip on her arm. What book was the man fixated on? There could be hundreds of old volumes in a house like Corbin Hall. Yet he seemed to think she had some connection with the object of his search. The only book she had brought to Scotland was the Psalter. She wondered if he were after *it*. If so, she wasn't about to let the brute know where her precious prayer book lay.

"What book?" she retorted. "I don't have a clue what you're talking about!"

"And dinna feign ignorance. Your play-acting willna fool me this time."

"I'm not—" she struggled for the right word and had to resort to using his old-fashioned terminology, "—Play-acting!"

He clutched her more tightly and drew her closer, nearly dragging her off the ground. "I will ask you one more time, and then I warn you, witch, I will cease to observe the fine points o' chivalry."

"You call grabbing me chivalrous?" She glared up at him. "This is no way to treat a lady!"

"You're no lady. You're a witch. And ye dinna deserve the time o' day from me." He clenched his jaw. "Now, where's my book? 'Tis not in the library here."

"That's it! I've had it with you!" Tara wriggled, trying to avoid the close proximity of his wide mouth and his white masculine teeth. The bulk of the man—the very heat of him—unnerved her but in an oddly arousing way. Every feminist sensibility within her warned her to ignore the primal beast in front of her. He was just an alpha male throwing his weight around. Any enlightened woman should be able to see through such posturing.

But the brute strength of him, his barely-contained fire, and his glittering eyes turned her will to water. She felt the primal feminine inside her unfurling with desire, aching to melt into him, to surrender to him. Such an unfamiliar physical reaction to a man alarmed her more than any external threat. She had to get away from him. Now.

"Mrs. MacMillan!" she yelled, praying the housekeeper was within earshot. "Somebody, help!"

"Silence!" the man hissed. He pulled her backward, away from the door. Then he glanced over his shoulder, as if looking for a place to drag her. The brute was going to abduct her!

Tara tried to bite the flesh of his fingers, but his hand held her fast. Instead, she remembered the self-defense moves she'd learned from her personal trainer. She threw her weight to the right, ignoring the pain that shot up her injured leg, raised her left knee, and stamped as hard as she could on the top of the man's long foot. Just as she'd hoped, his suede boot afforded little protection from the steel shank of her shoe heel.

"Faith!" he gasped and staggered back, releasing her just as the door burst open.

"What's going on?" Mrs. MacMillan called, her hand on the door handle.

"Mrs. MacMillan, thank God!"

But as soon as she uttered words of relief, Tara felt a sudden shift in the air, as a vacuum of silence fanned out behind her. She knew without looking for proof that the man in the blue robe had vanished once again.

"What's wrong, Miss Lewis?" The housekeeper looked around, perplexed.

"There was a man," she began, sweeping the air behind her.

"What?"

"A man. The man I saw in the library. He was here!"

Mrs. MacMillan paused, and then carefully folded her hands below her generous breasts, as if composing herself after an obvious false alarm. "Really?" she said.

Tara bristled at the woman's doubtful tone. "I'm telling you, Mrs. MacMillan, that man was here. He must have been hiding in the room. Didn't you hear him talking?"

"Nay, miss. I heard nothing."

"He was here. I swear!"

"Then where did he go?"

"I don't know. He disappeared. Just like the last time."

Mrs. MacMillan returned her stare with an indulgent smile. "David said you had quite the bump on the head. Maybe you should rest, Miss Lewis. And try not agitate yourself so much."

"I'm not agitated!"

"Come, come." The housekeeper grasped her shoulders. "You're in quite a state, miss."

"That's because no one believes me!" Tara glanced around the room, her eyes wild. "And I swear, that man can appear and disappear—into thin air!"

MacMillan clucked and shook her head. "Sounds like a ghost to me."

"I can't believe you can say such a thing with a straight face."

"As I said before. You're in Scotland. 'Tis a magical place, you'll soon find out."

Tara pressed her lips together, knowing that butting heads with the housekeeper would get her nowhere but more frustrated.

"Sit yourself down, dear." Mrs. MacMillan gently urged her to the couch. "I'll have a wee look around, just to be sure this man you think you saw is not about."

"Thanks." Tara glanced at the shadows of the windowless dressing room across the way. She hugged her chest. "I appreciate it."

Mrs. MacMillan marched to the bathroom and searched it, even moving the door back and forth, and checking out the linen closet. Then she paced to the bed and stooped to look under it. By the time the housekeeper had completed her condescending search, Tara had recovered from her scare and had vowed not to lose her cool ever again in the Corbin House—no matter what she saw.

As Tara walked the housekeeper to the door, she reminded herself that she was a strong, accomplished woman who had come amazingly far on her own. She was smart, practical and levelheaded. She could manage whatever came her way—even in a ghost-riddled country like Scotland. She would find a way to banish the doubt she saw in people's eyes when they looked at her.

Their doubt only made Tara more determined to deal with the man in blue on her own, should he appear to her again. The intruder was obviously a coward, ducking out whenever anyone else showed up. If she could handle an executive producer in Hollywood, she could certainly handle the big brute in the bathrobe.

A few moments later, she heard a light knock on her door.

"May I come in?" a voice called.

Tara recognized Morag's voice and was surprised that Morag was still at Corbin Hall. She thought David's friend had left with the others.

"Sure," she answered. She closed the cover of her laptop as Morag swept into the room.

"I thought you went with David," Tara commented.

"I was going to, but he and John decided to drive into Ayr to deal with the car insurance people. So I came back to keep you company. And from what Mrs. MacMillan tells me, you might need some help unpacking."

"How thoughtful of you." Tara would have preferred to spend the morning alone, but she didn't say anything. Part of getting to know David was getting to know his family and friends. And from what Tara could tell, it looked as if Morag had been an integral part of David's life in Scotland.

Plus, if she looked on the bright side, maybe the man in the blue robe would make a third appearance while Morag was in the room. She would have a witness then, and no one would be able to accuse her of "seeing things." Tara glanced around the room, searching for evidence that the boorish man was still with them, and hoped he'd show himself again—at least from a distance.

Morag drifted to the doorway of the walk-in closet. "You didn't bring that much luggage," Morag remarked.

"I pack light."

"If I were going somewhere for two weeks, I'd have two suitcases just for my shoes!"

Tara forced a smile. She expected Morag to say something like that. The woman obviously liked her clothes. Even for a simple morning visit, she was well groomed. She was dressed in a yellow cotton skirt and blouse with a cashmere cardigan in a faint leopard print of yellow and white. Pearls hung at her throat, her ears, and her wrist. She'd even put on pink lipstick after breakfast, which accentuated the soft curves of her mouth. Again, Morag's innate femininity made Tara feel under dressed and undersexed in her black slacks and simple pullover.

Tara was accustomed to having a stylist groom her for the show, but here in Scotland she was on her own. She would have to ramp up her routine if she was going to compete with Morag for center stage.

Morag picked up one of the suitcases and settled it on a luggage stand.

"You don't mind if I help you unpack, do you?" she asked, turning to glance at Tara. "I don't have a sister, so I'm not sure what sisters do." She smiled. "But I hope we can be like sisters. I've always wanted one."

"Me, too."

But not one that outshone her every time she turned around.

Tara watched Morag unzip the suitcase. The blond woman drew out the white box she found inside and held it up.

"My wedding gown," Tara remarked.

"Oh!" Morag beamed. "May I have a look?"

"Of course."

Morag set the box on the chest of drawers in the middle of the closet and then carefully pulled off the lid of the box. Tara held her breath as Morag lifted up her wedding gown and let the gleaming folds of satin cascade nearly to the floor.

"How interesting," Morag crooned, turning the simple garment this way and that to admire it. "Plain, but it has a certain elegance."

Tara's heart flopped in her chest as she surveyed the scrap of satin that would change her life forever. Did every bride feel such dreadful anticipation?

Tara ran her tongue over her suddenly dry lips. Maybe dread was a little strong. She didn't dread marrying David. She just couldn't predict how their life together would turn out, or if she would be able to bear being tied to one man for the rest of her days. To be honest, she was fearful of such unpredictability, even though she knew that she couldn't control every aspect of her life. Still, she had never felt joy at the thought of her upcoming marriage, only a stomach-churning thrill that didn't seem normal. Her chest tightened.

She wasn't about to let Morag Smithbank see the slightest sign of her distress. She had to distract herself, get her mind completely off the wedding. For starters, she had to quit looking at the dress.

"It needs to breathe," Tara commented, reaching for the cloud of netting of her veil. "And the veil, too."

"Won't you try the dress on for me?" Morag asked.

"That would be bad luck."

"Only if David were to see you in it."

Tara avoided a second look at the gleaming gown while she handed the veil to Morag, all the while trying to drag a decent breath into her lungs. "Maybe some other time, Morag." She lifted her injured foot. "When I'm not sporting this ugly bandage."

"Oh, all right then." Morag frowned prettily, but did as Tara asked, fussing with the gown and veil while Tara hung up her slacks and shirts. Besides the wedding gown and one little black dress, she didn't own anything but pants. She'd never realized until meeting Morag how infrequently she wore a dress or skirt.

She wondered if David cared what she wore, or if he even noticed. He rarely commented on her appearance. In fact, the compliment at the breakfast table had been a pleasant surprise. Maybe he didn't think he needed to compliment her when he knew she received thousands of fan letters a day. Still, David's praise had been nice to hear.

"So, are you married, Morag?" she asked, deciding to reach out to the other woman.

"No, I've never found a man to suit me."

"Oh?"

Morag shrugged. "I've walked a fine line all my life, Tara, being the reverend's daughter with no money, yet rubbing shoulders with the likes of the Corbins. It made me want more from life than a rented flat, four children, and a husband who spends every night at the pub. So off I went to Edinburgh to get an education."

"You seem to have done quite well for yourself."

"Yes, but it's still not quite enough." She regarded the shining gown as she continued. "We fight our way to the top, Tara. No, we *claw* our way to the top, don't we? And then find out it just isn't enough."

"I know. I've spent the last ten years sacrificing everything for my career. But the older I get, the more I realize I'd rather have a family than keep the sweet spot on Thursday night." Tara shook her head in wonder. "For someone who works in television, that's saying a lot!"

"I hear you, girlfriend."

Tara reached for another blouse. "Women like us want it all. With sugar on top."

Morag chuckled. "Exactly!" Then she sobered. "So you're a lucky lassie to have caught David's eye."

"He's a great guy."

Morag looked over her shoulder at Tara. "And I'm so happy you two are being married in the old chapel."

"You know about that?"

"I was the one who suggested it. If I were ever to marry, that's where I'd want to have the ceremony. It's going to be so romantic!"

"But isn't the chapel in a ruined old castle?"

"Yes, but just think how lovely it will be on an autumn night with candles burning and pipers playing as the sun sets. I can just picture it!"

Tara studied Morag's rapt face as she spoke. Morag was more into the wedding ceremony than she was. In fact, Tara had got only as far as the dress. The rest of the details she'd left up to David. And look where it had got her: getting married in a moldering old building—and on television if David had his way.

Morag smoothed down the satin skirt of the gown. "It's perfect that David should marry there. Absolutely perfect. Like a wheel turning full circle—do you know what I mean?"

Tara nodded but didn't really follow her.

"After so many years, he's come back to his roots. When the time was right."

"I see." Tara moved a shirt into place. She preferred a color-coded closet, which sped up wardrobe selection. Years of working in television had developed the habit in her.

"Scotland's like that, you know." Morag drew the veil out to its full length and fluffed it gently. "It calls a person back. There's a spirit here that can't be denied, once it calls out to you."

"Unless you've gone deaf—" Tara said wryly as she reached for her folded lingerie. "—From too many Snow Patrol concerts."

Morag froze, her hands still holding the ends of the veil. She stared at Tara. Her radiant smile had vanished. "You mock me."

"I'm not mocking you, Morag. I just don't believe in spirits and callings, and that sort of thing." Tara gave a small laugh, hoping to jog Morag out of her sudden seriousness. "It's my job to debunk such claims. I'm good at it. In fact, if David thinks that Lady in Green entity is going to make an appearance at our wedding and win him an Emmy, he's going to be sadly disappointed."

"You know about our Lady in Green?"

"He told me she comes out of the woodwork once a year, yes."

"But you don't believe it."

"Have you ever seen her, Morag?"

"No, but I am not of the Corbin family. The Lady in Green is most often seen by members of the family."

"Why?"

"No one knows."

"So who was she?"

"No one knows that either, I'm afraid."

"Just another convenient mystery," Tara drawled.

"Scotland is steeped in such mysteries. You'll see."

"Truthfully, I wish I would see." Tara arranged her underwear in a row, black to the back, white to the front. "I'd like to believe in life after death, in the ability to communicate with the spirit world. But frankly, Morag, I've never seen a shred of evidence to prove such a world exists. Or that our spirits live after our bodies expire."

"What about last night?"

"You mean the man in the library?"

"Yes, what about him?"

Tara shrugged. “Like David said. He could have been anyone.”

“What if he wasn’t?” Morag let the veil fall into place in the closet.

“What are you getting at?”

“What if the person you saw was a spirit? A ghost? A tortured soul who couldn’t find peace?”

“Then, as we Yanks say in America, I’d eat my hat.”

Tara stowed the empty suitcases in a cabinet and brushed her hands together, anxious to get out of the airless walk-in closet.

A car horn tooted outside. David must be back. Tara hobbled down the stairs behind Morag as David and his uncle walked into the main hall.

“I found your book,” David announced, holding up her purse.

“Well done, you!” Morag exclaimed before Tara got in a word edgewise.

“It was still there, safe and sound. No vampire blood. Nothing.”

“Thanks.” Tara took the bag. His sarcastic words stung her, squelching the question she had intended to ask him, if he had noticed the sarcophagus lid had been moved.

“Chris called and said the crew’s on their way. Ready to take some shots at the old castle after lunch?” He grabbed her hand. “Think you’re up to it?”

“No, David. And I’m not going to be.”

“Why?” he asked, throwing a quick glance at Morag.

“Because one, I’m on vacation for the first time in two years, and two—it just isn’t fair, springing this on me without notice.” She pulled out of his grip. “I don’t know anything about that castle or its legends. I won’t be able to give a decent rational viewpoint.”

“Right,” David grinned. “So maybe I’ll win for a change!”

“It’s not about winning. It’s about presenting alternative explanations for strange phenomena—science over superstition.”

“That’s easy for you to say, Tara. You’re the one who always gets to debunk everything I discover. And I’m the one who ends up standing there holding the mic and looking like an idiot.”

“I just don’t think it’s fair, David.”

“I think it’s a delicious challenge,” Morag put in, hugging Tara around her shoulders. Morag’s sweet perfume enveloped her in a cloud. “And one that you’re up to, Tara.”

“Hey, M!” David wailed in mock complaint. “Whose side are you on?”

“Besides that,” Morag added, “I think your audience is going to love the tables being turned for once. Don't you, John?"

"I don't pretend to know what Americans like," John answered, putting his cap on a small table by the stairs. "But I've told Davy once and I'll tell him again—that old masonry isn't going to last forever. So tell your lads to be careful. No climbing and no big equipment up there. That castle is a necessary revenue stream, and I don't want the Highland Council shutting me down."

Tara glanced at David in surprise. He had failed to mention the castle might be unsafe. She planted her hands on her hips and turned to her fiancé as Lord Corbin retired to his rooms on the first floor. "The castle is dangerous?"

"No, it isn't dangerous. Uncle John's just a worry wart." David shook his head in disgust. "Castle Corbin's been standing since William the Conqueror. It'll stand for a few more days."

"I don't know, David. I don't like the sound of all this."

"It'll be fine, darling. You'll see."

"And just for the record, I still haven't agreed to having the ceremony—"

David grabbed her hand, interrupting her. "We'll talk about that later." He squeezed her fingers. "Just wait until you see the place, Tare. I'd forgotten how cool it is. You're going to change your mind."

Chapter 6

After lunch, Tara and the *Fact or Fiction* crew, as well as Morag Smithbank and Susan Fritch, Tara's assistant, piled into three cars and a van and drove the short distance to the ancient seat of the Corbin family. The castle perched on a knoll at the north of the property, standing sentinel high above a firth. As the others chattered away about their trip, Tara sat silent in the car, watching the castle take shape through the rain.

The best thing about seeing Castle Corbin for the first time was that the rain finally let up when they got there. The worst thing was standing outside the curtain wall of the old fortress and contemplating a walk through the forbidding arched portcullis. Tara stared at the dank stone bastion, still dripping with rain. There was something eerily still about the castle, as if it were sitting there listening, waiting for someone. This place was not a desolate ruin. It was very much alive. Every instinct in Tara's being told her to think twice about trespassing. She paused.

David looked back at her. "What's wrong?"

"There's something not right here."

"Exactly! That's why we're going to do an episode on it!"

"Look at the place," Morag commented, her tone dwindling off in wonderment. "It's been ages since I saw it."

Tara scanned the front of the castle. It was built of sandstone blocks on an outcropping of rock too high for a man to scale without mountaineering equipment. The size of the castle surprised her. She had expected to see a much larger building, with lots of circular towers and soaring crenellated walls. But Castle Corbin was barely over three stories tall, with a square entry that jutted out from two plain walls that stretched only a hundred feet on either side. Three squat towers had been constructed at the north, east, and west corners, and looked more like rounded afterthoughts than actual towers. She could count the windows on one hand. Only four narrow arrow slits punctured the entire span of the east curtain wall.

She tipped back her head to get a better view, but all she could see above the gray wall was the roof line and gabled windows of a much newer gatehouse inside the castle wall. The gables gave the impression of someone standing on tiptoe to peer over the battlements at her. She shivered and wrapped her arms around her chest.

This castle did not evoke the image of knights and ladies and merry medieval feasts. This castle spoke of ancient wars, of brutality, of blood and bones and death. If Dracula *had* existed, and if he *had* decided to buy a piece of Caledonian real estate, this would have been it.

"Come on," David urged. "We're losing precious time."

Tara hung back. "I don't like this place."

"What?" David looked over his shoulder at her.

"I don't like it." She glanced at the dark maw of the portcullis again. The gate looked like a mouth full of jagged iron teeth, waiting to shred her flesh. "I don't want to go in."

David gave an uncomfortable laugh. "I've never seen you like this." He glanced at Morag, as if to apologize for Tara's behavior. "Tara's the one who always goes where others fear to tread."

"But that's the thing," Tara countered. "I usually know where I'm going and what I'm getting into. I don't know a thing about this place. And I'm fairly sure I don't want to, either."

"Oh, live on the edge for once," David teased.

"There's nothing here to harm you, Tara." Morag gently touched her forearm. "We used to play here when we were bairns and nothing ever happened."

"Morag's right. It's just a pile of old stones. People come here all the time, hoping to see the Lady in Green. Nothing happens to them, either."

Tara glanced at the portcullis again. She'd never gotten the creeps like this from an old pile of stones, and she'd seen some pretty old piles.

David turned to fully face her. "Don't tell me you're *scared*!"

"I'm not scared," she retorted, flushing. "I just don't like the looks of the place, is all."

"Once you're inside the walls, it isn't so grim." Morag took her hand and urged her toward the gate. Tara didn't budge. It felt awkward to have the woman holding her hand.

She slipped out of Morag's grasp. "No need to drag me. I'm coming."

Morag laughed, and the sound echoed around them.

They wound through a jagged cut in the rock designed to force visitors to approach in single file, and trudged up a steep incline to the dark portcullis.

Much to Tara's relief, the iron gate didn't crash down and shred her flesh and the drawbridge didn't slam shut behind them as doors always did in horror movies. Still, Tara found herself holding her breath as David barked instructions to the camera crew that had arrived moments after them.

"I want a wide shot," he said to Chris. "Of me walking through this area."

"The bailey," Morag put in.

"Right, of me walking through the bailey, and then coming upon Tara over there." He pointed to the keep, where the Corbin family would have lived in the old days. "Go over there, Tare, and pop out of the shadows. You know how you always do it."

Tara glanced at the hall as a microphone was attached to her and her assistant Susan brushed powder on her forehead and nose.

The double wooden doors of the great hall had rotted away long ago, leaving the entry to the ancient family living quarters bare to the elements. Lichen and moss covered the crumbling wall. Grass grew from cracks in the floor. In the overcast gloom of the fall afternoon, the hall looked dark and dank—no place for the living. The hairs on the back of Tara's neck stood on end.

"Is there enough light today?" Tara asked Chris, stalling for time.

"Just." He studied a meter he pointed in the direction she would take. "As long as we don't waste too much time."

"How's my make-up?" Tara asked, turning toward Susan.

Susan stepped forward and brushed her nose with powder again. Even in the Scottish mist, her blonde bob kept its bouncy shape. "It's fine, boss. You look fine."

"Thanks," Tara glanced down at her petite assistant, who never complained and was willing to do anything at anytime to prove that she had what it took to succeed in show business—a bit like herself, actually. Maybe too much like herself. Susan projected an image of a loyal assistant, and she really did seem to have Tara's best interests at heart, but Tara had learned the hard way that people in Hollywood were usually not as loyal as they seemed. Still, she was glad to have Susan at her side.

"What about the script?" Tara held out her arms as the technician fiddled with her mic. "I can't work without a script."

"Just act nervous," David replied. "The way you're doing. It'll be perfect."

Tara opened her mouth to deny that she was acting nervous but let the protest die. She knew that David was too self-absorbed at the moment to care about the difference between being scared and being prudent. Plus, she didn't want to waste time arguing. The sooner she got the shot over with, the sooner she could get out of the castle. And that wouldn't be soon enough for her.

Briskly, she walked across the yard to the ditch-like moat, which had dried up long ago, and on to the entry of the keep. She slipped through the fifteen-foot portal and around the corner, out of view of the camera. More stairs climbed into the gloom behind her.

"Perfect!" David called.

Tara backed to the front wall of the keep, forcing herself to concentrate on the work at hand, and refusing to gaze too deeply into the shadowy shells of the rooms on the ground floor. She could hear the drone of David's voice as he approached. She readied herself to step into his path.

"And here in the hall," David said, slowly backing up the stairs, "Is where the mysterious Lady in Green is said to appear to the members of the Corbin family."

The moment had come for Tara's appearance. She stepped away from the wall.

"Lady in Green?" she repeated in a scathing tone she often used on the show.

"Ah, Tara!" David smiled in mock surprise. "Just the person I didn't *want* to see. What are you doing in Scotland?"

"I'm here to set the record straight, as usual." She smiled at the camera, projecting more confidence than she felt inside.

"Not this time, Miss Lewis." David turned slightly, which put his back to the wide staircase and the old kitchen beyond it. The bones of the rooms were outlined by partially standing walls and two lines of columns marching to a huge fireplace. "This is one phenomena you won't be able to explain away."

"Cut!" Chris called out. "It's one phenome*non*, David."

"Shit!"

Chris made them repeat the entry scene two more times before he was satisfied. On the third take, just as Tara gave her reason for being in Scotland, she broke off. Something had moved in the shadows at the top of the stairs.

David whirled around. "Did you see something?" he asked, peering into the bowels of the building.

"Something moved." Tara pointed to the landing ten feet up the stairs. "Up there."

"I don't see anything." He squinted and took a few steps toward the staircase. Tara followed him as four cameramen trailed after them, continuing to film at multiple angles.

"The local folk claim the Lady in Green is a fairy or *gruigach*," David went on with his narrative. "Who often appears to members of the Corbin family. Some say the lady is a harbinger of bad news, that she shows up before tragedy befalls the house."

David's voice was nothing but a hum as Tara scanned the shadows on the stairs, straining to catch the slightest movement again or pick up on a telltale sound.

"But whatever the Lady in Green's reasons are for haunting Corbin Castle, she never fails to appear to the general public on October 11th. No one knows why she shows up on that particular date. But *Fact or Fiction* intends to catch the Lady in Green in action. We hope—for the first time in television history—to capture the image of a ghost on film."

He turned slightly, enough to allow Tara to share the shot with him. "And now the voice of reason—"

Tara choked. She had heard her cue. She knew her role well. She was supposed to offer a scientific explanation for how shifting filtered light could look like a figure moving in the distance, or how wind swirling through a chimney could produce a melancholy moan.

But five years of working on *Fact or Fiction* could not explain the vision that she was seeing now. She couldn't believe what was happening to her. Ever since she'd stepped foot on Scottish soil, she'd begun to see things—things that were not supposed to be there. Not in her world, anyway.

"Tara?" David's voice was closer this time. More insistent. Odd, how he didn't seem concerned that his bride-to-be was struck dumb with alarm.

"Tara?" Morag repeated from the sidelines.

Tara swallowed, her eyes glued to the figure she saw standing on the landing and staring back at her. The woman was tiny, probably less than five feet tall. She had a medieval headdress on that covered her hair, a veil that draped around her jaw and shoulders and framed her serious, narrow face, and huge blue eyes. She wore a green gown with long sleeves that hung nearly to the ground. And she just stood there, staring back at Tara as if trying to make out the modern woman as intently as Tara was trying to make sense of what she was seeing.

"Tara?" David clutched her arm. "What's wrong?"

"It's—it's her," Tara breathed, barely able to speak. "The Lady in Green."

The cameras pivoted and so did David.

"Where?"

"There." Tara pointed. "Up those stairs."

"I don't see anything," Morag slipped around Tara, keeping out of view of the cameras. "Where?"

"She's standing just there." Tara swallowed back her incredulity. "She's looking at us."

"I don't see anything," David exclaimed. "But maybe the cameras will pick up something."

Tara stared, awestruck by the vision. Then the Lady in Green suddenly sneezed, breaking the spell. Tara didn't have much experience with spirits, but she was pretty sure they didn't sneeze.

"Wait a minute!" Tara turned on her fiancé, infuriated. "It's a set-up!" She flushed with the realization that David and his Scottish sidekick had come up with a way to trick her, to essentially humiliate her on camera. "It's a God-damn set-up!"

"Mr. Corbin, are we done?" the lady in green wailed, pulling at the veil. "It's really cold up here!"

"Cut!" Chris yelled.

"Dammit, Tara!" David threw her a hard glance. "It was perfect. Why couldn't you just go along with it?"

"Because it isn't real!"

"It might be. It could happen. And it *might* happen in a few days."

"Then film it in a few days, David. And don't go toying with me!" Tara turned on her heel. Even though her ankle protested, she stomped away, furious at her cohost.

"Tara!" David called after her.

She refused to acknowledge him with a reply. Fuming, she strode across the yard and through the cramped tunnel entry, with Susan skittering to keep up with her in her platform wedgies. As they burst through the portcullis, a flutter of crows took flight, cawing and beating the air with their huge glossy wings, startling Tara.

Tara gulped back her shock, determined not to show the slightest weakness to anyone on *Fact or Fiction*. Something was going on there, but she wasn't sure what yet or who was involved.

"I want everything you can find on this castle, Susan," she said through clenched teeth. "I want to know more about this castle than all the Corbin family combined." She yanked open the car door. "Do you understand me?"

"Right, boss."

"I want to see everything you can find on the legend of the Lady in Green."

"Right." Susan wrote everything down in her little notebook as Tara dropped into the driver's seat. "And see if there's anything special about that date, October 11th."

"Okay."

"Now get in."

"But what about David and Miss Smithbank?"

"They can hitchhike back for all I care."

Tara turned on the engine with a sharp flick of her wrist. She'd never driven a car in the UK before, and it felt strange to be sitting on the other side of the vehicle. But there was no time like the present to learn to handle herself on the Scottish roads. And she was damned if she was going to ask anyone for favors. Tara roared away from the castle.

Chapter 7

Tara was still upset about David's shenanigans at the castle as she pulled the car up in front of Corbin Hall. She couldn't figure out what his motives were. Was he trying to show her up to his Scottish chum? Was he trying to undermine her credibility with the crew? Why? And why had he gone behind her back to arrange for the shoot at Castle Corbin? It was the first time in their partnership that he had done something without consulting her first. Deep in thought, Tara let herself into her room while Susan continued down the hall to her chamber, to start her research.

Tara limped across her room to the desk and set her purse down. Then she opened it, and pulled out the sandalwood box containing her Psalter. Whenever she was distraught or troubled, she often turned to the little book for solace. Not only were the ancient verses consoling, the illuminations were still as beautiful as the day they were painted and never ceased to lift her spirits. She had just set the box on the desk when John appeared at her open door.

"Settling in all right, are you, then, Tara?"

"Yes. Thanks." It was tough to modulate the anger out of her voice. John didn't seem to notice that she was troubled, so her acting must be convincing. She took a couple of deep calming breaths.

John strolled to the writing desk where she had arranged the items she had carried on the plane, items she was overjoyed to have back from the bramble-covered glen: her phone, the emerald necklace she'd bought for herself when she'd landed the television show, her tiny laptop, but most of all, the Psalter.

John glanced down at the sandalwood box in which she kept the prayer book. The box was as old as the Psalter, and boasted an intricately carved lid that depicted a crow, its wings outstretched, its talons clutching a sword.

"Did David give you this box?"

"Actually, no, but it's a strange coincidence, isn't it?" She drifted toward John. "David tells me the crow and sword are part of your family crest."

"They are."

"Perhaps that's why David and I were meant to be together. Maybe we're linked through the time and space continuum." She gave a quiet laugh. John smiled shallowly, but never took his stare off the box.

"You sound like your television program," he remarked.

"Do you get *Fact or Fiction* here in the UK?"

"Of course. I believe Mrs. MacMillan watches it every week. And I've seen it on occasion." He glanced at her and his gaze swept down her body and then back up to her face. "I feel as if I know you already, Miss Lewis."

Tara guessed he intended his words to convey friendly familiarity, but something in his eyes made the words turn dark—as if spoken by a voyeur or a detective with an ulterior motive. She forced a smile.

"Then you'll have to tell me more about the Corbin family history so I can get to know *you*."

"Whenever you like." He turned back to the sandalwood box sitting on the desk and motioned toward it with a slender hand. "But where did you get this curious box, if you don't mind me asking?"

"It's been in my family for ages. It's the only thing I have of theirs that's worth keeping."

"What about the Psalter? Has it been in your family, too?"

"Yes. It belonged to my mother." She stood near John's shoulder. "It's all I have of her."

"I see. And where did your mother get the book?"

"From her mother, I expect. People have written a series of names in the front of the book. I assume they're family names. But I don't know for sure. My mother—"

Tara paused. She didn't want to lie to a member of David's family, but she was trapped by publicity fabrications of her own design. Her fictionalized life story was well documented. "As you probably know, my mother died young before she could tell me."

"I see." He studied the box. "It seems valuable. I marvel that you travel with it."

"I take it with me wherever I go." Tara smiled quietly. "It's strange, but I find comfort from it."

"Really? From a Psalter?" He shot a glance at her. "David tells me you aren't the religious type."

"I'm not." She shrugged. "But there's one passage in the book—" She paused and closed her eyes, letting the words come to her. "*In peace I will both lie down and sleep; for Thou alone, O Lord, makest me dwell in safety*."

She opened her eyes to find Lord Corbin studying her, a dark look on his face. Unnerved, she gave a short laugh. "I have trouble sleeping."

"I see." He turned back to the book. "Have you ever had the Psalter evaluated by an expert?" he asked without looking at her.

Something about John put her on edge—perhaps because he remained cold to her.

"No." She shrugged, wondering why he was so curious.

"It might be worth quite a tidy sum, if it's anything like this box."

"I was never interested in finding out how much it's worth. I'd never sell it."

"That's what people always say." John finally lifted his gaze. "And how many questions must I pose before you allow me to look at your precious Psalter?"

Tara smiled. "I thought you weren't into books."

"But you have piqued my interest in this one. I'd like to see it."

"Sorry, John, but I usually don't handle it without gloves." She pulled the box toward her. "And unfortunately, the gloves I use were lost in the accident."

"How disappointing." John frowned. "I will look into getting some for you then. I believe Mrs. MacMillan may have a pair."

Before she could offer her thanks, Mrs. MacMillan appeared in the doorway.

"Excuse me, Lord Corbin, but there's a man here to see you. A Mr. Garry?"

John glanced at the housekeeper and frowned. Then he turned to Tara as Mrs. MacMillan ducked back out of the room. "If you will excuse me?" He seemed perturbed. "I must attend to this person."

"Of course. You can see the Psalter later."

"Indeed, I hope so. In the meantime, you might consider storing your book in the family vault."

"Do you think I need to? Your staff seems above reproach."

"They are."

"Then I prefer to keep the Psalter with me."

"As you wish." He strode to the door. "I'll see you at tea, my dear. Mrs. MacMillan will be serving it in a few minutes."

Tara glanced back at the sandalwood box, wondering if she were taking a foolish risk in leaving it out in the open on the desk. Then again, if she couldn't trust David's family, whom *could* she trust?

She picked up the box.

Just as John left, David appeared at her door.

"Still mad?" he asked, raising his eyebrows, his hand poised on the latch.

"What do you think?" She could barely look at him.

"We had to get the footage." He stepped gingerly into the room as if testing the state of her emotions. "Just in case."

"Really?" she glared at David, putting a halt to his forward motion. "Or are you planning something else you haven't told me about?"

"Like what?"

"Like tricking the audience with a bogus ghost."

David paled just enough to confirm her suspicions.

Tara set down the sandalwood box. "You're going to use fake footage in case the real Lady in Green doesn't show up. That's what you're going to do, aren't you?"

David guffawed. "No!"

She walked toward him, her anger mounting. "You would undermine the credibility of the show with fake footage!"

"I'd never do that, Tara!"

"For the first time in the history of *Fact or Fiction*, you'd stoop to doctoring footage."

"I never said I was going to do anything of the sort! But it couldn't hurt—for the ratings, I mean."

"What's happened to you, David?" She crossed her arms over her chest.

"What do you mean?"

"You get here a few days before I do and turn into someone I don't even know!"

"I could say the same for you, Tara." He planted a hand on his left hip as he drawled out her name.

"What's that supposed to mean?"

"Seeing things that aren't there."

Tara flushed. "The man I saw was *there*."

"So you say, darling. So you say."

Tara stared at him, knowing that they'd reached an impasse. She couldn't explain what she'd seen. Not yet, anyway. And David wouldn't admit to any wrongdoing.

"I'm going to run through the footage with Chris," David finally said. "Are you interested?"

"To see the Lady in Green—polyester? Hardly!"

"Have it your way, then." He gave her a mocking salute and ducked out of the doorway.

Tara watched David leave, surprised at his enthusiasm for the project. The situation was usually reversed, with her laboring over the editing process while he watched European football. At David's increasingly odd behavior, her suspicions that all was not right intensified. She frowned.

There was no time for looking at the Psalter now, with or without her gloves. Staying in her room during tea would be an insult to her host. Tara glanced at the wooden box in her hand. She wished she could take the Psalter with her. But that would be impractical. Instead, she carefully stowed it in the drawer of the night stand beside her bed. Then she headed down the stairs for the parlor.

"I'm knackered!" Someone exclaimed as Tara approached the doorway of the parlor.

Tara recognized Morag's too-familiar voice. The blonde must have decided to stay for tea. Tara wasn't surprised. She set her jaw, determined to hide her dismay at the omnipresence of David's chum, and hobbled into the room.

"High heels weren't meant for hiking around castles, that's for certain," Morag remarked, looking up at Tara as she rubbed her calf. "You are so sensible, Tara, with your sandals and slacks."

"But not nearly as fetching." Tara gave her a cool smile.

"I hope you aren't still mad at David." Morag's blue eyes studied her.

"I'll cope."

"Where is he, anyway?"

"I thought you would know," Tara replied, feeling a bit catty, but unable to bite back her words.

"He wanted to look at the footage," John explained. He motioned toward the couch. "Tara?"

"Thanks." Tara sank into the chintz-covered sofa, grateful to get off her feet. Low afternoon light filtered through the lace curtains, filling the room with mote-infused ether. A tea service had been set out, complete with sandwiches and scones. Tara's stomach rumbled at the sight of clotted cream and preserves sitting next to the fluffy white buns.

"So what did you think of the old castle, Tara?" John motioned for her to help herself.

"It was quite the experience." Tara reached for a scone. "I've never seen anything that old."

"Come on," Morag teased. "You hated it."

"I didn't hate it."

"She didn't want to go in, John." Morag winked at her. "I could swear she was spooked!"

"I was not spooked!" Tara retorted, flushing.

"It can have that effect," John replied. "It's a ramshackle old ruin, so it is, but I do my best to keep the walls from crumbling. There and here."

"I see no evidence of crumbling at Corbin Hall."

"Good. I'm doing my caretaker job well, then."

"Caretaker? I thought you owned the property."

"I do. But I think of myself as its caretaker. After me another Corbin will see that the estate survives intact."

"Unless it winds up like the Ayr place," Morag put in, stirring her tea.

"Over my dead body!" John exclaimed.

"Really?" Morag drawled. "I see no heirs running around."

"I still have some years in me. And there's always David. He will certainly have children." John straightened his shoulders. "A Corbin has held this property since William the Conqueror, and I won't see the tradition end with my generation. I'd rather jump off a cliff."

"Strong words." Morag smiled at Tara and took a sip of her tea.

"What happened with the Ayr place?" Tara inquired, anxious to make sense of their conversation. She took a bite of her scone and savored the sweet and creamy combination of spreads she'd piled on top.

"Oh, the old chap who owned it—Samuel Beck was his name." John put a third spoonful of sugar in his tea. "Went to his grave two years ago without producing an heir. The bloodline died with him."

"So what happens, then, when there is no heir to an estate?"

"Who would know?" Morag chuckled. "Someone always comes crawling out of the woodwork to stake a claim."

"It will be harder to make a claim this time, my girl," John put his cup back in the saucer. Tara noticed the flesh around his eyes was more careworn than David's, his cheeks and nose colored by a fragile network of tiny capillaries. "Old Beck left behind a sample of his DNA. Whoever comes forward will have to be a near perfect match."

Tara pressed for an answer. "But if no one appears?"

"Then the property goes up for auction." John sat back and sighed. His gaze shifted inward as he lapsed into thought, tapping his cup and saucer with his right index finger.

"I take it you would be interested in the place?" Tara ventured.

"Of course he would," Morag poured a second cup of tea. "The property borders the Corbin estate on the west. It would be a real coup to gain ownership of that land."

"Regain, you mean," John said. "That land once belonged to us."

"What happened?" Tara leaned forward, always ready to hear a story. "Was it lost somehow?"

"Hardly. One of my forefathers had to pay the price of royal disfavor by surrendering land to the Crown—which ended up being the Ayr estate. It was passed along to some half-naked barbarian—a Norseman—who had done a favor for the king. Probably slaughtered entire villages or some such thing. I'm not sure what."

"A Norseman? You mean from Norway?"

"The very same." John smiled. "Scotland's swimming with Viking genes and so is France—didn't you know?"

"I didn't, no. I really don't know much about the UK."

"Norsemen were forever raiding our coastlines. They were dominant in the area at one time, even making conquests in France. That's where the place name of Normandy comes from. Land of the north men."

"I never realized that!"

Morag crossed her shapely legs. "They were huge brutes for their time, taller than average and quite fierce. They must have seemed like monsters roaring out of the mist. I can almost picture it."

"Most likely smoke and mirrors were involved," Tara countered with a wry smile. "That's what it always is. Theatrics and advance PR."

"Well, not to worry," John put in. "After a thousand years, the Normans have been assimilated. The chances of meeting one of Morag's big brutes are slim."

"Still, one can hope," Morag purred. She wiggled her eyebrows at Tara.

Tara gave her a begrudging smile in return. Morag was beguiling. She'd give her that. But how much had the blond woman beguiled David? That was the real question.

She sipped her tea, her thoughts swirling. And that's when the jet lag hit.

Chapter 8

The rattle of something hitting the floor woke Tara from a deep sleep. She opened her eyes, struggling to adjust to the low light, and was surprised to find herself in bed. She could barely remember falling onto the comforter after tea, when she'd found herself overcome by the travel and trauma of the past two days. She did remember telling herself that she would shut her eyes for only a few seconds. But she must have napped for hours instead of minutes, because she had awakened to a room that was pitch black and chilly.

Then she saw movement by her desk. Someone small stood across the room with their back turned to the bed.

"Robbie?" Tara called out.

The figure turned. All Tara could make out was a dark wedge-like shape topped by a pale oval face.

"Robbie?" she repeated, even though she was fairly sure the boy's silhouette would not match the one by the desk. Still, the shape looked oddly familiar. Who else would be that small, but Robbie? Tara flung her legs over the side of the bed and dropped to the floor.

"Who's there?" she demanded.

Then it dawned on her. The chick from the shoot must be staying at Corbin Hall with the rest of the crew. Not only was she a fledgling actor, it appeared she was a thief as well—with the audacity to break into Tara Lewis' room and go snooping around her things. In fact, she was probably trying to steal Tara's necklace—only she had fumbled in the darkness and dropped the gems on the floor.

Tara snapped on the lamp near the bed. Light pooled around her but did little to illuminate the rest of the huge room. The couch, desk, and curtains at the far wall remained vague silhouettes.

"Get out!" Tara demanded. She pointed toward the door. "Now! Before I call the police."

The figure didn't move from her stance by the desk. Tara strained to get a clearer view. The desk stood at the far wall across the vast room and was still bathed in gloom. All she could see was the woman's white featureless face and the long dark dress.

"Better ditch the costume," Tara said, limping closer to make sure nothing on the desk was missing. "Cat burglars shouldn't wear long dresses. They get in the way."

The figure said nothing. The young woman must be petrified to have been discovered stealing.

Tara walked past the couch. "Stealing that necklace would be a felony in the States," she remarked. "I'd clear out if I were you. And I mean now." When the young woman didn't respond, Tara added, "I could press charges, you know."

Tara was close enough now to see the woman's features. Her face was pale and drawn, and though she was quite young—probably in her twenties—she looked haggard and worn out. In fact, she looked downright emaciated. But it was the woman's eyes that captured Tara's attention. The pale blue eyes, looming huge and feverish in the cavernous sockets of her skull, stared at her, studying her fiercely. They were eyes full of suffering and sadness and hungering intent.

Tara paused, momentarily stunned, as a shiver of unease passed over her. Whoever stood before her was not an actress. Not even the most driven, self-starving ingénue would be as thin as the woman by the desk. In fact, the figure didn't even seem all that human. Call it a trick of light, but up close the female image appeared to be semi-transparent. Tara could see the darker outlines of the desk through the woman's heavy skirt.

What was going on? First, the knight had appeared and disappeared in this room, and now she was being visited by an ephemeral wraith. What kind of Scottish trickery was this? Was this room a conduit for the paranormal? No wonder Robbie had fled from the chamber as soon as he could.

Tara took a step backward, her heart thudding, unsure what she was seeing or what kind of danger she might be in. There was a light switch ten feet behind her, and she intended to flick it on as soon as possible.

But before Tara could reach the switch, the woman lifted her right arm and slowly pointed toward the windowless closet across the room, as if the effort was almost more than she could manage. Her colorless lips mouthed two syllables, as if she had no voice, as if she hadn't the strength to push air from her lungs and up her throat. Tara stared, trying hard to make sense of the woman's behavior.

"What are you saying?" she demanded.

The woman repeated the soundless word, all the time staring at Tara as if she imagined her intense gaze had the power to brand the word into

Tara's thoughts. Tara could tell the word started with a "B" and had a "W" in it, but that was all she could decipher.

"I don't get what you're saying," Tara said.

The woman slumped, obviously disappointed. Then she put her hand over her heart. Slowly, she lifted her other arm and pointed at the window with fingers so skeletal, they looked like bird claws. Her eyes glowed like twin blue fires in the darkness, imploring Tara to understand her meaning.

"Sorry. I don't know mime," Tara commented, her voice tight with unease. She swiped the wall with her palm until she located the light switch. She turned it upward, and the room burst into light.

Tara blinked, disbelieving her own eyes. The bedchamber was empty, and the figure in green had vanished.

With her body still charged with adrenaline, Tara shoved her feet into her sandals and fled from the room, determined to make sense of what she'd just seen. She found David and John in the billiard room playing a game of snooker. When she barreled across the threshold of the room, David looked up, his lips parting in surprise.

"You're up," he commented. She could tell from his jaunty smile that he hoped she had slept off her anger toward him. She had no intention of letting him off that easily.

"Oh, I'm up all right." She plowed toward the billiard table, feeling her anger increase at the smile on David's face. John planted the end of his cue stick on the floor, as if to defend the room from her.

"Is there something wrong?" he asked.

"Yes, but I think it's between David and me."

"What's eating you now?" David glanced at her hair. "And I don't mind saying, Tara, you look a fright."

Tara put a hand to her hair, realizing what she must look like. She'd slept for hours and hadn't even thought to brush her hair. Worse, her hand was shaking. John stared at her, clutching his cue stick.

"Never mind how I look," she retorted, clamping her hands under her arms. "Where's that actress?"

"What actress?"

"The one you hired for the shoot. The imposter lady."

"I don't know." David shrugged. "I think she went into town with the crew."

"You think, but you aren't sure."

"What do I look like—a casting director?" David gave his trademark snort and glanced at his uncle. "I couldn't swear she went into town, no."

"Why do you ask?" John inquired.

"I believe she was up in my room just now."

David sighed and rolled his eyes. "Not this again."

His reaction rekindled the anger that had only smoldered while she slept. Now it flared up again, full force.

"David, I swear—" she began, before biting off the rest of her words. It took every ounce of her self-control to keep from slapping him. She clenched her fists at her sides.

"Swear what?" David's lip curled. "That you'll quit believing every God damn dream you have is real? That would be a step in the right direction."

"The things I'm seeing here are *not* dreams!"

"Right. Take the god damn pills the doctor gave you, get a decent night's sleep for once, and then we'll talk."

"You know I hate taking those pills."

"Because they make your thinking fuzzy," he mocked her in a high feminine tone, using the comment she had often made about her medication. "Well, if you want to know the truth, darling, your thinking hasn't been all that clear lately."

"You asshole!" Tara cried, lunging for him.

"Hold on there!" John caught her arm and held her back. "Both of you!" He propped his cue against the table. "Now Davy, you're being a bit hard on the lass. She's had a bump on the head. That's all."

"And she's taking it out on me!"

"That's not it at all!" Tara tried to yank out of John's grip. "I'm not the one who planned an entire shoot behind his cohost's back."

"It was last minute!" David yelled back. "Can't you get that through your head? It was last minute, Tara. And a stroke of genius!"

"Really? Or was it something that Morag Smithbag hatched?"

"It's Smith*bank*!"

"Whatever!"

"Children!" John shouted. "Right, you two!"

Tara glared at David. "Let go of me, John," she said through clenched teeth.

"If you promise not to scratch my nephew's eyes out."

"I will, if he promises to keep his so-called childhood chum out of my face."

John glanced at his nephew. "Davy?"

David crossed his arms. “I knew it was something about Morag.”

“It’s not about your dear old M,” Tara retorted. “It’s about you, David. Not confiding in me and not having faith in me.”

“Oh, come on.” David rolled his eyes again. “You give me proof of the man in the library and I’ll believe anything you say. You’re the proof-meister. Why don’t you show me some?”

“Oh, I’ll find proof, I can promise you that.” She pulled out of John’s grip.

John strode around the end of the bar and picked up a crystal decanter. “Right now, what you both need is a wee break and a stiff drink. Davy?”

“A double.” David let his arms fall free and stepped toward the bar.

“Tara?”

“I don’t usually drink hard liquor.”

“A stiff whisky will do you a world of good. It’s been a tough couple of days for you.”

John poured a generous portion of a fifteen-year-old single malt into a cut crystal tumbler and handed it to his nephew. “Now then, Davy, you get your relationship with Morag straightened out, or I’ll do it myself.”

“What relationship?” Tara stepped closer as John poured another drink for her.

“Davy?” John stared at his nephew, waiting for him to speak. Tara stared as well, wondering what connection there was between David and Morag. All along she’d sensed an undercurrent between them.

When David didn’t say anything, John added. “She expects to become the mistress of this house one day.” He gave the glass to Tara. “And she’s but a mere commoner. The daughter of small town preacher.”

“Oh?” Tara fought back a flush, wondering what John had made of her own background. “Is having a title a prerequisite for marrying David?”

“Hardly.” David swallowed his drink. “But John hasn’t accepted the twentieth century, let alone the twenty-first.”

“Some things don’t change over time, my boy,” John snapped. “And one of them is the importance of a person’s heritage.”

“Morag’s harmless.”

“Still, it’s time you told her that you aren’t interested. The woman’s wasting her life away waiting for you.”

Tara thought the conversation was odd in light of her upcoming wedding to David. There was no need to tell Morag to back off when David was going to be married in a few days.

Then a sudden thought occurred to Tara: David hadn't told his uncle about their upcoming marriage. John had no idea a wedding loomed on the horizon to another mere commoner. Her breath caught in her throat as anger and incredulity choked her. Out of fear or rudeness, David hadn't told his uncle that she and he were to be married on Saturday. No wonder he'd been acting funny. She turned to him, her anger mounting.

"Time to tell it like it is," John added.

"I agree, David. It's time you made your intentions clear— to everyone."

David shot her a warning glance. "In my own way, if you don't mind."

"How many years have you known her?" Tara asked.

He shrugged. "I don't know. I've lost count."

"Morag's spent over twenty-five years tending her friendship with David." John poured himself a second drink. "And her position here made known—always on the scene, always making sure she is part of the family."

"You never mentioned that."

David threw her a glance. "Why would I? Like I said. She means nothing to me."

"Then if she means nothing to you, Davy, let the girl know."

David plopped down on a chair and scowled. "You don't know Morag. She won't take no for an answer."

"She seems reasonable to me," Tara put in.

"She's like a terrier. Once she gets hold of an idea—"

"Well, she's simply got to understand that she hasn't a hope in hell of becoming your wife." John sipped his drink. "When you take a wife, it's going to be an advantageous match."

David rolled his eyes. "No, it isn't, Uncle John. It's going to be to someone of my own choosing."

"Maybe even someone like me," Tara put in, too angry to hold back for David's sake.

John gave her a scathing glance and then turned his attention back to his nephew. "You would take the chance of being disinherited?"

"Of this?" David swept the air with a slender hand. "You think I want this place? That I'd ever move back to Scotland? You're crazy!"

"David!" Tara couldn't believe he would throw away his birthright or insult his uncle so blatantly.

"It's your duty!" John slammed his glass on the bar, shocking Tara. "You will be the next lord of this house!"

"But it's my life!" David yelled back. "And it's not going to be lived in the UK!"

"You'd turn your back on your family?" John's gray eyes flashed. "Your history?"

"If you call a bunch of crumbling stones and a herd of sheep history, you're damn right I would."

John's face turned red. "I'll forget you said that."

"Why? It's the truth."

"These are hard times for old families like ours," John retorted. "But we've survived. We always survive. That's the Corbin legacy. Survival."

"Really?" David sneered. "Well, maybe I just don't see the allure."

John glared at him. "You think you've got the world by the tail with all your jet-setting, with all your stocks and bonds and fancy cars, don't you? Well, some of us chose to stay in Scotland and fight the good fight—like men!"

"So I'm a quitter, am I?" It was David's turn to slam down his glass. "A Nancy Boy. Is that what you're saying?"

Tara looked from one man to the other, amazed how easily the argument had shifted from David and Morag to David and his uncle. She had to do something before the two men came to blows. To defuse the situation, she held out her empty glass.

"You were right, John. The whisky has done the trick! May I have another, please?" She wiggled the cup in the air. "Before the civil war turns into a clan war?"

"The Corbins don't have a clan," David growled. "We're Lowland Scots. I've told you that before."

"In fact we're French," John added, tipping the decanter to her glass. "And have never had a thing to do with the barbarian horde up north."

"I see." She sipped her drink. "So can we all call a truce then, here in the Lowlands?"

"Aye." John glanced at his nephew, and David reluctantly nodded.

She could see the anger ease out of John's shoulders.

"Sorry, Tara. I didn't mean to go off like that." He poured a second drink and came around the bar.

"Right." David sighed and picked up his cue stick, willing to ignore his uncle's insult for the sake of family harmony, just as she hoped he would.

"I'm ready to finish the game, Uncle John."

"And then you and the lass can go upstairs and get ready for dinner,"

John set his glass on a nearby table. "And start behaving like civilized adults."

Tara walked up to the billiard table and stood beside David. "Before you go on with your game, would you mind answering a few questions?"

John paused, his drink at his lower lip. "About what?"

"First off, did you happen to see anything strange at the tomb this morning?"

"What do you mean, strange?" David glanced across at her, puzzled.

"You didn't see anything out of the ordinary?"

David shot a look at his uncle and then back at Tara. "Not that I noticed. What are you getting at?"

"What about the coffin itself? Did you happen to look at it?"

"Not really. I was concentrating on retrieving your things."

"So you didn't notice if the sarcophagus was open or not?"

"Now that you mention it," John put in, picking up his cue stick. "It was."

"Did you happen to see what was buried in that sarcophagus?"

"It was empty," John put in. "I did notice that."

"Which isn't surprising," David added. "People rob graves all the time. How else do you think the museums get their displays?"

Tara sighed and fell silent. David had provided her with a perfectly good explanation. Unfortunately his comments did not jibe with what she had experienced at the tomb the previous day. She bit back further questions, however, unwilling to suffer more comments about the state of her mind should she admit to seeing the sarcophagus lid move and smelling that horrible burned odor.

"Why do you ask, Tara?" John sat back. "Did you expect us to be molested in some way—maybe by a ghost?"

David patted Tara's hand that rested on the polished edge of the table. "Tara doesn't believe in ghosts. She'll be the first to say it."

"Don't you now?" John leveled his gaze on her.

"No, I don't. There's always a rational explanation for things. Always." She pulled her hand away from David, annoyed that he'd repeated Morag's condescending behavior at the breakfast table. "And that brings me to my second question."

"And what is that?" John sipped his drink.

"What's with Robbie and the room I'm staying in?"

"What do you mean, lass?"

"He acted like his feet were on fire the entire time he was in the room. Like he couldn't wait to get out."

"You know how lads are in the company of a pretty woman."

"That wasn't it," Tara countered, ignoring the implied compliment. "He wasn't nervous. He was frightened."

David and John exchanged a quick glance.

"He told me his mother advised him not to spend any time in the room. Why is that?"

David waved her off. "Old wives tales. Pay no attention to the boy."

"Really?" Tara turned to his uncle to find him studying the remains of his drink. "John?"

"Davy's right. Women round here tell stories to their bairns to put the fear of God into them." He met her gaze. "You'd find the tales laughable, my dear. They've stories about fairies, enchanted shirts, tree-people, you name it."

"Robbie's grandmother was the worst," David remarked. "She used to scare me silly when I was a kid."

"I see."

"Folks around here don't have your rational attitude," John added. "They believe in all kinds of things. Makes their lives more exciting, I suppose. Gives them a reason to believe in something more than the gritty day-to-day. In the old days, that's all they had, lass."

"Are there any hidden passages in that room?" she continued. "Any trap doors?"

"None that I know of," John put down his empty glass.

Tara studied the man, dissatisfied with the answers she'd received.

"Any more questions, Miss Lewis?" David asked, lining up for his shot. She could hear the impatience in his voice.

"Not right now. I'll leave you to your game." She headed for the door.

"Dinner's at eight," John called over his shoulder.

"Thanks. I'll be there this time."

By the time Tara got to the base of the massive staircase, the last of the autumn light had abandoned the old manse, leaving shadowed corners and dark hallways all around her. In the twilight, the house loomed larger than ever, and for the first time she became aware of a musty smell—the smell of draperies and furniture moldering into decay, the trappings of women long dead in childbirth, of men killed in battle, of old folk wasting away from madness. A chill washed over her as impressions of the past closed in upon her.

Tara hurried up the stairs, up through the old ghosts, anxious to get to her room. It wasn't like her to get swept away by sensations like this. What she needed was a long, hot shower and a reality check.

As soon as she got to her bedroom, she walked over to turn off the bedside lamp she'd left on. Leaning down, she noticed the drawer to the night stand had been left open a crack. It wasn't like her not to close a drawer. She yanked open the drawer, worried that someone had stolen her Psalter while she had been out of the room. To her immense relief, the sandalwood box was still where she'd put it earlier that day.

Tara straightened, holding the box to her chest. Who had been in her room, touching her things? Mrs. MacMillan? A household servant? It could have been anyone. Anyone who knew of the family crest would be curious about the box she'd carried from America.

Tara looked around the room. She had to find a hiding place for her book—not in the family vault—and somewhere the housekeeper and her staff wouldn't find it. By the looks of this chamber, however, it appeared that Mrs. MacMillan was a neat freak. She was probably the type who insisted that everything be dusted on a weekly basis—even items stored in closets. The best place to keep the book would be on her person, but that would be impractical. The Psalter was small—not much larger than a cell phone—but it would be awkward to put it in a pocket, and it would be prone to damage whenever she sat down. She'd have to find a method for carrying it around her neck or waist. That would be awkward, too, and hard to explain without more raised eyebrows regarding her state of mind.

No, she would have to find some other hiding place. Still holding the small sandalwood box, Tara ambled toward the nearest window and drew back the lace panel. Her room looked down upon the back of the house and the lawn and gardens, now just dark shapes in the autumn twilight. Beyond the lawn she could see the gleaming oval of a pond, fed by a gently flowing stream called the Dippol Burn. David had mentioned the stream as a place he'd often played when he was a child.

There had to be an old building out there somewhere, across the Dippol burn, somewhere safe where she could hide the Psalter for a few days. The first chance she got tomorrow, she'd explore the wooded area and see if she could find a place to temporarily stow her treasure.

Chapter 9

Tara thrashed in bed, caught up in her nightmare. She tried to keep her feet from taking her closer to the shadowed door, but she couldn't stop herself. As hard as she tried to hold back, an even stronger force pulled her forward, almost near enough now to reach for the doorknob. No! She didn't want to know what was happening. She didn't think she could bear to see. She could hear the angry male voice beyond the door, the woman's hysterical cries...

"Lass, wake up!" Someone urged at her ear.

Tara tried to drag herself out of the dream, but the pull of the nightmare was strong. She saw her hand reaching for the knob.

"Tara! Lass!"

Someone shook her, hard enough to break the nightmare's hold. She opened her eyes and gasped.

"You again!" she exclaimed, jerking up on both elbows.

Her sudden movement sent the Knight Templar stepping backward. He straightened to his full height, which was more than impressive from her supine position on the bed. Once again she was highly aware of his imposing masculine bulk. And once again he had violated her privacy.

"You were well and gone, witch," he said. "And to a dark place to be sure."

"It was just a nightmare."

"The likes of which I've never witnessed." He planted his hands on his slender hips. "No doubt you now reap the rewards of the black life you've led."

"It was just a *dream*." She glanced at the clock. It was three-thirty-three in the morning—the witching hour again. And here she was wide-awake, and her knight visitor was back. Was she still caught up in a nightmare? The man before her didn't seem like a dream, though. And he certainly hadn't felt like a one. His strong grip on her shoulders had been very real. Yet real men didn't appear and disappear into thin air. She felt a buzzing noise flare to life in her head, the same sound she heard when she couldn't comprehend a concept, or had unresolved emotions about an issue—like the buzz she experienced when she considered her upcoming nuptials.

“My life is none of your business,” she added.

“’Tis my business entirely,” he retorted. “Until your cursed spell is broken.”

“Would you just can the spell and witch talk?” She yanked the duvet up to her neck. Her hair was damp with sweat, but her body was trembling from the aftereffects of the dream.

“Can?” he repeated, momentarily puzzled.

“I’m not who you think I am. So why don’t you just get over it and leave me alone!”

“Because I dinna believe ye.”

“And what are you doing here anyway? It’s the middle of the night, for God’s sake.”

“Fie!” He crossed himself. “Beg forgiveness for your blasphemy!”

She couldn’t believe he was serious. She glanced at him and found him staring at her with an unwavering earnest expression.

“Beg!” he commanded.

“Pardon me, then,” she retorted, exasperated and embarrassed. “I usually don’t take the Lord’s name in vain, I’ll have you know.” Tara ran an impatient hand through her damp hair. “But swear words spring from my lips when strange men wake me up in the middle of the night.”

“Would you have preferred I leave you to your bad dream?”

She glared at him, unable to refute his logic. Then she reached for her cell phone sitting on the night stand. This time she intended to call David instead of shouting for help. Maybe then he’d catch the knight before he had time to disappear. But the knight caught her wrist in midair instead.

“No tricks,” he growled. He snatched the small phone from her hand and stared at it.

“What magical device is this?” he asked, releasing her.

She rubbed her wrist, even though he hadn’t really hurt her. “It’s a phone. And it isn’t all that magical. Believe me.”

“What does it do?”

“Like you don’t know.”

“I don’t.” His accent stretched the word into two syllables. *Doe-ant*.

She sighed and decided for the time being to play along with his innocence routine. “It allows two people to talk to each other. Pretty much incessantly.”

The knight turned the phone over in his hand, studying it. He looked up. "I need no such device to speak to another."

"You would if you wanted to talk to someone in another country. Say the pope in Rome. Or your relatives in Wales."

"I have no relatives." His tone constricted with a surprising amount of bitterness. Then he glared at her, as if weighing the truth of her words. From the look on his face, she guessed that he was experiencing a bit of his own mental buzz.

"Listen, mister," she began. "You need to understand something. I'm not who you think I am. I am not a witch. I didn't steal anything from you. And I didn't put you under a spell."

He began to protest, but she held up a hand.

"My name is Tara Lewis. I've never met you. This is the first time I've been to Scotland, in fact. I'm a Yank as you people say."

"Yank?"

"From the United States of America."

The knight paused and studied her. His lip curled. "I have never heard o' such a place."

"You don't know about the United States. Impossible." She studied him right back, wondering how such a vigorous, handsome man could be so out of touch with the modern world. Was he mentally ill perhaps, a person the rest of the household wished to keep a secret? Yet he didn't seem mentally incapacitated, and his entrance earlier that afternoon, when he'd materialized before her eyes, had been quite a feat of magic.

She decided to press for answers. "So tell me, is John Corbin your relative?"

"You mock me!"

"Your master?"

"You insult me!

"Then who *are* you?"

The man shifted, crossing his arms over his chest and planting his feet wide. "You know very well who I am. You said my name. You released me from the tomb."

"The tomb?" A shudder passed over her.

"Aye, the tomb." His blue eyes flashed at her.

"That's crazy." Tara edged away from him, bumping against the headboard.

"'Tis my sentiment as well. Nothing looks right t' me in this world. The people I've seen 'round here look strange. Their garments stranger still." He waved the air impatiently. "I was away many years in the Holy

Land, but not all that long, lass, not so long t' allow for such a turn of events!"

Tara evaluated him as he spoke. The man was definitely troubled, definitely frustrated. And he didn't seem to be play-acting.

"When did you return—to Scotland, I mean?"

"I came home from the crusade in the year of Our Lord 1223."

"You expect me to believe that."

"Aye!" His brows shot together. "Hugh Lachlan is no liar."

"You're Hugh Lachlan."

"Aye."

"The knight from the tomb."

"That's what I've been trying t' tell ye!"

"You expect me to believe that you are a man who was born in the eleven hundreds?"

"Aye, and put under a spell by a she-devil witch! And freed but a day ago."

"Do you have any idea what year it is now?"

"I expect you'll tell me."

"Two thousand and eight."

"Two thousand and eight?" His right brow shot up in surprise. The left brow's movement was much more restricted, dragged down by the scar tissue on the side of his face. "A jest, surely!"

"I'm not kidding. Look at the newspaper over there, if you don't believe me." She pointed at the paper folded neatly upon the coffee table.

She could tell by the confused expression on the knight's face that he didn't know what she referred to. But he clumped to the table and reached down.

"What manner of cloth is this?" he asked tilting the newspaper back and forth.

"It's paper. Made from trees."

Hugh sniffed the fold and jerked back.

Tara shook her head and smiled. "Look at the top right. You'll see a date there." She watched as he found the right area.

"What does it say?" she prodded.

"October 5, 2008."

"That's right," she answered as he put down the newspaper and retraced his steps to the bed. "It's 2008. So I can't be who you think I am. And I really doubt that you're who you say you are. But the bottom line is, Hugh old chap, you're going to have to find someone else to bother, or haunt, or whatever it is you think you do."

The knight was silent for a moment, and then all of a sudden he wilted. He plopped on the foot of the bed, tilting the mattress so precipitously that Tara nearly rolled forward. She recovered herself and pulled the duvet up to her chin again, amazed that her words could have such an effect on the big man.

He leaned his forearms on his knees, the picture of dejection.

"Blessed Holy Trinity," he muttered. "'Tis two thousand and eight."

Tara said nothing. She no longer feared the man. But she did wish he'd leave her alone.

"Everyone I've known is gone." He sighed. "Dead and buried."

"It looks that way."

"Everything I knew has passed."

Tara nodded.

He shot her a sidelong glance. "But how am I here? Explain that. How did you break the spell?"

"That I don't know."

"'Twas a miracle."

"That I am fairly sure is not the case."

He jumped up, full of vigor and enthusiasm again. "But it had to be a miracle. That I even survived being burnt was a miracle! The Lord must have saved me for a reason!"

She ignored his epiphany. "You say you were burned?"

"Aye. 'Twas my last memory, lass. And terrible, too. Like your nightmare. The smell of my own flesh burning at the stake. Thank the Holy Virgin that She swept me away before I knew too much pain. And then nothing. I felt nothing. Not until I heard your voice."

A sudden memory prickled over Tara. She remembered the disquieting smell that had wafted up from the stone sarcophagus in the tomb, a smell she had guessed was burnt human flesh. Her mouth went dry.

"You were burned at the stake?"

"Aye. By the bastard, Edouard Corbin."

"But surely someone saved you." Tara paused, cursing herself for momentarily buying into his tale. Nothing he had said was the least believable.

"I dinna ken." The knight shrugged. "'Twas all darkness from there."

They stared at one another, and Tara was suddenly struck by the outlandishness of the moment. There she was, in the wee hours of the morning, talking to a man in a costume standing at the foot of her bed, a man who claimed to have lived in the twelfth century—and acting as if it was the most normal thing in the world to do. If the paparazzi could only see her now, they would have a field day.

On the other hand, she imagined that handsome Hugh Lachlan, with his sharp features, high coloring and glossy hair, would photograph very well.

Hugh glanced at the door of the bedchamber. "'Tis back to the library, then."

"Good." She fluffed her pillow. "I need to try and get some sleep. A bride shouldn't have circles under her eyes on her wedding day. And I will if I don't get some decent sleep soon."

"You are getting married?"

"Yes. That's why I'm here in Scotland."

"What man do you marry?" He stepped closer, hovering over her again. "Surely not a Corbin."

"I'm marrying David Corbin, as a matter of fact."

"St. Andrew!" He studied her face, his expression dark, and his eyes almost black as his pupils dilated with alarm. "Tread carefully, milady."

His gravelly words sent a second shudder through her. For the first time someone had voiced a negative opinion about her upcoming marriage—and she had a strange feeling that she should heed the warning.

Still, she refused to take advice from a guy who wandered around in a blue bathrobe.

"David is wonderful," she countered. "You don't know him like I do."

"The Corbin man can hide his cold heart well. Mark my words. And they are all alike, I've been told. The lot o' them."

"Spoken like a true asshole."

"Milady, you misjudge me." He swept a bow.

She stared at his back, at his massive shoulders and bowed head. Men didn't bow like that anymore. The gesture should have appeared comical, overly dramatic even. But there was nothing remotely comical about Hugh Lachlan. Instead of amusing her, his chivalry sent a frisson of pleasure through her. *He pleased her.* On some fundamental level, the man before her simply pleased her. His figure, his eyes, his voice, and the way he expressed himself pleased her. She caught herself gazing at him in appreciation and swallowed a lump in her throat.

"I will prove my true colors." He rose back to his startling height. "Or my name is not Hugh Lachlan."

"Which I doubt it is."

He ignored her sarcasm. "Am I released?"

"What in the world is that supposed to mean?"

"Do you release me from your service?"

"Right." She waved him off, smiling at his old-fashioned manners. "Go, sir, and good riddance."

"I bid you good night then." He turned for the door.

"Try knocking the next time," she commented to his back. "If there has to *be* a next time."

He pivoted to face her again. "I shall try. But when I am summoned, it seems I must obey immediately."

"Summoned?"

"Aye. By you."

Tara tilted her head. "I didn't summon you."

"Ye did. Your voice, your distress—I am compelled to answer them both. I believe 'tis part of the spell."

"So you're like my personal knight," she replied. "My knight in shining armor."

"It would seem so, milady. But now, you must excuse me. I have a book to find." He bowed again and strode out of the room.

Tara watched him go, more wide-awake than she had ever been in her life. She couldn't begin to sort out the conflicting sensations that coursed through her—doubt, fascination, concern, and undeniable sexual attraction for the man who had just left the room.

There was no way she could sleep in her present condition. If she wanted to be halfway conscious tomorrow morning, she would have to resort to taking one of the sleeping tablets the doctor had prescribed. Tara pulled out the drawer of the night stand and retrieved her bottle of sleeping pills. She swallowed two tablets and leaned back on the pillows. As she waited for the drug to settle her nerves, her thoughts kept returning to the man who claimed to be Hugh Lachlan.

Someone at Corbin Hall must know who the man in blue really was. And there had to be a logical explanation for his strange comings and goings. His—and that disappearing act of the tricky little actress. She was determined to find the answers—or *her* name was not Tara Lewis.

Chapter 10

"Good morning," Tara announced the next day as she swept into the parlor. She'd slept in and missed breakfast, and had almost missed this wedding briefing with Mrs. MacMillan and David.

David glanced at his watch. "What's with you this morning? It's ten, Tara."

"I know, sorry."

"It's not like you to sleep in."

"I didn't sleep well." She sat down near the coffee table where brochures, lists, and color swatches were laid out neatly by a tea service. She barely looked at them. "But at least I found out who the strange man is—or who he *claims* to be."

"What man?" Morag asked from the doorway.

Tara glanced up, surprised to see David's childhood chum. She flushed. She thought she had made herself clear to David about Morag Smithbank. But there she was, ready and willing to insert herself into their lives once again.

This time Morag had ridden a horse to the manse, so she was dressed in dun colored tight-fitting pants, riding boots and a muted plaid blazer and vest. Her legs had never looked longer. And her skin was still flushed and glowing from her exercise in the crisp morning air.

Once again, Morag had outshone Tara. Though Tara had taken care in dressing, choosing khaki slacks and a sage-colored sweater that fit her slender body to a tee, she knew her complexion bore the marks of both the accident and her sleepless nights. No amount of concealer could mask the tired lines forming around her eyes.

"Oh, there you are, M." David jumped to his feet and hurried to her side. Then he turned and shot a glance at Tara.

"I asked Morag to help out with the wedding plans."

"Really," Tara replied, taken aback. So Morag was not only choosing the wedding location, but other details as well.

"I could never say no to David," Morag purred. "I hope you don't mind, Tara."

Tara couldn't believe David would do such a thing without consulting her first, or that he would blatantly ignore her request to keep Morag out of the house. "Of course not," she answered, trying to keep her voice level. Mustering every ounce of graciousness she possessed, she indicated a chair beside the couch. "The more the merrier." She watched David guide Morag to a chair beside him.

"Morag's helped her father with hundreds of ceremonies. She knows everything there is to know about what goes on."

"And as to that, David Corbin," Mrs. MacMillan put in. "You need to tell your uncle about everything before this goes on too long."

"I will. I will."

"I don't like going behind Lord Corbin's back, I don't mind saying—not even for you."

Tara turned to her fiancé. "You still haven't told him?"

"After that row last night? Not on your life."

"David seems to think John will object. Maybe even try to stop the wedding." Morag sank gracefully into the chair and crossed her ankles. "How's that for a real shocker?"

Tara whirled to face her fiancé. "He couldn't stop the wedding, could he?"

"Of course not." David waved her off. "I'm an adult."

"Then why haven't you told him?" Tara pressed. "He's going to be more angry that you've waited. And he's going to be angry enough as it is."

"He'll be mad no matter what. He's a crotchety old bastard. I've told you that a hundred times."

"But we're getting married on Saturday."

"I know! I know. I'll tell him right after this meeting, I promise." He picked up a brochure and studied it as if hoping to deflect any more questions. "Now let's do something productive."

"Men!" Morag laughed and gazed over at Tara. "The great communicators. But we interrupted you, Tara. What were you saying about the man in your room?"

"I was saying," Tara answered, trying to put David's behavior out of her mind. "I found out who the man in the library is."

David glanced up from the pamphlet in his hand. "You saw him again? When?"

"Last night."

It was Mrs. MacMillan's turn to look up in surprise. "Where, Miss Lewis?"

"In my room, as a matter of fact. That's why I was up half the night."

"And he told you his name?" David frowned. "Who is the bastard?"

"He claims to be someone named Hugh Lachlan."

"Hugh Lachlan?" Morag repeated, her voice rising with surprise.

Tara glanced at her, hopeful she might be on the heels of an answer at last. "Do you know him?"

"I should say not!" Morag reached for a brochure. "The Hugh Lachlan I know about has been dead for hundreds of years."

"Maybe he's a relative," David put in.

"I don't think so." Morag's fine eyebrows drew together. "I know of no Lachlans in the immediate vicinity."

"Aren't there a lot of MacLachlans up north, around Loch Fyne?"

"Yes," Morag nodded. "But the man in question apparently isn't a member of that clan."

"Aye," Mrs. MacMillan put in. "With the shortened last name and all."

Tara was confused. "Does the Mac part of the name have some special significance?"

"It means 'son of.'"

"In your stalker's case," Morag drawled, "Son of Lachlan."

"Or not, as the case may be," Tara mused.

"Whoever he is," David pivoted to face the housekeeper. "He shouldn't be allowed to wander around the house frightening our guests. Should he, Mrs. MacMillan?" He gave her a pointed look.

"Certainly not!" she retorted, indignant. "I'll see to it, Master David. Even if the locks have to be changed. Don't you worry, sir."

"Thank you."

"Now, then." Mrs. MacMillan bent forward and picked up a list from the table. "I'd like to show you what Morag and I have planned for the morning of the wedding, and then we'll talk about the reception. Let's start with the floral arrangements. Pink gladioli were recommended to me as—."

"Excuse me, Mrs. MacMillan," Tara put in. "But I had one more question before we start in on the wedding."

"Yes, dear?"

"About Hugh Lachlan."

Tara noticed David's shoulders stiffen with impatience. Still, her hunger for an answer was stronger than her concern about David's state of mind. She turned to Morag.

"The Hugh Lachlan you mentioned—what do you know about him?"

"He was a Knight Templar," Morag explained. "He was burned at the stake."

"How do you know that, M?" David asked, surprised.

"I used to read the records at the church for fun," Morag smiled warmly at her childhood chum. "Until I found out that coming over here was a lot more exciting."

David patted her hand and smiled. Tara ignored their exchange of mutual admiration, and demanded Morag's attention again. "Was that Hugh Lachlan from around here?"

"I'm not sure. My father might know. He's somewhat of a history buff."

"Why would a Knight Templar be burned at the stake? Weren't they part of the church?"

"They were," David said.

"Yes, but this one did something wrong. Let's see." Morag looked toward the ceiling, searching her memory. "As I recall, it said in the book that he was found guilty of sodomy." She gave a warm chuckle. "That's right. I remember being confused about the word sodomy and asking my father what it meant. That's when I learned to keep my questions to myself and use the dictionary!"

Tara thought Morag's merriment was out of place during a discussion about a man who had been burned to death. Perhaps Morag didn't grasp the tragedy of the situation because she hadn't met Hugh. She didn't know how wrong it seemed to have snuffed out the life of such a vibrant human being—especially in so barbaric a way as fire. Thinking about scribbled lines in a book was one thing. Pondering the death of a real man was quite another.

Yet, Tara still couldn't accept the fact that she had met the real Hugh Lachlan. To accept the idea that the knight from her bedroom was the same man mentioned in the church records meant that she had seen a spirit. To accept the existence of the Knight Templar, she would have to admit that a different plane existed, a different world.

She just couldn't stretch her belief system that much. If she were to accept the existence of a spirit world, she would have to reexamine everything she'd disproved on *Fact or Fiction*. She would have to think through every truth she'd clung to for the past twenty years. She'd worked too hard to want to go back and form her belief structure all over again. Besides, her world as it was made sense. And if *Fact or Fiction* had taught her one thing, it was that there was always a reasonable explanation for any mystery. Always.

Still, she had seen Hugh Lachlan materialize with her very own eyes. Her very own skeptical eyes.

Her ears began to buzz.

"Miss Lewis?" Mrs. MacMillan called.

Tara realized that everyone was staring at her. She jerked back to the present.

"What do you think? Do you like the pink?"

Tara took a deep breath and shifted her attention to the brochure the housekeeper was holding in front of her nose. Photographs of floral arrangements came into focus.

"Pink is nice," she answered, still only halfway present.

"Are you certain?" Morag reached for the brochure. "It's a fall wedding after all. The beginning of October. Wouldn't yellow or orange be more appropriate?"

Tara flashed back to the outfit Morag had worn the day before. Her sweater and skirt set had been the color of lemon chiffon pie.

"Now that I think about it," Tara replied. "I don't really like yellow."

"Then pink it is." David slapped the table with the palm of his hand. "Next?"

\

Not until mid-afternoon did Tara get the chance to break away so she could look for a place to hide her Psalter. She went to her room, put the sandalwood box in a plastic shopping bag, and headed down the stairs to the morning room. She prayed no one would intercept her and ask her where she was going.

Her prayers went unanswered. Just as she put out her hand to open the French door leading to the veranda, she heard a voice behind her.

"Taking a walk?"

Tara turned slightly to find Mrs. MacMillan standing in the center of the morning room, her hands clasped beneath her large breasts.

"Yes. Just getting some air."

The housekeeper's glance slanted down to the bag in her hand.

Tara lifted the bag. "Sketching supplies."

"You're an artist?"

"Not a very good one. But I try." She opened the door.

"Do you think you're up to a walk on that ankle of yours?"

"It's not so bad. I'll be fine."

"Then a word of warning, Miss Lewis."

Tara froze, ready for anything—a threat, advice, or even a joke. She hadn't yet determined if Mrs. MacMillan approved of her as a future member of the Corbin family or not. Mrs. MacMillan had fawned over David all morning but had been cool to Tara—probably because she hadn't shown enough interest in the elaborate wedding plans Mrs. MacMillan had arranged.

"Yes?" she ventured.

"Have a care if you go past the gardens."

"Oh?"

"There are holes in the ground you could fall into. The bottleneck dungeons."

"What are bottleneck dungeons?"

"Places they kept prisoners in the old days. Have a care where you walk. Some of the holes are covered over by vines and grass."

"Thank you for the warning. I'll watch my step."

"Do you have a cell phone with you?"

"Yes." Tara patted the rear pocket of her slacks.

"Good. We wouldn't want Master David's bonny bride getting lost or hurt, now would we?"

Tara studied Mrs. MacMillan's expression, looking for signs of the old woman's true intent. She couldn't tell if sarcasm or solicitousness hung in the housekeeper's frosty words.

"Don't worry, Mrs. MacMillan," Tara replied just as coolly. "I can take care of myself."

"And don't stay out too long. Remember the dinner party this evening. David is looking forward to introducing you."

"I'll be there. Bye."

She let herself out of the house, aware of the housekeeper's hard gaze on her all the way across the lawn.

The wood was denser than Tara had first guessed. The ancient stand of oak was crowded in by trunks of struggling young alders and the forest floor was covered by a healthy growth of brambles. The air hung heavy with the fragrance of loam and moss, a thick verdant smell that clung to her nostrils. Tara could hear the trickle of a brook ahead and guessed that it was the Dippol Burn that David had told her about. She walked toward it, favoring her injured leg. Still, she was grateful to be out of the house and away from talk of the wedding. The entire morning had been claustrophobic.

The Dippol Burn turned out to be a small creek, not more than four feet across. It ran clear and clean but was the color of tea, stained by the peat bogs it meandered through. She picked her way down a rocky path to the bank of the stream as the light grew dimmer and the atmosphere cooler. She wished she had thought to bring a sweater.

Tara glanced up through the break in the foliage, and was surprised at the change in the sky. No wonder the light had faded so precipitously. A storm front had moved in, pushing purplish-blue clouds across the heavens. Tara shivered at the sudden chill. She had to find a hiding place for the Psalter soon or be caught in what looked like a horrendous downpour.

Tara glanced right and left. The banks on either side of her were blocked by bramble bushes nearly as tall as she was. She had no choice but to cross the stream or retrace her steps. Tara splashed through the burn and hurried up the path, which had dwindled almost to nothing as it followed the slope of the hill. She forced herself to keep walking, turned a bend, and then spotted a small stone building, nearly shielded from view by a grove of rowan trees. She could see no sign of a trail to the structure and no evidence of anyone having been in the area lately.

"Perfect," she murmured. She tore her way through a line of stickers that scratched her wrists and snagged her slacks. Ivy grew rampant over the roof of the small building and cascaded over the doorway, forming a curtain of green.

Trying not to think about spiders and bugs, Tara swept the ivy aside and peered into the tiny narrow space. At first she thought she had discovered an abandoned chapel. But not a crucifix was to be seen. Instead, the sandstone blocks of the interior walls were carved with a band of symbols that reminded her of Celtic knots. The border ran along the top of all four walls. On the opposite wall to the door was a stone face of a man with a beard and curly hair. Part of his nose had been broken off. He stared at her, unblinking, and she had to look away from his piercing gaze.

Piles of crudely dressed flagstones littered the packed earth beneath her feet, as if someone had intended to install a floor but had been interrupted in their ancient task. She could hide her book among the stones. It would remain dry and concealed, and completely out of the weather.

"Perfect," she said again. Carefully, she folded the edges of the plastic bag around the sandalwood box. Then she set it upon a flat stone, and stacked others around it in a casual manner. When she was done, she straightened, brushed her palms on her slacks and inspected her work, satisfied with the job. No one looking at the flagstones would guess that anything had been hidden there.

When the wedding was over on Saturday, she would slip back out here and get her book. Problem solved.

As she let herself out of the strange little building, she heard lightning crack above her head, and a far off roll of thunder. She would have to high tail it back to Corbin Hall if she wanted to beat the rain.

Jogging was out of the question, but she forced herself to trot as fast as her bad ankle allowed. Just as she reached the bend in the trail, she heard the unmistakable sound of a horse galloping toward her. Tara froze. The last thing she wanted was to be seen anywhere near the hiding place of the Psalter. She plunged into the woods to her right, hoping she could dash out of sight before the horseman made it up the slope.

Tara heard the jangle of a bridle and the swat of a whip.

"Faster!" a woman demanded. The whip slashed again.

Tara wasn't the only one determined to outrun the storm.

The horse pounded closer, and Tara squatted behind a bush, praying she wouldn't be seen.

The horsewoman came tearing around the bend, and Tara was shocked to see Morag astride a dappled gelding. The blond woman had said her good-byes two hours ago, after the wedding pow-wow, and Tara had assumed she had left the house. Where had she been since then? She watched Morag strike the horse's flanks once more and then disappear around another bend.

Moments later, Tara emerged from her hiding place, thankful that she hadn't been spotted, but still wondering about Morag. She glanced at the path she'd forged through a dangerous patch of nettles. No sense returning that way and taking a chance on getting stung. She'd had enough bumps and bruises for one trip to Scotland.

Lightning cracked again, flashing through the sky like quicksilver.

Tara took off to the right, hobbling over a patch of rocky ledges, her mind focused on getting back to the house, her eyes straining to find a path through the brush ahead.

She hadn't taken more than a few steps when the world beneath her dropped away.

Chapter 11

Tara plunged downward through a rocky shaft, scraping her shoulders on the rough stone and crashing feet first onto a hard surface. She had enough presence of mind to blunt the force of her fall by bending her knees and rolling to the side, and took most of the shattering impact on her butt. Pain flared in her right hip and barreled down her injured leg. She prayed she hadn't broken her pelvis this time.

Stunned, she looked around her. She'd fallen into an underground room carved out of sandstone. She squinted, peering through the dim light at her surrounds. Faded straw rotted in the corners, cloudy bottles lay on their sides, along with tatters of woolen cloth. Thankfully she could see no evidence of rats or snakes. Then she spotted rusted shackles fastened to the far wall, and she realized where she was—in one of the bottleneck dungeons Mrs. MacMillan had warned her about.

"Great," Tara muttered. Carefully, she got to her feet, testing her bones. Nothing seemed to be seriously injured, which heartened her. But when she stood to her full height and reached up as far as she could, her fingertips were more than ten feet shy of the bottom of the shaft. No need for a lock and key on this dungeon. No one thrown in this hole would get out alone—including her.

"Great." Tara would have to call David and get someone to rescue her. She could just picture Mrs. MacMillan shaking her head and making clucking noises. Tara flushed, her pride hurting more than her ass and ankle put together.

She reached for her phone, flipped it open, and saw that she had no signal in the rocky hole. She waited, studying the screen, hoping she would see the bars climb. But no such luck.

"Crap," she muttered.

Tara sank down to the floor of the cell, her mind racing through possible options and coming up with only one. She would have to wait to be found. And how long would it be before anyone decided she was overdue—teatime? And then where would they look for her? She hadn't told the housekeeper where she was going, and the Corbin property was vast. They might think to look in the bottleneck dungeons, once they realized something had happened to her, but did they know the locations of all the dungeons? Mrs. MacMillian had made it sound as if they were scattered all over the place.

Tara sat in silence, her ears straining to pick up on any outward noise other than the wind in the trees. At the slightest sound of human presence, she would shout for help. She lost track of how long she sat there. But after a while, she noticed the light fading. Drops of rain fell down the shaft as the storm moved directly above her.

She scooted out of the way of the rain, and struggled to her feet. The stone floor was hard and cold, and the chill had seeped into her bones. She rubbed her arms and limped around the chamber, trying to get warm. The temperature plummeted as the day faded and the storm raged in earnest.

Thunder rumbled overhead, and lightning cracked, sounding as if it stuck nearby trees. The roar of the rain soon blotted out all hope of Tara hearing signs of rescue. Besides, no one in his right mind would chance getting struck by lightning to search for her. Even if the Corbins had realized she was missing, they would have to wait out the storm. Tara tried not to think about the coming night, and the possibility of not being found until the next day.

A rivulet of water suddenly plunged over the edge of the shaft and splashed onto the floor. Tara swore and moved away, knowing how dangerous it would be for her to get wet.

She paced the dungeon, avoiding the puddle of water forming in the center of the room, and muttered songs under her breath to keep her mind off her predicament. She pulled out her phone numerous times to make sure it was actually dead. It remained unresponsive.

After a good long while, her stomach grumbled, and she realized the afternoon had given way to night. She could no longer see her hand in front of her face. The brunt of the storm had passed, but rain still fell in earnest.

It was then she heard someone calling her name in the distance. She jumped, hope flaring to life.

"Here!" she shouted up the shaft, uncaring that the rain pelted her face. "I'm down here!"

"Tara!" The rain muffled the syllables of her name. It sounded like David's voice.

"I'm down here!" she yelled back. "David, I'm down here!"

He called her name again and she realized with a sick feeling that he wasn't getting any closer. He must not be able to hear her.

She cupped her stiff hands around her mouth and called his name. She shouted until her throat felt shredded. But after a few minutes, she could hear the search party moving away, their calls getting fainter and fainter, until she couldn't hear them anymore.

Devastated, Tara sank to the cold, hard floor. She hugged her knees and blinked back hot tears that threatened to fall. Crying wouldn't help. And should she be found—*when* she was found—she wasn't about to let anyone know how afraid she'd been by displaying red, bleary eyes.

She chided herself for losing hope. She *would* be rescued. It was just a matter of time. She might have to spend the night in this hellhole and miss the dinner party, but in the morning they would be desperate to find her. They'd probably get search and rescue dogs to locate her trail. For that matter, Morag Smithbank probably owned a whole kennel of rescue dogs, and would find her in the morning without breaking so much as a lemon chiffon-colored heel.

Her stomach growled again. She sank her chin between her knees and tried to find warmth in her own body. She couldn't believe how cold an autumn evening could be in Scotland. It had to be in the forties. Tara hugged herself tighter. The Scots called this early fall? She'd spent warmer nights in California in the dead of *winter*.

Not until much later, when the sky above the shaft was inky black and when she had shivered so much that her jaw ached, did an idea drift into her frozen brain.

Just like on her television program, she could put Hugh Lachlan to the test. He claimed to be able to hear her call him, to be attuned to her distress. If he was the man he claimed to be, and under a magic spell, she could call him right now and he'd appear. She'd done an admirable job of calming her own fears as she huddled in the dungeon, so a distress call might not have reached him yet. But what if she called him by name? What if he could actually materialize and help her?

She shook her head at such a preposterous hypothesis. She wasn't desperate enough to start believing in ghosts and fairies. Such beliefs were for the unenlightened and the self-deluded. When rescue came, it would be by real men with mortal bodies—and preferably a warm wool blanket.

Another hour dragged by. Her fingertips grew numb and white from the chill. She clamped her hands under her armpits, seeking warmth. But even the normal hot spots on her body were cold now. Tara got to her feet and paced the floor in a circle, unable to see the confines of her prison in the darkness, and not wanting to step in the puddle directly below the shaft.

The longer she paced, the louder her other self shouted to be heard—the self that relied on intuition and emotions and the self she often suppressed. As she paced, the buzzing in her ears roared to a deafening cacophony. What would it hurt to try, a voice said in time to her march around the puddle. What would it hurt to try?

"All right!" Tara exclaimed to the dark void, her voice tight with impatience.

She could handle being trapped in a dungeon. But the buzzing noise in her own head was too much to bear.

"All right!" she said again, steadying her nerves. She crossed her arms over her cold breasts and hugged her torso.

"If you're out there, Hugh Lachlan," she began. Then she paused, wondering if the knight would hear her exact words. She felt like saying, "Get your ass over here right now." Instead, once she gave in to the idea of calling him, she found herself uttering a shockingly plaintive request.

"If you're out there, Hugh Lachlan, please, come to my aid. If you really exist on some paranormal plane, sir, if you can hear me, Hugh, please, please find me." She closed her eyes and visualized his scarred face for good measure. "I call you to my side, Hugh Lachlan."

While her eyes were still closed, she heard the wind kick up above her head. Trembling, she slowly opened her eyes, reluctant to see what her words had manifested. As she stood there, gaping up the shaft, she saw the same eerie blue light she'd witnessed in the tomb. It glowed in a ball for an instant and then flowed outward into a tall cloud of glitter near the shaft opening.

As Tara watched Hugh materialize above her, the world as she knew it crumbled around her feet into brittle little bits of useless logic. Beyond all rational explanation, Hugh had heard her and responded.

In only moments the knight came into full and glorious focus. He stared down at her, backlit by the rising moon, his hands on his hips.

"What have we here?" he inquired, his scarred mouth quirking into a small smile.

"A lady in distress, obviously," Tara retorted, her teeth chattering. She bobbed a stiff curtsey.

"You have been here long?"

"Since the afternoon. And I'm frozen to the bone." She hated to ask for help, and from him of all people, but she was desperate. "Would you please help me get out?"

"Is there nothing down there with ye?" he asked. "No lumber, no rope?"

"Nothing. Some old straw. That's it."

He reached for his belt. "Did not the Corbins search for you?"

"Yes, but they didn't find me." The sides of her throat clenched together, hot with tears. She struggled to control her voice. The last thing she wanted was to show weakness in front of the knight. "I called and called, but they didn't hear me."

Despite her best effort at keeping herself under control, she was chagrined to feel tears slipping out of her eyes. She swiped them away with the sleeve of her shirt.

"Dinna ye worry, lass," the knight said. The rumble of his deep voice was surprisingly comforting to her. "I'll get ye out o' there."

"Thanks." She sucked in a ragged breath. Her chest heaved with sobs that she fought to hold back.

"We must make a rope of our clothing. Remove what ye can."

"Okay." She was so cold now and so close to rescue, that her control seemed to be slipping in all areas. Her limbs quaked so much that she could barely strip off her knit top. Worse, she was even willing to surrender herself to a phantom's direction. Worse still, her mind had ceased questioning his existence.

Above her, she heard the clank of the knight's belt buckle and a grunt as he divested himself of his long robe.

"Tie what ye have together, lass."

"Okay." With numb fingers that were clumsy with cold, she fumbled with the clasp of her slacks. Finally she managed to unfasten it and pulled off her pants. It took every ounce of her concentration to master her hands enough to knot her top and slacks together.

"I am sending my end down," Hugh called. "Fasten your garments to mine."

Tara blinked away the tears that continued to squeeze out of the corners of her eyes. She clenched her chattering jaw together as she stood in bra and panties and reached for the robe he lowered down the shaft.

Between the two of them, their clothes barely made a long enough rope to span the height of the dungeon and the shaft.

"Make a loop at the bottom, lass. One for your foot."

"I'll try."

"Unless ye have the strength t' grab onto a knot, and hold yourself while I pull you up."

"I doubt my hands could hold that long. They're frozen."

"'Tis a loop then." He leaned closer. "Make it secure, Tara, so ye dinna fall again."

She nodded and formed a loop with the sleeve of her top.

"Ready?" Hugh asked.

"Yes." She lifted her leg and wedged her foot in the loop.

"Test it first," he urged. She felt a steady pull on the rope of cloth. "Is it holding?"

"It seems to be."

"Put your full weight into the loop."

She obeyed his command, and gasped when she swung toward the left.

"'Tis holding still?" he called.

"Yes!"

"I'll pull ye up now, Tara. Hold on."

She gripped the leg of her slacks, praying the light cloth would support her weight. Slowly, Hugh heaved her upward until she spun and banged against the lower opening of the shaft.

"Ye alright, lass?"

"Yes!"

"'Tis not long now. Hold on." He grunted, and she felt a strong tug.

Tara hung on for dear life as Hugh dragged her hand over hand through the narrow passage and up to the surface.

As soon as she was close enough to reach, Hugh clasped her around the wrist. The moment she felt his warm grip around her arm, she knew she was saved. She knew the knight would not let go, would not drop her, and that she was safe at last.

The last of her poise disintegrated as he dragged her onto the rocky ledge at the side of the hole. Then, instead of pulling away from him, she flung herself against his chest.

"You came!" she exclaimed.

"Ah, milady!" he gasped. "You're like ice!"

She threw her arms around his neck and hugged him with her last ounce of strength. "You came, Hugh! You came to me!"

"Ye called," he replied simply.

His arms wrapped around her as she collapsed against him. His body was a blazing furnace, his chest a bastion of security. Skin to skin they stood pressed together, breathing heavily and unwilling to release their grip on one another.

"You actually came!" Tara whispered in awe.

"Aye." His voice slipped to a much quieter tone. She felt his breath on the small of her shoulder as he lowered his head. His arms gathered her even closer, and his large capable hands swept up and down her back, leaving a wake of delicious warmth and awareness along her spine.

At the touch of Hugh's hands, all thoughts of being trapped in the dungeon vanished. In fact, all thought disappeared completely. Instead, her feminine awareness took over, savoring the heat and strength of the man whose arms surrounded her. She melted into him, wanting more closeness. And she could tell by the sound of Hugh's long appreciative breaths that she was having a similar effect on him.

"Ah, lass," he gasped at her left ear. His words sent ripples of pleasure through her, awakening her from a longtime sleep she had not realized she'd been slumbering in. A feeling she had never experienced—joy and desire and longing all mixed together—swelled inside her, so big and hot that she felt as if she would burst. She sank her cold nose into the space just below his jaw and closed her eyes, drinking in his hard embrace. He shifted, and her lips brushed the pulsing heat of his throat. She ached to kiss him, to discover what he tasted like, to feel his mouth close over hers.

"Milady," he gasped again, his muscles suddenly hardening as reality descended upon them both.

He raised his head, taking his delicious warmth with him.

Tara swallowed and stepped backward, slowly drawing her hands from his powerful torso.

"I must get ye back," he said, averting his gaze from her near nakedness. "To a fire and something hot to drink."

"Yes," she blurted. Her command of the English language seemed to have deserted her. She reached for the line of clothing he had dropped on the ground. But she was in such a state that she could only fumble helplessly with the knots.

"Allow me," he said, taking over the task. He had stripped down to a pair of rough woolen stockings strapped to the drawstring of old-fashioned boxers. On any other man, the odd outfit might have appeared comical. But not on Hugh Lachlan. In fact, the linen breeches did little to conceal the hard planes of his thoroughly masculine figure—from his small round ass to his bulging calves. She didn't glance at his crotch to see if it was bulging. They'd shared a far too intimate moment as it was.

Within seconds Hugh had untied the garments. He handed her the knit top and slacks, which she slipped into as quickly as possible. She stole glances at him as he pulled his robe over his head. As he raised his arms, the flesh of his abdomen drew taut in the moonlight, displaying his perfectly sculptured musculature. She'd never seen such a beautiful male body in real life.

And then she remembered why Hugh had been burned at the stake. He'd been accused of sodomy. He'd been a warrior priest accused of sexual violation. Hugh was most likely gay. She stole another glance at him as he buckled the belt at his narrow hips, finding the story hard to believe.

Yes, that ass of his was the ass of a beautiful male all right—a far too beautiful ass to belong to a typical male. And his calling had surrounded him with male priests. Even his military career had isolated him from women—perhaps to his liking. Not that there was anything wrong with a beautiful gay man. But she just didn't buy it.

"Come," Hugh said, holding out his hands to her. "Here t' me, Tara."

She was glad for the darkness that hid her thoughts from him. She obeyed him and hobbled closer. Before she could protest, he swept her into his arms.

"What are you doing!" she sputtered.

"You're in no condition t' walk," he replied. "I'm carryin' ye."

"No way!" She remembered with chagrin how David had panted after carrying her up the stairs. She had no desire to embarrass herself and Hugh with a repeat performance. "It's at least a mile!"

"'Tis but a stroll, lass. Ye're light as a feather, so you are."

"Really, I can walk!"

"Wiest now. I'll have no more of your blether."

He clumped off through the woods with her. She decided not to protest and locked her arms around his massive neck. Her weight didn't seem to faze him. His breathing was not labored in the least as he picked his way through the thicket to arrive safely back at the path.

Tara let him carry her in silence, glad for his strong arms, glad for the heat of his body, and glad for his supposed sexual preference. She'd felt far too much in his arms for her own peace of mind. If he were a heterosexual male with a lust for her that equaled hers for him, she would be in serious trouble as far as loyalty to David was concerned.

Tara allowed a finger to stoke a strand of hair at Hugh's neck. The gesture only made her want to run her entire hand through his glossy locks. She sucked in a deep breath and chided herself for her lack of control.

Hugh shifted her body in his arms and took a deep breath of his own. She glanced at the side of his face. He stared straight ahead, ignoring her gaze. But when the moonlight struck his profile, she saw that his jaw was clenched—hard.

Perhaps Hugh Lachlan fought inner demons of his own. Perhaps she had an effect on him. The possibility intrigued her.

Chapter 12

Hugh tramped to a halt just outside the pool of light that spilled from the back of the house.

"'Tis all lit up," he commented as Tara slid out of his arms.

"They were having a dinner party," she replied. "In my honor, as a matter of fact." She glanced over her shoulder. "God knows what time it is."

"Blasphemy again," he chided.

"Sorry." She held out her hand. "Listen, I have to go, Hugh. Thank you so much for rescuing me."

"'Twas my pleasure." Instead of shaking her hand, he bent over and planted a kiss on it.

She pulled away quickly to cut off the tingles that zipped up her arm.

"Good night," she said.

"That I am," he bowed and rose up, smiling. "And you'll soon realize as much."

His sense of humor hadn't surfaced until now. Perhaps he revealed more of himself because of the embrace they'd shared, or because he sensed her begrudging acceptance of him.

"Maybe I *am* beginning to realize it."

"Good." He stepped back. "I am released from service, then?"

She had to smile at his quaint manners. "Yes. Thanks."

As he saluted and faded from sight, Tara turned to face the house, her thoughts still very much with the vanishing knight.

Though she'd had a bone-chilling experience in the woods, she felt an uncommon warmth radiating through her heart. She wished she could simply stand there and savor the residual effect of being with Hugh. But the real world and its obligations waited for her in Corbin Hall.

Sighing in resignation, Tara limped across the lawn to the veranda, and then to the French doors of the morning room. The instant she opened the door and heard the voices of the guests in the house, her fairy-tale moment with Hugh ended. Dinner hadn't been canceled because of her disappearance. She glanced at the antique clock on the mantel of the fireplace. It was eight pm.

Tara was not about to allow anyone to see her in her disheveled condition—especially a reporter from the local paper—in case one had been invited. David would be mortified to have such a picture run in his hometown newspaper. She hurried to the servants' staircase between the morning room and the kitchen. As quickly as her protesting ankle allowed, she limped up the stairs.

She gained the second floor to discover David, dressed in a suit and tie, pacing the hallway, a phone clamped to his ear. He was arguing heatedly with someone. The moment he caught sight of her, he broke off, stared at her for a moment, and returned to the phone.

"Hold on, she's here!" he barked. Then he flipped shut the phone and rushed to her.

"Tara, thank God! Where have you been?"

She couldn't explain how she'd been rescued. It would sound too preposterous. She'd have to lie.

"I got lost!" She allowed him to hug her.

"Are you okay?"

"Yes. Just a bit scratched up."

"Come on," he clutched her elbow. "Do you think you can get ready in ten minutes? I'll stall them downstairs."

"I can try."

"That's my girl." He guided her into the bedroom and stood near the couch as she peeled off her clothes.

"The damn police wouldn't come out to look for you until twenty-four hours had passed. You could have been out there the entire night for all they cared!"

"I believe that's normal procedure." She padded into the bathroom and started the shower. David trailed after her.

"We looked everywhere for you!"

"I heard you, and I called, but you didn't hear me."

"Good God, I thought something terrible had happened to you."

"Sorry, David." She pulled back her hair and fastened it with a clip. "You must have been in quite a state, with the guests arriving for dinner and everything."

He waved off her words. "I couldn't tell them you were lost. And to have to go on with the damn dinner when I was worried sick about you—that was the worst of it."

"Well I'm back. And I'm glad to be here!" Tara stepped into the shower.

"What will you wear?" David called. "I'll have Susan get it out."

"The little black dress I brought."

He ducked back into the main room, and she reached for the soap.

Susan rushed in a moment later and dug out her dress, shoes, and jewelry as Tara wrapped a towel around her hair.

"Glad to hear you're okay, Tara," Susan called.

"Thanks." Tara walked to the bathroom doorway. "Have any luck with the research?"

"Not much. I'll e-mail you what I have so far."

"Thanks. And look up anything on local witches. That would be Ayrshire witches. That's what they call the area. See what you can find." She rubbed her hair. "Oh, and the crusades of the thirteenth century. See what went on and who were the major players."

"Right, boss."

Ten minutes later, Tara grabbed David's outstretched hand as he practically dragged her downstairs. Her hair was still damp at the nape of her neck, and she worried that she might have forgotten one of her diamond earrings. But at least she was going to make it to the dinner. All the way down the staircase she forced herself to calm down and take deep breaths. By the time she reached the main floor, she was the poised and contained Tara Lewis that everyone thought they knew.

Getting to the dining room was like running a gauntlet. Each person they met wanted to shake her hand and comment on her show. But at least every other person asked David where Morag was. Why wasn't she here? She was practically part of the family. They hadn't seen her in ages and were looking forward to chatting with her. Each time he was asked, David replied that Morag had been called away by her work. Tara trailed through the small crowd of local dignitaries and businessmen, wondering why David's family was not in attendance. He never spoke about his Scottish family, but she had assumed he had a cousin or two.

By the time they sat down to roast beef and Yorkshire pudding, Tara was tired of hearing Morag's name.

"You never let on that Morag had played such a big part in your life," she said, arranging her napkin on her lap.

"We grew apart over the years." David shrugged one shoulder, acting almost too casual about her question. "I never thought to mention her." He reached for his champagne. "I'm ashamed to say I'd almost forgotten her."

"Really? No one else seems to have."

David paused, his drink at his mouth. "Do I detect a hint of jealousy, my love?"

"Of course not," Tara retorted. "But I would have thought tonight would be more about us and less about *her*."

"You can't fault the old folks. That's their way. What else do they have to talk about with someone like you and me?"

Their Morag conversation was cut short when John stood up at the head of the table and raised his champagne flute.

"Thank you all for coming," he began. "And may I present my guests of honor tonight—my nephew, David Corbin and his cohost of the brilliant television series *Fact or Fiction*—Miss Tara Lewis."

David got to his feet and reached down for Tara.

Surprised that John hadn't mentioned their upcoming wedding, she grabbed her napkin and stood up. She raised her chin—all the while wondering if she still looked as if she'd spent the afternoon in a pit. She smiled at the crowd, bowing her head slightly as they clapped.

Tara glanced around the table, at the friendly faces beaming up at her. She could tell by the way the crowd was looking at her and David that they were waiting for a speech. She'd make it short and sweet, so they could get down to the business of eating—which was high on her list of priorities.

"Thank you for coming," she began. "This is my first visit to your beautiful country," she began. "And I have to say that Scotland just takes my breath away. It feels so magical. In fact, David tells me that if I stay here long enough, I may even begin to believe in fairies!"

"Not you, Miss Lewis!" a man called from the back. "Never!"

She grinned at him while her mind flashed back to the image of Hugh Lachlan pulling her out of the dungeon. How relieved she'd been to see the mysterious knight. And how real he'd seemed. She blinked away the vision and forced herself back to reality.

David squeezed her hand. "Tara and I would like to take this opportunity to make an announcement. We're engaged."

"Engaged?" John sputtered while the dinner guests clapped. He glanced up at David and then at Tara, balling his hands into fists on either side of his plate. Tara stared back, appalled by his reaction. He was definitely surprised by the news, and definitely not happy. And David had definitely not kept his promise to tell his uncle about their wedding.

Upset, she tried to pull away from David's hand, but he only gripped her harder.

"I decided to take the cohost gig to a whole new level." David dragged Tara's hand up and pushed a giant diamond ring onto her finger. She gaped at the pear-shaped gem as it flashed in the candlelight, branding her as his choice for everyone to see. "And Tara said yes!"

"You're getting married?" John struggled to keep his voice under control. "When is the special day?"

"Saturday, actually."

"Saturday?" John's neck flushed red above the white collar of his dress shirt.

David released Tara's hand and leaned over to his uncle. "We'll talk later. And not to worry, Uncle John, we have it all handled. We didn't want you to go to any trouble. That's why we didn't say anything sooner."

"Good God!" John muttered under his breath so that only Tara and David could hear. But he stood up, forcing a smile, and raised his glass.

"To Davy—may Saint Andrew protect him!" he toasted, and without looking at Tara, he added. "And to his bride-to-be."

"Hear, hear!" Someone exclaimed.

David stood beside Tara and grinned as the guests clinked their glasses together. Tara hung somewhere beside him in stunned silence, feeling as if she were outside of her physical body. The dinner had morphed into a bad dream—one that she wanted no part of.

She should have been brimming with happiness and love for David as their new partnership was being announced to the world. But as the crowd drank to their health and happiness, the faces around the dining table dimmed and the image of Hugh Lachlan came into full focus—that of him staring down the shaft at her, backlit by the moon. She could almost feel him pulling her against his solid frame again. Her chest swelled with longing, and she drew away from David's side, wanting to disengage from him, wanting to stay in the other moment with Hugh. Out of the corner of her eye, she saw David glance at her in surprise.

"And now, let's eat!" John exclaimed, holding his arms out in a grand gesture. He lowered to his seat and never once looked her way as he attacked his dinner. She could tell he was fuming.

Tara sat back down. A servant slipped a plate in front of her. She stared down at the slices of roast beef, which were pink and bloody at the center and black at the edges, like charred flesh. She picked up her napkin to hide her disgust and for the first time noticed the cloth was blue, just like the knight's blue robe.

She had to get a grip. She had to quit fantasizing about the Knight Templar and concentrate on the real problems facing her. God knows she had a doozy to deal with in regard to Lord Corbin.

"See?" David bent to her ear. "It wasn't so bad."

She didn't look at him. Words couldn't explain how mortified she felt about what he'd just done to his uncle.

Resolute, Tara reached for her fork. She could do anything if she put her mind to it, and that included banishing the knight from her private thoughts—a world he had no business intruding upon. She was also determined to put the best face she could on the strained atmosphere of the table. She would eat the beef. She would talk animatedly with her dinner companions. And she would pretend to enjoy them all.

Not until midnight did the last guest leave. David walked Tara to her bedroom, his fingers loosely laced with hers. He didn't say much, which struck Tara as odd. Usually after a dinner party, it was common practice to chat about the guests and their behavior. The crowd at dinner had been as eccentric as any other, providing plenty of fodder for discussion.

"That Hannah MacLaren," Tara began, as they gained the top of the stairs. "She could be a movie star, she's so pretty."

"Always was. But content to be a hometown girl."

"Nothing wrong with that." Tara opened her door and turned. "But your uncle, David. I'm concerned about him and the way he took the news. Why didn't you didn't tell him beforehand, instead of shocking him like that in front of everyone?"

"He'll get over it."

"I'm not so sure."

"Look, he was going to be upset one way or another." David swept the air with an impatient wave. "He'll have time to digest the news tonight, on his own. Trust me, it'll be better that way."

Tara nodded but still wasn't convinced. She crossed her arms. "And I was surprised by the guest list."

"What do you mean?"

"I was hoping to meet some of your family." She shrugged. "I assumed you had a nice loud Scottish clan."

"Actually, I don't. I've told you before—I'm Uncle John's only heir. The Corbins aren't a prolific bunch."

"So you don't have a granny or a cousin or anything?"

"Nope. I'm it."

"Oh." Tara couldn't hide her disappointment.

David bent close to look her in the eye and laughed. "What? I'm not enough?"

"I didn't mean that." She leaned against the doorjamb. The red wine they'd had for dinner and the port afterward had warmed her blood—almost as much as Hugh's embrace had fired her. She put a hand on David's chest, wanting reassurance that she could feel the same warmth from him, wanting to re-establish the connection they had lost with each other.

"And I didn't mean to complain," she murmured. "It was a wonderful dinner for the most part, David."

"I'm glad you liked it." He covered her hand with his own. "And I'm glad you didn't have to spend the night outside."

"Speaking of spending the night, what about you with me?" She tried to move her hand, to caress the plane of his left breast, but David clamped her hand in place.

"I'd love to," he said. "It just wouldn't be right."

"Why?"

"That room, this house—"

"What about them?"

"It would feel—" He let go of her hand and stepped backward. "Wrong."

"Wrong?"

"Like screwing with my family watching."

"I see." Tara studied him. "And put so romantically."

"Sorry, Tare, but I—" David began to speak and then broke off. He swept a hand down the front of his body, as if brushing away her touch. He was probably unconscious of what he'd just done, but the underlying meaning of the gesture was not lost on Tara. "Let's just say I wouldn't be good company."

"I wasn't asking for an Olympic performance. I just had a traumatic day," Tara reached out for him once more, seeking to purge the dangerous memory of the knight from her thoughts with a renewed appreciation of her fiancé. "And was hoping for a bit of one on one with the man who claims to love me."

"Darling, I love you." He sighed and put his arms around her. He pulled her close and pressed his cheek to hers. "It's no empty claim. You know that."

"Oh, David," she whispered at his ear. "What's happening to us here?"

"Nothing," he said. "Nothing is happening."

Tara didn't agree, but she didn't say anything more. Instead she stood in his arms, evaluating his embrace and comparing it to Hugh Lachlan's. The Knight Templar had felt like fire in her arms. David felt like wood. His arms were as wiry and unresponsive as the branches of a shrub, and his chest felt like a cutting board draped in a tie. She'd always considered David as brusque—not a man for chatter and foreplay—and his modus operandi had been fine when she was busy with her career, with only a few hours to spend with him at a time. But now that she had the luxury to observe him away from the set, she realized his brusque nature was edged with a remoteness she had never picked up on before. Had it always been there?

She flushed with the memory of Hugh's hands on her back, remembering how his touch had sent swirls of delight up and down her spine. David's hand's felt like oven mitts. Or was it her changing reaction to David that was the problem?

"I love you, too," she said, forcing herself to remember why she cared about this man, and how he had once made her feel special. He'd swept her into a whirlwind of fund-raisers and gallery openings. He'd mesmerized her with his television experience and networking skills, and impressed her with the sleek organization of his home. Yet deep in her heart, she'd always known he lacked a certain spark for her—in his embrace, in his kiss. But she'd always thought things would get better between them, once they weren't so busy.

She leaned closer and put her lips on his, trying hard not to compare his slight figure to Hugh's towering frame. She didn't even have to stand on tiptoe to reach David's mouth. She opened her lips, inviting him to kiss her back. He encircled her waist with his hands, pressed her lips for a moment, and then pulled back with a chuckle.

"If I didn't know better, Miss Lewis," he laughed. "I'd think you were trying to seduce me."

"Maybe I am." She hugged him again, ignoring his protests. His torso felt like a cardboard box under his suit jacket.

"Maybe I have to take a rain check," he murmured, reaching for her arms to disengage her grip.

"Maybe that would disappoint me."

"Maybe you've had too much to drink."

Tara pulled back, offended. "You think I'm drunk?"

"Well, you usually don't try something like this on me!" He smiled, but she could see that he was trying hard to step away with grace.

"Maybe it's time I did."

"And I'm flattered." He flicked her chin. "But the timing's not right, darling. You know it isn't."

"Oh?" She crossed her arms, and leaned against the woodwork of the door.

Unfailingly fastidious, he adjusted the knot of his tie. "We'll have plenty of time for fun and games on the honeymoon."

"Just like we always do—in between calls?" she shot back. "Maybe you'd be more interested in *phone* sex than real sex!"

"Please," he admonished. "Keep your voice down!"

"Why?" she retorted. "Afraid your Mrs. MacMillan might think we've had premarital intercourse?"

"Jesus, Tara. What's gotten into you?"

"Nothing!" She pulled away from the doorjamb. "Good night, David. Maybe one of us will be able to sleep. But it won't be me!"

"Don't lay that guilt trip on me, Tara. It won't work."

"Like anything does!" She slammed the door and strode to the bathroom, expecting David to trail after her with an apology.

Much to her surprise, he left her alone.

Deep in the night, someone shook her awake again. Tara dragged herself to consciousness and opened her eyes. She wasn't all that shocked to find Hugh standing at the side of the bed. But she *was* surprised when he squeezed her shoulder in warning and put a finger to his lips. He pointed toward the wardrobe with his other hand.

Without moving, Tara stared into the darkness in the direction of his hand. She heard rustling coming from the windowless room that served as a dressing area. Her heart flopped in her chest. Someone was in her room! She strained to see whom it was, and could just make out a figure draped in black with a hood covering its head. She couldn't tell from the shape if the intruder was male or female. But she could see very well that the figure was rifling through the clothes she had worn earlier in the day.

Outrage and alarm flashed through her. Someone was going through her clothes. She should do something, but what—simply feign sleep, challenge the intruder, or call for help? She was not a feigning sleep kind of gal.

As if Hugh could read her mind and her intention to take action, he motioned for her to stay in bed. Then he padded across the room, treading surprisingly quietly for a man of his bulk. She watched him, feeling confident of his ability to handle the situation—any situation as a matter of fact. Once the intruder noticed the hulking knight standing at his elbow, the figure would drop what they were searching and beg for mercy.

Yet nothing like that happened. The intruder didn't even seem to notice Hugh was there. Tara watched Hugh walk around the intruder and bend to inspect his face, while the intruder kept on with the search. Whoever was in the wardrobe obviously couldn't see Hugh. A chill prickled her scalp. She could see the knight but others couldn't? How was that possible?

If the intruder couldn't see Hugh, they probably couldn't touch him either and vice versa. That meant that Hugh could not defend her against anyone, as he apparently had no physical form with anyone other than herself. She was on her own.

Then Hugh purposely pulled a shoe off a shelf and dropped it to the floor. The intruder jumped and stared down at the pump. Wildly, the figure turned and glanced at the bed. Tara jerked up to a sitting position.

"You there!" she cried. She jumped out of bed.

For a moment the figure froze in the darkness. Then, with a lurch, the intruder lunged for the door.

Tara scrambled after the person in the black robe as they flung open her bedroom door and raced down the hall.

"Stop!" she yelled.

The figure tore down the stairs, kicking up the hem of the robe. Tara could just make out the sole of a masculine shoe. She limped down the stairs, her hip as well as her ankle complaining about the speed. She would never catch the man.

"Bastard!" she shouted.

Hugh joined her on the landing.

"Did you see who it was?" she panted.

"The lord of the house," Hugh glared after the disappearing figure. "John Corbin."

"David's uncle?" she replied, incredulous.

Hugh nodded grimly. "The same."

A door creaked behind them and Tara turned to see David stumbling out to the hall, wrapping a dressing gown around his spare frame.

"What's going on?" he asked, his voice rough with sleep. "Tara?"

"Someone was in my room." She glanced at Hugh, who stood to one side, glaring at David, his navy eyes glowering. If looks could kill, David would be a smoking cinder lying on the floor.

"Who was it?"

Hugh turned, a finger once again pressed to his lips.

Tara paused.

"Who was it, Tara?" David tied the belt at his waist.

"I didn't get a good enough look to tell." She brushed her hair back from her forehead as David stepped closer.

He cupped her shoulders. "Are you okay?"

"Yes. Whoever it was didn't hurt me. They just looked through my clothes."

"Was it your man from the library again?"

"No, this man was smaller." Tara glanced up at Hugh, who now stood near her bedroom door with his arms folded over his chest, waiting impatiently for David to finish his interview.

"God, Tara," David exclaimed, rattling the handle of her door. "Didn't you lock this last night? I thought you would have locked it, after the so-called actress incident."

"The door *was* locked."

"So whoever the person was had a key." David rolled his eyes. "It was probably the dreaded Mrs. MacMillan making sure you're keeping your virginity intact until the wedding."

Tara gaped at her fiancé, amazed that he could make a joke of the break-in. "David, it's not funny!"

"I agree. It's not funny. It's tiresome, that's what it is." He released the door handle with a frustrated flip of his fingers. "Why is it that you're the only one having all these strange visitors? Hmm?"

"Because of that room!" She jabbed a finger at the door.

"There's nothing special about that room." David turned toward his own door. "Just get that out of your head."

Their eyes locked and held. For once Tara refused to back down for the sake of the relationship. David's demeanor had changed since he'd come back to Scotland, and she didn't appreciate the way the new David had been treating her. It was his turn to make a conciliatory gesture.

For once, David picked up on her mood. He shook his head and heaved a dramatic sigh. "Okay, so what do I do to make it all better?" He reached for her shoulders.

"I don't know, David." Tara stepped out of range. "You think of something this time."

"Want me to check out the room?" David looked at the door of her bedchamber and gave no clue as to whether he could see the knight. He did, however, seem annoyed at the prospect of searching her chamber in the middle of the night. He yawned. "Will that make you happy?"

"That won't be necessary."

"Do you want me to come in for a few minutes? Until you can get back to sleep?"

Tara thought of his behavior earlier that night, when he'd brushed off her invitation as well as her touch.

"Thanks, but I'll be okay. The danger's probably passed by now." Plus, she had a huge warrior standing at her elbow.

"Good. We can call the police, if you like. But if there's no harm done—"

"Don't bother." The greatest harm so far had come from her own fiancé with his flippant dismissal of her fears. Disappointed in him yet again, she pushed open her bedroom door. "Good night, David."

He stepped forward to kiss her on the mouth, but missed in his haste to return to bed. His lips brushed the side of her cheek instead. "Good night."

Hugh followed Tara into the room. She shut the door and turned to him.

"Why didn't you want me to tell David who the intruder was?" she demanded.

"I dinna trust the man."

"Well, I do. He's going to be my husband in a few days."

"He doesn't kiss ye like a husband."

"What would you know about that?" she countered. "Weren't the Knights Templar supposed to be celibate?"

"Celibacy doesn't affect a man's perception."

"I thought celibacy would drive most men crazy."

"Perhaps," Hugh growled, his expression growing even darker. "But I am not most men."

He strode to the cluster of furniture in front of the fire. "So you will ignore my warnings about the Corbins and go through with this marriage?"

"Yes." She threw back her shoulders. "David is right for me. We'll make a good team."

"A good team." His lip curled. "I hear nothing o' love when you speak of him."

"So?" She planted her hands on her hips. "That's not why I decided to marry him."

"And why did you decide to marry him?" Hugh asked frostily.

"Because I have a theory."

"And what is that, prithee?"

"I don't think marriage is about love. It's about communication and friendship."

The knight regarded her, his eyes glinting. She couldn't tell if he was going to nod in agreement or laugh at her, so she pressed on, determined to make her point.

"I've seen too many so-called love matches fail. In fact, bad marriages go way back in my family. So I decided long ago that I would choose a mate who is a good match, not because I was all gaga over the guy. I would choose a man whose world view was the same as mine. Someone whose way of life and drive were similar to my own. That kind of thing. And when David came along, he met all my criteria."

"So you choose a man because you think you have the least chance of failing with him? Not because you wish to spend the rest of your life with him." He shook his head. His disgusted expression made her feel ten years old. She bristled.

"Relationships are a crapshoot, Hugh. So I made a logical decision and I intend to stick to it!"

"Aye." He shook his head again as he bent in front of the fireplace. "I hear ye, lass. All brains and no heart."

"It's not that at all. I've got plenty of heart. I'm just not going to open myself up to hurt like the rest of the women in my family."

"Tis like showing up for a fight," Hugh commented, glancing over at her. "Dressed in your heaviest chain mail, your stoutest helm. But carryin' no sword. Like not wantin' t' truly engage."

"It's not that I don't care for David."

"Fie. 'Tis obvious ye don't." He shoved a poker into the fire with more force than necessary. "If ye have the luxury of a choice in marriage, and it seems ye do, Tara, ye should marry a man ye canna live without. Someone ye love deep in your bones. Not a man who fills some bill ye've written out in your head!"

Tara glared at the knight. It was as if her conscience had popped out of her head, taken human form, and was lecturing her—as if she hadn't thought about this issue a million times. She launched back out of the chair, more disturbed by his words than she wanted to acknowledge to anyone-especially to herself.

"Well, that's where we differ, Hugh," she retorted. "I don't believe such bone-deep love exists."

"Ye don't?"

"No. That kind of feeling is a hormonal ruse. It's Mother Nature's way of getting men and women together for a while-enough time to have a few offspring. And then it fades."

"I dinna believe ye." Hugh rose to his feet, towering above her when she stood so close to him. "'Tis one o' the reasons why I wanted to leave the order. I knew there was something more t' life. Something I was missing deep in my bones. Something I wanted t' experience in this life."

"Like I said," she limped away from his compelling gaze. "We have different views. You're entitled to yours. And I'm entitled to mine." She hugged her chest and stared at the fire, not as sure of her convictions as her tone implied. "Besides, even if I wanted to call off the wedding, I couldn't do it now. All the arrangements have been made. I'm committed."

"You'd tie your wagon to a bunch of flowers and a cake then?"

When put that way, the wedding preparations didn't seem all that important. Tara hobbled to the sofa as Hugh poured coal on the file. "I can't back out now," she added. "When I think of all the trouble people have gone to just getting here—the *Fact or Fiction* crew—"

"Morag Smithbank—" he added, raising a brow.

She glared at him. "I can't call it off. I would look like an idiot to the entire world—and especially John Corbin. He's upset enough. And that's one thing that really strikes me as odd—"

"What is that?"

"John Corbin's reaction to our engagement. It's like he doesn't approve of me or something. And yet it was his idea that David and I come to Scotland to visit him."

"Then ye have t' ask yourself why." Hugh stood up and leveled his steady gaze on her.

Tara stared up at him, her thoughts swirling, her ears buzzing. "What do you mean?"

"As I said. Ye canna trust the man."

"You expect me to take you seriously?"

"Aye."

"A person—" she swept the air in front of him. "A *thing* that no one can see but me? You expect me to take advice from an imaginary friend?"

"If that's what ye'd like t' call me. Aye."

"A man whom I know nothing about?"

"What d'ye want t' know, milady?"

Tara sank to the couch, too wide-awake now to ever get back to sleep. "I want to know who you are, Hugh Lachlan. Right now. I want to know what happened to you. The whole story."

"I can only tell ye what I know."

"Then have at it."

Chapter 13

Hugh replaced the fire screen and then turned at the hearth, his expression serious and his eyes hard.

"There is not much t' tell."

"Like I said, tell me what you know." She leaned back. "I intend to figure out who and what you are, but I need facts to work with."

"Work with?"

"I have many ways to research a subject, and people to help me. Give me some facts, and I'll soon have your life story laid out with names, dates, and the brand of your father's favorite whisky."

"That's fascinatin'," he retorted. "Seein' how I dinna ken who the man was."

"What about your mother?"

Hugh shrugged and looked toward the far window, the same one he had gazed out of the previous day when he'd claimed everything had changed. "She died when I was young."

"What was her name?"

"Agnes."

"Agnes what? Lachlan?"

"Agnes is all that I know."

"So Lachlan was the name of your father?"

"I dinna ken."

"Didn't you want to know?"

"Lots of lads had no fathers. I was no different."

Still, Tara noticed a flush rising on Hugh's cheekbones that belied his indifference.

"So you were illegitimate?"

"Aye. A bastard. That's me."

"So maybe the last name was a reference to your social status. Maybe Lachlan means you lacked land."

"Nay. The name means 'warrior from the north'."

Tara's gaze ran down Hugh's tall, powerful frame. She could imagine that he came from a long line of warrior stock.

"Where were you born then?"

"They tell me somewhere in the Borders."

"You don't know for sure?"

"I don't."

"And your mother?"

"Of her I know even less. When I was a bairn, she took me north, no one knows why, and died of a wasting disease outside Ballantrae."

"How old were you then?"

"Four. Five. I dinna recall. I barely remember my mother's face."

Tara nodded solemnly. Her background was similar to Hugh's. She'd been five years old the last time she'd seen her mother. And like Hugh, she could barely remember her mother's face. But then again, she'd purposely buried every vision of her childhood. Tara cut off thoughts of her past and turned her attention back to Hugh.

"Then what happened?"

"I lived like a wild thing until the church took me in."

"You were raised in an orphanage?"

Hugh shook his head. "Nay, for some reason, the Knights Templar found me and raised me. I have known nothing all my life but the brotherhood."

"The Templars didn't usually take in orphans?"

"Hardly. And to confer knighthood to a landless bastard?" Hugh paced the floor in front of the fire. "Twas highly unusual."

"Why do you think they did it?"

"I never knew. I only knew that I was grateful, that I owed everything to my God, my grand master and my brothers. Everything that I had in life. Everything."

Tara stared at Hugh. She'd never heard such quiet vehemence from another human being. His sincerity humbled her into silence. Hugh continued his story.

"I worked hard for all that I had. I wanted t' prove that I was as good as my brothers who came from noble families, who had land and gold. They could renounce their wealth much easier than I could ignore my lack of it, ye see. I excelled in all forms of combat. My height was an advantage and my cunning a secret weapon. I became the best of the best, Tara, the equal of my noble brethren and more."

"I could imagine," she murmured.

"When the brotherhood was called to the Levant, I went willingly, full o' righteousness and full o' myself."

"I could imagine that, too," she said kindly.

He glanced down at her and smiled, but his expression was full of sad remembrance.

"But I was in for a shock. War was not the glory I imagined."

"I've heard that it never is when you're on the front line."

"I lost many friends." He paused. "Templars never surrender. Do you know that? We fought to the death."

"Why?"

"We did not believe in the practice of ransom, as the Saracens and secular soldiers did. To be captured and forced t' renounce our God at the hands of the Saracens—'twas a fate more heinous to us than death."

"But you escaped death."

"By the grace of God, aye. I escaped physical death." He stared off into space again, his eyes glittering.

Tara wondered what had happened to him. She usually didn't shrink from posing piercing questions to guests on her show, but she was reluctant to ask Hugh to relive what seemed to be a painful time in his life. She found herself strangely protective of the man and didn't wish to hurt him. Yet she also felt the need to press on, hoping for more information than the sparse facts he had relayed so far.

"But you encountered something else?" she ventured. "Something that troubled you?"

"Fighting in the Holy Land was far different than jousting with my brethren." He sank into a chair and slumped forward. "My fellow Christians did not just kill soldiers of Allah. There were times we trapped entire villages inside their mosques and slaughtered them. Men, women, children. Bairns. In the Name of God, Tara. In the Name of my merciful God."

Tara was silent, sensing that Hugh was confessing to her more than conversing.

He glanced up at her, his eyes glinting with moisture and emotion. "The brotherhood to whom I owed my life and soul was party t' slaughter that stained my very soul. I could not shrug it off like the others. I could not wash away the stain with prayer or hair shirts. I began t' change."

"In what way?"

"I wanted God to smite me down, to end my days as a Knight Templar. I could not quit the order. I could not walk away with honor. Only death would release me from my vows."

Tara stared at him, wondering if there existed a modern human being with such conviction. She doubted it.

"So what happened?"

"I took dangerous chances. I dared to go where the strongest among us feared t' tread. My name became legendary, Tara. I became a hero. A *hero*!" He sank his head in his hands, pushing his long fingers through his ebony hair. "I became a hero for perpetratin' the very acts I abhorred."

Tara longed to reach out to him, to stroke him, to whisper that it was all right, that it was all over. But she knew that nothing she could say would absolve Hugh of the guilt he suffered.

"Then," he took a deep breath, "Then I discovered that wickedness is everywhere. Not just in the Corbin house, but in God's house."

"What do you mean?"

"I witnessed the rape of a Saracen woman. By my own master."

Tara could tell such a violent betrayal had scarred Hugh, probably as much as it had scarred the poor woman. Tara shook her head at a tale that never seemed to change, no matter how evolved a civilization became. "Sorry to say, but it's still happening—priests taking advantage of those who are vulnerable."

"Aye. But 'twas shattering t' me. I was raised in th' church, lass. I knew nothing of th' outside world and the gray areas that most men live in. Things t' me were black or white. Right or wrong. I knew the rape was wrong and I called my master out. But I was silenced."

"They punished you?"

"Aye. I was accused of a crime I'd never commit in a million years and thrown in prison, t' await trial." He gave a dark laugh. "If found guilty, I would be stripped of my robe, my weapons—my whole world. I would be marooned in the Levant, a penniless bastard with no honor, no friends, no family, and nowhere to go."

"God!" Tara gasped, catching herself immediately as Hugh shot her a warning glance. "Sorry."

He nodded and continued. "The poverty I could handle. The loss of honor," he closed his eyes for a moment. "That I could not."

Tara said nothing. She waited for him to continue his story, fascinated by the tale and by the man.

"In prison, I had time t' think. Who was I fighting for? For my God, my beliefs? Or some twisted bastards with a taste for Muslim gold and women? I wondered if I had been lied to my entire life. I started t' question everything I believed in. 'Twas a terrible time."

"How long were you in prison?"

"Nearly a year. Until one day, I was summoned by a high-ranking brother. I didn't know who he was. He was cloaked. I could tell he was gravely ill. Most likely a leper. He told me that not all Templars were cut from th' same cloth as my master, and that he had a mission for me.

And should I complete the mission, I would not only be acquitted of any wrongdoing, I could leave the order with grace as long as I assumed another name and never mentioned my connection to th' brotherhood. He also said that I would come into my own at last."

"I assume you accepted the job?"

"Aye. It seemed simple enough. And it restored my faith in the order somewhat. I just didna realize how dangerous the task would be."

"So what was the mission?"

"To deliver a cipher t' Merristone chapel in Edinburgh."

"A cipher?" Tara was intrigued. "Do you mean a code?"

"Aye. Written in an innocent wee Psalter."

Tara nearly choked. "Really?" she blurted.

"Aye. 'Tis the book I seek, lass. Th' book I believe is somewhere still about this house."

"And you think someone stole it from you—a witch?"

"I know she did." Hugh sat back in the chair and cupped the ends of the chair arms with his big hands. "'Twas my own fault. The order taught us to avoid women. I failed. She entranced me. And I succumbed."

Tara felt a twinge of jealousy. "You mean by a spell or romantically?"

"'Tis little difference between the two."

His answer didn't satisfy her, but she decided not to pursue the possibility of Hugh's past love life. "So what happened?"

"I let down my guard." He sighed and looked toward the wall, his eyes unfocused. "Ah, lass, ye canna conceive what 'twas like t' return to this bonny land o' my youth. I'd been ten years in the desert. For all those years, my world was sand and blood, Tara. Sand and heat and blood."

She nodded, surprised that a warrior could speak in such poetic terms.

"All the way back I was beset by those who wanted the Psalter. Someone knew its value. Someone with a thirst for it. All the way back to Scotland I slept with one eye open. I canna tell ye the number of times I had t' defend that wee book with my sword."

"But you got to Scotland in one piece?"

"Aye. My heart sang when I saw my homeland. I canna describe th' feelin' I had, seeing the mist, the glens, the green. Ah, 'twas brae!" He paused for a moment and smiled. The expression transformed his stern face. For a moment Tara could imagine the boy that had once lived inside the warrior. "And for a few days I let down my guard." The smile vanished. He sucked in a deep breath and let it out in a long sigh. "I landed in the west. I had only to get to Edinburgh, to the east, and my mission would be accomplished. I would be a free man at last. Ready to start livin' a life I knew I had been denied all my days."

"So what happened?"

"I met the master of Castle Corbin on the road. He was on his way home from France with his new bride. They suggested that I ride with them until our paths separated. Theirs was a jolly company, so I joined them." He looked down at the floor. "I was not accustomed to rich food and wine—or the company of women. I confess I enjoyed them all."

"So you crashed someone's honeymoon."

"So to speak. Aye." He rubbed the side of his face where the scars shone. "And that is where I first met the witch."

"She was the bride, I take it."

Hugh gave her a sharp glance. "Aye. She was." His face hardened. "She was bonny. Hair as fair as new laid straw. Eyes the color of cornflowers. Skin like milk and rosebuds. In one day, I was half in love with her."

"Not a good thing for a priest, was it?"

"Or any man. She was wed to another."

"What did you do?"

"Nothin'! She was already carryin' her lord's child." He tapped his fingers on the arm of the chair. "But she made her intentions quite clear to me, that she did."

"She seduced you?" Tara gave a small laugh. "Somehow I can't picture anyone taking advantage of you!"

Hugh glanced at her again. "Ye can't?"

"No. You're huge!"

"But innocent of women, milady. Innocent as a wee lamb."

"I'll bet." She shook her head. "So what happened? Did the husband find out that she had the hots for you?"

"Not immediately. He came into far more dangerous information."

"And what was that?"

"Who I really was."

"So what happened?"

"When the time came for us to part company—his party to Ayr and me to Edinburgh, he had me bound and gagged and thrown into a wagon."

"Nice guy."

"At first I thought 'twas because he'd discovered what his wife intended to do with me. But it soon became apparent that he was after th' cipher."

"What did he do with you?"

"He threw me into the dungeon at Castle Corbin, which once stood very near this place."

"I've been there," she commented. "It's the creepiest place I've ever seen."

"As well it should be. 'Twas the center of wickedness."

Tara leaned forward. "But what happened at the castle—to you, I mean?"

"Edouard de Corbin, the French master of the place, tortured me for weeks, seeking the knowledge I carried from the Levant."

"Why didn't he just take the Psalter?"

Hugh chuckled bitterly. "He wasna aware th' book held the secret he sought. He thought it was just a prayer book. He mocked me for clinging to my beliefs and my pretty wee book. I let him."

"And no matter what he did to you, you couldn't tell him anything?"

"Aye, because I had no idea what 'twas in that wee book."

"What did the book look like?"

"As I said, 'twas small," he held up both hands to indicate the dimensions of the book. "Three inches by five at most. Leather bound. Dyed red. Tooled on the cover with the image of a tree. I always assumed 'twas the Tree of Knowledge. A pun, ye ken, on what was written inside."

Tara fought to keep a poker face. Hugh had just described her family heirloom in stunning detail. Again, her thoughts ran wild. She wasn't sure what to do about the Psalter. Hugh was sincere and she couldn't help but like the man, but he was—she had to admit it once and for all—a ghost. There was no other term to describe a person who could appear and disappear and roam unseen in a house full of humans. Hugh Lachlan was a ghost. But more importantly, he had already lived an earthly life. And his life among the living was over. Hers was not. If she gave up her precious book to the Knight Templar, she would never see it again. Such a sacrifice would do neither of them any good.

Hugh might argue that to finish his quest would be reason enough to take possession of the book. But if Hugh completed his mission in the 21st century, whose hands would he put the book in? No modern day priest could possibly know the true purpose of the little Psalter. The only outcome of Hugh's quest would be that her valuable book would lay forgotten and rotting in an old church, and she'd never see her precious

Psalter again.

Lost in her thoughts, Tara knew she was being far too quiet, and Hugh would wonder why. She decided to fill the silence with more questions.

"So what were you supposed to do with the Psalter once you got to Edinburgh? Hand it over to another Grand Master?"

"Nay. Leave it."

"Where?"

"At the altar. I was told there is a stone where men knelt to be knighted. The stone is not set in mortar but fitted so well as to lay solidly in place. Beneath that stone is a chamber. The Psalter was to be placed in the chamber and I was to leave."

"But I thought you would be rewarded in some way for completing the mission."

Hugh shrugged. "Those were my instructions. I assumed that my actions would be observed and that those in charge would know of my movements ever after. I would be contacted. That was the way of the brethren."

"Certainly that wouldn't happen now. Who would know what the Psalter was all about? Or who you were?"

Hugh leveled his navy eyes upon her. "Dinna underestimate the brethren, milady. I would wager my life that the brotherhood has survived in some fashion all these years, as surely as I sit here with ye."

"But what good would it do to relinquish the Psalter now? No disrespect, Hugh, but your life is over. You're not a mortal man."

He flushed. "'Tis a matter of honor. Of keepin' a promise. God would know that I had kept my word, and that would be enough."

Tara felt the tips of her ears burning beneath his smoldering gaze and eased back in her chair, her pulse racing. Hugh Lachlan was a force to be reckoned with, like a bulldozer in a forest, inexorable, stubborn, and persistent. She knew he would not give up his search until he found the book and completed his quest—unless she could change his mind.

"I've heard a lot of stories about ghosts just like you."

"Truly?"

"Yes, they wander around, earthbound, because they can't let go of something that happened in their mortal life."

"And what is wrong wi' that?"

"It prevents that person from passing to the other side." Tara leaned forward. "Nothing on earth is worth denying the progress of the soul. The life we know on earth is full of meaningless illusions, Hugh, that's what I'm told."

"And what do you believe?"

Tara flushed again. Once she would have answered his question with a quick retort, that when a person died, they died. End of story. End of person. Dust to dust. But now—she wasn't so sure.

"Personally?" she replied, stalling.

"Aye, what do ye think? That I want t' know what your Aunt Edna believes?"

Tara swallowed. "Well, until recently, I believed that a person's life force ended when their physical body expired."

"And ye dinna believe that any longer?"

"Well, it's hard to cling to such a theory," she swept the air between them, "When I have you sitting there as big as Mike."

"Who is Mike?"

"It's just an expression." She studied his face, searching for the tiniest chink in his armor, the smallest clue that he was not really who he said he was, that it was all a trick. Part of her—the *Fact or Fiction* part of her—refused to accept Hugh Lachlan, and insisted that Tara beware of being made a fool—or worse, giving up her most valuable possession for nothing.

She would like to help Hugh. But once he put the Psalter under that stone in the chapel, she would never get it back, regardless of the true state of the afterlife.

"Think about it, Hugh," she urged. "Your brothers lied to you before and treated you unfairly. What if the same is true of your mission? What if you are staking the rest of your existence—your eternity—on another man's lie?"

Hugh stared at her. She could see his thoughts racing. She wondered if his ears buzzed as much as hers did when he was around.

"Nay," he said finally, his voice deep and even. 'Tis enough for me to know I did everything I could as a man." He set his jaw. "What other men do is their domain. As for me, I pray that in the end, God will know my heart, and deliver me."

If He happens to be watching, Tara thought to herself. *Or even caring.* She chose not to verbalize her jaded view of the Almighty, knowing Hugh would accuse her of blasphemy again.

She decided to change the subject.

"You haven't finished your story," she said, hoping that to switch the subject would divert Hugh's focus off her religious beliefs.

"I have not. But 'tis nearly done."

"So you were tortured by Edouard de Corbin."

"Aye. But Edouard's young bride took pity on me. She would come at night and visit me. She cleaned my wounds, gave me powders to ease the pain. Little did I know she was a witch."

"She doesn't sound like a witch."

"Sometimes ye canna tell from outward appearance."

"What was her name?"

"Anne. And I dinna ken her other names or where she hailed from." He slid her a dark look and then let his gaze settle on a far off vision.

"But what was her interest in you? Why help you?"

"She hated Edouard de Corbin. She'd been forced into marriage with him. She wanted to heal me. She wanted me to take her away from Castle Corbin."

"So what happened?"

"Edouard de Corbin's torture surpassed Anne's healing arts. I knew I would not survive many more days. When I knew I would never leave the dungeon, I begged her to deliver my Psalter. She promised that she would."

"But she didn't."

"Nay. 'Twas the devil in disguise she was." Hugh shook his head, his wide mouth grim, his jaw set. "I should have known. I was a fool!"

"So she knew about the secret of the Psalter?"

"She must have. The day after I gave it to her, I was dragged before her lord and master, where my crime of sodomy was resurrected. They knew who I was for certain by then, probably thanks to her. And Corbin was determined to teach me a lesson for standing up to him. He had me stripped naked before the village and burned at the stake."

Hugh broke off, staring down at his clasped hands, which were perched beyond his knees. His hands looked strangely bare, as if he should be holding a mace or claymore.

"And that's where your story ends."

"Aye. That's where it ends." Hugh snorted. "Torture could not break me. But a woman's wiles ruined me."

"So how do you account for the crypt, for that inscription on your tomb?"

"What inscription?"

"About healing you. Someone went to a lot of trouble for you after your death. Surely it wasn't Edouard de Corbin."

Hugh glanced at her in surprise. "I didn't take notice of th' tomb. I quit the place as soon as I could."

"I don't blame you."

"What was in the tomb?"

"An inscription on your sarcophagus, about healing you. It was kind of like a chant. And then there was a poem carved into the side," she continued. "Something about a crow and Michaelmas. I couldn't make heads or tails of it. But I think whoever buried you, wanted you to live."

"Little good it will do me now," Hugh growled. "I have no Psalter. I have nowhere to go. I am back to where I started in the Levant."

"But whoever put you in that tomb must have had some kind of magical power. You did heal. Fairly well, as far as I can tell."

Hugh stroked the side of his face. "Aye." He held out his long hands. "My fingers have healed, 'tis true. Corbin broke them all. My legs as well. And my skin—I should be covered with burns and bruises."

Tara winced at the thought of what the knight had endured. But apparently he had healed. Yet he was in spirit form for the most part. Maybe all spirits assumed a more perfected form than they had possessed in real life. She wondered what Hugh's physical condition would be if the spell was fully broken, allowing him to return to his mortal form. Would he resume his mortal life where it left off and have to take on the extensive physical damage he'd suffered at the end of his life? She wouldn't wish that agony on anyone.

"So what will you do?" she asked gently.

"I have yet to search the entire contents of this house. It is a vast place. I will continue the hunt."

"The Psalter might not even be here, though. It would be considered an ancient relic today. It might be in a museum."

"A museum?"

"A place where people keep and display old things, so others can look at them and learn about history. Kind of like looking at you."

He gave her a dark look. "No. The book is here. I feel its presence. I felt it with you."

"Really?" Tara flushed. "That's odd."

"That's why I thought you were Anne, the witch." He studied her.

"Well, I can assure you, I'm not."

Hugh looked around the room. "That wee book spent days next to my breast. I protected it with my blood, and it comforted me in my darkest hour. That book and I have more than just a passing friendship, Tara. I know that it is close." He stabbed the arm of the chair with his forefinger. "That it is nearby."

"I hope you find it," she lied.

"Aye." He rose, his large frame suddenly filling up the space near the fireplace. Tara got to her feet as well, shocked to discover that it was four o'clock in the morning. She and Hugh had talked for hours.

He saw her look at the clock. "'Tis late. I leave you to your bed." He swept her a bow.

"You will come again?" she asked, reluctant to see him go. She hadn't talked to another human being in such an intimate fashion for as long as she could remember.

"O' course. I look forward t' hearin' my life story in all its glory, as relayed by Tara Lewis and her minions." He smiled down at her. Without thinking, Tara raised her hand to him.

He kissed her fingertips.

She surveyed his glossy hair as his lips grazed her flesh. It appeared he hadn't had a haircut in a long time, but the unruly locks looked good on him, and hinted at the rebellious nature she was sure he kept on a tight leash. "Maybe you could tour the old castle ruins with me tomorrow," she ventured. "I'd like to see the place from your perspective."

"'Twould be my pleasure, milady." He straightened.

"I'm not sure when I'll be free though."

"You need only call," he replied, still trapping her fingertips with his thumb. His gaze held hers, strong and steady and full of warmth. "And I shall answer."

Her heart skipped a beat.

"Okay, I'll see you tomorrow then." She was so conscious of the heat between them that she barely heard the words she'd just uttered. Hugh was so close to her, and the moment was so intimate, that she could feel his life force pulsing through the air. She ached for him to engulf her hand, to draw her to him and lean down and kiss her—to break the bonds of whatever vows still held him.

She could tell that he was thinking about it. But then he cut off his heated, searching gaze.

"Until then, milady, farewell." He released her hand, gave her a quick nod, and strode out of the room as any mortal man would, closing the door behind him.

Tara let out the breath she'd been holding with a sigh and for a moment simply stared at the door, her senses swirling and her heart aching. If she really wanted to, she could call Hugh back in an instant, just by saying his name out loud. But what excuse would she use? She couldn't tell him the truth—that she was starving for companionship, his in particular. Until this night and the conversation she'd just had with Hugh, she hadn't realized how abysmally lonely she was.

And that was the last thing she would ever admit to anyone.

Tara marched to the door and locked it, determined to get back on an even emotional keel. No ghost from the thirteenth century was going to rock her boat. She'd had a traumatic couple of days and a big change coming up in her personal life. That was all that was the matter with her.

Still, Tara knew she would not sleep. She felt more vital and awake than she had in years, as if something had leaped to life inside her. Instead of taking sleeping pills and waiting for the drugs to plunge her into unconsciousness, she sat down with her computer instead, to see what Susan had found out about Hugh and the castle. She had a feeling that she would not be successful in making David call off his plans for filming his episode. If that were the case, she intended to be prepared.

But more than that, she sought proof for herself of Hugh's life story. It was one thing to conceal one's identity in the thirteenth century, to change one's name, and slip into obscurity. It was another thing altogether in the twenty-first century. These days, with computer databases kept by everyone and their grandmothers, a person couldn't even skip out on a parking ticket.

When Tara finished reading Susan's e-mail, she closed her computer and stared into space. Susan's research had given her some valuable tips about the Lady in Green. She was often spotted in the upper rooms of the keep or in the chapel. Tara planned to investigate both areas to see what made those locations special. Mold and other plant material could often make humans hallucinate. There was plenty of mold and lichen on the walls of Castle Corbin—maybe enough to affect a human being in the right weather conditions. The ruin might also be giving off dangerous chemicals as it rotted away in the rain. It wasn't unusual to find ancient buildings full of lead, arsenic, and mercury—all mind-altering or fatal. There might be mirrors or other shiny surfaces combining with limited light coming through those arrow slits that could create the illusion of a figure moving around.

Whatever it was, Tara was confident she would discover the underlying secret to the Lady in Green's spooky visitations. And that would be the end of the mystery. Smiling, she got into bed and lay back.

Now that she was armed with information, she looked forward to the next day at Castle Corbin. Debunking old myths was half the fun of doing *Fact or Fiction*. Granted, she hadn't been able to explain Hugh Lachlan's presence to her scientific satisfaction, but she was determined to expose the Lady in Green. Tomorrow might even be fun, especially if Morag Smithbank wasn't part of the entourage.

But there was one thing about tomorrow that she didn't look forward to. Tara flopped on her side. Before she went debunking anywhere, she had to confront the master of the house.

Chapter 14

The next morning, Tara found John Corbin at the stables, dressed in a hunting outfit and waiting for the groom to saddle up a bay gelding. When he caught sight of Tara approaching, he tucked his shotgun into the crook of his arm and looked over his shoulder at her. He didn't smile.

"Good morning," Tara called.

"Good morning." John's reply was stiff.

"Going hunting?"

"Aye. Something is killing my sheep." He shifted the gun in his arm. "And my gamekeeper just passed away. So it's up to me for now."

"Sorry to hear it."

"No worries. I'll see what's at the bottom of it." Lord Corbin raked her with his cold eyes. "To what do I owe the pleasure, Miss Lewis?"

"I wanted to apologize."

"For what?" He looked down his thin nose at her.

"I had no idea David was keeping our engagement from you. I'm sorry for that. It must have been quite a shock."

"I can't say it wasn't." John turned to his groom. "Hurry it up, man. I haven't got all morning!"

"Sir." The groom bobbed his head and tested the cinch.

Tara stepped closer. "And I had a question—about last night."

"What about it?"

"I wondered why you were in my room so late." Tara studied John's reaction. Not a muscle stiffened. Not an eyelid fluttered. His self-control amazed her. For a second, Tara wondered if Hugh had been wrong about whom he'd seen in her room. "Did you misplace something?"

"I beg your pardon?" John's jaw dropped open a fraction, but he immediately pressed his lips together. The groom handed the reins of the bay to the master of the house and ducked back into the stables.

"You were in my room. It was you, wasn't it?" She had to be careful and not alienate David's uncle any more than he was, but she was determined to let him know she didn't appreciate him rifling through her things. "Was there something in particular you were looking for that I could help you with?"

"What in the name of Heaven are you going on about!"

"Wasn't that you going through my clothes last night?"

He drew himself up to his full height, which wasn't much greater than her own. "It certainly was not!"

"Really? I could have sworn it was you." She watched him carefully as she shrugged.

John shoved a shining boot into the left stirrup. "It wasn't me, and no, there's nothing I require, thank you." He swung onto his mount and glared down at her.

"All right, then." She gave him a quick smile. "Just wanted to be sure there wasn't something I could help you with."

"You should see a doctor." John gave a curt nod at her head, his eyes flashing. "Have that brain of yours examined before you cause any more trouble around here." He jerked the horse's head around, and the bay danced nervously. "And a word of warning, Miss Lewis."

"Oh?"

"As I told David, we Corbins pride ourselves on our bloodline. And I'm not at all happy about your arrangement with my nephew."

Tara flushed. "In what way?"

"David could do much better than to marry a woman of questionable background and psychological makeup."

Tara's flush darkened. She had taken great pains to distance herself from her Tennessee upbringing, including changing her name. Had someone in the Corbin family uncovered her hidden past? "What are you talking about?" she countered.

"David may not care about what kind of stock you spring from. But even he would think twice about marrying someone in the midst of a nervous breakdown."

"My mental condition is just fine."

"Really? Have a care, Tara." He adjusted the gun at his elbow. "I advise you to keep quiet about what you think is going on in your bedchamber. People might get the wrong impression about you. Do we understand each other?"

She clenched her jaw. "Perfectly."

John gave her a hard glare and then kicked his mount into a gallop.

She watched him go, wondering if it had been a mistake to confront him. If he was guilty, he was pulling off a great acting job with no way for her to prove he'd been the person in the robe. If he was innocent, she'd just made an enemy for life.

"I want to investigate two areas," Tara announced at Castle Corbin later that morning. She stood in the yard with Susan, David, and the rest of the crew. "With or without cameras."

"The guys are here," Chris replied, indicating the four men standing with their cameras perched on their shoulders. "We might as well shoot it."

"What two places are you talking about?" David asked, his demeanor still frosty from their words during the night.

"The bower and the chapel."

"Why?"

"According to Susan's research—that's where the Lady in Green makes the bulk of her appearances."

David raised his chin. "Somebody's been doing their homework."

Tara met his chilly gaze. "Did you think I'd sit around eating bonbons?"

"No, I expected you'd be busy with wedding arrangements."

"I assumed your friend Morag was handling all that."

Chris smothered a chuckle behind his hand, and David shot him a dark look.

"I believe you said she knew everything about weddings, didn't you?" Tara continued. "Scottish ones in particular."

"Come on, Tara, let's not fight."

"Fight?" Tara shrugged one shoulder. "This isn't fighting."

"You could have fooled me."

"You'll know when it's a fight, David." She glanced up the rocky face of the hall. "Besides, planning a wedding isn't half as much fun as taping a surprise episode of *Fact or Fiction*." She looked over her shoulder at her fiancé. "I'm so glad you thought of it."

Before David could make a flip reply, she turned to the director. "Come on, Chris. Let's tackle the upper rooms in the hall first."

Out of the corner of her eye she caught David's scowl. He no longer had the upper hand. And as long as she continued to talk and focus her mind on the science aspect of the show, she could keep Castle Corbin's dark spirit at bay. She tried not to breathe too deeply. The stench of malevolence hung heavy in the air.

Though the keep was only three stories high, each level was a good twenty feet tall. They clanked up the sandstone staircase, which rose sharply in the center of the building, flattened to a landing halfway up, and then continued its steep ascent to the main level of the keep.

They fanned out into a huge room with a dais at the far end set off by an arch and columns and two huge fireplaces on either side of the chamber. In modern days, the room would be described as an atrium, because the ceiling went all the way up to the top of the keep, allowing the third level rooms to surround it in a ring. Gray light filtered down from the top, where the roof had long ago rotted away.

"I don't know why you want to go all the way up," David complained at the top of the first set of stairs. He paused to catch his breath. "The great hall was where all the action happened."

"Susan's research was clear. The Lady in Green is seen on the upper level."

"Nobody goes up there." David wiped the sweat from his forehead with a handkerchief. "I really doubt we'll find anything. The place is just a bunch of empty rooms."

"Perhaps to the naked eye." Tara scanned the colonnade of the minstrel's gallery above the dais. Odd how the stone arches reminded her of a rib cage. She could definitely sense that the rooms were not empty. Even though she tried to deny it, she could feel a presence of something or someone.

Chris ambled toward one of the massive fireplaces. "Let's get some shots here anyway. We might want some footage of the actual living space of the occupants."

"And I want to take some samples of the moss as well as the water in the puddles," Tara added. "Let's be sure to get that on film as well."

"Right."

"Wasting your time," David chided, shaking his head. "You're never going to explain this one away with science, Tara. Never."

By the time they finished filming in the great hall, it was already way past noon. They broke for lunch, packed for them by Mrs. MacMillan, and then resumed their work.

"Okay, how do we get up to the third story?" Tara asked at the top of the main stairs.

"We go that way." David pointed to the left, to a dark doorway that led to a much more narrow set of stairs. The doorway had been roped off, probably by Lord Corbin, with a sign hanging on it that said "Danger, Keep Out."

Tara limped over to the rope with David at her heels.

"I'm telling you, Tara, we don't need to go up there."

She ignored him. "Why does the sign say it's dangerous?"

"Maybe the place is starting to crumble from the top down."

"Have you ever been up there?"

"Sure, when I was a kid."

Tara stuck her head into the stairwell and looked up. They would have to lug the heavy cameras up a steep and winding spiral staircase that had no handrails and no light source whatsoever. It was so dark in the stairwell that she couldn't see all the way to the top. Even if the stairs held, the climb would be dangerous.

"Maybe we should take just one camera, Chris."

"Whatever you say."

Tara unfastened the rope barrier and set it to one side.

"You're not really going up there," David began.

Tara turned to face him. "Do you want me to find your Lady in Green, or don't you?"

"That's not why you're doing this." David crossed his arms. "You're dying to undermine this whole shoot—and my idea."

"Does that mean you aren't coming?"

"Oh, I'm coming!" He replied.

One of the cameramen gave Tara a small flashlight, and she took the lead, every sense on high alert. With one hand on the cold wall, she made her way upward, slowly going round and round and guiding the small party through the gloom, until she'd lost track of how many steps she'd taken. She couldn't imagine maneuvering this path in a long gown and slippers or while balancing a tray of food.

Behind her no one spoke. They were too busy trying to catch their breath and watch their footing on the precipitous pie-shaped stairs. Their shuffling footsteps echoed through the stairwell.

When at last they got to the top, Tara turned off the flashlight and limped down the gallery to allow the rest of the crew room to maneuver. She tested the stone balustrade, which was substantial enough but seemed dangerously low in comparison to the height of modern day men. A person could easily tumble over the railing and onto the stone slabs of the great hall. No wonder John had cordoned off the stairs.

Chris and the crew set up the lights, and they did some takes in the gallery. Slowly, Tara walked its length, looking for clues as to what might cause the illusion of a ghost, all the while keeping up a running commentary with David for the sake of their audience.

Afterward they moved into the great chamber, where the Corbin family would have slept and spent private time. While the cameras rolled, Tara continued her exploration. No mirrors hung on the walls. In fact, no furniture remained, not even a scrap of tapestry. She was amazed to discover that the chamber still had a roof, as structures this old usually stood bare to the elements. In fact, the room boasted a wall of wood panels that was in surprisingly good condition.

Tara moved forward. She couldn't smell any noxious fumes, either. Still, the farther she walked to the back of the chamber, the more a strange awareness unfurled. She passed through a doorway into a smaller chamber and confronted a sudden cold draft.

"Do you feel that?" she asked.

David moved to her side. "Cold air." He held up both his hands, palms facing outward. "That usually means there's a spirit close by!"

Tara studied the little room and the shadowed fireplace. She could see no arrow slits. No windows at all, in fact. The place should have been musty and airless. She limped to the fireplace, bent down on one knee, switched on the flashlight and trained the beam up the chimney.

"Must be a draft from the fireplace," she theorized.

"Then why don't I feel the cold spot there?" David countered. "It's only here." He planted his feet across the room, where a small alcove jutted back from the main wall.

Tara glanced his way.

That's when she saw something out of the corner of her eye—a flutter of movement just behind him. She froze and swung the flashlight around.

"What?" David demanded.

"I thought I saw something," Tara replied.

"Where?"

"Behind you." She rose and switched off the light. Again, she saw the fluttering movement, like light dancing through the limbs of a tree and hitting the wall—except this light was green.

Tara stared at the alcove, her senses on fire, her ears straining, her eyes burning. Nothing moved. She sighed and began to turn away, and caught the fluttering again.

Tara whirled around, trying to catch a good glimpse of the entity before it vanished. But each time she concentrated on the vision, it dissipated.

She glanced at the cameramen, wondering if this was another one of David's stunts.

"Did you guys move anything? The lights?" she asked.

"Nope," Chris replied. "Not a thing."

She glanced at her fiancé. "David, is this your doing?"

"No, I swear!"

Tara turned back to the alcove. There it was again. This time more distinct—a strangely familiar triangle of darkness topped by the white oval. A shiver shot down her spine.

"What?" David demanded, slowly pivoting to scan the room. "What are you seeing?"

"Something. But every time I *try* to look at it, it isn't there."

"What's it look like?"

"It's just a faint movement. It has to be light coming from somewhere. I bet there's a crack in the mortared wall opposite you."

She looked up at the wall opposite the alcove, searching for a light source, but knowing in her heart that what she had just seen behind David was not a trick of light—not unless the same exact trick had occurred in her bedroom at Corbin Hall.

"Take plenty of shots," David said, indicating the alcove. "We might get something on film even if we can't see it with the naked eye."

"Right," Chris answered. The cameraman moved in.

David stood to one side. "Try it without the lights now."

"Okay." Chris motioned toward the crew.

They shut down the lights, and the room was plunged into darkness.

"Feel that?" Tara whispered.

"What?" David moved silently behind her.

"Something just went past me." Tara grabbed David's hand. "Something just brushed past me!"

"Good God!" David exclaimed.

"It's leaving."

David stepped away, leaning into the darkness. "Where? I don't see a thing!"

"That way!" Tara pointed toward the main room. She concentrated on not looking directly in front of her, and every once in a while could detect the fluttering. She trailed after the vision, her heart pounding in her chest, her senses tuned into an entirely new dimension for her. She was barely aware of the floor beneath her feet, the sounds around her, or the people behind her. The vision was sucking her into a trancelike state that she felt compelled to give in to.

Though she didn't trust whatever lived in this dank old fortress, she had no power to fight it. Like falling into a dark pit, she succumbed.

Chapter 15

Tara moved across the floor of the great chamber, seduced by the strange force and her own curiosity. She shuffled into the gallery and down the spiral staircase, barely conscious of the danger of descending the stairs without a light. Every time she paused for a moment, wondering what in the world she was doing, she'd catch a glimpse of the fluttering figure in green, which compelled her to continue.

She followed the vision. Down they went again, from the great hall to the ground floor and out the main portal.

"Do you still see it?" David asked. He followed closely at her heels, and yet his voice sounded far away. Tara tried to answer, that yes, she was still catching glimpses of the entity, but her voice failed her. It was like being in a dream where she couldn't speak and where the air around her felt like syrup—thick and difficult to pass through. But even in the dreamlike state, she was very much awake.

"David, she's getting really pale," she heard Susan comment. "Maybe we should stop her now."

Pale? Tara didn't feel pale. In fact, she felt hot, almost feverish. Her ears began to buzz, which blotted out David's reply. She walked onward, following the wraith across the drawbridge and down a gravel path.

The path led to what Tara guessed was the chapel. Its timber roof had long since disintegrated, leaving the perimeter walls to wear away to a scalloped line around the doorways and arched lancet windows. Fallen leaves covered the stone floor in a gray-brown carpet dotted with scarlet, which looked like drops of blood on the flesh of the earth.

The closer Tara got to the chapel, the slower her breathing became, and the more she felt as if she were enclosed in a glass bubble, which distorted the world around her and muffled both voice and thought. Her brain felt sluggish, and as she stepped across the threshold of the old chapel, a crushing sadness descended upon her.

Tara paused and stood in the damp leaves as she watched the wraith drift to the end of the chapel. She could see the entity now without having to shift her focus, but the shape of the being was still blurred around the edges. Tara could discern that the entity was a woman in a long dress, but that was all. The figure stopped at the end of the large room where a raised area had been built with two short flights of stairs bordering it on either side. Tara guessed that the raised area had served as an altar for a priest, and the room beyond as a crypt for the family.

It was there, between the two flights of stairs that the entity sank to her knees before a giant crucifix carved into the stone wall. Her downward movement echoed inside Tara with a sudden lurch of sorrow. Grief swept through her, a sharp and cutting wind that brought tears to her eyes and clutched tightly around her throat. She stumbled closer, compelled to share her grief with the woman in the green dress.

She could see the woman clearly now—her white starched headdress, the silk veil wrapped around her throat, her green gown hanging on her skeletal frame, her hands and face deathly white. She was the same person Tara had discovered in her bedroom. Yet the emaciated lady seemed completely unaware of Tara. The lady bowed her head, her hands pressed together, her lips hovering above the tips of her fingers.

Tara was stunned when the vision began to speak. This time she could hear the woman's words, which floated on the still air in an ethereal whisper.

"Lord in Heaven," she prayed. "I am Thy servant, Thy cur, Thy castoff. I know I am not worthy of Thy regard, but I beseech Thee to hear me, for I live in hell for my sins and my wickedness."

"Sins and wickedness." The words took flight and swirled around Tara, repeating over and over again in an eerie echo. *"Sins and wickedness."*

Tara moved forward, the leaves sticking to her shoes, mesmerized by the plaintive prayer.

"Please, Lord, please hear my prayer, from a most unworthy and penitent soul."

Tara stared at the wraith as sadness swelled within her, pressing in on her, pressing down. She couldn't bear much more.

"I pray for the soul of one who *is* worthy. One who does not deserve to be barred from the gates of Heaven."

Gates of Heaven. Gates of Heaven.

"I beg of You, in the name of the most merciful Jesus, of His blessed Mother Mary, let this poor soul break the bonds of darkness and come to Thee."

Bonds of darkness. Bonds of darkness.

Tears streamed down the lady's face, but she did nothing to wipe them away. Instead, she laced her fingers together, squeezing so hard that her pale fingertips turned red. Then she pressed her lips to her knuckles.

"I suffer eternal damnation. I pay the price, Lord. I pay the price in this unholy prison! Forgive this wretched creature her one transgression. Forgive me, Lord, forgive me. Look into my heart, Lord, and see the truth. My heart is not black. I did not betray the truth. In the end, I did what was right. Please forgive me and release us. I am your most wretched and repentant daughter, Lord. Please forgive me!"

Forgive me. Forgive me.

At that moment, a flock of crows flew over the chapel, swirling together as one to form a black vortex, as if to snatch away her prayer and devour it.

The lady broke into sobs and flung herself to the ground. The woman's pain and despair knocked Tara to her knees. She collapsed onto the leaves and stone, her body wracked with the same longing and hopelessness that the wraith suffered. Tears ran down Tara's cheeks and her limbs trembled, but she had no power to stop them. Grief immobilized her. She couldn't think, she couldn't speak, and she suddenly lost all awareness of the outlines of her body.

"David!" Susan screamed nearby. "Something's wrong with Tara!"

"My God!" David exclaimed. "Oh, my God!"

As footsteps pounded toward her, Tara felt herself falling into a vast and hollow darkness. But just before she hit the stone floor of the chapel, she felt two strong arms cradle her fall.

"Lass!" a deep voice said close to her ear. "Dinna let her enchant ye."

"Hugh?" Tara murmured, barely able to form a coherent thought, let alone open her eyes to see who held her. But she didn't need to open her eyes. She knew that voice. She knew the strength of the arms that held her and recognized the warm, spicy fragrance of the knight. He might have spent years lying in a dank Scottish tomb, but the sun and spice of the Holy Land still lingered upon him like an exotic cologne.

"Fight her, lass." His warm palm brushed her cheek. "She's evil."

"She's sad," Tara countered as Hugh gently laid her upon the ground. Her lips felt puffy and dry. "She's so sad—"

"The others come for you now." His warmth drew away.

"Hugh, don't leave me!"

"I'll not be far."

"Hugh!"

Tara felt the air change as someone knelt beside her and looked down at her. She could sense the person's scrutiny even though she could not open her eyes.

"Jesus," David exclaimed, touching her forehead. "She's burning up."

"What was she saying?" Susan asked.

"Who knows? She's delirious. She must have hit her head when she collapsed." The leaves rustled as David stood up.

"Chris, give me a hand, will you?" David called. "We've got to get Tara back to the hall."

"Right."

"I'll call Mrs. MacMillan," Susan put in. "And have her get a doctor."

And that was the last Tara heard.

Tara woke up in her bed at Corbin Hall to find David and Morag standing by the couch and conversing with a man in a rumpled suit. She could hear them talking and saw them throwing worried glances at her, but she couldn't understand anything they said. In fact, she saw the room as if she were looking through a fish-eye lens, all curved and blurry around the edges. And she still couldn't move her limbs. What was the matter with her?

Frantic, Tara shifted her glance—her eyes seemed to be the only part of her body that she could control—and spotted Hugh standing silently near her bed, his arms folded over his chest.

"Quiet now," he urged. "You've had a shock."

"How can I hear *you*?" she asked, worried. "But I can't understand them?"

"Ye're hoverin', I expect."

"Hovering?"

"Between one world and th' other, as I am."

"What other world?"

"The world of the spirit, lass." He glanced over his shoulder, suddenly alert. "Hold on—"

"What?"

"'Tis a weapon." His arms slowly dropped as he came to full attention. "'Tis a wee weapon they have."

"What are you talking about?" Tara struggled to follow his line of sight, and spotted the man in the suit coming toward her with a hypodermic needle.

"No!" Tara tried to shout, but nothing came out.

"What manner of sorcery is this?" Hugh asked, stepping closer to the bed, ready to defend her.

"It's a hypodermic needle. They're going to drug me."

"A draught could plunge ye into darkness again," he growled. "The witch could get her claws into you forever!"

David walked to the end of the bed and looked down at her. "Miss Lewis hasn't slept for days," he commented. Tara could hear him clearly now. "She refuses to take her medication."

"David's also told me that she has recurring nightmares," Morag added. "Which sound like they stem from deeply repressed childhood trauma."

Outraged, Tara glared at David. He'd not only been spending an inordinate amount of time with his childhood chum, he'd discussed her personal problems with the woman. Tara felt a sharp stab of betrayal and violation.

"And now look at her," David said. "Eyes open. But nobody home. It's creepy!"

"She has been deeply traumatized," the physician explained. "She's in some kind of fugue state." He lifted her arm and rotated her wrist. "But this sedative will help."

"The poor thing's had a rough time of it," Morag added.

Poor thing my ass. Tara tried to wrench away from the doctor's grip, but her muscles wouldn't obey her. Her heart began to pound as the doctor loomed over her. They were going to drug her like a wild animal, like a maniac in a mental institution, and she couldn't do a thing to stop them.

This was worse than any nightmare. "No!" she tried to scream.

The doctor primed the needle, forcing a glistening bead out of the tip.

Then he lowered it toward the crook of her arm. But just before the sharp tip punctured her skin, Hugh knocked the syringe away.

"What the hell?" David gasped.

"Good Lord!" the doctor said. "Something just hit my hand!"

"Where'd the syringe go?" David sputtered.

Morag stepped closer. "I think it went under the bed."

David dropped to his knees and searched for a few moments. "I don't see it."

"I'll get another." The doctor returned to his bag on the coffee table. He shook his head as he returned to the bedside, still puzzled by the disappearance of the first needle.

"This time, try to be more careful, would you?" David commented.

The doctor shot him a dark look. "I'll have you know I'm always careful, young man. People's lives are in my hands. Every day."

Again, he primed the hypodermic needle and bent over Tara. This time Hugh snatched the shot out of the doctor's hands.

"What in hell is going on here?" David exclaimed, throwing wild glances around.

Morag smiled. "Tara's been saying all along that strange things happen in this room."

David turned on her. "Don't you start, too, Morag."

She shrugged her soft feminine shoulders and smiled again, not bothered by David's harsh tone. "Just thought I'd bring it up, D."

"Unfortunately," the doctor commented. "I don't carry a stockpile of that drug with me." He frowned. "If we don't find those syringes, I'm afraid I can't do anything for Miss Lewis."

"I'll have another look." David knelt on the floor again and flipped up the dust ruffle of the bed.

Morag stepped closer and smoothed the wrinkles from the comforter while the doctor lifted the edges of the pillows. While they quietly searched the area, Hugh held up both syringes and smiled down at Tara, lifting his expressive brows. Tara felt heartened. At least one person in Scotland—one entity at least— was on her team.

David scrambled to his feet. "There's nothing under the bed," he announced, brushing his hands together.

"Nothing here, either." The doctor sighed. "And there's nothing else I can do, not without the sedative. However, you could take her to hospital."

David glanced down at Tara. "That doesn't seem necessary. Looks like she's quieting down. At least she's not shaking anymore."

"Or babbling," Morag added.

"Perhaps what she needs is simply a good long rest." The doctor retrieved his bag. "I have other patients to attend to, but if she doesn't improve, call me, and I'll come back this evening."

"All right."

"And if she wakes up soon, insist that she take her pills. A decent amount of sleep will do wonders for her."

"Right."

"But have someone stay by her side in the meantime. If her condition deteriorates, call me immediately."

David nodded and left the room to show the doctor out.

Morag remained by the side of the bed, gazing down at Tara. She reached out and gently brushed the hair from her forehead.

"I believe you have a lot of secrets, my dear," she murmured. "Secrets you don't want to look at. Secrets that David should know."

Morag's words chilled Tara to her bones. She struggled to move her head. She didn't want Morag Smithbank touching her or psychoanalyzing her. But in her present state, she could do nothing but lie there and take it.

Moments later, David came back into the room. He joined Morag at the bedside and looked down.

"Can you stay with her for a few minutes?" he asked.

"David, no!" Tara tried to yell.

"Chris just caught me in the hall. Says he wants me to see something."

"Something on film?"

"Yes. We might have something! Really have something!"

"That's wonderful, David!" Morag grabbed his hands and beamed up at him.

"David, don't leave me with her!" Tara screamed, but her cry was nothing more than a silent torrent of emotion.

Oblivious to Tara's distress, David leaned down and kissed Morag, very close to her lips. Morag closed her eyes and leaned into him, her hands closing around his wrists.

"Thanks, M," David murmured. "What would I have done without you these past few days?"

Tara glanced at Hugh, who watched David's overly intimate display, his countenance stormy, his blue eyes dark with condemnation.

"I'll be back as soon as I can."

"No hurry, D." Morag patted his arm and smiled at him. David paused for a moment and gazed at her, with more tenderness in his eyes than he'd ever shown to Tara.

"Thanks, love."

Tara paled, shocked by the intimacy of his tone. She watched David walk away, as she burned with confusion and hurt. He'd insisted that Morag meant nothing to him. But his actions just now made his words ring false.

As soon as David closed the door, Morag sank to the mattress beside Tara's hip. She unclasped the locket around her neck and held it up to the dim light of the lamp.

"Now then," Morag crooned, letting the locket sway on its chain. "Calm yourself, Tara. Take a nice deep breath and just listen to the sound of my voice. You have had a couple of bad days, haven't you, sweetie? But I'm here to help. I can make you feel better. Just relax now, Tara Ann. And watch the shining gold ball. There. That's right. It's beautiful, the way it catches the light, isn't it?"

Chapter 16

"You are drifting back now, Tara."

Morag's voice hung above her in a soft cloud, urging her to give in, to sink back and relax, to let go of the tight grip she held on herself.

"Let yourself go back, Tara Ann, to the time you didn't have to be so strong, when there was someone else with you, holding your hand—"

Tara was shocked to suddenly feel the warmth of someone's hand enclose her fingers.

"Who is it?"

"My mommy." Tara's heart lurched in her chest. Had she been able to run, she would have bolted out of the room before she allowed her mother to touch her like this. She didn't want to see the past, her mother, or the world she had once inhabited. It had taken her years to crawl out of that hole, and she had no intention of falling back in.

Tara tried to hold back, but the hypnosis swept her under, to a time she was more innocent of the weaknesses of people. She felt the heat of her anger dissipate as her mother's fingers tightened around hers. Her analyzing was suddenly eclipsed by pure feeling. She had forgotten the wonderful sensation of holding her mother's hand. When her mother held her like that, everything felt right, everything felt whole. She looked up for a glimpse of the woman who had betrayed her. It had been almost thirty years since she'd seen her.

And there she was hovering over her—her beautiful waif-like mother, with her long, ash brown hair rippling to her waist and her tired hazel eyes full of love. Tara stared up at her, her heart breaking all over again.

"Mommy?" she whispered in disbelief, afraid that the vision would disappear if she spoke too loudly. "Is that you?" Her voice sounded strangely high-pitched.

"Yes, pumpkin, it's me. Wake up now, little one."

The woman gently touched her cheek, her hands rough but warm. She wore her coat with the tattered furry collar and she smelled good, like baby powder. "Come, Tara," her mother said, reaching down for her. "We're going to town. But we must be very, very quiet. Can you use your quiet voice?"

Tara nodded. She would do anything her mother asked—just to keep her with her for as long as entirely possible this time.

"What are you doing with your mother, Tara?" Morag asked.

"She's lifting me out of bed. We're going to town."

"Why?"

"I don't know. I hope for ice cream." Tara had little patience for Morag's questions. She longed to stay in the world with her mother. She'd missed her mom, but had buried her aching loneliness under years of hard work and a thick skin. Now, however, the ache flared full force, burning through the barriers she'd built.

"How old are you, Tara?"

"I'm five." She held up her hand, with all five fingers splayed. "This many."

"Is your mother nice to you?" Morag asked. "Do you like her?"

"Oh, yes!" Tara smiled as she wrapped her arms around her mother's neck, pressing her soft brown hair against the nubby fabric of her coat and giving in to the joy of her much younger self. She'd forgotten how silky and full her mother's hair had been, very much like her own was now.

She let her mother slip a sweater and pants on her, and kept her feet still as she pushed on her shoes and buckled them.

"Are we going to get ice cream?" Tara asked. Most times when they went to town, her father said they didn't have enough money for ice cream. But it was her favorite treat, and she was always hopeful.

"Maybe tomorrow, baby. The ice cream store is closed right now."

"Oh."

"Is Pa coming? Or Grandma?"

"Not this time." Her mother tugged on her coat and knelt to fasten it. "Maybe next time, pumpkin."

That was strange. They never went into town without her father. Even stranger, her mother swept her into the air and settled her on her hip, even though Tara was big enough to walk just about anywhere. "Quiet now. Let's not say anything more until we get past the barn."

"Okay."

They crept down the stairs. Her mother went really slowly, trying not to make the wooden treads creak, and clutched the railing to steady herself on the steep narrow stairs. For some reason her mother hadn't turned on the light in the stairwell. And for some reason, Tara's heart began to thud in her chest.

"No—" she stammered.

"What's happening?" Morag asked.

"I don't like the stairs."

"What stairs?"

"The stairway is dark. Mommy is shaking."

"Hush!" her mother warned.

Much to Tara's relief, they made it to the bottom of the stairs and turned for the door that led to the rickety back porch. The long enclosed porch was even darker than the stairs. Her mother reached for the rusty door knob and turned it, just as a light flipped on, blinding them.

Tara felt her mother's body stiffen with fright. She wiggled around in her mother's arms and spotted a familiar silhouette standing in the kitchen doorway.

"Where in the hell do you think you're going?" a deep voice boomed.

Tara's heart seized with panic. She didn't like it when her father yelled at her mother.

"Give me the girl." He held out his hands.

"No!" Tara clung to her mother, burying her face in her soft hair.

"What's happening?" Morag asked.

"It's my father."

"What's he doing?"

"He wants me."

"Do you want to go to him?"

"No. His arms are hard. He always squeezes me."

"Give her here," her father snarled. "I'm not asking twice."

Tara could tell her mother was sad and frightened. Slowly, she peeled Tara away and held her in the air in front of her.

"You spineless coward," her father sneered at her mother. "Trying to sneak off, weren't you?"

Her mother stood silent.

Tara stuck her thumb in her mouth, sensing that now was a time to be really quiet. Her father grabbed her and slung her over his hip, not caring that he clutched her leg so hard that it pinched her thigh. Tara tried to wiggle away, but he only tightened his grip.

"Think I wouldn't hear?" He snorted. "You were like a herd of cattle coming down the stairs." His face looked mean. Tara glanced at her mother, who looked really scared. Why didn't her mother just run away? She could run out the door and into the forest, and hide until her father gave up searching for her. "Think I'm too drunk to know what you're up to, you little slut?"

"I'm not a slut!" her mother cried, bursting into tears. "I've never cheated on you!"

"Don't back talk me!" Her father grabbed the front of her mother's coat, lifted her onto her tiptoes, and flung her against the door. "You know better than to back talk me!"

"No!" Tara cried, struggling to escape the iron band of his arm. "Don't hurt my mom!"

"And you shut up, you little brat!" Her father flung her through the open door of the kitchen. Tara flailed the air, trying to keep to her feet while her heart pounded in her ears. Her father had never done more than spank her or give her a slap. He'd never thrown her down before. She landed on the linoleum floor with a painful thump, and sat there, momentarily stunned.

"See what you're teaching my little girl?" her father shouted, pointing behind him. "Back talk! No good back talk! I have half a notion to punish the both of you!"

"No, Eddie!" Her mother cried. "She didn't mean it. She's just a little girl!"

"Learning all her mother's bad habits." Her father grabbed her mother's arm. "Get in the house, Tatiana. Right now. Nobody's going nowhere!"

He unbuckled his belt as her mother skittered into the kitchen and stood in front of Tara.

"No!" Tara cried, sure of what was coming. She couldn't bear to see it. She couldn't bear to watch her beautiful mother being beaten like one her father's hunting dogs. "No!"

"What's your father going to do?" Morag asked, her voice sounding distant and fuzzy.

"He's going to hurt her!" Tara wailed, her voice cracking with fear. "Don't let him hurt her!"

"Enough!" someone roared.

Tara blinked, confused by the strange voice but at the same time hugely relieved. Who was in the kitchen with them? She recognized the man's voice, but it was so out of context, she couldn't remember to whom the voice belonged—only that the person was good. Desperate, she jerked around, searching for the someone she knew would help her mother for once.

"Enough!" the voice roared again.

Tara heard a small metallic object hit the wooden floor of the bedchamber, and the mist of her childhood memory shifted toward the horizon.

"What in the world?" Morag gasped.

Suddenly, the spell Tara had been under lifted. Her thoughts cleared, her vision switched from the shabby kitchen in Tennessee to the stately bedchamber of Corbin Hall. A hand cradled her left cheek—a hand that felt much larger and more callused than her mother's.

"Ye all right, lass?" the familiar voice asked.

Tara looked up, into the worried face of the medieval knight. She'd never been as happy to see him as she was at that moment.

"Yes, thanks."

A movement caught her eye. At the side of the bed, Morag knelt on hands and knees, searching for her golden locket. Tara frowned, remembering everything now. Morag had hypnotized her so she could psychically snoop into her past. Tara wondered how much the blond woman had discovered, and how much she believed to be true. Angry at being forced to relive a time in her life that she preferred to leave in the past, Tara jerked up and threw off the covers.

"Get out, Morag," Tara demanded.

Still on her hands and knees, Morag glanced up at Tara. For a moment, she couldn't disguise her surprise. But she quickly hid it with a smile.

"You're awake!" She settled back on her haunches. "Wonderful!"

"No thanks to you. Now get out." Tara stabbed the air in the direction of the door.

"Not a problem, but I seem to have lost my necklace."

"Mrs. MacMillan will look for it." Tara stood on the floor, with Morag at her feet. "Get out, Morag, before I report you to the Royal Medical Society."

"Are you serious?" Morag rose, her smile faltering. "Whatever for?"

"For hypnotizing me without my consent."

"It was for your own good!" Morag brushed her hands together. "And it worked. See?" She swept the air in front of Tara. "You're as good as new."

"And stay away from David."

Morag raised her chin. "Why should I?"

"Because he's going to be married in four days. To me."

"That won't change anything," Morag retorted. "I'll always be welcome at Corbin Hall. In fact, I'm more a member of this family than you'll ever hope to be."

"But I'm the one who's going to share his bed."

"Like you are now?" Morag smiled and winked at her.

Tara flushed as a second wave of betrayal swept through her. Obviously, David had revealed the complete catalog of their intimate details during his *tête–à–têtes* with Morag.

"We're respecting the wishes of his uncle."

"Is that what he told you?" Morag planted a hand on her shapely hip. "He didn't mention that he was having second thoughts?"

"He isn't."

"That your behavior is worrisome?"

Tara stared at her.

Morag's lip curled in disdain. "That I've been asked to do a complete psychological profile on you?"

"You're lying!"

"David might very well be the next Lord Corbin. He can't be too careful when choosing the mother of his children."

"No one's asking your opinion, Morag."

"Don't fool yourself." Morag dropped her hand from her hip, stared at Tara for a long moment, and then turned on her heel and marched out of the room.

Tara watched her go, and then slowly sank to the edge of the bed behind her, trying to make sense of the last few minutes. The glimpse of her mother had been bittersweet, as her childlike love for her parent was intertwined with adult resentment. Her mother had abandoned her. After that incident in the kitchen, her mother *had* run away, leaving Tara to take the brunt of her father's rage until she was old enough to run away herself. Heartsick, Tara struggled to shut out the memory, relegating it to the useless past where it belonged.

But having looked at her past just now, she saw that her childhood had molded her adult life more than she had realized. She had become a person who would rather die than to be poor and ignorant or live in an environment she could not control, but most of all, to surrender her independence to anyone. She would never sneak down a set of stairs like her mother had, or bow her head and weep instead of fighting for herself. And she would never—*ever*—abandon a five-year-old child—no matter what price she might have to pay.

Still thinking of her painful childhood, Tara let her gaze follow Hugh as he closed the door behind Morag, and then turned. Something about him looked different, and she suddenly realized he wasn't wearing his long blue robe. Instead, he had on a pair of jeans and a blue long-sleeved buttoned-down-collar shirt. In the jeans, his legs looked long and lean, especially in contrast to his muscular torso. Before she could ask where he'd come by the modern clothes, he barreled toward her.

"Morag thinks you do not qualify to be a wife to a Corbin?" he asked.

"Apparently."

"You are a commoner?" He regarded her closely.

"Yes. That's what the United States of America is all about, presumably. Equality. The land of opportunity."

"Ye dinna seem like a commoner."

"Thanks." Tara glanced up at the knight. "I think."

"Your hands are soft." He reached for her and smoothed a large thumb over her palm. Every inch of her flesh tingled where he touched her. She felt her anger toward Morag and her mother easing.

Hugh stepped closer until his knee brushed hers. He stroked her cheek, his palm hot. "Your skin as well. You do no menial work."

"Not lately." She closed her eyes, savoring his surprisingly gentle touch. For a long while he caressed her hand, and she could tell that he was studying her face.

"I was fearful for ye, lass," he said at last, his voice more intimate than she'd ever heard. "I had to stop what Morag was doin' t' ye."

"Thank you for that, Hugh." She kept her eyes closed, hoping he would continue to touch her but denying herself the pleasure of touching him back. She knew she would go too far once she allowed herself to embrace him.

"But I have such limited power in this world."

"I was glad you were here—in any capacity."

"Your father—he was a cruel man?"

"Yes, and worse when he drank."

"I am sorry t' hear it."

"Thanks for intervening with Morag. And being there at the castle, too. That was an experience I never want to repeat."

"The witch got her claws in ye—for what I pray is the last time."

"So the Lady in Green is your witch?"

"Aye. Ye can see what she does t' a person."

"I couldn't seem to control my own thoughts." Tara shook her head. "Her sadness became my own somehow—"

And to see ye so distraught, Tara." He sank to one knee in front of her. "And me not being able t' do a thing about it—it cut me t' the quick!"

The intensity of his tone made her open her eyes.

He glanced at her and then raised her hand to his mouth and turned her palm upward. Then he kissed her just below the mound of her thumb. The gesture was full of reverence and devotion. She sat without moving, transfixed by the sudden shift in their relationship. Hugh's lips were warmer than she'd ever imagined and far softer than they appeared.

Tara stared at the top of his head, wondering at the depth of his sudden and serious display of sentiment. Then something hard cracked inside her, very like the joyful pain she'd felt in seeing her mother. It was as if her soul recognized Hugh on a level far deeper than anyone she'd ever met.

"Who are you?" she murmured, awestruck.

He said nothing. Instead, he kissed her wrist and curved her fingers around his feverish face, pressing her hand to his skin. She felt a thousand sensations there—the heat of his flesh, the bumpy line of his scar, the rasp of his beard, but most of all the tightly bound pulse of his desire. For a while, he simply held her hand to his cheek as his breath fanned hot and hard over her skin, and his big rib cage heaved up and down.

Tara could no longer hold back. She could not leave his soulful caress unanswered. As if watching her own movie, she saw her free hand reach out for his glossy black hair, just as she had longed to do since the night they had met. She pushed her fingers into his silken locks and sent her hand around the curve of his head to the back of his neck, urging him closer. With a sigh, Hugh gave in. He sank into her, his nose pressed into the well between her breasts as his arms encircled her torso to crush her against him.

"Ah, lass!" His muffled words warmed her through her clothing and tunneled all the way to her heart. She embraced his neck and shoulders, holding him against her, aching to pull him all the way inside her, to weld his strength and heat to hers. His hair tickled her throat and breast—so light a touch compared to the massive man in her arms. Still kneeling, Hugh caressed her back, just beneath her shoulders, and she could tell that his fingertips were branding the landscape of her flesh into his memory. Tara was aware of a hundred points of contact between them—like star bursts—each flare of light awakening her. She clung to him, knowing she would be forever changed by his embrace.

"Milady!" Hugh murmured.

She'd never been held like this by a man before. Hugh's embrace was part prayer, part celebration, and part begrudging surrender. She could see the spiritual surrender in the curve of his neck, but felt the mortal desire in the crush of his arms. He wanted her, but he was begging for forgiveness with each touch of her flesh. Hugh's inner turmoil set her on fire.

Tara reached out to either side of his face and urged him to meet her gaze. His navy eyes looked feverish, all humor gone. They stared into each other's eyes, aware that a point had arrived that was no small marker in the road. Neither of them spoke. Neither of them pulled away.

Then Tara leaned forward, slightly tilting her head, and slowly touched her lips to his. Hugh froze in stunned silence, his back ramrod straight.

His mouth was incredibly soft, incredibly warm. Still holding his face between her hands, she kissed his lower lip, his grizzled chin, and even the scar that cut a jagged swath from the left corner of his mouth and up his cheek. He closed his eyes, shutting off his fierceness and transforming into a much younger-looking man—the man he should have been—could have been—without the atrocities of war that scarred him.

Tara's heart burst with joy at seeing Hugh's secret self emerge at her touch. His face glowed with tenderness and hope, smoothing away the careworn lines cut by sun and sadness. At that moment, he was the most gloriously handsome man she had ever seen.

Warmth poured out of her heart and diffused through her entire being, like a hidden halo. She'd never experienced such a sensation. Enraptured, she closed her eyes and opened her mouth over his, kissing him in earnest, driven by hunger and the curious molten feeling in her heart. She held his head and neck tightly, not allowing him to back away. At that moment, she wanted Hugh more than she had ever wanted a man.

Her deep kiss unlocked something in the knight. He suddenly met her kiss with intentions of his own, pressing her back, grabbing fistfuls of her hair, and arching over her. It was as if he couldn't get enough of her. He curved his hand around her left breast and passed his thumb over her rock-hard nipple, as his tongue found the perimeter of her lips. She drew him into her mouth, well aware that the action was the harbinger of something more they both desperately wanted.

Then with a moan, Hugh rose to his feet, dragging her with him, his mouth still locked upon hers, one strong forearm under her hips. She let him pull her off the bed and off her feet, barely conscious of where his body ended and hers began. He crushed her against him, easily holding her off the floor. She let her head fall backward, exposing her throat to him.

Then Hugh consumed her. There was no other way to describe how he kissed her throat, her breast, and jaw line. He staggered backward, tasting her, feasting on her flesh, until he turned her to the paneled wall. There, he wedged her against the polished wood, his nose at the small of her neck, his breath hot. Her legs wrapped around his hips, as he shoved up against her and cried out in anguish. Then he went still and sighed. His head slowly rose.

"I canna do this," he breathed.

Frantic that he had cut off his assault, she kissed the hard line of his jaw and found his mouth again. She knew she shouldn't tempt him, and she knew it was wrong to be with anyone besides David, but she wanted Hugh with blind intensity. Her body was driven to join to him. Overcome by her kisses, he ground against her again, groaning.

"Lord God in Heaven!" he gasped. He staggered backward, easing her to the floor at the same time. Then he ran his hands through his hair, as if to wipe the madness of the last few minutes from his mind. "I must go!"

"Don't!" Tara collapsed against the wall behind her. "Don't go. Not yet—"

"So help me, 'tis wrong!"

She met his smoldering gaze, her breath coming as hard as his. "But it feels right, doesn't it, Hugh?"

For a moment he stared at her.

"Aye." He finally said, his voice gravelly. Then he gradually raised his chin, steeling himself. "But there's nae dignity in being someone's secret lover."

"I know."

"Cuckolding anyone, even a Corbin, is not for me, Tara."

"I know." His sense of honor shamed her and brought her to her senses. She sank her forehead in the wing of her hand. "Oh, God, what am I going to do?"

"Blasphemy," he reminded her kindly. Hugh stepped forward and took both her shoulders in his big hands, but stayed a prudent distance from the rest of her body.

Tara let her hand fall and glanced up at him. "I get married on Saturday. How can I go through with it?"

"Only you know the answer to that, lass."

She nodded glumly. "I thought I knew all the answers. But suddenly, I realize I don't! Not after this—"

"Tara," he bent slightly to meet the level of her gaze. "It was just a kiss."

"It wasn't just a kiss!"

"'Twas just a wee kiss," he continued firmly, dousing all thought of further protest. "Don't let a stolen kiss ruin your life as it did mine."

She said nothing. She stared into his serious dark eyes, listening to every word, as each syllable sank into her bones.

"Our natures make us seek each other physically," he continued. "But 'tis up to our minds to control the beast within."

"Maybe our natures are trying to tell us something!"

He ignored her comment. "'Tis my fault," he went on. "The dishonor lies with me, for having crossed the line."

"There is no fault," she countered. "I felt no dishonor." She should have, but she didn't.

"But I did. I am a priest, lass, bound by solemn vows, until I finish my quest." He shook his head. "It is not meant to be, Tara. 'Tis as simple as that. Some things are just not meant t' be. We must make peace with each other and go on."

"How can you say that!" She had spent a lifetime making circumstances bend to her will, pushing herself to rise from nothing into becoming the youngest television host on prime time, of molding and shaping herself until she got what she wanted from life. She refused to accept Hugh's take on the situation. Instead, she reached for his cheek.

At her touch, his eyes blazed down at her, and he grabbed her wrist. But he did not pull her hand away.

"Is that all you want from life?" she demanded. "Peace?"

"No. But I am determined to find it in this."

"What about me? How will I cope?"

"You must find a way."

"What if I don't want to?"

"You must. Our worlds are not suited for each other. You are a beautiful woman, Tara, with your whole life ahead of you. And I?" he drew her hand away and stepped back. "I am nothing but a shade, with one foot in the grave."

"Hugh, don't just give up like this." She took a step toward him, and in return, he stepped back.

"I'm not giving up," he retorted.

"You are!" She held out her arms. "There is something between us, something special, you can't deny it—"

"Something forbidden—"

"Something we shouldn't turn our backs on—"

"Something we *must* turn our backs on." His eyes blazed at her.

She reached out to him one last time, and he stepped back, crossing himself against her, as if she were an evil that must be avoided, as if she were a monster in a horror movie instead of a flesh and blood woman trying to free him of outdated ideals. Furious at his refusal to bend, she caught his hand as it traveled toward his heart.

He glanced at her, his eyes widening in surprise for a fraction of a second. Then his glance turned dark and deadly.

"Do not," he growled. "Ever do that again." He yanked his hand out of her grip, and stood in the center of the room, seething.

His glare unnerved her for an instant, but she pressed on, determined to make her point. "Be your own master for once, dammit," she challenged. "No one cares what you do. No one's watching. Especially God. He's forsaken you—or haven't you figured that out yet?"

"He will never forsake me!" Hugh bellowed. "And do not mock my faith!" He strode toward the door. Then he pivoted, his chest heaving.

"Am I released from your service?"

"No!"

"Am I released?" he repeated, his voice cold.

She glared up at the ceiling, fighting back tears of frustration and disappointment. She clenched her jaw.

"Release me!" he roared.

"Okay!" she flung her arms wide. "Okay, then! Go! Run, Hugh Lachlan! Run back to your self-limiting little fantasy life!"

Still glaring back at her, he vanished into the air.

Chapter 17

Tara was still staring at the spot where Hugh had disappeared when she heard the latch on the door turn. She stepped away from the wall just as David burst into the room.

"So you *are* up," he exclaimed, smiling. He made no comment about her flushed and disheveled state and didn't seem to notice that she had been arguing with someone as he approached the bedchamber. "Morag said you had recovered."

"Did she also mention that she hypnotized me?"

"What?" David laughed.

"She hypnotized me, David." Tara marched toward the bathroom, still angry with Hugh but trying not to show it.

David trailed after her. "Morag wouldn't do something like that."

"Really?" Tara clenched her jaw. "She said she's been asked to check me out."

"That's bullocks!" David hung in the doorway of the bathroom while Tara angrily brushed her hair. "Why would she do that?"

"To prove that I'm not mentally fit to be your wife." She met his glance in the mirror.

"Bullocks again." He smiled at her, but the expression didn't reach his eyes.

"I want her out of here, David." Tara slammed the brush down on the counter. "Not tomorrow, not after the wedding. Now!"

"But for how long?"

Tara shot him a hard stare. "What do you mean, for how long? Forever!"

"I can't just toss her out." David slumped against the doorjamb. "Morag's like part of the family. It would be like disowning a—a sister."

"So she's going to be hanging around for the rest of our married life? Even your uncle told you to get rid of her."

"She'll learn her place. She'll keep her distance."

Tara turned at the sink. "You're telling me that I will have to put up with Morag Smithbank for the rest of my life with you?"

"Oh, darling!" David reached for her shoulders. "It won't be that bad. She'll come to accept you. I promise."

"Maybe I don't want to accept her!"

"She's a good person, deep down," David continued. "She's just jealous." He squeezed her shoulders. "And I'm sure you can handle her."

He leaned forward and pressed a cool kiss on her lips. Tara let him kiss her, struck by her lack of reaction to him, and was amazed that he made no comment about the foreign scent on her skin. She could smell the spicy fragrance of Hugh's embrace hanging like a cloud around her.

When the quick kiss ended, David stepped back. "So are you up for some dinner?"

"Yes, but what about going out? Just the two of us?" She had no desire to sit across the dinner table from John and Morag.

David's eyes lit up. "Well, there's a place in Ayr we could go. It used to be quite good."

"That sounds fine." Tara put away the brush. "But what about the footage we took at the castle? I'd like to see it before we go."

A shadow crossed over David's pale face. "That? Maybe later, Tara."

"Why later? I thought we might have got something this time."

"Not really." He grabbed her hand. "Come on. Get dressed. I'm starving."

She didn't budge. "There was no footage of the Lady in Green?"

"Unfortunately, no."

Tara regarded him for a long moment. His answers had been too flat and far too dismissive. She didn't believe him.

After dinner in the nearby town of Ayr, Tara and David returned to Corbin Hall. David retired for the evening, grumbling that she hadn't said more than two words at dinner, which was true. She had been too preoccupied for idle chatter.

Tara left David at his bedroom door, and headed toward the third story to find Chris. She was determined to have a look at the day's footage, no matter what David had said about it. She was also determined to block Hugh Lachlan from her thoughts. During dinner, she hadn't been able to get him out of her mind.

Her last few minutes with Hugh had run over and over again in her mind, leaving her more distraught than she would have imagined. The man had essentially told her to get lost. She should have walked away with grace. Walking away would have been the best recourse, as Hugh Lachlan's presence was a monumental complication in the life she had planned for her and David. But she hadn't been able to disengage. And she'd lashed out at him.

She could still see Hugh's face glowering at her. Just like all the other times, she flushed at the memory. She'd hurt the man's feelings. No, that wasn't what she'd done. Her cuts had gone much deeper. She'd mocked his most fundamental beliefs. Tara flushed again and glared up at the ceiling, ashamed of herself. When had she become so insensitive?

Still burning with embarrassment, she mounted the staircase to the third floor. She found Chris in a sitting room watching English soccer with two of the cameramen. The room was littered with equipment and damp clothing tossed on the furniture. Tara wondered if Mrs. MacMillan had seen the state of the room yet.

"Hey, Tara," Chris greeted, looking up from his beer. "How are you feeling?"

"Fine, thanks." She motioned toward the laptop sitting open on the desk by the window. "Mind if I take a look at what we got today?"

Chris paused, with the beer at his mouth. "Not worth your time, Tara."

"Why not?"

"Didn't get a thing."

"What did you get?"

"Mostly you just walking around."

"Are you certain?" She frowned. "What I saw was so real."

Chris nodded. "Yeah, but maybe you were the only one who *could* see it."

"Still, I'd like to have a look."

"I don't know." Chris rose. "David might not be too happy about letting you watch it."

"Why?"

"He thinks it'll upset you."

"Since when was David in charge of everything?"

Chris shrugged. "Well, you guys *are* getting married."

"We aren't married yet. And even when we are, he won't dictate to me." Tara marched across the floor pointed to a computer surrounded by cords and plastic cases.

"Is a copy on here, Chris?" she asked.

"Yes, but just raw footage."

Tara picked up the computer. "I'll bring this back in the morning."

"Wait a sec!" Chris tried to grab the laptop, but she whipped it away. "What I am going to tell David?"

"Anything you like."

Tara left Chris hanging in the doorway with a worried expression wrinkling his face. Quickly, she returned to her room, glad to discover that her ankle was almost as good as new. She slipped into her bedroom and put the computer on the coffee table. Then she kicked off her shoes and sat down.

She was glad to have something to distract her from her personal life, as she was still upset about her argument with Hugh, her growing dissatisfaction with David, and her increasing misgivings about her upcoming wedding. Maybe a few minutes with Castle Corbin's past would get her mind off the present, and allow her to get a decent night's sleep for once.

Mrs. MacMillan had left a glass of port for her on a silver tray, along with a pair of snow-white cotton gloves. Tara looked at the gloves and frowned. She'd have no excuse now to keep from showing the Psalter to John if he asked to see it. How would she explain to him that she didn't trust anyone enough at Corbin Hall to keep the book in the house? She would have to think of an excuse if he inquired about the Psalter. As her frown deepened, Tara picked up the glass of port, started the video footage, and settled back on the couch to watch.

After a few minutes she grew impatient and fast-forwarded through the film until she got to the shots in the great chamber, when she had first felt the presence of the spirit. Sipping her port, she watched the image of herself pause in surprise at feeling the cool draft going by. Tara leaned forward, studying the details of the room. She saw nothing but herself and David looking around. Then she headed for the gallery and stairs. The camera followed, shooting a dim and bumpy version of her initial trek. There was no sign of the Lady in Green.

Tara took another sip of port and rewound the video and replayed it again, looking hard for clues but finding none on the second go around. Then she let the video play until she left the hall for the chapel. And that's when the video went awry.

Tara had a good memory. In fact, she was pretty sure she had a photographic memory. She could distinctly remember standing at the door of the chapel and watching the Lady in Green weeping and praying. She could remember the leaves on her shoes and the sadness she had felt. And she could remember finally trudging forward and falling to her knees with grief.

But that's not what the video portrayed. Instead, Tara watched herself trail through the leaves without stopping, saw herself dropping to her knees and crying out for mercy, just as the Lady in Green had done.

A dark sense of unease snaked through Tara. "Wait a minute," she said out loud. She slid the status bar of the video to the left to rewind it, disbelieving what she had just seen on film.

She watched the scene a second time, her incredulity mounting with each second. Everything the ghost of the Lady in Green had said and done that morning had been performed in minute detail by flesh and blood Tara Ann Lewis.

Tara sat back, stunned and perplexed. No wonder the Corbins thought she was losing her mind. She had been absolutely ranting in the chapel. She'd been so disturbed, she'd even collapsed and lost consciousness. And it had been caught on film—every hysterical minute of it.

Worried, Tara clicked the stop button, located the file of the video, and deleted it. She prayed it was the only copy, and made a mental note to ask Chris to destroy the master. Then, with a trembling hand, she lifted her glass and drained the rest of the port.

"I've got to get out of here," she said to herself, rising and glancing around. The room was bathed in shadows, each one threatening to reveal another mystery. "I've got to get out of this God-forsaken place before I really do lose it."

Then as if on cue, she saw a movement by the desk. Almost afraid to look, Tara turned. In the darkness glowed an all-too familiar figure—a white oval atop a spare triangle. The Lady in Green.

"See me," the figure said, her voice a raspy whisper.

"Go away," Tara retorted. "I don't *want* to see you."

"See me. I beg of thee."

"You're a witch."

"Nay, I am not."

"And you may have just ruined my future here."

The lady fell silent. Her eerie eyes glowed like electric blue bulbs, and her stare never wavered from Tara's face. The ghost gave her the creeps. She tried to break from the woman's gaze, but couldn't.

"I saw him," the Lady in Green began again. "With thee, there, this day."

"Who?"

"Hugh Lachlan."

To hear Hugh's name on the spirit's lips sent a chill through her. "Stay away from Hugh," Tara warned. "You've done enough to him already."

"'Twas not my intention!" the lady stepped closer, her drawn face contorting.

"Stay back!" Tara held up her hand. This ghost had sucked her into a dangerous vortex earlier in the day. She wasn't about to be swept away like that again. "Don't come any closer!"

"He lives!"

"No, he doesn't. He's a ghost—just like you."

"But he has risen. Someone has raised him from his healing sleep. I saw him."

Tara paused. How did the Lady in Green know about Hugh's healing sleep?

"Yet he refused to look upon me," the lady added in her mournful voice. "He would not look once upon me!"

"That's because he distrusts you. You betrayed him in some way."

"I never meant to." She raised her fingertips to her lips, as if she were about to pray again. "Thou must believe me!"

"According to Hugh, you took something from him—a book."

The lady's frail shoulder's sagged. "I never meant for all that happened to befall him. You must tell him that. Please, you must tell him for me. I was detained. I could not get to him!"

"Love to," Tara replied, crossing her arms, and wondering what she would look like on film now, chatting up thin air over a vacant desk. "But I doubt I'll see him again. Plus, I'm leaving."

"Thou canst!" the lady sank against the desk, her hand at her throat. She looked so pale and worn that Tara thought she would fade from sight. "Please," the ghost implored. "Thou art my only hope. Thou alone seest me, hear me."

"Like that's a treat. You made me look like a crazy person this morning."

"Please, you mustn't leave. You must help Hugh."

"Really? How?"

"He has a chance to break the spell. On Michaelmas. Tell him to face the fire again—to face the fire and he will break the cycle and the spell."

Tara stared. The words sounded familiar. Then she remembered the cryptic message on Hugh's sarcophagus, about the craven crow and Michaelmas. She wondered if the Lady in Green had been behind the elaborate burial of the knight, and opened her mouth to ask.

But the lady was in no condition to be questioned. She had sunk her head in her claw-like hands and her shoulders shook with sobs. "He thinks I abandoned him. How my heart doth break at that. How my heart doth verily break in two—"

Tara gazed at the Lady in Green. She knew the other side of abandonment, and how many tears a little girl could cry when left to face the world alone at far too young an age. Something in her soul flowed up and outward, toward the emaciated lady. She staggered backward, wary of making a connection to the witch. She'd almost lost herself to the witch's sorrow that morning, and she was sure it would be dangerous to allow another emotional merge. Tara shuffled backward, toward the light switch.

The lady looked up, as if she sensed Tara's intent to banish her. Her figure began to flicker, becoming intermittently indistinct except for her luminous eyes. "Promise me that you will help him."

"The man hates me."

"Promise me."

"Prove to me that you are real then," Tara countered. "That you are not just a figment of my imagination. And maybe I'll consider staying another day."

"The alcove," the lady said, growing faint. "Look in the alcove—"

Chapter 18

"The alcove?" David repeated the next day as they crossed the bailey of Castle Corbin. A light rain fell, pattering upon the hood of Tara's raincoat, given to her to wear by Mrs. MacMillan. The sky hung low with clouds, making the castle appear drearier than ever.

David came up behind her. "Why the alcove?"

"I just want to check something."

"The chapel is a lot more interesting, from a visual standpoint."

"We can go back there later when the rain lets up." Tara stepped onto the first stair leading to the great hall. "Right now, I want to look at the master chamber upstairs."

"You know it's hard for the camera guys to lug their equipment up those stairs, not to mention getting the lights hooked up to the van. And if Uncle John ever found out—"

"I know. But it may be worth the effort."

"So you had a vision last night, did you?" David chided, struggling to keep up with her as he followed her up the steps. "Or did some fairy stop by for a chat?"

Tara ignored his sarcasm. He had no idea how close he was to the truth. But if she told him the truth, she would only add to his doubts about her.

The crew trudged up the stairs in silence after them, first to the main floor and then up the winding side staircase that spiraled to the gallery above. Tara threw back the hood of her raincoat so she could see and hear better, and led the group to the great chamber of the lord of the house.

"Set up over there," she instructed, pointing at the old fireplace while Susan helped her divest herself of the rain slicker. "Where you can get a good shot of this alcove." She walked briskly to the arched wall and ran her palm across the expanse of milled walnut.

"Right," Chris said.

The crew jostled into place and ran a few light and sound tests while Susan smoothed down Tara's hair and dabbed raindrops off David's forehead. Then Chris gave the go ahead as he held his monitor in front of him.

"What's so special about this alcove?" David asked.

"My research shows that it may have something to do with the Lady in Green?"

"In what way?"

Tara made up an answer for the benefit of the viewers. "This location is where she has appeared frequently."

David cocked his head. "So you think there's something special about this part of the castle?"

"Yes." Tara flicked on her flashlight and trained the beam on the ancient wood. She ran the circle of light around the arc of dressed stones that bordered the opening and then stepped into the recess to inspect the wall. She ran her fingers across the joints. Time and damp air had worn away any surface clues that might have existed in the twelfth century as to why the alcove was special to the Lady in Green. Frustrated, Tara shot the beam toward the ceiling, where the roof lay in shadow over their heads. Nothing struck her as odd.

"So?" David asked. "Finding anything, Miss Lewis?"

She shook her head. "Not really. Only—" She stepped out of the alcove and switched off the flashlight. "Only that I find it strange that the décor is different in this part of the room."

"Why is that strange?"

"Why the curved arch and then the wood paneling? It doesn't make for good design. Usually there's symmetry in these old buildings. And except for the minstrel's gallery out in the hallway, there are very few arched features in the castle."

"So what are you saying?"

"I'm just wondering why the builders put a Gothic style arch in the master's chamber, when the rest of the hall is comprised of simpler, Romanesque-style elements."

"Maybe someone did a medieval remodel?" David suggested, smiling at the camera.

"Maybe."

"So no hidden levers?" David teased. "No loose stones?"

"Nothing." Disappointed, Tara tapped the flashlight on her right palm. The Lady in Green had promised her proof, but she had not delivered. Or if she had, Tara couldn't see it. There was nothing out of the ordinary about the alcove. She frowned. "There's nothing here after all, unfortunately."

She was about to step out of the alcove when her ears started to buzz. She paused. She could see David talking, but his voice suddenly became distant and his words unintelligible. Tara blinked in surprise, sensing that her world was shifting to another plane—the spirit plane, as Hugh had termed it. She stood in silence, hoping to tap into the other world to get more information. And she didn't have long to wait.

"See me."

The haunting words sounded like a whisper on the wind. Tara whirled around, wondering where the words had come from, and wondering where the Lady in Green was.

"See me," the voice repeated.

"I can't," Tara replied, uncaring what David thought of her behavior. "Where are you?"

"See me."

Tara felt a chilling draft, and then caught sight of an even chillier vision—that of the Lady in Green passing through the paneled wall of the alcove and coming toward her.

Tara stared, every sense of her being on high alert, as she tried to understand what the spirit was telling her.

"What is it?" David exclaimed, grabbing her arm.

Tara shook him off, intent upon watching the Lady in Green and afraid he would destroy her concentration. The spirit walked through the alcove wall effortlessly—as if the panel weren't even there. Her gown flowed smoothly as she passed through the opening on a floor that had once been a much larger expanse of planks.

"That's it!" Tara cried.

"What?" David grabbed her again.

"It's a false wall!"

David stared at her and then broke away to study the alcove more closely. "You mean this?" He flattened both hands on the wooden panels.

"Yes, it must be a false wall!"

In her altered state, she could see now that the space the lady walked through was bordered not by the archway but by squared-off columns, much more in keeping with the rest of the architecture of the castle. The archway was an addition, just as she had suspected.

Tara turned to confirm her suspicions with the spirit, but the Lady in Green had vanished as quickly as she had appeared.

"The archway is an add-on," Tara said, touching the curved border. "And that wall you're standing in front of is blocking the way to a hidden room. I'm sure of it."

David glanced over his shoulder at her. "There's no record of a hidden room in the castle."

"That's because no one knows about it." She joined him at the wall. "But if we take this down, I'll bet we'll find something. Something really interesting."

"Take it down?" David turned to face her.

"That's what I said."

"No way. My uncle would kill me."

"Even if the wall was fake?"

"Not even. Castle Corbin is his pride and joy. No way is he going to allow anyone to knock down a wall."

"What if the reveal could make him a lot of money?"

"What do you mean?" David made a motion for Chris to stop the cameras and turned back to face his fiancée.

"What if we took a small look first? We could remove a couple of panels, so the wall isn't destroyed. If we did find something interesting behind the wall, we could make a TV special about it—like when they opened that tomb in Egypt—"

"No, Tara." David took her shoulders and stared into her eyes. "I'm not even going to ask him. I know what he'd say. And that would be no."

Tara stared right back, her mind made up. She'd had plenty of people tell her no. And the word no had never stopped her. When they got back from the day's shoot, she'd charm her way back into John's good graces, and somehow, some way convince him to let her break through the wall.

The rest of the day they spent doing background shots, covering the history of the castle for filler. When they got to the chapel, Tara had to force herself to step into the old shell. Her spirit still resonated with the grief she'd felt here the last time.

"Let's check out the crypt," David suggested. "We haven't done that yet."

Tara nodded and trailed after him, her senses on fire. So far, however, the Lady in Green had not made an appearance since her morning visit at the alcove. In the center of the chapel, Tara paused while the rest of the crew tramped past her. She cast a glance around the ruined sanctuary and suddenly felt very much alone in the mist, very much a stranger to the rest of the company.

For a few moments she stood unmoving in the fading afternoon light, fighting the ache of alone that this place intensified inside her. Then a movement caught her eye. A huge crow bobbed its sooty black body in the tree to her right. It cawed raucously, making her jump, and soared down from the tree, very close to her head. Tara flung both arms up to ward him off, and then straightened, her heart pounding.

Fighting to regain her composure, Tara focused on a scrap of poetry that came to her mind. She muttered it out loud, as she stared at the creature that had just frightened her out of her wits.

"Find refuge from the craven crow."

Susan appeared at her elbow.

"What did you say?" she asked, staring at the bird.

"Find refuge from the craven crow." Tara kept her eyes on the bird until it appeared it wasn't going to attack again. "It was something I saw on a tomb here."

"Oh." Susan clutched her windbreaker at her throat. "The crows are kind of big around here, aren't they?"

"I'll say. That one nearly took some hair with him."

"Did I tell you that in my research I discovered the name Corbin means crow?"

"I should have guessed," Tara murmured. "From the family crest. The crow and sword."

"Refuge from the craven crow?" Susan turned to follow the crew. "Sounds like maybe someone was hiding an enemy of the Corbins."

"I think you might be right."

Someone had been hiding a Corbin enemy all right. Someone had hidden half-dead Hugh Lachlan, and that someone had been the Lady in Green—Tara would stake her life on it. At the thought of Hugh, a painful sense of loss radiated through her, making her feel more alone than ever. She hadn't seen Hugh for almost an entire day and wondered if he'd ever appear to her again. His absence left a hole in her world that no one else seemed to fill.

Tara shut off the feeling. No man was going to make her ache, especially a mere ghost of a man. Tara climbed the stairs to the left of the large crucifix, just as David appeared at the top.

"Come on, Tare," he urged. "We're ready for you down in the crypt."

At the top of the stairs was a large room full of sarcophagi, with stone effigies marking the burial places of the Corbin family. But down a steep flight of stairs at the end of the room was the oldest part of the crypt, the original vault where Corbins had lain since the twelfth century.

Lights had been set up with an expert's eye for drama, casting eerie silhouettes on the wall. David took her hand and pulled her into the dank old room, which probably hadn't been illuminated for hundreds of years. Leaves littered the floor and piled against the bases of the sarcophagi. Cobwebs festooned the corners in thick white veils. English ivy snaked around the coffins and up and over the stone figures.

"Let's take it from here," David said. "And get Tara's first impression. It's always so good."

Tara gave her rain slicker to Susan again, and waited for the sound guy to mic her while she stood at the bottom of the old stone stairs. She was anxious to inspect the tombs in front of her—especially those of Edouard and Anne Corbin.

"Like it, don't you?" David beamed.

"Yes. It's fascinating."

"So will our viewers. I just know it!"

Chris held up his hand. "Okay, ready?"

Tara shuffled closer to David and looked at him seriously.

"Roll 'em," Chris said, lowering his hand.

"We're here in the family vault of the Corbin family," David explained to the audience. "A place where the most ancient lords and ladies of the house were laid to rest."

"The family has lived in England and Scotland since the eleventh century," Tara put in, providing background information as usual. "They came here after William the Conqueror landed in England and killed King Harold at the Battle of Hastings. The Corbin family was French. They spoke French and observed French customs. In fact, the Lady in Green may very well have been French, and the young wife of Edouard Corbin."

"Really?" David glanced at her in true surprise. "Where did you come up with that idea?"

"Research." Tara smiled, hoping her love of history and research would inspire young viewers. "You never know what interesting tidbits a little digging will unearth."

"Well, Tara," David drawled. "You may not have your facts right this time."

"What do you mean?"

"Come this way." David took her elbow and guided her toward the end of the stone chamber. "I have something to show you."

Chris grinned and looked down at his handheld monitor. He gave them a thumbs up.

Curious, Tara allowed herself to be led down the aisle, through a dozen pairs of Lord and Lady Corbins lying side by side, looking eternally peaceful in their marble repose.

David chanted each name out loud as he walked past, as if announcing nobility at a ball.

"Stephen and Isobel Corbin."

"Guy and Anne-Sophie Corbin."

"Guillaume and Maude Corbin."

His voice droned in the background as Tara scanned every stone face for clues about the couple's true personalities. Had they been happy together? Did they hate each other? Did they want to be lying next to each other for all time? She glanced at David, wondering if she would want to be linked to him like this for all time and eternity. One day, should they become Lord and Lady Corbin, she could very well by interred in the family plot, just like this. The thought made her want to turn and run—as fast as she could.

Only David's next words kept her from dashing out of the tomb.

"But look, Tara," he said, standing near the end of the vault. "Here lies Edouard Corbin. Alone. There's no lady at his side."

"What?" Tara looked down at the impassive visage of Edouard Corbin and saw the same narrow face and slight stature of his twenty-first century counterparts. But, as David had just announced, there was no matching tomb beside him.

"Why isn't there a tomb for his wife?" Tara asked, shocked.

"He obviously didn't have one."

"But he was married!"

"How do you know?"

"My research." She thought back to Hugh's fascinating recount of his life, how Edouard had traveled to Ayr with his new wife. Had Hugh lied to her? Had she misunderstood something? Proof that Edouard Corbin had been a bachelor was staring her in the face.

"Maybe there was more than one Edouard Corbin." David bent closer to look at the dates. "This one died in 1240."

"That would be the one I researched." Slowly, Tara pivoted to stare down the length of the room, searching for anything that would solve the mystery of the missing wife.

"So you think the Lady in Green was married to Edouard Corbin?"

"Yes," Tara replied, shaking her head. Hugh would not have lied to her. There had to be some other explanation.

"So where is she, then?"

"That's what I'm going to find out." Tara turned to him.

"Cut!" Chris gave a victory sign. He squeezed the monitor and gave a hoot. “This is perfect, guys!” He looked up. “This is absolute dyn-o-mite!”

As much as Tara hated to see Morag Smithbank’s car sitting in the drive when they returned to Corbin Hall, she lost no time locating the woman. Morag sat in the rear parlor, a less formal room at the back of the house, sipping tea with Mrs. MacMillan.

“There you are,” Morag called. She seemed to have put aside the chilly words they had exchanged the previous day.

“Morag,” Tara greeted. “Mrs. MacMillan.”

“Where’s David?” Morag asked.

“He’ll be down soon. He’s changing.” Tara strode across the room. “But I wanted to ask a favor of you before it got too late in the day.”

“Oh?” Morag smiled. She knew how much it cost Tara to make a request. “A favor? How intriguing.”

“You know that book you talked about? The one where you could look up local births and deaths?”

“The parish records?”

“Would there be a Catholic version somewhere—one the Corbin family might show up in?”

Mrs. MacMillan put down her teacup. “What are you looking for, Miss Lewis?”

Tara glanced at the white-haired woman. “I’m trying to find out if one of David’s ancestors was married or not—to the Lady in Green.”

“The Lady in Green?” Mrs. MacMillan gasped.

“She’s got to be connected to the family. Why else would she hang around for centuries?”

“Interesting,” Morag murmured. “I could make a few phone calls for you.”

“No need,” Mrs. MacMillan struggled out of her chair. “The Corbins have their own family record. In fact, I know exactly where it is. Come.”

She motioned for Tara to follow her down the hall. Morag trailed behind them, uncharacteristically quiet. The housekeeper took them to the library and marched to the east wall of books, where she pulled out a large brown volume.

“Lord Corbin has been researching the family for years,” she commented, as she carried the book to the desk. “He’s quite the genealogy fanatic. He’s always got his nose in this book.”

“He told me he didn’t like books.”

"Fiction, not so much. But family history? He's always buying old documents and maps, and making charts. He knows everything about this family, and then some—would be my guess."

Carefully, Mrs. MacMillan deposited the heavy book on the desk blotter. "I'm sure there must be something about Edouard Corbin in here."

Tara looked down at the book. Something didn't ring true. John had made himself out to be an outdoorsman, not a scholar.

Morag reached for the book, eager for answers.

"Shouldn't we use gloves?" Tara asked.

"Right you are." Mrs. MacMillan opened a desk drawer and handed her a pair of white cotton gloves. "You must be a bit of an expert yourself, Miss Lewis."

"I've been to a few national archives in my day." Tara slipped on the gloves and reached for the leather-bound book as Morag stepped away with a frown, not happy at taking a back seat.

With careful fingers, Tara opened the cover of the old book. The pages hung loose in the binding, and were dry and fragile. A musty fragrance wafted up of leather and ink and age—a smell that had always promised the thrill of discovery to Tara.

"This book ought to be kept in a controlled environment," she commented. "Before it falls apart."

"Oh, aye," Mrs. MacMillan nodded, clutching her hands under her breasts.

"There should be marriage notations somewhere," Morag put in. "That's what you're looking for."

"Here." Tara leaned closer to scan the pages at the front of the book, where names and dates and notations had been written since the dawn of the Corbin family. "Here they are."

She paused for a moment. She'd never seen the course of history so poignantly displayed in such far-reaching records of birth, marriage, and death, year upon year, century upon century. The fainter the ink was upon the page, the more she felt herself plunging backward in time.

"Look at the dates," Morag suggested impatiently. "You'll find your answer sooner."

The blond woman's voice broke the spell Tara had been slipping under. She would much rather have had this book to herself, to savor it on her own time. "I'm getting there," she murmured.

The housekeeper stepped closer. "When did this Edouard Corbin live?"

"The late eleven hundreds." Tara ran her finger through the lines of handwriting, making sure not to actually touch the page with her glove unless absolutely necessary. "Ah, here."

The other two women leaned over the desk, intent on hearing the results.

Tara strained to read the ancient handwriting, which was much more angular than modern day cursive.

"Edouard Corbin, born 1180. Married to Anne de Montclair 1223." Tara glanced up, grinning with victory. "There! Anne—the Lady in Green!"

"How do you know that?" Morag asked, frowning.

Tara ignored the question as she continued to scan the text. "There's more." She read the notation as she deciphered it. "Marriage annulled 1224."

"Annulled?" Mrs. MacMillan straightened. "Strange. That didn't happen very often in the old days."

"So what happened to your Lady in Green after that?" Morag asked.

Tara looked through the text on the page. "There's nothing. But there shouldn't be anything. Not if the marriage was dissolved."

The ancient handwriting blurred before Tara's eyes as her thoughts swirled. It made sense. Anne had cheated on her new husband or had been suspected of cheating with the Knight Templar. Edouard had annulled his marriage to her and had never taken another wife.

"It doesn't look like Edouard ever married again," Tara commented reading down the page.

"How would the line have continued then?" Mrs. MacMillan inquired.

Tara glanced at her. "A bastard son, maybe. A younger brother."

"A nephew," Morag put in.

Mrs. MacMillan nodded, and then pointed down at the book. "But what's that, Miss Lewis—that paper sticking out?"

Tara knew what the housekeeper was talking about. She'd seen the newer piece of paper that had been folded and placed in the center of the book. But she'd wanted to find the Edouard Corbin citation before she investigated the more modern information.

Gently, Tara opened the book to its center, and lowered the two halves slowly to the blotter. Then she slipped out the paper and just as carefully unfolded it.

The document was a long piece of paper in an nonstandard size, as if cut from a larger sheet and folded in quarters. On the paper was drawn an extensive family tree. Tara glanced at the beginning name, the fount from which had sprung the entire tree. She frowned, perplexed, and then glanced at the tip of the tree, which culminated in a single pair of names. And when she saw what names were written on the page, she had to brace her palms on the desk to keep from fainting out of stunned surprise.

Chapter 19

What's going on in here?" a male voice called out.

Tara looked up to see John Corbin standing in the doorway of the library, still wearing his Burberry trench coat and hat. She straightened, forcing all signs of shock at what she'd just seen from her face. Still, she knew she must look pale.

"I do beg your pardon, Lord Corbin!" Mrs. MacMillan scurried toward him. "I didn't hear your car—what with the storm and all."

"No matter." John pulled off his hat and handed it to her. "What do you have there?" He stepped toward the desk.

"I had a question about Corbin history for the show," Tara motioned toward the book. "And Mrs. MacMillan was kind enough to direct me to this book. I hope you don't mind."

"What question was that?" John took off his coat. "Perhaps I can help." He strolled toward the desk as Mrs. MacMillan hurried out of the library with his wet outer garments.

"We were at the family crypt today, in the chapel. And I thought it was strange that Edouard Corbin was buried alone. David said he must not have had a wife. But I was sure I'd read somewhere that he had been married."

"Edouard Corbin was married but for only a short time. The marriage was annulled."

"Do you know why?"

"Why does anyone end a marriage?" John walked closer. "Unfaithfulness. And I'm happy to report that his failed marriage was an exception to the rule in regard to the Corbin family."

"Do you know anything about his wife, Anne de Montclair?"

"There isn't much information on the woman. Only that she came from France. From a very wealthy family."

Tara nodded thoughtfully, digesting the information, and wondering how it might apply to the situation.

Morag chuckled. "Tara thinks the naughty bride may be the Lady in Green."

John shot her a sharp look. "You do, do you?"

"It's just a hunch." Tara pointed at the family tree laid across the desk, hoping to get a reaction from the master of the house. "And it seems someone else has wondered about Anne, too."

John glanced at the paper. "It does."

His face remained impassive and unreadable. Tara couldn't tell if he was intimately connected to the authorship of the Montclair family tree or not. She pressed on, determined to get as much information from him as she could, before he suspected anything. "Why would the Corbins be interested in a woman who was a member of the family for so short a time?"

"I couldn't tell you. But that's all there is about the woman. The entries about the marriage and annulment and that family tree." John nodded toward the gloves on her hands. "I suggest you put things back where they were found, and join us in the parlor for tea. There's no more for you here."

Tara's ears stung. He hadn't blatantly chastised her for snooping, but he'd come close enough for her to tell he didn't appreciate her sniffing through the family records on her own.

"All right," she replied, keeping her voice even.

At that moment, David swept into the room.

"What's everyone doing?" he asked, smiling. He'd changed into a pair of navy wool slacks and sweater that complimented Morag's light blue skirt.

Morag ambled toward him. "We were looking up Edouard Corbin in the family records."

"Find anything?" he asked.

Tara pulled off the white gloves. "Apparently his marriage was annulled. That's why he has no wife buried next to him."

"Did Tara tell you she thinks the Lady in Green was Edouard's wife?" Morag slipped her hand through the crook of David's elbow.

"Yes." David laughed and patted her wrist. "We've been filming all day trying to find that ghost." David waited in the doorway as Tara carefully replaced the book in the shelf, exactly were Mrs. MacMillan had pulled it out. "Tara, did you ask Uncle John about the alcove yet?"

The question hung in the air for a moment as Tara stood at the bookshelf, appalled at how stupid David could be sometimes. Didn't he realize that it would take a lot of finesse to get his uncle to consent to defacing a castle wall? A person couldn't just ask for permission and hope for the best. The process had to be done very carefully, with reason and intent well laid out beforehand. But David in his insensitivity had just ruined her chances at getting the go ahead.

Tara pushed the book in line with its shelf mates and turned, trying to hide her anger and dismay.

"What alcove?" John asked, predictably.

"Tara thinks there's a hidden room in Castle Corbin. Up in the master bedroom."

"Preposterous."

"The architecture's different," Tara explained. "My research suggests that there might be a false wall in the master chamber."

"What research?" John crossed his arms.

Tara glanced at him, knowing she could not support her claim with mortal facts. The only proof she had came the from the spirit world, a world that John Corbin had warned her against mentioning. She found it ironic that the people she had met in Scotland had chided her for not believing in ghosts and fairies. And yet when she claimed to have seen something otherworldly in her bedroom, they all doubted her sanity. She wasn't about to tell John how she'd received her information.

"It was something my assistant found," she said finally. It wasn't an out and out lie. The Lady in Green had become somewhat of a silent partner to her.

"Well, your assistant should double-check her sources. There is no hidden room at Castle Corbin."

"But couldn't we remove a couple of panels, just to be sure?"

"Remove?" John stared at her, horrified.

"We'd only need to loosen one or two panels to see if my theory is correct."

"And compromise the integrity of the castle?" John swept the air in front of him. "Do you know how rare it is for a structure that old to have wooden components still intact? It's a historical miracle!"

"If the panels are removed correctly, no one would ever be able to tell."

"And you've done something like this before, have you, Miss Lewis?"

"No." Tara threw back her shoulders. "But I've read about it. There must be local tradesmen who—"

"Absolutely not!" John swept the air again and shook his head for emphasis.

"But Uncle John," David put in. "What if there's something of historical significance behind the wall?"

"No! It's all conjecture. No one is going to move a single board."

"We could make a television special," David added. "Castle Corbin could be famous!"

"I said no!" John thundered. "And I forbid you from going up there again. Next thing you know someone will get hurt and sue me!"

"What if we signed a waiver?" Tara put in.

John stared at her.

Encouraged, she stepped toward him. "What if we took out insurance that guaranteed the rebuilding of the wall, should anything happen to the castle or to us."

"No." John's lip curled. "You can't rebuild history. You can't just rebuild an old structure and think it will ever be the same again." He rolled his eyes and turned to leave the room.

"Americans just don't grasp the significance of ancient roots," Morag purred.

"You have that right, Morag. And you, Davy—" John brushed past his nephew as he stomped out of the library. "I'm ashamed of you for even thinking of doing such a thing!"

Tara glanced at David, who had turned bright red at his uncle's words. His hot gaze rose to Tara's.

"I told you," he hissed through clenched teeth.

Morag squeezed his arm. "He'll get over it, D. Let's go make him a nice drink and smooth things over."

Tara knew it was useless to discuss the subject further. She glanced at Morag, who gazed back at her with a smug smile hovering around her perfect lips.

"Good idea, Morag." Tara walked past them. "Go smooth things over."

"Where are you going?" David demanded.

"For a drive," Tara called over her shoulder. She had to get away, and find some peace and quiet where she could make a decision about her future with David. She knew for a fact now that she would never find peace at Corbin Hall.

"But we're having tea."

"I'm not in the mood. And I don't think John's in the mood for me." She hurried to the coat closet before anyone could say another word.

Tara drove the car out of the parking lot and didn't look back. In fact, she had half a notion to drive away and never *come* back. She hadn't had a civilized conversation since she'd arrived at Corbin Hall, except for her chats with Hugh. And she certainly hadn't got a decent night's sleep since coming here. But most of all, she knew a showdown with John Corbin was imminent. She hadn't been the only one doing their homework. John must know everything about her. He would never approve of her marriage to David.

The thought of standing at the altar with David and having John call out an impediment to the marriage mortified her. He could very well accuse her of misrepresenting herself in front of the crew, the producers, and the entire television audience—if David had his way about filming the wedding. Should John object to the marriage, Tara knew she would be on her own, stripped bare before the public, without anyone to defend her. Having witnessed David's behavior in his uncle's presence, Tara knew that David wouldn't stand up for her. But even more, she didn't *want* him to stand up for her. Since coming to Scotland, she was discovering that his views weren't as similar to hers as she had once believed. And the closer they got to tying the knot, the more controlling David was becoming. She didn't want such a man speaking on her behalf.

Maybe it was best to not even marry him.

Tara stopped the car. She had half a mind to turn around, march back into Corbin Hall, and call off the wedding. She paused, her foot on the brake, the wipers beating furiously. A burning flush seared through her at the thought of changing her world so drastically. Everything in her life revolved around her relationship with David—her career, her social life, and especially her dream of rising above her shabby roots and creating a real family. If she left David and Corbin Hall, she would have to start completely over.

She knew how difficult starting over could be, especially now. Ratings were slipping and her looks would soon start to fade. Worse, in a few years she would be too old to have a child. The thought of living out her life without having a child to love was almost too much to bear. She had always looked toward motherhood as finally giving real meaning to her existence. And now her deepest dream was in danger of being snatched away from her.

Tara squeezed the steering wheel. Hard. It wasn't like her to turn her back on the practical aspects of a situation. She'd seen women throw their lives away over the foolish pitter patter of their hearts and their "gut feelings"—including her own mother and grandmother. She had vowed to never be that naive. Plus she was no quitter. When things got tough, she was no mere terrier like Morag. Tara was a Rottweiler—stubborn, determined, and in your face. She wouldn't just shake something until it surrendered. She would plow it into the ground and demolish it.

No, she would not quit. Not yet. Tara took her foot off the brake and roared out of the parking lot. If there were a way to achieve her goal and get around John Corbin, she would find it. But did she really want to? She had to decide, and decide today. Tara knew the next few hours, which she intended to spend deep in thought over a cup of coffee in a quiet inn, were crucial to the rest of her life.

But as she turned the bend at the long line of beech trees to head for the main road, she lost her way in the rain. Before she realized how far off course she was, she came around a curve and spied the silhouette of Castle Corbin looming in the mist.

"Crap!" Tara exclaimed. She had arrived at the absolute last place she wished to be, especially alone. She wondered if she could find her way to Ayr from here, and looked for a navigation system in the car. But there was none.

Tara glanced out the side of the car, hoping to catch sight of a familiar landmark in the storm. Lightning flashed, lighting up the sky in ghostly blues and lavenders. It was then she spotted a tall figure standing in the center of a clearing, seemingly unmindful of the storm. Tara would recognize the set of those shoulders and the lean line of those legs anywhere. It was the Knight Templar standing there. The sight of him filled her with a startling amount of relief. She needed a friend right now. And Hugh Lachlan was the only person she could depend on in Scotland. She stopped the car and rolled down the window.

"Hugh!"

He didn't look her way.

She cupped her hands around her mouth. "Hugh!"

He crossed his arms over his big chest, but didn't turn around. He'd heard her, but he chose to ignore her.

Tara frowned, turned off the engine, and slipped out of the car. Rain pelted her, but she hadn't brought an umbrella or the rain slicker. Trying to keep from getting drenched, she pulled her coat up over her hair and scampered across the wet grass of the clearing.

"What are you doing out here?" Tara called. "You could get struck by lightning!"

At last he turned to her, his face pale in the darkness. "Does it matter?"

She was shocked at the cold expression in his hard eyes and grim mouth, but knew she was partly to blame for his reaction at seeing her.

"Look, Hugh, I'm sorry that I upset you the other day."

"You spoke what was in your heart." He turned away again.

"Sometimes I say things just to rile people up." She stepped closer to his back. "I didn't realize how much it would hurt you."

"Perhaps you should be more mindful of what you say."

"I'm not used to people being so serious about things—so sincere."

"I am sorry for you then." He swept her a haughty look over his shoulder. "You must live in a world without meaning."

Tara paused. She *did* live in a world without meaning. There was lots of work in her world—too much work most of the time—and lots of traveling and parties, but very little meaning. He'd picked up on the very issue she'd been struggling with for the past few years.

"You're right. And I'm sorry, Hugh. But can we be friends again, at least?" she ventured. "If I promise not to mock you? I am truly, truly sorry for that."

He turned a bit to study her for a moment, as if gauging her sincerity. "If you wish," he said at last. "Aye, I suppose we may still be friends."

"Great!" Tara's heart brimmed with happiness at his acceptance of her apology. She wanted to pump his hand, she was so happy. But she held back, not sure he wanted to be touched by her again, and not wanting to put him off.

"Listen," she clutched the coat tighter instead. "Can we get out of this rain, and talk a few minutes? A lot has happened since we—since the argument."

"I am at your command, as always."

He followed her to the car, and she opened the door for him.

"You sit there," she indicated the leather seat of the Mercedes. Hugh bent down, dwarfing the car door next to him. Somehow he managed to get his bulky shoulders inside the sedan.

Tara joined him in the car, and dabbed her wet face with a tissue. "What were you doing out there, anyway?"

"Thinkin' about life," he replied. He ran his fingers over the dashboard, exploring the vehicle in the dim light. "And death. 'Twas where they burned me, this clearing."

Tara looked out the window. "Where?"

"Right where I was standin'. There once was a village here, with a town square. 'Tis all gone now. Rotted into th' ground, as I should be."

"Why would you come to such a place?"

"To find answers. Any answers as to why I'm here." He turned to her. His dark hair looked blacker than ever when it was wet, and raindrops glistened on his lashes, making them appear longer than normal. He sensed her regard and ran his hands through his sodden hair, transforming it into damp ridges and ringlets. "And you? Why are ye out alone on a night like this?"

"I'm looking for answers, too," she replied, trying to ignore how handsome he was, and how close he was. His large frame and dominating presence filled up the small car as well as her thoughts. She could still recall the softness of his lips and the way he had devoured her. Desire soared through her, but she blocked it out. Now was not the time for such thoughts. She had some serious thinking to do. Sex and romance would only cloud her mind.

To keep from reaching out to him, she gripped the steering wheel. "My world's been changing since I came to Scotland, Hugh. Since I met you, in fact. I'm not so sure any more."

"Of what?"

"Of anything." She gripped the wheel tighter. "I thought I knew what I wanted. I had it all arranged. But I'm not sure I should go through with the wedding because for starters, I know John Corbin hates me."

"Since when would ye let somethin' like that stop ye?"

She flashed him a quiet smile at his faith in her. "Since I think he might stop the wedding. I'd be so embarrassed, Hugh."

"Why?"

"To have everyone find out what kind of family I'm from? I'd rather die first." She clenched her jaw. "The Tara Lewis everyone thinks they know doesn't even exist. I made her up years ago, complete with a stellar bio and sob story about wealthy parents dying in a boating accident. For the past twenty-five years I've been nothing but a cardboard cutout."

"Cardboard?"

"A fake."

"Ye seem real t' me."

She laughed bitterly. "Easy for *you* to say."

Hugh ignored her sarcasm. "Why do you think John Corbin knows of your past?"

"He's got this family tree. I saw it today in the library. And that's one of the things I wanted to talk to you about."

"Go on."

"The family tree starts with Anne de Montclair. Your Anne."

"Nay, now." Hugh held up a hand. "She's no Anne of mine."

"She seems to think so."

Hugh shot her a dark glance. "Dinna tell me ye've had more contact with the witch."

"I have, and I think I know now why she's got a hold on me."

"Why? Has she cast another spell, from beyond the grave?"

"No. From what I can tell of that family tree, Anne de Montclair and I are related."

"Ye jest!"

"No. My parents are on the end of that family tree. So someone has been trying to make a connection between Anne and Tara Briden."

"Your real name."

"Yes, but whoever's been doing the research may not have made the connection to Tara Lewis yet." She frowned, thinking of the entry upon entry on the family tree. "And there's something else."

"What?"

"There's a book in my family—a little—" She bit off the word Psalter, remembering suddenly that she had never admitted to owning the little prayer book that she suspected Hugh was looking for. "A little book that's been handed down in my family. It's got names written in it, going back generations. The same names as that matrilineal family tree."

"Blessed Holy Trinity!" Hugh sat back and blew out a long breath. "Ye're part o' this. I should have known."

"Someone has been researching my family. And I think it's John."

"I told ye the man was not t' be trusted."

"Maybe he was making sure of my bloodline. The Corbins seem bent on making advantageous marriages."

"Or maybe 'tis something else."

"Like what?"

"He's looking for the Psalter." Hugh rubbed his chin. "I gave that Psalter t' Anne, believing she would deliver it for me. But she never did. And maybe the Corbins know that. Maybe they are still searchin' for the wee book. Just as much as I am."

"But why? What was so special about that book?"

He rolled his head to glance at her. "Do you not know how the Templars came t' power, lass?"

"Not really."

"'Twas bankers, they were. When a pilgrim wanted to take up the Cross and go to the Holy Land, they would entrust their estates to the Templars."

"Why?"

"So they'd have something t' come back to, lass. And something t' sustain their trip."

"In what way?"

"The Templars would give them a document, encoded so that only another Templar could read it. The pilgrim would travel to a distant city, find a Templar, show the document, and they would be given a certain amount of gold, and a notation on their document t' indicate the transaction. 'Twas like carryin' money, but much safer."

"So what does that have to do with your Psalter?"

"I believe the Psalter belonged to a powerful lord whose holdings were entrusted to the Templars, and who upon his death in the Levant, was sending his note back to Scotland t' be cashed."

"In the form of a book?"

"Aye. Where the code is hidden. In the wee book."

"So that book could be worth a lot of money."

Hugh nodded. "'Tis my guess."

"Would someone be able to read it in this day and age, though? Would the money still be there?"

"Aye. Mark my words, Tara. There are those who will be able to read the cipher, if the brotherhood is anything like the one I knew. And they would honor the pledge as well."

"I see." It all made sense now: John digging up information on Anne de Montclair's family, his interest in Tara's book in the sandalwood box, and in his midnight visit to her bedroom.

Tara shivered, breaking his gaze. "Let's get out of this storm and go somewhere to talk—somewhere warm. I need to really talk with you, Hugh. Will you come?"

"Aye, but not a public house where I'm not visible. You'll look like a madwoman talking t' thin air."

"Where then?"

"I have found a place where we can make a fire."

"Where?"

"A guardhouse overlooking the firth. I have been staying there to keep out of the elements."

"Is there a road?"

"Aye."

"Then hold on, Sir Hugh. You're about to have your first ride in a car."

Chapter 20

Tara pulled back onto the road while Hugh held on for dear life, clutching the armrest of the door and the side of Tara's seat.

"By all the saints!" he gasped.

"This is nothing." She sped back down the lane. "This car could probably go 180 miles per hour—easily."

"In one hour?" Hugh gaped at her.

"Right now we're going twenty miles an hour."

"That means we could be in Ayr in half an hour, not half a day."

"Yes."

"Amazing!"

"There are planes, too, that go a lot faster. I'm sure you've seen them in the sky."

"Carryin' folk?"

"Yes."

"Amazing. Truly amazing." He stroked the dashboard again and sat back. "I will master this vehicle."

She smiled at him. "Maybe someday. Right now, though, I need directions to the guardhouse."

"'Tis up the road there, on the right."

Tara followed the path he indicated. Five minutes later, they rolled across a flat field to a guardhouse perched on the high bank of the River Ayr. Tara could see the gleam of the water a hundred feet below. She set the emergency brake and got out.

"This place served as the first line of defense," Hugh explained as he got out of the car. "Should an attack be made from the water."

"It's hard to believe anyone would try to climb up those rocks."

"You'd be surprised." Hugh pushed open the door of the guardhouse and stood back to allow her to go in first. "Desperate men will try anything."

Tara walked past Hugh into the small stone building. From what she could see in the fading light, the place had been maintained over the years and updated with plank floors, a plastic radio upon the mantel, a settee before the fire, a sink and countertop, a table and chairs, and a bed in the far corner. Perhaps the old gamekeeper had lived here.

Hugh's blue robe had been neatly folded and placed at the head of the bed, as if he had used it for a pillow. She glanced at the knight, and found it difficult to visualize him lying in bed sleeping like an ordinary man—or lying next to him and watching him sleep. A second wave of heat rolled over her.

Tara shook off the dangerous image and distracted herself by strolling to the window by the table while Hugh strode to the fireplace. She looked through the cloudy panes of glass to discover a stunning vista of the river gorge, which plunged straight down from the foundation of the building. A guard would be able to see anyone scaling the rocks below, but it was a terrifying view. With a shiver, Tara pulled back from the window and turned her attention to the rest of the room. A bottle of HP sauce sat on the table, looking very much out of place.

"Looks as if someone recently lived here," Tara remarked.

"A shepherd perhaps. Or an old family retainer." Hugh knelt upon one knee at the hearth. "I'll make a fire so we have some light."

"Good idea."

She ambled across the floor to stand behind him, and gazed down at the muscular span of his wide back.

"Where did you get the shirt you're wearing?" she asked.

"Shir?" Hugh asked, confused by the word.

Tara nodded at his wool shirt. "The garment you're wearing on top. We call it a shirt. With a T on the end."

"Ah. This *scyrte*. Aye. *Shirt*." Hugh tried the word on his tongue and then glanced up at her. "I found it on a line. And aye, it was stealin'. But I shall repay the person the first chance I get."

She smiled. "I don't doubt you will."

He struck the flint at the kindling, and soon had a small flame. "The clothes I was buried in did not lend themselves to much activity."

"I'm surprised you found clothes that were big enough." She longed to throw her arms around him and rediscover how big he really was.

"Aye. 'Twas lucky for me." Carefully, he fanned the flames that licked the edges of the squares of peat piled in the grate.

Tara sank to the settee and soon found herself watching the fire dance and succumbing to the comfort of being in this small warm place with Hugh while rain fell outside. She couldn't remember the last time she felt so secure.

"There's tea if ye like," he said, rising. "I see ye modern folk drinkin' it all th' time."

"Really?" she glanced at the minimal kitchen. "I would love some. I'm so cold and damp-my feet are freezing."

Hugh pumped water into a pan and carried it to the fire. Then, before she could protest, he picked up her left foot and slipped off her shoe.

"The most important task of a soldier's day," he commented, "is keepin' his footwear dry." With surprising gentleness, he rolled down her trouser sock and slipped it off. Then, turning at the waist, he arranged both items in front of the fire. A moment later, he picked up her chilled foot again and held it to his chest, placing both of his big blazing hands over her skin.

"Ah!" Tara murmured, closing her eyes. "You might be a ghost, Hugh, but you feel like flesh and blood. You're a furnace!"

"Always was." He rubbed her foot briskly, kneading it back to life. "Is that better now, lass?"

"Yes." She marveled at his attention. Most men would rub a woman's feet only at the beginning of a relationship, when they were hoping to barter such intimacy for sex. But she was sure Hugh had no such agenda, which made his attentions seem all the more genuine.

"Now the other." He reached for her right foot, and she gladly surrendered to his ministrations. Had it been any other day, had he been any other man, she would have melted into his arms and demanded to be kissed. But Hugh had made it clear that he was off limits.

"You should have been a massage therapist," she murmured.

"A what?"

"Someone who gives massages." Tara sighed. "That's heavenly, Hugh." She opened her eyes to find him gazing across at her, his eyes full of soft sad lights. The expression struck her to the core.

"I like th' sound of my name on your lips," he remarked. "So few have called me by my Christian name. And with such tenderness."

"I like your name. It's a strong name." She allowed her glance to wander over his figure. "Or perhaps it's strong because it belongs to you."

He gazed at her a moment too long to keep his feelings from showing. For a few seconds she considered leaning forward, flinging her arms around his shoulders, and kissing him as she longed to kiss him. But she wanted his friendship more than she wanted his body. And should she throw herself at him a second time, he might walk out the door forever. So she pulled back, slipping her foot out of his hands.

"Water's boiling," Hugh remarked gruffly. He rose to his feet in the fluid motion that, for a man of his size, never ceased to amaze her.

"Thank you," she said, slumping against the back of the settee. "That was nice."

Neither of them said anything as he prepared the tea and waited for it to steep. Tara moved the settee closer to the fire so she could toast her feet while they talked. Then she sat down and poked at the fire, her mind blissfully idle for the first time in a long while. A few minutes later, Hugh carried a steaming china cup to her—another incongruity in the old shack. He grabbed a nearby chair and dragged it toward the fire.

"So, what else did ye want t' talk t' me about?" he asked, sitting down.

She wrapped her hands around the warm cup. "I hardly know where to start."

"Start with Anne. That's the part that has me the most worried." He propped his forearms on his thighs.

"Okay." Tara tried to take a sip of her tea, but it was far too hot.

"What has passed between the two o' you?"

"She has visited me twice. I don't think she's what you think she is."

"A lyin', thievin' witch?"

"No. In fact she seems to be pretty torn up about you—especially that you wouldn't even acknowledge her. She asked me to tell you that she was detained."

"Detained?" Hugh rolled his eyes. "'Tis an innocent wee word that. Detained?" He snorted in derision.

"She seemed adamant that I tell you she tried her best to get to you."

Hugh lifted his head and regarded her silently.

"She cried, Hugh, when she was talking about how you must have thought she abandoned you. She seemed really sad that you would think badly of her."

"She's an actress of th' first order." He slumped back down.

"No. She wasn't acting. I know acting, believe me."

He turned his head to glance up at her. "Ye think she truly meant t' help me?"

"Yes. That day in the old chapel, I heard her praying for forgiveness. It almost broke my heart." Tara sipped her tea. "No witch would pray like that."

"She would if she finally realized how sinful she'd been."

"But she knew about your tomb, too, about your healing sleep, she called it. I think she went to a lot of trouble to try to save your life."

"With a spell and an enchanted tomb."

"Okay, maybe she used witchcraft. But she was trying to keep you from dying. She wanted to give you a second chance."

"So she could raise me up to do her bidding!"

"You're wrong, Hugh."

"How do ye know?"

Tara paused, searching her memories for some kind of proof in what Anne had told her but finding none. Frustrated, she shook her head. "I can't believe I'm saying this, but I know what I saw in her. And what I saw was love."

True love. She'd gone from doubting its very existence to claiming she could now see it in action—and if she were honest with herself—to feeling it in her own heart. Stunned, she stared at Hugh. She suddenly knew what true love felt like. It was the fullest, most burgeoning feeling of warmth and selfless good will she had ever experienced. And that's what she felt for Hugh.

She loved him. She loved him without limitations, without parameters, and without second-guessing her heart. She loved him! It took every ounce of her self-control to keep from blurting out the truth that had suddenly unfurled within her.

"You're sayin' that Anne loved me."

"I'm sure of it." *And me, too*, she longed to add.

Hugh ran a hand through his hair. "'Tis not what I expected."

"I don't think she meant to leave you all those years, stuck in that dark place. There must have been some magic she was going to perform to make you whole. But something held her up."

"For a thousand years?" Hugh jumped to his feet. "And did ye ask her what she did with my book?"

"I didn't, no. I didn't think I'd ever see you again. I was so upset, I was going to leave Scotland. But she asked me to stay and help you."

Hugh looked down at her, the space between his dark brows furrowed in thought.

"Perhaps I misjudged th' woman."

"She said you'd get a second chance. At Michaelmas."

"Michaelmas?" Hugh frowned. He counted something on his fingers.

Tara took another sip. "What is Michaelmas, anyway?"

He glanced at her, but was preoccupied. "'Tis a feast day. The Feast of St. Michael. A day of settling accounts with the master of the manor." He counted his fingers again.

"That sounds appropriate, knowing your past with the master of Castle Corbin."

"And the day th' devil was kicked out o' heaven."

"That sounds even better. I'd like to see someone pay for what was done to you." She finished her tea. "So when is Michaelmas?"

"To my reckoning?" Hugh held up a couple of long fingers. "In two days."

"Are you sure?"

"Michaelmas is celebrated on October eleventh. I believe that is two days from now, is it not?"

Tara felt a chill course down her spine. "That's Saturday. The day of the wedding."

"So it is." Hugh crossed his arms. "So, if Lady Anne has told you the truth—perhaps it will be a day of reckoning for the both of us."

They studied each other silently, contemplating a fate that could connect them more than they ever imagined.

"In two days," Tara murmured. "Our lives might never be the same."

"Aye." He tramped to the fire, as lost in thought as she was.

For a long moment she regarded his silhouette—the intelligent tilt of his head, the strength of his shoulders, the slenderness of his hips, and the way he planted his feet solidly upon the ground. He was the picture of unyielding strength, of dependability and truth. If there was anyone she would choose to go through a reckoning with, it was Hugh. She wanted to tell him as much, but she bit her lip, struggling to find the right words to convey her sentiments to him. She wanted to be sincere and heartfelt for once in her life, without couching her feelings for him in a shallow caress or worse, a flippant remark.

She stood up. "I may not have the chance again to tell you this," she began, wetting her lips. "We have no way of knowing what will happen by Saturday."

"Aye?" Hugh raised his glance and leveled it upon her.

"But I want you to know something." She took a deep breath, forcing herself to continue, no matter how lame she might appear to him. "And it's going to sound pathetic, Hugh." She blinked and met his gaze. "But you're the only real friend I've ever had."

"Lass." A soft smile warmed his face. "Am I now?"

"I can talk to you. I've never been able to talk to anyone the way I can talk to you."

"Because ye're not tryin' t' be anyone but simple Tara Briden with me, lass. You're your own true self."

"I know. And I'm not sure why. Maybe because you aren't real."

"'Tis not that. 'Tis because ye trust me." He held out a hand to her. "And ye do, don't you?"

"Yes." Slowly she raised her hand to his and just as slowly he wrapped his fingers around hers, never breaking her gaze. She felt as if he were pulling her into a slow, romantic dance in a slow, romantic dream.

Tara could hide her feelings no longer. Tears welled up inside her as she brought his hand to her cheek. "Oh, Hugh! What am I going to do? I have to decide. One way or another, I have to decide about David. Tonight."

"You know what you must do," he replied, his voice gentle. "In your heart."

"But I'm so tired!" she replied.

"Of what, lass?"

"Of being alone. That's the main reason I'm getting married. And how stupid is that?" She lowered his hand and gazed up at him with eyes hot with emotion. "I wanted to make a home so badly, and have a family—a real family of my very own—that I convinced myself this marriage to David was right."

"But it isn't right for you now?"

"Not as it stands! Everything is so off kilter!" She pressed her lips together. "David has changed since he came back to Scotland—so much I barely know him any more."

"Has he changed, lass?" Hugh asked kindly, letting his hand smooth down her hair to the back of her neck. "Or has the one to be doing all the changin' been you?"

She stared up at him, startled by his perceptive question.

He placed a hand on each of her shoulders. "Do you think your loneliness will fade, marrying David on Saturday? Answer me that—as Tara Briden and not Tara Lewis."

She shook her head, tears slipping out of the corners of her eyes. "No, I'll still feel alone." *Without you*, she wanted to add. "I know that now. And you?"

"I am never alone."

"I wish I had your faith." Tara shrugged, feeling his hands heavy on her shoulders. "But I don't. And I know you hate it when I say such things, but I don't believe there *is* a God or that He intervenes in our puny little lives. Or even cares."

Hugh leaned down and looked directly into her eyes, studying her, his expression intense but kind. "Do you not ever wonder that in my case you might *be* the Hand of God?"

"What?" She was sure she'd heard him wrong.

"You might be the Hand of God, sent here t' set me free."

"That's crazy!"

"Perhaps not. I have been pondering this thought. You might be my angel. *My* knight in shining armor."

"Are you kidding?" She had to smile at the visual of her in a suit of armor, kneeling before a cross. "I'm about the most irreligious person on the face of the earth!"

He raised a brow. "That is often how the Lord works."

"But why would He wait so long to help you?"

"Perhaps t' test me." Hugh squeezed her shoulders. "Or perhaps it took a thousand years."

"For what?"

"For th' right person t' come along." His steady gaze held hers until the smile faded from her lips. Hugh had just bestowed an enormous burden on her, heavier than the plaintive request of the Lady in Green. It was the last thing she needed, to be responsible for a dead Scottish warrior. And it was much more than she wanted to deal with right now.

But the names she had seen on Anne de Montclair's family tree entangled her with this knight in ways she couldn't even imagine. And if she were honest, she wanted to be entangled with him, as tangled up as possible—body, heart, and soul.

She shot him a tremulous smile. "That's some theory, sir."

"And one I shall believe in until I draw my last breath." He cupped her cheek and smiled down at her. "I've decided you're an angel, Tara Briden. My personal angel. And come Michaelmas, we will prevail."

She gazed at him, her smile fleeing as quickly as it had arrived at the thought of the days to come and what might happen. She'd found true love at last, only to face losing Hugh in less than forty-eight hours if the spell went wrong on Michaelmas.

"What? Ye doubt me?" he asked gently.

"It's not that. I'm just thinking about my life in the States—how strange it will seem after having…now that…well after this trip to Scotland."

"Your eyes have been opened to new possibilities then?"

New possibilities? What an understatement. Her heart felt absolute brand spanking new, shining like a polished copper kettle, and bursting inside her chest every time she looked at him. She could barely breathe she was so full of love. But she couldn't tell him that she loved him. Not yet. Not if he were to push her away again. But she ached to tell him *something.*

"Yes, I've been opened to possibilities. Because of meeting you."

He nodded and let his hand fall from her cheek. He was drawing away. She couldn't bear the thought.

"And having met you," she said, reaching for his arm. "How do you propose that I go on with my humdrum life, with my boring acquaintances and my meaningless work, knowing you're out there in the ether?"

"Ye will, Tara." He stroked her hair again with his free hand. "Remember—I'm just a dream."

"One that I don't want to wake up from."

"Nor I, lass. Nor I."

She didn't know if she moved forward or he stepped toward her, but suddenly she was curling into the warmth of his torso and he was bending to embrace her. Tara buried her nose between his elbow and chest and felt his arms slipping down her back to hold her fast. She pressed into him and hugged him tightly, as tight as her arms could hold him.

"What if we lose this connection, Hugh? What if nothing changes on Michaelmas and I go back to America and you have to stay here, tied to the Corbin estate?"

"We'll cross that bridge when we come t' it."

"But I won't be able to bear it—losing your friendship. It was tough enough the last two days when you were mad at me and stayed away."

"Have faith, Tara." She could feel his sad smile. "God made us strong enough to bear anything." He drew her hair to one side so he could see her face. He ran a finger down the edge of her hairline to the front of her ear and then slowly down her neck, sending tingles coursing just under her skin. "Even this physical hunger between us."

"But you don't have to bear it. Let yourself be human for once. And just hold me for a while."

"Ye tempt me, lass," he murmured. "Were I a real man—"

She looked up, her throat burning with unshed tears. "You are real to me, Hugh. More real than any man I've ever met."

"With a real future—"

"The future doesn't matter!" She clutched his wrist.

"Ye know it does, lass. And we're but spirits passing through time, wavin' at each other. It canna last. Not like we both want it to."

"Then let's grasp each other's hands and hold on for as long as we can. It will be enough for me, Hugh, enough for now."

"But 'tis far more than a handshake I want from ye, Tara." He gazed down at her and stroked her face with his thumb, just under her cheekbone, his gaze fastened upon her mouth. "Ye know that, don't you?"

"Yes." She breathed, her heart surging in her chest.

"So ye'll not be marryin' that David Corbin then?"

"How could I now?" she replied, feeling gloriously free at finally making the decision to call off the wedding. In fact, Tara felt as if her life were just beginning. She turned to kiss the side of Hugh's thumb. "Do you have any idea the effect you have upon me?"

"Not half th' effect ye have on me." He dragged the pad of his thumb over her lower lip, as if contemplating what he was about to do to her mouth, and then with a growl, swept her off her feet.

Chapter 21

Hugh carried Tara to the small bed, kissing her all the way across the room. Then, still kissing her throat, he laid her upon the old quilt. She reached for his shoulders, but he stood up and took a step back from the bed.

"Will you show yourself to me, Tara?" he asked, his arms at his sides. "I've never seen a naked woman."

She rose on one elbow. "You can't be serious."

He blushed slightly. "I have known the flesh of a woman. But I have never seen one completely bare o' clothes."

"Really?" Tara held back a smile of delight. She'd never been with such an innocent man. "Then if you want to see me naked, you'll have to undress me. That's part of the game."

"Game?" His eyes darkened. "'Tis no game with me."

"Me either, actually." She was glad to hear his serious remark, for she had never taken lovemaking lightly. Her definition of real lovemaking was not a game but the deepest conversation two human beings could have. And with Hugh, she believed she would be capable of sustaining such a conversation for the first time in her life.

Part of the process was showing Hugh what she wanted in a lover by being such a lover to him. She patted the bed beside her. "Hugh, come and sit down. Let's start over."

He gave her a questioning look and then slowly sank to the mattress beside her. She kissed him, and got to her feet, nudging so close to his knees that he was obliged to open his legs. He inhaled sharply and grabbed her hips, nearly dragging her off her feet.

To stop her free fall toward him, Tara planted a hand on his chest and then rose up to look him in the eyes. She began her conversation with him by framing his face between her palms.

"Do you have any idea how incredibly handsome you are?" she asked.

"I hardly think so, scarred as I am."

"I don't even notice your scars. I see your eyes—so dark blue. As dark as the evening sky. And so kind." She brushed the hair off his forehead and kissed the arch of each eyebrow. "I see your big, Scottish beak that gives your face character." She pressed three kisses down the length of his sharp high-bridged nose. "And your mouth. How determined it looks, and yet how soft it can be." He tipped his head, expecting a real kiss, but she teased him by drawing away without touching his lips. Hugh eased back on the palms of his hands, a half-smile on his mouth.

Tara reached for the top button of his shirt. "I've wanted to see you naked, too. For the longest time." She unfastened the first button, and felt Hugh's thighs tighten against hers. She kissed him just above the open placket of his shirt, wondering what she would find beneath the wool cloth.

"I'm warnin' ye, Tara. I'm a warhorse. I'm no' pretty."

"What makes you think I like pretty?" She released the next two buttons and slipped her hand in the opening. Then she closed her eyes, trying to visualize what he would look like using only her fingertips. His flesh was hot and smooth, free of hair, and ridged with muscles she'd never encountered in a lover.

Tara felt a surge of desire so strong that her knees went weak. She had to reach out for support by grabbing his shoulder.

"Ye swoon at the feel o' me," he growled, straightening. "Back away, lass. Ye dinna have t' continue."

Tara stood her ground and met his feverish gaze. She leaned down. "Wild horses couldn't stop me, Hugh Lachlan."

For a moment, he stared at her, trying to comprehend her meaning and intent. Then his serious face relaxed into the most engaging smile she'd ever seen.

She could barely keep from ravishing him on the spot.

Sucking in a deep breath to steady herself, she unfastened the last three buttons and opened his shirt to get her first good look at Hugh's torso.

She had imagined he'd be built. She'd expected he'd be scarred. But she was not prepared for what she saw before her. He was crisscrossed with lines, in both white and purple, and marred with splotches like giant snowflakes where flames had left their mark on his flesh. But beneath each wound, his muscular prowess beamed through like a beacon, undaunted and unyielding, no matter how many times he'd been struck, no matter what horrific pain he'd endured. Beneath the scars, his abdomen was as taut as a hunk of tanned leather, ridged with muscle, his flat male breasts like ledges of stone, his shoulders and neck like that of a wild beast, strapped with sinew and steel.

"Hugh," she breathed, stunned that so harsh and tragic a story had been written across such an exquisite physique.

He stared at her, the whites of his eyes gleaming with an unspoken challenge that she not turn away in disgust.

"Oh, Hugh!" She sank forward and kissed him in the center of his chest, on the hot indentation of his breastbone, hoping her kisses might someday wipe away the tragic history inscribed upon his flesh. She turned her head and pressed her cheek against his thudding heart while she hugged him fiercely.

"Have ye seen enough, lass?" he asked, his voice husky with emotion. He reached for the arms wrapped around his neck.

She drew back. "Not nearly enough." She grasped the edges of his shirt and drew the cloth down his massive arms, until he was forced to let her take it all the way off. Then without speaking, she ran her hands down his biceps and over the backs of his arms to the vast expanse of his back, caught up by her first exploration of his body. She melted into him, swept away.

He glowed against her. Even through her sweater she could feel the heat of his muscular chest. For a while she caressed his back, reveling in the sensation of being so close to the man she had come to love. Soon she had slipped into a far more intimate space than the old stone guardhouse with its glowing fire. Her world had coalesced to a delicious cocoon, where all she knew was the touch of Hugh's fiery skin, the flames of heat in her own body, and the sound of their breathing. She could tell by Hugh's sighs that her fingers and kisses had swept him into her private world as well. And when he slowly reclined, drawing her down to his naked torso, she followed as smoothly as if she were attached to him.

Tara embraced him, and then rose slightly, kissing Hugh just under his chin, then down his neck and his chest to the rise and fall of his ribbed abdomen. She licked the tight skin around his navel and slowly dragged the tip of her tongue downward, following the feathery trail of hair that disappeared into his jeans.

Hugh froze.

Tara didn't have to look at him to know he had propped himself up on his elbows and was watching her.

Deftly she unfastened the metal button of the jeans with one hand as she slipped her other hand over the denim stretched tightly across his crotch. He sucked in a breath and so did she. Hugh was as hard and massive as the rest of his warrior's body. Tara felt herself go wet with desire at the thought that this powerful being had submitted to her, but could rise up at any moment and devour her. Closing her eyes, she bent down and kissed the warm fabric near the zipper of his jeans, following the line of the most private part of him.

"St. Andrew," Hugh murmured, sinking back down on the quilt.

Tara unzipped his jeans, and then, not able to stand another moment disengaged from him, straddled his hips.

She sank down upon him, her entire body thudding with need as she aligned the silhouette of his desire with hers. Hugh encircled her waist with his large hands and went silent, suspended in disbelief. Then, forgetting all about her slow timetable of love, Tara pushed her hips forward and back, rocking over him and moaning with pleasure.

The sound of her moan broke Hugh's self-control. Gasping her name, he clutched her hips and pressed her down upon him, pinning her to him as if she might rise off and disappear. Then before she knew what had happened, he had rolled on top of her and was kissing her with both desperation and blatant intent.

His huge frame dwarfed hers, but somehow he kept his weight off her, as he pushed against her, his slender hips made to fit between hers. She wrapped her legs around him, meeting every undulating thrust with her own, desperate to know how what it would feel like to have him truly inside her.

"Hugh!" she gasped as he thrust so hard the bed frame slammed against the wall.

She had unleashed him much sooner than she had planned. She had thought to undress him, and then herself, teasing him beyond endurance, but never actually having sex with him. But he had cracked much sooner than she had guessed he would. And so had she.

"Hugh!" she cried, struggling to get out from under him so she could at least slip out of her slacks.

Hugh didn't seem to hear her. He thrust against her, his nose at the small of her shoulder, his breath bursting over her skin like a wild bull in rut, his hands pushing her sweater up her blazing torso.

The bed slammed against the wall a second time, a third, and then with a sudden crash, collapsed at the corner, sending Tara and Hugh sliding to the floor.

His reactions were as nimble as ever, even in the throes of lovemaking. He rolled to his back and caught her against his tall body, cradling her fall.

"Ye alright?" he gasped, struggling to sit up.

Shocked, Tara raised her head and stared at the old bed, while a cold draft swept over her, cooling her runaway lust. "What happened?" she exclaimed.

She felt the rumble of Hugh's laugh before she heard it. "'Tis someone tryin' t' tell us to stop such carryin' on."

She glanced down at him and found the hunger in his eyes had turned to humor.

"Carrying on?" She flushed hotly and straightened to a kneeling position. "That was all it was to you?"

"Nay, now." He sobered and caressed her left arm. "'Twas the bonniest feelin' I've ever had. The absolute bonniest, Tara."

She studied his intense gaze and realized he was telling the truth.

"And we'll pick up where we left off." He shifted, and she climbed off him, knowing their chance for intimacy had passed. "As soon as I see t' the poor wee bed."

Tara yanked down her sweater and knelt on the floor as Hugh rose to his feet. "Wait a minute," she said, ducking closer for a better view of the floor beneath the bed. "It wasn't the bed that broke. The leg fell through the floor."

"What?" Hugh knelt on one knee beside her.

"Can you lift the bed?" Tara questioned, anxiously. "Or move it back?"

"Aye." Hugh tilted the bed on two legs as if it were as light as a cardboard box. He held it off the ground as Tara made a closer inspection.

In the dim light, Tara leaned forward, tracing the old planks with one hand. "There's a line in the floor—like a seam—where the leg fell through." She straightened. "Can you move the bed away, Hugh, to the middle of the room?"

He rose, pulled the bed away from the corner of the guardhouse, and tramped back to her side. Light from the fire now illuminated the corner, enough to reveal a separate panel in the floor that had been hidden under the bed.

"Look!" Tara pointed at a rusted ring.

"'Tis a trap door!" Hugh bent and grabbed the ring, pulling the door open with a loud creak. A cold musty smell wafted up from below, where stairs disappeared into inky blackness. Tara's thoughts of lovemaking dissipated in a cloud of goose bumps.

"Where do you think those stairs go?" she asked. "To a dungeon?"

"Perhaps. But more likely to the end of a passageway."

"Coming from where?"

"The castle. A castle always has an escape route. Usually from the master chamber, so the lord of the castle can get out if under duress." He studied the dark abyss. "Since this guardhouse is close to the water, I'd wager this building marks the end of an escape route should the master wish to flee by boat."

"But how would the other end of the passage be marked?" Tara thought back to the large master chamber she'd visited twice. "I don't remember seeing an interior door in the master bedroom."

"Oh, 'twould be hidden, lass. No one but Edouard Corbin would have known of it."

A hidden passage. A secret door. Maybe even a false wall concealing a hidden room. Tara's mind raced with possibilities.

She clutched Hugh's forearm. "Are you saying that if we took those stairs and went along the passage, we might end up in a secret chamber of the master bedroom?"

"Aye." Hugh glanced at her, and suddenly understood her intention. "Ye mean to go now, don't you?"

"Yes!"

"Why would ye want to take such a trek?"

"Because we might find out the truth—the truth Anne wants me to discover." She grabbed her socks and shoes and put them on as she talked. "I think there's a secret hidden behind a false wall in the castle—maybe one we can access from that tunnel."

"Ye jest."

"No, I'm serious." She turned. "Will you go with me, Hugh?"

"I have no choice *but* t' go with you." He reached for his discarded wool shirt.

"Good." Tara headed for the door. "I'll see if there's a flashlight in the car."

"A flashlight?"

She turned. "It'll be easier if I just show you what I'm talking about. Wait here."

Moments later, with the newfangled flashlight in his hand and his shirt buttoned, Hugh led the way down the stone steps. When he got to the bottom of the stairs, he reached for Tara.

"Steady now, lass," he said. "'Tis uneven ground from here." He swept the beam of light in an arc to illuminate the path in front of them, revealing a cramped tunnel carved out of earth and rock. Tara could hear water dripping in the distance.

"How far do you think it is?"

"A mile or so." He looked down at her. "Sure you're up t' it?"

She nodded, determined to get to the end. "Let's go."

They trudged through the tunnel in silence, batting away cobwebs and stepping over puddles of groundwater. Tara tried not to think how far underground they were, or what would happen if the passageway caved in. She focused her mind on getting to the end and what she might discover there.

Hugh tramped forward, his pace brisk enough to make her have to jog to keep up. She snatched glimpses of his figure, and each time a rush of desire mixed with alarm flared within her. She had nearly made love with a ghost. If the bed hadn't collapsed, she would have had unprotected intercourse with a thousand year old warrior. Who knew what the consequences might have been? Tara didn't know whether to be thankful or not for having been interrupted. She only knew that being with Hugh felt right, that each moment in his arms had been like a wonderful gift. Even now, she felt an undeniable sense of camaraderie with the knight.

After fifteen minutes, the passageway walls turned to solid rock. Hugh looked over his shoulder.

"We're under the castle now," he commented. "Castle Corbin was built on a rock outcropping. This must be it."

"And look!" She touched his back and pointed at the darkness ahead. "I think I see stairs."

"Aye," he grabbed her hand. "We've come to th' end."

"Thank goodness!"

"'Tis a climb now." He tugged her forward.

Tara didn't pull out of his grip. His hand around hers felt as natural as breathing. She let him guide her up the narrow stairs, which switched back and forth in a steep incline, bounded on two sides by claustrophobically-close stone walls.

"We must be inside a wall," Tara mused.

"Aye. An interior wall that doesna need to be as impenetrable as an exterior one."

Hugh kept the pace up, even on the stairs. Tara puffed while the knight's respiration barely changed. He must be accustomed to rigorous exercise. Walking around in chain mail and armor in the desert heat must have required not only physical strength but incredible endurance, both of which he apparently possessed in abundance.

"How far do you think we have to go?" she gasped.

"Ye laggin'?" He stopped to look down at her.

"What do you think? I'm a TV personality, not a superhero!"

"Ye wish t' wait here, while I'll go on ahead?"

"Are you kidding?" She gave his butt a friendly push. "Keep going, you big lug!"

He chuckled and turned to resume the climb.

A few minutes later, Tara felt an awareness filtering over her. All thoughts of her relationship with Hugh disappeared. All bodily sensations—her tired legs and aching lungs—diminished in the wake of a soundless melancholy that pervaded the stairwell.

"Here," Tara said, pausing to place her palm on the cold wall. She drew her other hand out of his grasp.

Hugh turned around and pointed the light at the wall beside her. "What do you see?" he asked.

"It's not what I see. It's what I feel." She stopped to allow the sadness to guide her. She closed her eyes and stroked the wall. "Anne and I are connected. I don't know how or why. Maybe our bloodline is strong enough to link us. But I can feel echoes of what she feels."

"What're ye feelin' then?"

"A vast hopelessness," Tara swallowed, "that is almost too much to bear."

Hugh scanned the wall with the light. "There is always a concealed latch," he explained. "If this is the right spot, we have only to find the latch."

Tara joined him in the search by sweeping her hands over the blocks of stone, pushing at them one by one, looking for a lever but finding none.

"What about further up the stairs, at the landing?"

"'Twould be too obvious a door." Hugh studied the wall in front of him. "Nay, I put more stock in your gut feeling, Tara."

She stared at Hugh, surprised in the amount of faith he had in her. Since arriving in Scotland, she'd suffered nothing but scornful looks and raised eyebrows, which had taken a toll on her.

Heartened, she turned back to the wall. She glided her hands over the rough stones, searching for a clue. And suddenly she found one.

A narrow stone, set vertically, as if to compensate for the neighboring short block, stuck out a few millimeters from the rest of the stones. She pushed it, but nothing happened.

"Hugh," she called over her shoulder.

He tramped down the few stairs to her side and stood behind her. His looming presence sent a wave of longing over her. She had to close her eyes to block the sensation.

"Can you move this one?" She showed him the narrow block. "This small one?"

She moved out of the way to allow Hugh to get closer. He studied the block, pushing at it with his fingers, shoving it with the heel of his hand, but nothing happened.

"I'll wager a sword hilt would do th' trick," he commented, frowning. "If I but had one."

"Use the flashlight."

"What if I should ruin it? We'd be in total darkness."

"We could find our way back. I'm not afraid of the dark." *Not as long as Hugh was at her side.* She crowded close to his elbow. "Use the handle. Try to wedge it under the lower edge of the stone."

"As you wish." Hugh positioned the handle of the flashlight under the edge of the stone, sending distorted shadows across the wall and stairs. Once he flipped the light upside down, they could no longer see the stone.

"Give it a whack, Hugh," she urged. "See what happens."

Hugh pounded the lens cover with the edge of his hand. Tara heard a muffled creak inside the wall.

"Again!" she exclaimed.

Hugh hit the flashlight, causing the bulb to flicker dangerously.

The stone jerked upward and out, creating a lever.

Hugh shoved the light in her hands. "Hold the lamp!" he commanded, reaching for the jutting narrow block. With one powerful heave, he pulled the lever downward. Something answered within the wall—rusted wheels turning on crusted pins, blocks grating against blocks. Then Tara heard a scraping sound just behind her shoulder. She turned.

A portion of the wall had moved a few inches into the passageway.

"Hugh!" she cried. "It's a door!"

"I see it!" He squeezed around her, and shoved his hands in the crack of the wall. Grunting against the weight, he pulled the stone door open as Tara's heart pounded like thunder in her chest.

She trained the flashlight on the space behind the door, and slipped inside as soon as Hugh had pulled the door open far enough. Hugh came up beside her.

"Oh, God!" she gasped.

For the first time since she'd met him, Hugh didn't scold her for swearing. He was too caught up by the pitiful sight before him.

"Blessed Virgin," he murmured, crossing himself. He fell to one knee. "Holy Mother of God."

Chapter 22

Tara whipped out her phone and dialed David's number.

"Tara," David's voice shot over the line like a bullet. "Where are you?"

"At the castle." She leaned against the wall, her knees still trembling. "I've found it!"

"What?"

"The secret room. You'll never believe what's in here."

"You're in the secret room?"

"Yes, it's part of an escape route built in the walls." She glanced at the ceiling of the tiny chamber—anywhere but at the shape next to her. "And don't worry. I didn't have to destroy anything."

She watched as Hugh, still kneeling, bowed his head, pressed his palms together and began to pray. As a courtesy, she removed herself from the secret chamber and walked back into the gloomy passage while she talked. "Listen, David. We have to film this room. We just have to. I've never stumbled on such a story. Tell the crew to meet me here at first light tomorrow."

"Does that mean you aren't coming back tonight?" His voice was frosty.

"Probably not. I need some rest. I haven't had a decent night's sleep since I got to Corbin Hall."

"Where are you going to stay?"

"Somewhere in Ayr."

"Tara, darling." He lowered his voice as if afraid of being overheard. "If you're getting cold feet, you could destroy both our careers. Our producer is coming to the wedding!"

"I know. I know."

"And what will Uncle John think? He thought it was rude enough of you to skip tea without a word to him."

"John will never have a good thing to say about me. That's half the problem."

"But it all reflects on me!" he exclaimed. "You're making me look like an idiot!"

"Vice versa, David."

"You don't need any help with that." She could hear him rolling his eyes. "You're doing enough on your own as it is."

She paused, not wishing to prolong the conversation or the argument.

"Tara, don't stay in a hotel tonight." David whined. "How do you think *that* will make me look?"

"I don't know, David." She cupped her hand around her elbow. "Maybe how it makes me look when dear old M drapes herself over you, and you just stand there smirking." Tara scowled and clicked off the connection.

She didn't love David. She didn't even like him any longer. She would never be able to abide living with him or being a part of his world. She knew that now. But it would be difficult to end her relationship with him and still remain a cohost of *Fact or Fiction*. Maybe it would be impossible. Maybe her career was going to nosedive regardless of what she did.

Hugh walked forward, his broad shoulders filling up the opening of the secret room.

"Anne was truly detained," he said, his voice hushed by sadness. "I see that now."

"You're sure it's her?"

"I recognize th' green dress. What's left of it, anyway."

Tara glanced up at the tall knight, at his somber face and grim mouth. Life was not a joke to Hugh Lachlan. Integrity was not a thing to be taken off like a damp overcoat when he was out of the public eye. Truth wasn't something to be twisted for personal gain or bent for the greater good. This was the type of man she wanted to have in her life. Her heart swelled with love again and burned with compassion for what he had lived through. He'd given his life to keep a promise to a dying comrade and was determined to carry through long after it mattered to anyone but himself.

But what kind of woman was *she*? What had *she* done? She had withheld the truth from the only being who meant anything to her. She had kept the Psalter from Hugh, the book that would allow him to finish his quest, to achieve peace at last, and to attain the freedom he longed for—even if it meant merely breaking the bonds of the spell and crumbling to dust. He would be free of his promise, of the vows he had taken at far too young an age to know his own heart, and free of a world that was far too wicked for a man with a spirit as pure as his.

Yet to give Hugh the Psalter might very well snatch him from her arms. She swallowed, knowing if she really loved the Knight Templar, she would have to take the chance of losing him. His freedom and admitting the truth to him was worth the price she might have to pay.

"Hugh," she began, reaching out to touch his forearm, more to steady her nerves than anything. "I have something to confess."

His glance locked on hers. "Aye?"

"I've lied to you."

His eyebrows shot up.

"Well, not exactly lied. Withheld the truth."

Hugh pulled away from her. She could feel his trust in her pulling away as well. "What are ye sayin'?"

"I know where the Psalter is. Your book. I've had it all along."

He stared at her, his lips parting for a moment before he clenched his jaw again. Then his face took on a formidable expression. His navy blue eyes darkened to shards of sapphire. His arched brows sank into a scowl, and his lips turned white around their edges. For the first time, Tara saw him not as a courtly knight but as a glowering warrior.

Shocked by the transformation, she took a step backward. "There are reasons why I didn't tell you—"

"Fie!" He waved her off, his color high. "I thought we were fightin' the same battle. Under the same flag!"

"We are!"

"And ye kept this from me?" he cried. "You're no friend o' mine!"

"I was afraid!"

"Of what?" he thundered.

"Of losing the book forever. Of losing the only tie I had to a family!"

He glared at her, studying her, his scarred mouth twitching in anger.

"I had nothing but the names in that book!" She swept the air with her hand. "I had no one, Hugh! No one!"

"So why give it up now?"

"Because." She paused, unwilling to tell him how she felt about him—not in this dark and evil place, and not while he was glaring at her. "Because I realize that I don't need it now. Because I have—I'm—"

He waved her off, impatient with her stammering. "Ye knew it was everything t' me, and ye didna say a word!" His voice rang through the narrow corridor. "What else haven't ye told me? What else are ye plottin' and plannin'?"

"Hugh!"

"You *are* like her. You're Anne de Monclair all over again. I should have seen it comin'!"

"You're wrong!"

He took a threatening step toward her. "Where's my Psalter, woman?"

His eyes burned holes in her. She could feel her hope withering.

"Tell me where my book is, or I'll throttle ye!"

She crossed her arms over her chest. "It's in a little stone building. Near that bottleneck dungeon where you rescued me the other night."

He studied her face, looking for more lies. She felt a blush flooding her cheeks and forehead.

"It's under some stones," she added. "In a plastic bag."

Hugh gave her a chilly once over and turned to leave.

"Say that you release me," he growled, his back to her.

"I release you," she answered, willing to do almost anything to get back in his good graces. "But I'd like to go with you."

"I dinna want company the likes o' you."

"What about the flashlight?" She bent to snatch it from the floor and held it out to him.

"Keep it."

"But you'll be in the dark."

"'Tis where you like t' keep me, is it not?" His voice was gruff with emotion.

"Hugh!" She ran toward him, but he held up a hand to stop her forward progress.

"Nay. Stay here. 'Tis where you belong."

"You don't mean that!"

"You made your bed, Tara Briden." He raised his chin and met her eyes. "Now you must lie in it. With the Corbins."

He jerked away and galloped down the stairs.

"Hugh!" she cried, trailing after his quickly descending form. "I made a mistake! I'm sorry! I'm only human!"

He didn't look back.

"Hugh, don't leave me!"

The knight disappeared in the gloom.

Tara sank against the wall, holding the flashlight against her knees as the sound of Hugh's footsteps faded. She could still hear her words ringing in her ears. How pathetic she had sounded, calling after him like that. What had happened to the proud Tara Lewis who had vowed never to let a man get to her? Tara's heart ached in answer. That cardboard version of her was gone forever.

Gloom seeped into Tara's heart, darker than the shadows that surrounded her. She should have told Hugh about the Psalter days ago. And yet, she'd only just met him days ago. How then, could she be so certain that she loved him? It didn't make sense. Still, she had never felt more certain of something in her entire life. But little good would true love do her now.

"Hugh!" she breathed, shutting her eyes against hot tears that threatened to spill out. He'd left her. And once he got the Psalter, he'd probably never come back.

See me.

The voice came a like a whisper. At first, Tara thought she was hearing the echo of Hugh's steps. But there it was again, closer this time.

See me.

The voice came louder, and the familiar phrase sent a chill down her spine. Tara opened her eyes and pulled away from the wall. A faint figure in a green dress hung in the doorway of the secret room.

"Anne!" Tara exclaimed.

The woman's gaunt face glowed more distinctly. For a fraction of a second, Tara caught a glimpse of a weary smile, and then the vision faltered.

"He prayed for my soul!" Anne said, her voice just above a whisper. "Hugh forgave me!"

At least he had forgiven one person. Maybe in another thousand years, he'd forgive *her*. Tara stepped toward the secret room to try to get a better look at the Lady in Green. "Can you manifest yourself a bit more? I can't see you very well."

"I cannot. I am leaving this place. I am free!" Her tired voice sang with joy. "At long last, I am free!"

"But what happened to you, Anne? Tell me! People need to know what happened in that room."

"I cannot linger," Anne replied. "I am weary of this world. It takes all my strength just to speak to you."

"But tell me why he did this to you! It was Edouard Corbin, right?"

"Yes, but I will come to thee anon," the lady promised. "In a dream. I will come to thee if I am able."

Tara stepped closer, as if she could keep the spirit within grasping range. "When?"

"Soon, Tara. Soon." The Lady in Green faded.

"Don't go!" Tara cried, searching for the ghost with the flashlight but finding nothing but gray stones.

"I must." Anne's disembodied voice hung in the air. "There is someone coming. Oh, how lovely!" The Lady in Green shimmered for a moment, turning into an ethereal collage of lime green and cerulean almost too bright to look at. The glitter hung in the air like a fairy cloud, twinkling and undulating. Then Anne's voice broke through one last time. "My thanks to thee, Tara Briden!" she called.

And then she was gone in a burst of white.

Tara knew in her heart that the Lady in Green had appeared at Castle Corbin for the last time. She stared after the ghost of Anne de Montclair, with the reverse of the glittering image dancing in her vision for many moments afterward.

Then she shook herself back to reality. She was alone in Castle Corbin with nothing but a flashlight. Who knew how long the batteries would last? She had to locate the latch that would open the panel into the master chamber, and then get out of the castle as quickly as she could. But most importantly, she had to get to the little stone house before Hugh.

A half hour later, Tara drove back to Corbin Hall and rolled into the parking lot with the lights off to make her arrival less noticeable. She parked next to Morag's Jaguar and jumped out of the car.

The grounds of the estate and the path to the Dippol Burn looked much different in the dark. Tara hurried through the wet grass at the back of the house and down the rocky trail. The distance seemed twice as long as before, and soon she was puffing from the run. But she forced herself to keep up the quick pace.

She saw no sign of the knight, but then again, he could be coming from the opposite direction. The path that Morag had taken on horseback the night Tara had fallen into the dungeon might lead to a shortcut from the castle to the Dippol Burn. If that were the case, Hugh could have already been to the stone house and gone.

Though she ran through drizzling rain, Tara panted from the heat generated beneath her light jacket. Sweat mingled with rain in her hair as she pulled open the rickety door of the tiny building. She prayed that she wasn't too late.

The small chamber was empty and dark.

Tara ran her light around the room. The face on the far wall stared down at her, distorted by the artificial light into a malevolent mask. She shuddered as she crossed the room. Then she sank to one knee and propped the flashlight on a nearby stone.

Carefully, Tara lifted the rocks from the pile she had stacked around the Psalter. In a few seconds, she saw the fold of the plastic bag. Just as she drew the bag from the stones, she heard a step behind her.

Tara wheeled around and was totally relieved to see Hugh standing in the doorway.

"Here it is!" she exclaimed holding out the plastic bag.

He didn't take the bag from her. "I told ye I didn't want ye t' come."

"I had to."

He scowled.

"It was the least I could do. Here." She rose and picked up the light, and then held the bag out again. "Take it. It's yours."

After an uncomfortable moment, he grabbed the bag.

"Are you going to go now?" she asked. "To that chapel you spoke of?"

"Aye."

"Do you plan to come back?"

"What is there t' come back to?" He stared down his sharp nose at her.

She fought to keep her desperation at bay. "What about Michaelmas?"

"What about it?"

"What if you still need to do something about the spell on Michaelmas?"

"Then my Lord God will direct me."

"I could drive you to Edinburgh. It would be a lot faster."

He frowned. "I dinna want your help."

Hugh broke off his stare and stuffed a hand inside the bag to pull out the sandalwood box. He gazed down at the family crest, his lip twitching.

"That's the Corbin family crest." She ventured closer.

"I am well aware of that."

"Someone put the Psalter in a Corbin keepsake long ago."

"A blasphemy." Hugh tossed the bag aside.

"Maybe the Corbins had your book at one time but didn't realize its worth."

Hugh didn't answer. He pulled at the lid, but it didn't budge.

"There's a button on the left side," Tara instructed. She trained the beam of light on the decorative band of the box. "There, where the inlaid pieces join."

Hugh frowned and fumbled with the contraption, until the lid popped open a fraction of an inch. Carefully the knight raised the lid and stared down at the contents of the box. Tara could see a flush creep up his neck.

"What?" she asked, stepping closer.

"You toy with me."

"What?" she tried to look into the box, but Hugh held it high, out of her reach.

"The collected works of Robert Burns?" he thundered. "Who in the name of Hades is he?"

"What?" Tara cried, flabbergasted. "Where's the Psalter?"

"'Tis another trick!" Hugh spat. "I am sick to death of tricks!" He flung the box at the wall, and it fell to the floor in pieces.

"Hugh!" Tara shouted, mortified.

"When will th' games ever end with you people?" he shouted. "When will I ever learn t' trust no one—especially women!" He stomped out of the building.

Tara dashed for the sandalwood box, intent on discovering what Hugh had seen inside it. She picked up the splintered box, the lid that had been ripped off, and then the small volume that had been placed inside.

Tara held the book in her hand. It was old and heavy, and perfectly proportioned to fit inside the box, but it was not her Psalter. Someone had tricked her as well, by replacing the Psalter with a book of equal dimension and weight. But whom?

She stuffed the remnants of the box and the book into the bag and ran out of the stone building, hoping to catch the knight before he vanished.

"Hugh!" she called into the wet black night.

He didn't answer.

"This was none of my doing!" she yelled. "Please, you have to believe me!"

She whipped the flashlight right and left, searching for a sign of the knight, even though she knew he could disappear into thin air.

"Someone has tricked me, too!" She ran out to the path. "We're in this together Hugh Lachlan! Together, dammit!"

She waited for a few moments, her hands at her sides, hoping Hugh might change his mind and come back to her. But he didn't make an appearance.

"Crap," she muttered.

With a heavy heart, she struck out down the path, retracing her steps to the car as her mind raced.

She thought back to the last time she'd held the Psalter in her hands. It had been on the plane crossing the Atlantic, when she couldn't sleep, and everyone around her was dozing in their seats or hooked up to their mp3 players. She'd read through at least a quarter of the book and gazed for minutes on end at the illuminated illustrations. She hadn't actually looked at the Psalter since coming to Scotland. But the only time it had been out of her hands was the night she'd left it in her purse at Hugh's crypt and then the brief span of time when she had stored it in the night stand drawer of her bedchamber.

It was obvious that someone at Corbin Hall had stolen her book and replaced it with another. But who? Her first suspect was John Corbin, but he'd looked through her clothes the day she'd hidden the Psalter near the bottleneck dungeon. If he had stolen the book before that time, why would he be searching for it later? That made no sense at all. She discarded the idea.

While thoughts of her lost treasure and her lost love churned in Tara's mind, her stomach growled loudly, reminding her that she hadn't eaten since breakfast. And she still had to find her way to Ayr and locate a hotel room. It was going to be a long and lonely night.

Most of the lights of Corbin Hall were out by the time she got back to the parking lot. She opened the car door and threw the bag in the back. Then, rising, she noticed car lights coming up the drive.

Tara's heart sank. The only people coming to Corbin Hall at this time of night would be someone connected to the family or one of the wedding guests arriving early. She would never get away tonight.

Tara closed the car door and adjusted her clothing. Then she brushed back her hair, hoping no one would be able to tell where she'd been or what she'd been doing.

An older couple got out of the car.

"Tara!" The man called, holding out his hand. It was Bob Knickerbocker, one of the producers, and his wife, Emily. "How good to see you!"

Tara shook his hand, and made the usual small talk as her mind continued to race. The next opportunity she would have to look for Hugh would be tomorrow after the shoot, which could easily go until dinnertime. Then the next day was Saturday. Her wedding day. She would have only one night to find Hugh and make things right between them.

Just as Tara reached for the door to let the visitors in, she was surprised when it burst open on its own accord, and she came face to face with Morag Smithbank. Equally shocked, the blonde woman paused on the threshold, her smile faltering.

"Tara!" she exclaimed. "I thought you weren't coming back tonight."

"Change of plans."

"I was just leaving."

Tara stepped aside. "Don't let me stop you."

Morag glanced at the visitors and then at Tara, expecting to be introduced, but Tara remained silent, unwilling to prolong Morag's departure or satisfy her curiosity. If Morag wanted to discover the identities of the wedding guests, she could ask her usual informant.

"Well, cheerio then." Morag forced a gay wave.

"Bye." Tara didn't give her a second glance as she showed her guests into the house.

Chapter 23

The next morning dawned gray and stormy—with wind and rain sweeping sideways—as Tara, David, and the crew rumbled up the lane to Castle Corbin and the heartbreaking story that awaited them. All day they worked like fiends to capture enough footage to make Tara's Secret Chamber episode, and didn't even stop for lunch. No one seemed to have an appetite anyway. The grisly tableau that had been hidden for hundreds of years put them all in a serious frame of mind. Even Bob Knickerbocker, who stopped by for an hour and usually caused a needless uproar on the set, stood in uncharacteristic silence, watching their progress. As the shadows deepened at Castle Corbin and their filming wrapped up, Tara realized for the first time in her memory, the crew hadn't laughed or joked the entire day.

Tara's work, however, was only partially done. She still had to write the background story that would explain the reason the Lady in Green had met such a horrific end. But for that, Tara had to wait for the dream visit Anne had promised to make. She prayed that Anne would have the strength and ability to return to the mortal plane one last time.

After they left Castle Corbin, Tara couldn't escape dinner with the producer and his wife, as well as the *Fact or Fiction* crew. For all intents and purposes the meal was their rehearsal dinner, and David was in high form, spurred on by his nervousness about the day to come and Tara's indecision about their future. But Tara couldn't shake the anxious feeling burning in her. All she could think about was the coming day and what might happen to Hugh Lachlan.

She looked down at her wine glass as the voices around the table blurred into a loud buzz. The verse from Hugh's tomb came to mind as if by magic, each word as clear to her as if they'd been chiseled onto the backs of her eyes.

On Michaelmas shalt thou rise anew,
A mortal man, again to face the fire.

Together we shall change our fates,
And thou shalt be mine heart's desire.

Mine heart's desire. Tara lifted her glass as a sharp ache stabbed her heart. *Thou shalt be mine heart's desire.* How she wanted Hugh to be hers alone—in her arms, in her world, and in her future. Without even tasting the fine Bordeaux, Tara gulped a swallow of the wine, her thoughts far from the dining room.

What had Anne meant in regard to Michaelmas? Would Hugh become a man tomorrow? Would he transform into real flesh and blood that other people could see and hear? And then what? He would have to face an actual fire? Or was facing a fire a metaphor for a cataclysm that he would have to overcome? Would that also occur tomorrow?

Soon she would know the answers. In less than five hours, the clock would strike midnight. Michaelmas would then arrive. The day of reckoning.

Dinner dragged on until nine-thirty. Tara finally broke it up by announcing she needed her beauty rest for her big day. She was not surprised when David offered to walk upstairs with her.

"Thanks for coming back," he said, as they got to her bedroom door. He touched her elbow. "Last night, I mean."

She pulled out of his grip. "David, we have to talk."

"And about tomorrow," he interrupted, searching her face. "If you don't want to film the wedding, I suppose I can live with that."

David's mention of the wedding made her feel pushed in on all sides by claustrophobia. And she could tell from the look on his face that he was not going to let her bow out gracefully. Tara smoothed back her hair as she fought down the urge to scream. "David, filming the ceremony is the least of my—"

"If it rains, we'll hold the ceremony in the sunroom on the second floor. Mrs. MacMillan has been working on the arrangements for the past few days—which you'd know if you were here."

"I've had a lot on my mind, David." She clenched her jaw, determined to speak her mind. "In fact, I know now that I just can't—"

"Listen, Tare." He clutched both her upper arms. "I think I know what you're going to say. But please don't. Not until you hear me out."

"Nothing you say will—"

"I don't know what's happened between us," David interrupted her again, his words tumbling out in a rush. "But there's no denying something has. I'm just asking you as a friend and colleague to go through with the ceremony."

She listened to him, but it took every ounce of forbearance she possessed to stand in the hall and let him talk. The subject of the their life together suffocated her.

"There's so much at stake here, Tare. You know how it is in tinsel town. One little thing can become a tipping point. Our wedding could be one. If Bob thinks you and I are having personal problems—he'll sack one of us or cancel the show."

"He wouldn't!"

"He would. He says the show needs a breath of fresh air—I'm telling you. He said it again tonight."

David sighed and released her arms. "Look, stay with me on this. Marry me tomorrow. Go through the motions for the show's sake. I won't hold you to anything but the ceremony, I promise. Then, when the ratings get better, we can quietly get a divorce."

She studied him, amazed that David would go to such lengths for a television show.

"I'm telling you, Tara, the ratings are bound to go through the roof with this Secret Chamber episode. We'll be on top again!"

Tara stared at him. "You would take vows that you have no intention of keeping in front of everyone you know?"

David gave an uneasy laugh. "It's not like we'll be fooling each other. That's the important thing."

She looked at the ceiling, while an image of her career as the Hindenburg zeppelin bursting into flames and disintegrating came to mind. If what David said was correct, to back out of the wedding would sound the death knell on her career. Still, she could see no other way than to face that particular fire.

"We've been a good team, you and I," he added, cupping her cheek. "We could make a good life with each other still—if you'd give it a chance. Maybe not fireworks. But a certain understanding—"

"David, I'm sorry." She drew his hand away from her face. "It's my fault—this mess we're in. I mistook teamwork for love."

"Love *is* teamwork," he countered.

"But so much more. I want more than just an understanding partner. I want to be in *love* with my husband. I'm sorry, David. I really am." She turned and opened her door.

"Shit!" he exclaimed behind her. "I should never have brought you to Scotland!"

"It's better that it happened sooner than later. Before our lives got intertwined and complicated."

"But what about the show? You've always done anything for the show!"

"Not anymore." She turned at the threshold, expecting him to leave.

"What's happened to you?" he screeched. "You've turned into someone I don't even know!"

How true. She was turning into her real self.

Tara swung the door toward him. "Good night, David."

He wedged his foot in the door as she closed it. "So, that's it? Good night, David?" he demanded. "What about tomorrow?"

"Do you want me to leave tonight?" she asked. "I will, if you wish."

"What are you talking about? I don't want you to leave! I want you to take one of those god damn sleeping pills, get a good night's sleep, and get back to the Tara Lewis I know and love!"

"No pill is going to bring her back."

"Just sleep on it, Tara. Don't go running off tonight. Think about what I said. Think about how this is going to make me look—how it will make both of us look."

"David." Tara sighed. "We can finish this tonight or drag it on through tomorrow. Nothing is going to change."

"Just sleep on it," he held up both hands. "That's all I ask!"

David slipped his foot out of the doorway and turned to leave without meeting her glance. She watched him hurry down the hall, his shoulders thrust back, his head high. She felt sorry for him and guilty about breaking off the engagement so late, but pity and guilt were not good enough reasons to marry.

Tara had no intention of getting a good night's sleep. As soon as David left her, she took a shower and changed into a pair of black slacks and a sage-colored sweater. Carefully she applied her makeup, hoping to look her best if she happened to get lucky enough to see Hugh again. She simply had to find him and make things right between them. Tara left her hair long and put on gold hoop earrings and the short gold necklace she had bought during a trip to Mexico. Then she waited for the house to quiet down for the night.

By eleven, everyone had retired. Tara grabbed a warm coat and slipped out of her bedroom. Silently, she snatched the car keys from the cabinet near the side entrance, and hurried out to the parking lot.

She drove all over the estate, but Hugh was not to be found. The last place he might be was the guardhouse. Tara sped down the rutted road to the old building and parked the car behind a copse of rowan trees, so Hugh wouldn't see the vehicle. Then she hurried to the small stone house and pushed open the door. Hugh was not there either. Disappointed, Tara decided to build a fire and wait for him. Surely he would come back here sometime during the night. She struggled to light the peat fire, and then paced the floor, aware that valuable time was slipping away.

By midnight Hugh hadn't shown. Dejected, Tara sat upon the bed, which the knight had put back in place. She pulled his blue robe to her face and held it to her nose, savoring the fragrance of him. The velvet fabric was lush and soft, much thicker than any velvet she remembered touching. She closed her eyes.

"Hugh," she whispered fervently. "I demand that you come to me."

She waited in the flickering light, listening for a sign of his approach, but the knight didn't make an appearance. Perhaps he no longer had to obey her commands, now that Michaelmas had arrived.

"Hugh, please!" She hugged the robe tighter, investing every shred of sincerity she possessed into her request. "Come to me!"

But Hugh didn't show.

Minutes went by. Then an hour. Still, Tara remained, stubbornly refusing to believe that Hugh would abandon her. After an hour went by, she felt her eyes growing heavy as the many sleepless nights caught up with her. She could just as well wait for Hugh in a prone position. Forming the robe into a small pillow, she tucked it under her head and reclined upon the cot. Before she knew it, she was fast asleep.

"See me."

Tara blinked awake, but knew she was not really awake. Her body still slept as the all-too-familiar voice drew her to a higher level of consciousness. She looked up to see the Lady in Green standing before her—only this Lady in Green was not emaciated and ethereal. This version of Anne was as she must have appeared as a mortal woman—petite—full-bodied and beautiful, with hair so blond and skin so creamy that she seemed to emit a golden glow. Even her wide blue eyes glowed with a soft radiance. No wonder men had fallen under her spell.

Anne reached out to her. "Come."

Tara sat up and extended her hand. Anne wrapped her fingers around hers and gazed at her, her face serious.

"Now thou shalt know my tale."

The moment Tara stood up, she was instantly transported to a dark hallway with a door at the end—the same door she had seen a hundred times in her nightmares.

"Come." Anne urged her forward.

"No!" Tara tried to shout, but the word didn't have any sound attached to it.

Resolutely, Anne tugged her down the hallway. The door opened as if by magic onto a scene of someone giving birth in a huge bed hung with gold brocade drapery. Candles flickered beside the bed and a fire crackled in the grate, but the mellow light did nothing to mute the sounds of a female in the throes of childbirth.

Tara moved closer, shocked to discover the woman in the bed was Anne de Montclair, writhing in agony, with two older women attending her, and a young woman sitting near the side of the bed, holding her hand—probably a lady-in-waiting.

When the contraction waned, Anne clutched her lady-in-waiting's hand. "Remember what I told thee!" she gasped.

"Quiet now," her companion replied. "Save thy strength, milady!"

"Should I die in this bed, thou must see that my child gets the possessions in the green chest. And thou must read the instructions I have writ for thee. And follow them. Doest thou understand?"

"Yes, milady! I will do as thee ask."

Anne sank back to the pillow just as a man burst into the room.

He was short, slightly built, with reddish hair and a dark brown beard cut to a precise border along his jaw line. He marched to the window and turned. His flat pale eyes regarded the women while his mouth twitched with barely controlled anger.

"Get my son from her!" he barked. "She's had enough time!"

Tara knew without being introduced that the man was Edouard Corbin.

"I don't care if you have to cut the child from her. Get it out!"

The women shot dark looks at him, and then turned back to their task, their hands bloody and their faces running with sweat. Anne screamed, her cry echoing through the cavernous room. Her lady-in-waiting babbled encouragement to her while she threw fearful glances at Edouard. Anne panted and cried out, and then collapsed backward.

Everything went still for a moment. Then the silence was shattered by the wail of a baby. At the sound, Edouard swept into action.

"Take the babe away!" he bellowed. "See to it!"

One of the midwives straightened. "Do you not wish to see your child?"

"I shall see it soon enough. Get out!"

"But milady—" the midwife gestured toward her mistress, who lay nearly lifeless on the sheets, her thighs still bloody. "The afterbirth—"

"I shall attend to her." Edouard motioned toward the door. "Get thee gone! You, too, Madelaine."

As soon as the midwives and the lady-in-waiting had scurried out of the room, Edouard bent to a wooden chest and grabbed a gown out of it. He threw the garment at Anne.

Surprised, she rose weakly on an elbow.

"Get thee dressed!"

"My lord?" She stared at him, incredulity and worry in her eyes.

Edouard strode to the bed. "Have thee gone deaf?"

"But I have just birthed your babe."

"Which thee held on to far too long."

"It was as the Lord wished it."

"Fie!" Edouard slapped her. "God has nothing to do with a witch such as thee!"

Anne held her stinging cheek and stared up at him, her pupils dilating with alarm.

Edward loomed over her. "I have been told that you took his body."

"Whose body?"

"Don't play the fool with me!" Edouard slapped her again. "You know very well of whom I speak!"

Outraged, Tara tried to lunge forward, but her dream body would not obey her. There was nothing she could do but watch helplessly as Edouard abused his wife.

Anne clutched the green gown to her breast, as if the cloth could shield her from his wrath.

Edward narrowed his eyes. "I have been told that you worked thy black magic upon him—"

"'Twas not my handiwork! I but solicited a gifted healer to—"

"—And that he still lives." He grabbed a handful of her damp hair and twisted it cruelly. "Where is the Templar?"

"My lord!" Anne pleaded. "Have mercy!"

"Why should I? Thou hast betrayed me. Thou hast fornicated with the man!"

"I have not!"

"Thou hast plotted to run away with him!"

"Nay!"

"Liar!" He shoved her away in disgust. This time Anne burst into tears, hunching over in miserable submission, just as Tara's mother had always done. Edouard dragged her crouching body from the bed and forced her to stand. With shaking hands, Anne pulled down her bloody shift to cover her nakedness as Edouard grabbed the gown and thrust it against her flaccid abdomen. She cried out in pain.

"Now, my wicked wife, I will tell thee one time more." He pushed each word through his clenched teeth. "Put on the dress."

Sobbing, Anne fumbled for the opening of the garment. Tara was amazed Anne had the strength to stand, let alone dress herself.

"Wear the vestments of thy seduction," Edward commanded, yanking the skirt into place. "As thou attired thyself for thy worthless knight!"

Before Anne could fasten the strings of the gown, Edouard grabbed her elbow and dragged her across the floor.

"My lord, have mercy!" Anne gasped. "I cannot walk! I shall swoon!"

He ignored her. Punching a panel on the wall, he released the latch that allowed the wall to rotate open. Anne gaped in terror as he dragged her into the dank space beyond.

Without physically moving through the master chamber, the Lady in Green and Tara were transported into the small chamber off the escape route, where the master of the house had dragged his lady.

Edouard shoved Anne into a chair made of bulky timbers and iron rings. Metal cuffs were attached to the legs with heavy chains that snaked around the base.

"A gift for a lady," Edouard growled, "Who cuckolds her sire."

Terrified, Anne struggled to rise from the chair, but Edouard shoved her back down.

"Be still!" he shouted. "Or I shall strangle thee with mine own hands."

"Edouard, no!"

"I should suffer no blame as well, shouldst I rid the world of a witch and an adulterous fornicating whore!"

"I beg you, do not do this! I am no witch!"

"Tell me where thy precious knight is, and I will grant thee full pardon."

Anne fell silent.

"I thought as much." Edouard bent and snapped a cuff around her left ankle and locked it with a large key. Then he locked her right ankle as well.

"My lord, please!" Anne began to sob.

"You shall remain here until you confess to your sins." Edouard reached for a hammer. "And the location of the Knight Templar."

"I know naught!"

"Liar!" With a grunt, he brought down the hammer and drove a nail through the top of her right hand, pinning it to the massive arm of the chair. Anne cried out in agony and clutched at her impaled flesh with her free hand until Edouard pinned her left forearm down with his knee.

"Silence!" he roared. "'Twas good enough for our Savior, Jesus Christ." He drove a spike through her left hand. "'Tis good enough for thee!"

Anne slumped in the chair, her eyes rolling back in shock, as both punctured hands blossomed with blood.

Edouard stepped away and tossed the hammer against the wall.

"Tell me where Lachlan is and I shall release you."

Anne didn't reply. She panted, her eyes closed, obviously in as much pain as she had experienced while giving birth to her child.

"My babe!" she wailed, her voice wavering. "My child!"

"You shall never see it. No child of mine shall suckle at the breast of a whore."

Edouard marched to the opening of the room and whirled around. "I shall return at dawn. Tell me all, and thou shalt be released from thy punishment."

Anne licked her lips, which grew more colorless by the minute, but made no reply.

With a triumphant smile, Edouard closed the door, and the secret room plunged into blackness.

The edges of Tara's dream turned black as well, as the scene dissolved before her.

"The bastard!" Tara exclaimed, horrified.

"And there I stayed," Anne replied, her voice full of melancholy. "Until I died of fever and thirst."

Tara stared at her, outraged. "How could he get away with such a thing?"

"It happened all the time." Anne patted her hand. "Women were often locked away in cupboards by their fathers and their husbands for transgressions, imagined or not. Women were the chattels of their lords, to do with as they wished."

"Oh, Anne!" Tara turned to embrace the woman who had suffered so much for the man she had loved. Tears streamed down her face. "Anne!"

The Lady in Green stroked her back, giving Tara a surprising amount of comfort. "Edouard would have killed me for one reason or another. Even if I had confessed to loving Hugh Lachlan. I knew that. He would have killed me and desecrated Hugh's grave and ruined any chance for his resurrection. So I kept silent."

"You died in that room—"

"In that reeking darkness, nailed to that horrific chair."

"And Hugh never knew."

"Nay. Not until you brought him hence." Anne smoothed back Tara's hair and looked lovingly into her eyes, much as a mother would do. "And for that, I give thee eternal thanks."

Tara gazed at her through the tears hanging in her lashes.

"You are the strong one, Tara," Anne continued. "You may be able to break the cycle that has cursed us for centuries. Follow your heart. And do not give up."

"You were a lot stronger than me. Dying alone must have taken an incredible amount of courage."

"Nay, I let things linger until I had no choice but to die." She looked toward the wall, her eyes unfocused. "Had I left Edouard long before and struck out on my own, I would never have been locked in that room. But I was pregnant. I thought I had no choice but to stay."

"It wasn't so easy for women back then."

"It is never easy." Anne touched her cheek and stepped back. "But you, Tara. You know in your heart what is right. And you must get away from the Corbins."

"Yes." Tara nodded and wiped the tears away with the tips of her fingers.

Anne reached out again. "And now, if you have the strength for it, I have one more vision for you."

Curious, Tara raised her hand to link to the spirit again.

"My gift to you, Tara Briden, from beyond the grave."

Chapter 24

Tara was whisked to the hallway with the door a second time. For the second time, she tried to resist, but the Lady in Green urged her forward. Tara could hear strident voices beyond the door, the same shouting she had heard a thousand times in her nightmares. She could now make out the strings of profanity her father shouted at her mother.

Sweat popped out on Tara's forehead, and her mouth went dry as the spirit moved her closer and closer to the door. She writhed in the spirit's grip, trying to pull back, and dug in her heels to keep from being propelled forward.

"No!" Tara yelled. This time she could hear the sound of her own voice. "Please, no!"

Why would the Lady in Green want her to relive the day her mother left her? It had taken her years to turn her gut-wrenching feeling of abandonment to mere bitterness. Knowing what she knew now, that her mother would never bother to come back for her, and that she would be forced to watch Tatiana drive away without her a second time, Tara knew her heart would break all over again—maybe beyond repair.

Still, the hand of the spirit pulled her forward. Anne reached for the doorknob and looked back at her.

"I'm not going there!" Tara cried. Her voice sounded reedy, like that of a child.

"Lass," a new voice broke in, much deeper than the others. "'Tis Michaelmas. 'Tis time to face the truth."

Tara struggled to see whom the voice belonged to, even though she knew it was Hugh. But in her dream state, she couldn't open her eyes.

Blindly, she clutched at empty air. "Hugh!"

"Aye. I'm here." He took up her other hand. Even in her dream state, she felt his hand warming her cold fingers. Tara's heart lifted, knowing he had come back and was now beside her.

"'Tis only a dream, Tara. Ye must face it. Conquer it. And put it behind you."

Even though Hugh stood by her, Tara had no intention of revisiting her childhood. She glanced around the hallway, searching for a route of escape, but the only way out was forward, through the door that now opened.

Without moving her own limbs, she was transported to the garage at the tattered farm in the Tennessee hills where she'd grown up. The garage, not more than a shed between the house and barn, was small and dirty with a rotting plank floor, and cluttered with oily machine parts stacked everywhere, tools scattered on each surface, a motorcycle with a ripped seat and missing wheel, and a rusty Ford pickup truck. Morning light filtered through the single window fogged with grime, crowning the head of a woman who stood next to the truck. Tatiana Briden, dressed in her Sunday coat and shoes, cowered in front of the pickup door with a suitcase at her feet. Her knees shook.

Tara dashed toward her mother, but her father grabbed the collar of her shirt and dragged her backward.

"Go ahead and leave, bitch!" Tara's father shouted. He was so angry that spittle flew from his mouth. "Get out of my sight!"

"But Tara—"

"I said get!" He shoved Tatiana against the door of the pickup with the heel of his hand. "And don't come crawling back here, ever."

Warily, Tatiana reached for the suitcase, her stare never leaving Eddie's face, as if fearful that any quick movement might provoke him to more violence.

"I don't want to see your smirking, self-righteous face here ever again. You hear me?"

Tying hard to ignore his verbal abuse, Tatiana made no answer and lifted the suitcase just as he swung his leg to give it a kick. She hoisted the bag into the bed of the pickup. Then, with trembling hands, she pulled open the rusty door. She glanced over her shoulder at Tara and looked more pale and frightened than she'd ever appeared.

"I'll come back, Tara, and get you," Tatiana said. "I promise."

"No, she won't." Eddie grabbed the back of Tara's neck and yanked her hard against his bony thigh. She could smell bourbon on his breath and cigarette smoke on his clothes. "Your ma's nothin' but a lyin', cheatin' whore. She's never comin' back. Never."

"Mama!" Tara cried. She tried to pull away, but she was caught in the trap of her father's hand. Her heart thudded with terror at being left behind.

"You stay with me, girl." Eddie tightened his grip by pinching the tendons on either side of her spine. "We're better off without no-good vermin like your ma."

"Mama!" Tara cried again, tears streaming down her face. How could her mother leave her? She'd never been away from her mother a single day in her life. How could she think of going anywhere without her—and leave her with her drunken father and her senile grandmother?

Tatiana slanted a helpless look at her from the cab of the truck, and then with a loud clunk of the gears, backed out of the garage. The engine burped and popped, and for a moment, Tara hoped the vehicle would die, which would force her mother to stay home. But Tatiana successfully shifted gears, turned the truck, and rolled across the yard to the rickety gate and the winding lane beyond.

"Mama!" Tara screamed.

Tara's father spit viciously and swore at the retreating vehicle. Then, as Tara wept inconsolably, he dragged her out of the garage and marched her toward the house, her neck still clutched in his vice-like grip. They plowed across the side yard.

Tara's gaunt grandmother rose up from her stance at the laundry basket where she'd been hanging clothes out to dry.

"What's going on?" Grandma Briden asked, squinting after the truck. A cigarette hung from the corner of her wrinkled lips.

"Never you mind, old woman." Eddie thrust Tara toward her grandmother, almost knocking her down with the sudden force of his hand. Tara stumbled toward the wet pile of clothes, struggling to regain her balance. "Just make sure the kid don't run off."

"Where you goin', Eddie Jim?"

"Huntin'." Ed Briden loped toward the paint-starved farmhouse as Tara watched, her adult eyes and comprehension seeing much more than her five-year-old sensibility had taken in. A feeling of dread rose up from the damp grass and into the marrow of her bones. Her father hadn't been good for much. But he had been an expert in two areas: Tennessee Sipping Whiskey and guns. She watched him dash into the house as a cold wall of understanding closed in upon her. This was what her subconscious had been trying to get her to see for the last thirty years.

The dream dissolved.

"He's going to kill her." Tara squeezed Hugh's hand hard. "He's going to kill her!"

"Ah, lass!"

Tears ran down Tara's face, both in the dream and in her strangely conscious dream state where she knew the knight was at her side. Hugh stroked her arm in a gesture full of sympathy.

"Ye need t' know the truth." Hugh's voice rumbled gently in the aura of her awareness. "The truth will free you of your demons."

She felt Anne stroke her shoulder. "Come, Tara. She wants you to know all."

"No!" Tara gasped. She'd witnessed enough domestic violence to last her a lifetime. "I don't want to see any more!"

"Go," Hugh urged. "Be strong, Tara Briden! I'm here with you."

Before she could protest any further, Tara found herself standing on a steep brush-covered riverbank. Kudzu grew rampant, over the ground, up the trees, all the way to the rocks of the river, shrouding the ravine in a verdant canopy. Berry bushes threw canes across the kudzu, searching for purchase in the damp soil and reminding Tara of the blackberry jungle surrounding Hugh's crypt in Scotland. She gazed down at the river, not sure why she'd been brought here in the dream.

Anne touched her shoulder again and pointed to the right.

"There," Anne said. "Thou seest the truth?"

"I'm not following you," Tara began, but her voice trailed off as she suddenly discerned a familiar shape sticking out of the kudzu—a rubber tire suspended in the air. In an instant, her mind connected the dots, and she detected the unmistakable shape of a rolled vehicle perched on the riverbank, hidden under a blanket of kudzu.

Tara dashed through the vines, tripping and swearing, desperate to identify the vehicle. She swept away the vines to reveal the rusted door of the old Ford. She stuck her head in the open window and spotted her mother's worn black purse, still wedged under the brake pedal after thirty years.

Like a scavenger hunt in a horror movie, Tara found a shoe, and then a scrap of her mother's coat. And then, further down the bank, just above the flood line, Tara discovered the proof that Hugh and Anne had brought her here to find. Her heart cracked open, and a flood of tears rushed in.

"She didn't abandon me," Tara choked, dropping to her knees in the kudzu.

Her mother hadn't gone off to make a life for herself and forgotten about the little girl she'd left behind. She hadn't turned her back on her child. She hadn't been the spineless, whimpering coward Tara had made her out to be in her adolescent mind. She'd been here all along, lying on the riverbank with a bullet hole in her head. She'd never even made it off the farm.

"She didn't leave me after all," Tara murmured.

"She was *detained*," Hugh added, his voice full of sympathy.

Overcome, Tara sank her face in her hands and wept, openly displaying her wounds for the first time in her life. She felt Hugh's big hand splay over the nape of her neck as his voice lowered to a reverent rumble.

"*In peace I will both lie down and sleep; for thou alone, O Lord, makest me dwell in safety.*"

Tara swallowed back her tears. She couldn't believe what she'd just heard. Hugh knew her favorite passage from the Psalter by heart. And he had recited it now, when it meant the world to her. She bowed her head, knowing this moment on the riverbank had both rewritten her history and forever changed her being.

"Such a poignant scene." A familiar voice broke in, shattering Tara's newfound sense of balance. She jerked fully awake to discover Hugh sitting beside her on the bed and John Corbin standing in the doorway of the guardhouse.

Alarmed to see David's uncle, Tara struggled to sit up. "John?" she mumbled, her tongue thick from crying.

"All torn up about the wedding, I see." He took a step closer, and she saw that he cradled a shotgun in the crook of his arm. "And having to part with your lover." John ran a disdainful look across Hugh's figure as the knight slowly rose to his feet.

Tara glanced at Hugh. So he *was* visible to others now that Michaelmas had arrived, just as she had suspected he might be.

"I knew something was going on with you, young lady." John continued. "I just didn't think it would be this despicable."

Tara scrambled to her feet. "I can explain—"

"Nay." Hugh put his hand out, as if to shield her from John's wrath. "Ye dinna have t' explain a thing."

"Oh?" John's lip curled in anger. "And who might you be?"

"Lachlan." Hugh turned to fully face David's uncle, and crossed his big arms over his chest. "Hugh Lachlan."

John gave him a quick once over and was forced to look up to take in Hugh's unusual height. "You've known Miss Lewis long, I take it?"

"'Tis none of your concern."

"It is when she's about to marry my nephew!"

"She has no intention of marryin' a Corbin."

John whirled to face Tara. "Is this true?"

Tara straightened her shoulders. "Yes."

A procession of emotions flew across John's features—surprise, relief, confusion and then back to anger. He lowered the gun. "What do you mean, you aren't marrying David?"

"I've had a change of heart."

"Have you told him?"

"Yes, but he wouldn't listen to me."

John pressed his thin lips together and studied her for a long moment, his eyes cold.

"Do you have any idea how embarrassing this will be for the family?"

"Yes, and I'm sorry for that." Tara kept her chin high. "But surely, you can't be disappointed."

John's eyes glittered.

"You didn't approve of the wedding anyway," Tara continued. "You were part of the reason I decided to call it off."

"Don't lay the blame at my feet," John seethed. "Not when you were having an affair behind Davy's back."

"There's been no affair."

"What do you call this?" John swept the air with his left hand. "You tucked away with your lover. It sickens me!"

"You have no idea what I've been going through here."

"Oh? I'm not stupid, Miss Lewis. No one has to draw me a picture!"

"Are ye callin' the lady a liar?" Hugh took a menacing step toward John. The older man glanced up at the knight and grabbed his weapon with both hands.

"No, I'm calling her a whore."

Hugh lunged for John, and Tara lunged for Hugh, who she knew was dangerously innocent of the power of firearms.

"Hugh!" she shouted, pulling at his arm. "It's not worth it!"

Startled by the knight's quick temper, John stepped back, raising his gun. But once he trained his weapon on Hugh, John seemed to regain his composure. "Yes, Hugh, she's not worth it!" He mocked them with a sneering drawl.

"Stand back!" Hugh warned. He shook off her hand, but she clutched him again.

"Hugh, he could kill you with a single shot."

"From that wee thing?" Hugh glanced down at the firearm.

"Yes!"

Hugh paused, both hands raised as he studied the gun.

John smiled cruelly. "And it would all be for nothing, Romeo.

Because I really don't give a damn about you and Miss Lewis."

"Ye bastard!"

"But I do give a damn about the Psalter." He pivoted slightly to aim the gun at Tara. "I want it, Miss Lewis. And I'm asking you for the last time. Hand over the book."

Tara wondered how she would explain the loss of the Psalter to John in a way that he would believe her.

"So it comes down to th' Psalter again, does it?" Hugh growled.

John slanted a dark glance at him. "It's always been about the Psalter." He turned back to Tara. "You don't think I actually wanted to meet the host of a lowbrow television program, did you?"

Tara forced her chin to remain high, even though his words offended her.

"I knew if I could get Davy to bring you across to Scotland, you'd bring your book with you."

"How could you be so sure?"

"Davy mentioned that you never leave it." John smiled shallowly. "And I'm fairly confident that your book is the one I seek."

"It matters naught," Hugh put in. "She doesna have it."

"And how do you know?"

"Because I'm after it myself. 'Tis mine."

"Really? I don't think so." John gave a derisive laugh. "From what I've discovered, that book belongs to the Corbins—handed down from mother to daughter for centuries."

Tara felt a chill go down her spine at hearing John confirm what she had only suspected to be true.

"Isn't that true, Tara?" John leveled his frosty eyes on her face.

"How should I know?"

"Because you're a Corbin. On your father's side."

She paled, not only because John obviously knew everything about her now, but that she shared a bloodline with the monster that had killed Anne de Montclair. She was a Corbin. No wonder the Lady in Green had appeared to her. No wonder the sound of Hugh's Scottish burr had resonated within her. Ancient blood flowed in her veins, connecting her to these people, to this land, and to a story that needed to be told—and finally ended.

"Isn't that right, Tara?" John continued, his voice hard. "And your surname isn't really Lewis, is it?"

Tara stared at him, refusing to play his game.

"Is it, Tara?" He pointed the gun at her.

"No."

"It's Briden." John gloated. "It took me a while to track you down to your white trash roots. But I did it. And it will be worth it."

"Your efforts are in vain," Hugh commented.

"I don't think so."

"Someone else has the Psalter."

"You expect me to believe that?" John sneered. "Who do you think you're dealing with?" He curled his lip at Hugh. "You might have cuckolded my nephew, but you'll never cuckold me. Not John Corbin!"

"He's telling the truth," Tara said. "Someone took the Psalter and put a book of Burns poetry in its place. I didn't know until yesterday."

"Spare me your pathetic lies." John raised his gun. "Now where's the Psalter?"

"She doesna have it!" Hugh bellowed.

"And you—" John countered. "Shut the hell up!"

Hugh barreled forward, intent on protecting Tara. In a lightning quick reaction, John set the shotgun to the small of his shoulder and fired.

Hugh staggered backward, holding his chest, his face draining of color as Tara screamed. Then the knight's eyes rolled back in his head, and he toppled over, hitting his skull on the edge of the settee as he crashed to the floor.

"Hugh!" Tara cried, rushing to his side. Blood covered the hand he held to his chest, but he was still breathing. She patted his cheek, desperate for him to open his eyes. But Hugh remained unconscious.

"Get up!" John commanded, kicking her thigh.

Tara glanced up, and saw in John's vicious expression that he had run out of patience.

"I'll shoot you as well if I have to."

"You wouldn't!"

"Don't tempt me." He waved the barrel of the gun at her. "Now get up!"

Tara obeyed, hoping to buy time until she had a chance to get away, and get help for Hugh.

"You're going to take me to the Psalter, Miss Lewis. Now."

Tara walked to the door of the guardhouse with John close behind. He nudged her in the back with the end of the gun.

"Outside, you self-serving bitch."

Tara stumbled into the darkness. Rain pelted her head and shoulders. She turned slightly. "I don't have it, John!" she cried.

"Liar!" He pushed her forward with the heel of his hand. "I'll give you ten seconds to tell me where the Psalter is. And then I'm going to shoot."

Tara glared at him. "You'll never get away with this!"

"Hunting accident, my dear. Thought you were the wild cat that's been taking down my lambs." He waved the barrel at her. "Now get going!"

"I don't know where the book is!"

"One, two, three…"

"You bastard!"

"Four, five, six…"

Tara dashed into the rain, hoping to hide in the rowan trees and then double back to help Hugh.

"Seven, eight, nine…"

Hoping to dodge the bullet when John fired, Tara dove onto the wet ground, scraping her hands and arms, and sliding across a patch of slick wild garlic. The shot whizzed by, nicking her shoulder, and leaving a burning scratch along the top of her arm. She heard Hugh's voice ring out.

"Ye blackguard!" he shouted.

Holding her shoulder, Tara rose up on her knees in the pungent herbs and looked back at the guardhouse.

Chapter 25

Through the rain, Tara could just make out two silhouettes struggling in the light cast from the doorway. She guessed that Hugh would normally have bested the smaller man, as the knight was accustomed to hand-to-hand combat and had a distinct physical advantage over David's uncle. But Hugh was wounded and likely suffering from a concussion, so there was no way to predict the outcome of the fight. At least Hugh had knocked the shotgun away.

Tara scrambled to her feet and dashed back through the rain. If she could find John's gun, she could put and end to the senseless fight. Tara searched the ground. But without a flashlight, she couldn't see much in the dark. Behind her she could hear the two men grunting and punching each other as they battled dangerously close to the edge of the sandstone chasm. Then John's voice rang out, stopping her in her tracks.

"Back off, Lachlan!" John wheezed. "Or I'll aim for your head this time."

Tara whirled around, shocked to see that John had produced a small handgun from his coat.

"No!" Tara screamed.

Hugh dove for John's shins.

John fired as he lurched backward. He yanked his left foot out of Hugh's grip and stepped into another patch of wild garlic. For a moment, John struggled to keep to his feet in the slippery mass. But he couldn't keep from sliding toward the edge of the cliff. He flapped his arms, fighting for balance, his face contorted with terror as he realized his feet would never find purchase. Shouting his disbelief, he teetered backward, hung for an instant in midair, and then fell into the darkness and disappeared. His voice grew fainter as he plunged toward the river, and then it broke off with a thud.

"Oh, my God!" Tara exclaimed, rushing forward.

"Careful!" Hugh grabbed her arm. "'Tis dangerous!"

"He fell!" Tara gasped, staring into the blackness. "Oh, my God, Hugh! He fell!" She strained to see the bottom of the chasm at her feet, but saw nothing but the faint gleam of moving water. "How can we get down there?"

"We canna. Not in the dark. He's a dead man, Tara. There's nothing we can do."

"Oh, my God!"

Hugh wrapped his arm around her shoulders. "Many men have died for th' Psalter. May John Corbin be the last."

"I've got to tell David!" She pivoted in his warm embrace. "And get you some medical attention." She grabbed his hand. "Come on."

He held back, his face deathly pale, his eyes deadly serious, and his torso covered in blood. "Tara, I have something I must say t' you."

"It'll have to wait." She tugged his hand. "Come on!"

Dawn broke as Tara drove up to the front of Corbin Hall. She promised Hugh she'd be right back and left him resting in the car as she dashed into the house. She planned to get help for John, tell David about his uncle, and then rush Hugh to the nearest emergency room. The knight had been dangerously quiet during the drive back to Corbin Hall, and she worried that he had lost too much blood as well as suffered a serious head injury.

Noiselessly, Tara slipped into Corbin Hall. The house was quiet and full of shifting gray shadows as the sun rose. No one was up yet, for which Tara was grateful. She hurried up the stairs, and dashed into her room to grab her phone and necklace. She had no intention of coming back to this room.

Just as she straightened from the desk and opened her phone to dial 9-9-9, she heard a step behind her.

"Put down the phone," a familiar voice demanded. "And give me the necklace."

Tara whirled around, surprised to see Morag standing a few feet away. She was dressed in wool trousers and a jacket, as calm and well-groomed as ever.

"I need something personal of yours," the blond woman said. "Something that means a lot to you."

"What?" Tara couldn't make sense of what Morag was saying. "What are you *doing* here?"

Morag didn't smile. She nodded at the desk. "Give me that necklace."

"What—are you crazy?" Tara brushed past her. "I have to call for help and tell David—right now!"

As she ran past Morag, the woman grabbed her wounded arm.

Tara stared at the woman and was alarmed to see cruel lights glinting in Morag's pretty blue eyes. Pain shot up her arm from Morag's strong grip. She stuffed her phone in her back pocket.

"What's got into you, Morag!" Tara demanded. "Let me go!"

"Give me the necklace."

"Listen, you!" Tara countered. "John's had a fall. He may be dead!"

"So you gather up your things to leave instead of getting help for him?" Morag's gaze raked over her. "How thoughtful of you."

With a sudden jerk, Morag wrenched the necklace chain through Tara's fingers and shoved her away. Tara lurched backward toward the bathroom, astounded at the strength of the woman. She wouldn't have thought such a petite and manicured female could possess such power.

Morag held up the emerald necklace as Tara watched, shocked into inaction. The green stone glowed in the pale light of morning, drawing Tara's attention, oddly mesmerizing her. In the back of her mind, she knew she had something important to do, but she suddenly couldn't remember what it was.

The necklace swung in front of her face like a bejeweled pendulum.

"You're feeling calm," Morag purred. "You are feeling relaxed now, Tara."

She was. Tara felt her cares falling from her shoulders, releasing her from her intense week in Scotland. All the things that had disturbed her, all the things that had kept her awake faded into the foggy distance, leaving her numb with exhaustion. She yawned.

"That's right," Morag crooned. "Just relax, Tara. You've had such a terrible time these past few days. You deserve a little rest."

Still swinging the necklace, Morag reached for Tara's elbow and tugged at her gently. "Come, I know a place you can rest without being disturbed."

Morag guided her to the dressing room near the bathroom, the chamber with no windows that Tara had never felt comfortable in. She paused at the doorway, trying to recall something someone had told her about this room. A warning…

"Come, Tara. Rest a while, and you will feel refreshed, ready for our big day."

She did feel tired. She could barely put one foot in front of the other. In fact, she should have questioned Morag's use of the word "our," but she was too tired to care that much. Tara shuffled into the dressing room and stood like a zombie near the upholstered bench at the center of the small chamber.

Still swinging the necklace in front of Tara's face, Morag urged her to sit with a slight pressure to her shoulder. Tara plopped down. Then Morag dropped the necklace onto the bench and picked up a belt, which she wrapped around Tara's torso, pinning her arms to her sides. Without the necklace swinging in the air, Tara felt her head begin to clear, but not enough to break from the trance. Tara sat numbly, fighting the exhaustion and fog. She sensed something was wrong about all of this, but she couldn't seem to make a move. She couldn't even protest when she saw that Morag was binding her feet and legs. Only when Morag bunched a sock into a ball and brought it toward her mouth did Tara's faculties completely clear.

"What in the world are you doing?" Tara gasped.

"I'm setting things right." Morag stuffed the sock into Tara's mouth, choking her. Tara gagged and blinked as tears popped out of her eyes.

Morag straightened. "It is, after all, Michaelmas." She reached for the necklace. "Well, not technically Michaelmas. Technically, the holiday has already passed. But I'm celebrating the holiday on its rightful day, its old day, when it was marked by the moon and not a number on a calendar. Did you know the moon has a lot of magical power, Tara?"

Tara stared at Morag as she tried to force the sock out of her mouth, but the movement of her tongue only made her gag more.

"I have a lot to settle with the Corbins." Morag stepped back. "Especially with that blue-nosed bastard, John."

Warily, Tara kept her eyes on the blond woman, worried that she was about to produce a weapon.

"He thinks I'm not good enough for David. Did you know that? Yet my family was here long before the Corbins. He seems to have overlooked that little detail." She glared at the wall for a moment, as if focusing on her past instead of her prisoner. Then she snapped back to the present.

"Now then. It's David's wedding day, isn't it? And I should have been his beautiful bride." Morag clasped the necklace around her throat. "Something borrowed," she purred. "And something…" she reached into her jacket and held up a small familiar object. "…red."

Tara's eyes widened in shock. Morag had the Psalter.

"Surprised?" Morag asked, leaning closer to grin at her. "You are, aren't you?"

Tara refused to acknowledge the question. The woman was

obviously unbalanced, and the sooner she got away from her and out of the wardrobe, the better. She writhed desperately, but the bindings held tight.

"I found it the night we rescued you in the crypt." Morag smiled. "I noticed that you left your purse. So I went back later, curious to find out what kind of woman my David thought he was going to marry." Morag pressed the book between her shapely breasts. "You don't know what a lucky day that was for me."

A string of swear words passed through Tara's mind. She tried to convey them mentally—including 'put a sock in it,' but Morag didn't seem to notice.

"David was going to be my ticket to glory," Morag continued. "My step up the ladder. I had it all planned. But then you came along with something much better—the legendary Ayr Psalter."

Tara grimaced. Obviously, everyone in Scotland knew more about her Psalter than she did.

"This book will make me rich, so rich I'll be able to spit on John Corbin. And David, too! They'll come crawling to me for favors." She grinned. "Thanks, girlfriend!"

Tara narrowed her eyes, all the while struggling to wiggle out of the belts.

"You've kept this book quite close to you, haven't you, Tara?" Morag closed her eyes. "I can feel its strong connection to you. And its amazing power. I knew it had great power the moment I touched it." Morag took a deep breath. "Blood has been spilled over this little book. Blood that has strengthened it over and over again."

Tara wriggled, trying to free herself of the belts, but Morag had buckled her tightly. Sweat broke out on her forehead as she struggled to break free.

"I waited until the last moment. I was willing to give David the chance to choose me over you. But he didn't. He wouldn't call off the wedding. So now he'll have to pay."

Tara chafed her wrists trying to yank free.

Morag laughed softly. "You waste your strength, Tara. Nothing will save you now." She reached for the satin gown that hung nearby and yanked it off its hanger. She shook it in front of Tara's nose.

"And what were you thinking when you bought this dress? This rag is not worthy of the future Lady Corbin. Had you no sense of the family you were marrying into?" She yanked it back. "Of course you didn't. You were the dumb American who wanted to destroy Castle Corbin."

Morag glared at her as she pulled a small object out of her jacket pocket. She flicked her thumb and a small flame leapt upward.

A lighter! Tara stared as Morag held the flame to the hem of the wedding gown until the satin ignited in a sudden puff of yellow. Then the blonde tossed the flaming garment into the closet. The fire caught quickly, licking the edges of her slacks and blouses.

"Well—" Morag stepped into the bed chamber. "Cheerio, Tara! And Happy Michaelmas!"

She slammed the door shut. Tara looked at the flames, which had already engulfed the entire rack of clothes. Smoke wafted up, filling the room. Tara struggled to stand and hopped toward the door. Somehow, she had to find a way to open it. Then she heard the tumblers turn over. Morag had locked her in.

Tara slumped against the door, her heart thudding with panic, yet at the same time her mind clearing now that Morag had left. She was locked in a windowless room with no way to call for help, her arms and legs bound, and left to die—just as the Lady in Green had been left to perish in the secret chamber. All along, Tara had thought that she lived outside the tragic story of Anne de Montclair, and that she could tell the tale to the world and vindicate the woman. But now she realized that she was a part of the story—and that the tale might be far from over.

No one might ever know who had locked her in the dressing room and caused her death.

Frantic, Tara flung herself against the door, trying to force it open. But all she did was bruise her shoulder. She yanked at the belts that bound her until she chafed her skin. But she could not break free. Beyond the door she could hear Morag throwing things around, destroying the bedchamber and probably starting more fires. Tara tried to recall the layout of the bedroom. Had there been smoke detectors in the room? A sprinkler system? She didn't think so.

As the dressing room clouded with smoke, Tara hopped as far from the flames as she could get, struggling for a decent breath of air, and wondering if she would die here, with no one to know or care. Her last thought was of Hugh, how he'd looked sitting in the car in the parking lot, his head propped against the door, his face drained of color, and his eyes closed, waiting once again for a woman to come back to help him.

"Hugh!" Tara tried to cry out, but her words were muffled by the sock. She sank to the floor. She would never see him again.

"Hugh!"

At the sound of Tara's heartfelt cry, Hugh battled back to consciousness. He opened his eyes and struggled to bring Corbin Hall into focus. Something had happened to Tara to make her cry out. His eyeballs hurt when he moved them, and his head was on fire, but he scanned the property thoroughly, trying to locate her. He couldn't see her anywhere. And yet her voice had sounded so close at hand.

Hugh shut his aching eyes and rolled his head back against the seat of the car as he swiftly sorted through his options. Now that he was a mortal man, he couldn't just materialize in front of Tara if she needed him. He would have to go in after her.

Setting his jaw against the pain, Hugh dropped his palm on the handle of the car door. Every movement was an effort of sheer will. Pain throbbed in his chest. He raised his left hand and gingerly inspected the bullet hole. Even a bolt from a crossbow didn't wreak this much havoc on human flesh. His head roared, too, and his vision kept narrowing to a dark-edged tunnel. He vaguely recalled Tara's voice urging him to hold on, that she'd be right back. But it seemed as if she'd been gone for hours. And the cry he'd heard just now—was it merely part of his delirium? Or was she really in trouble?

"Lord, give me strength for one last task," he prayed between his teeth. "And I shall serve You all my days."

With a grunt, Hugh pushed open the door and tumbled onto the gravel parking lot. Pain shot through his chest, leaving him gasping for breath and unable to see. For a moment he thought he was going to swoon. But after a brief rest, he managed to pull himself onto his hands and knees, and then he rose to his feet, swaying and trembling.

"I have judged harshly," Hugh muttered, making his mind grind away so he could better ignore the agony of his body. He took a faltering step toward the house, rallying his strength through focused prayer as he had oftentimes done during battle. "I am not You, Lord. 'Tis not my place to pass judgment on my brethren." He took another step, a steadier one this time, forcing himself into the determined trance he had frequently employed to endure pain, torture, and loneliness. "Who among us is perfect? Certainly not this sinner." He took another step and felt a glimmer of his old strength rising inside him. "Allow me one last chance, Lord, one last chance to redeem myself in her eyes. I pray thee!"

Hugh broke off the prayer and trudged toward the hall, his mind commanding his ruined body to keep marching forward.

As soon as he opened the door to Corbin Hall, Hugh smelled smoke. His blood ran cold. A voice in his head bellowed for him to run away, and the surface of his skin retracted in fear. Every minute detail of his agonizing death by fire came rushing back—the smell, the sound, and the strange searing coldness that turned to excruciating heat. Sweat washed over him, mingling with his spilled blood, as he fought to stay true to his intent. No matter what he had to face in this house, he would find Tara and rescue her.

A movement in the library caught his eye. He jerked toward the room, hoping Tara was there, and they could leave the hall before the building burst into flame. He could hear a rumbling sound on the second floor. His entrails twisted in fear.

“Tara!” he called, stumbling through the doorway of the library.

A blond woman turned, holding a small lighted device and a wad of the printed paper the likes of which Tara had shown him days ago. It was Morag Smithbank standing there. Tara’s enemy. Morag’s mouth fell open at the sight of him.

“Who the hell are you?” she gasped. The paper caught fire in her hand, but she didn’t seem to notice. Her stare raked over him, and she was forced to tilt her head back to take in his full height.

Hugh stared back, appalled. Morag Smithbank was setting fire to the library, and had likely set blazes in the rooms upstairs.

The fire brought her back to her senses by burning the tips of her fingers. She dropped the paper.

“What evil have you wrought here?” he thundered. He lunged forward. “Where is Tara?”

Frozen in place, Morag stared at the knight, her eyes wide with alarm and confusion while the burning paper ignited the fringe of the Persian carpet at her feet.

Just as Hugh reached Morag, she broke from her daze, and ducked under his arm. He grabbed her, wrenching his wounded shoulder. He had to clench his teeth to choke back a cry.

Morag glared at him, her eyes wild, as she struggled to pull of out his grip.

“Where’s Tara?” Hugh demanded.

“Who cares!” Morag spat back.

“Hag!” Hugh had no time for questions, not when he was certain that Tara was in trouble, and still in Corbin Hall. He pushed Morag away in disgust.

Morag fell backward, skidding along the floor. Something tumbled out of the folds of her outer garment, catching Hugh's eye.

He stared at the object, his vision swimming. He thought for a moment that he was in a dream, that all that he saw was fantasy—for there on the floor of the library lay his Psalter, its tooled red leather cover glinting in the firelight.

"God's Blood!" he exclaimed. He lunged for the book, just as Morag realized what she'd lost. She scrambled to her hands and knees, racing to get to the book before Hugh. He dove to the floor, covering the Psalter with his body, while Morag leaped on top of him. The impact of her weight stunned him momentarily as pain fanned out in a white cloud.

Morag took his swoon as surrender. "Give me that book, you monster!" She pulled at his hair.

Hugh grimaced and thrust up and to one side, throwing her off. Morag rolled across the carpet, kicking her arms and legs and spewing swear words he'd never heard pass a woman's lips. He struggled to his feet as her profanity turned into a shriek.

Hugh glanced down, horrified to discover that Morag had rolled into the fire. Her hair ignited, and she jumped to her feet, dancing upon the carpet in terror, while flames raced up the bookcase behind her. Before he could react, her trousers caught fire, then her coat. He caught a glimpse of her face, and she stared at him in horrified disbelief as she was engulfed by fire.

Desperately Morag whirled, which only served to feed the fire, until she burst into a cloud of orange and yellow flame. She staggered around the carpet, trying to find an escape from her nightmare.

Hugh knew only too well that there was no escape. There was nothing he could do for the woman. He slipped the Psalter into the chest pouch of his shirt and turned for the library door.

By the time he got to the bottom of the main staircase, the house was billowing with smoke, and members of the household were streaming down the stairs, screaming and crying. Though Hugh received a few startled glances as he staggered up the steps, no one challenged his presence in the house.

Then he spotted David Corbin stumbling down the stairs, one thin hand on the banister and the other holding a handkerchief to his nose. Hugh grabbed the man's forearm and nearly pulled him off his feet. David gaped up at him, his eyes lit with alarm.

"What the devil?" he gasped.

Hugh squeezed his arm. “Where is Tara?”

“How should I know!”

“Bastard!” Hugh threw him off and lurched upward. His eyes stung, and he could hardly breathe, but he knew in his heart that Tara was somewhere in the house. A rafter gave way above the stairs, and with a crack the beam spiraled toward the floor below. Hugh heard shouts behind him, but he didn’t look back. There was no going back. Only forward.

Chapter 26

Tara awoke to find an oxygen mask pressed to her face and David hovering over her. A medic knelt by her side, his dark eyes inspecting her intently.

She was alive. Someone had rescued her from the burning bedchamber and released her from the belts. Sirens wailed around her, and people ran past, crying and coughing.

But all she could think about was Hugh. She rose up on an elbow, searching for a glimpse of the car she had left him in.

"Don't strain yourself, miss," the medic said, pressing her back down. "You've had quite a shock."

"Who did this to you?" David asked.

"Morag."

"Morag?" David countered in disbelief.

"She stole my Psalter. She wanted to punish—"

"Hush, now," David urged. "She's dead. We found her in the library, burned, nearly unrecognizable."

And David, your uncle—"

"Please, Miss Lewis." The medic adjusted the mask. "Try not to talk."

"And who the hell was that guy?" David asked, bending closer.

"What guy?" Tara rasped. Smoke and heat had burned her throat. Her face felt crispy.

"The huge guy that barged into the house after you." David glared at her. "Who was he?"

"Hugh? Hugh saved me?" Tara couldn't believe Hugh had possessed enough strength to get out of the car, let alone walk to the hall. She rose up again and searched the crowd huddled on the lawn, watching the firemen struggle to put out the blaze. The whole of Corbin Hall was on fire now. She could see Mrs. MacMillan with her hands to her mouth, watching her entire world go up in smoke, and Robbie standing very close to his mother, too old to hold her hand, but wanting to be reassured that everything would be all right. She saw that each member of the *Fact or Fiction* crew had made it out of the house unscathed, as well as her producer and his wife. But the subject of her swift search—the Knight Templar—was nowhere to be seen. "Where is he?"

"He's being looked after, miss." The medic struggled to hold the oxygen to her face. "Now if you please—"

Tara snatched away the mask and sat up. "Where is he?" she demanded, staring at the medic.

"In the ambulance."

Tara jumped to her feet, wavered for an instant as her vision swirled, and then headed for the emergency vehicle.

"Tara!" David called after her, his voice full of exasperation.

Tara ignored him. She had to see Hugh. If he had run into the house to rescue her, he might be in worse shape than the condition she'd left him in. At least he was getting medical attention.

She got to the ambulance just as they were closing the doors.

"Wait!" she cried.

A short red-haired medic turned, his expression grim. Tara felt her heart flop over in her chest.

"Tara Lewis?" he gasped in surprise. "Of *Fact or Fiction*?"

"Yes. Can I see the man inside?" Tara reached for the door handle. "What happened to him?"

"He's very badly burned. Plus he has a gunshot wound and a head injury. We must get him to the hospital immediately."

"Can I go with you? He saved my life!"

The medic frowned, and then opened the door. "Okay, hop in. But don't touch anything. Or him."

The medic helped her crawl into the back of the ambulance where Hugh lay ominously still. His long form stretched nearly to the rear doors. She couldn't see him breathing, but he had an oxygen mask on his face and was hooked up to a monitor. His face was black with soot, his eyes were closed beneath singed brows, and the skin on his throat was a worrisome pink color. But what worried her most was his silence. Of all the things Hugh Lachlan wouldn't do, one of them was to lie there so quiet—unless he was close to death. She stood above the knight, gazing at him in dismay, her heart breaking, as David ran up to the back of the ambulance.

"Where are you going?" he demanded.

"To the hospital with Hugh."

"You can't leave! What about me?"

"You'll live."

She turned her attention back to Hugh as the medic closed the door.

"You've got some explaining to do, young lady!" David shouted after them.

The siren turned on and the vehicle jerked into motion. She plopped to the bench seat along the side of the van.

"Oh, Hugh!" Tara murmured, longing to enfold the knight in her arms. She leaned toward him, her forearms crossed over her thighs, while the medic inserted IVs in both of Hugh's arms.

"Will he live?" she asked.

"We're doing everything we can, miss." The medic adjusted one of the drips. "I'm giving him something to ease the pain now."

"Wait!" Tara cried. She was sure she'd seen Hugh's lips move. "Before you drug him—I think he wants to say something!"

"I don't believe he's capable of speaking."

"I saw his lips move!"

"He's not even conscious, miss."

"There!" Tara dropped to her knees beside the knight, searching his face for more signs of life.

"Don't touch him," the medic warned. "Whatever you do. His skin is fragile."

"Hugh!" Tara called, her heart wrenching painfully. "Hugh!"

Hugh's scarred mouth trembled. She glimpsed a flash of his white teeth, whiter than ever against his sooty skin.

"Hugh!" Tears welled up in her eyes as she studied him. "We're going to help you! You're going to be all right!"

"Salt," he mumbled, his voice barely above a whisper.

"The Psalter?" Tara brushed away her tears with the sleeve of her jacket. She had to remain strong so that Hugh didn't know the gravity of his condition. "Morag had it!" She swallowed. "Sorry, Hugh, but it's gone."

"Shir." His eyes rolled beneath his sooty lids.

"What? Shir?" Tara fought back the urge to grab his hand. "Yes, I'm sure! Corbin Hall is nearly burned to the ground."

"Shir," Hugh repeated. His Adam's apple bobbed in his muscular neck. "T."

"Shirt?" His meaning suddenly dawned on her. She raked a glance over his ragged bloody shirt. A slight lump showed in the left chest pocket. She reached for it.

"Miss Lewis!" the medic exclaimed. "Don't touch him!"

Tara ignored the EMT and carefully slipped her fingers into the pocket of Hugh's shirt. His breath caught in his throat from the pain of being touched. She drew out the object she found there, and knew when her fingertips touched tooled leather that she was holding the Psalter.

"I have it!" Tara cried. "I'll deliver it for you, Hugh. I promise! Merristone Chapel, right?"

He swallowed again. She thought she saw the corner of his mouth lift.

"Miss, please!" The medic moved closer, holding a large pad of wet gauze. "You're disturbing him. It could be too much for him!"

"Okay, okay!" Tara sat back on her seat and hugged the Psalter to her chest as the medic lay the sterile dressing over Hugh's burned flesh. Tears streamed down her face, making Hugh's bulky shape blur. But she refused to take her eyes off him. She knew only too well that each breath Hugh took might be his last.

It was Michaelmas. And Hugh had faced the fire once more to save her life and had probably given his own in return.

She heard him sigh, and for a horrible moment she thought he had released his final breath. But then she realized that the morphine must be taking effect.

He reached out his left hand. Tara fell to her knees again and clutched it gently, drawing it to her damp face.

"Forgive," he murmured, still not able to open his eyes. How she longed to look into his eyes once more. "Me."

"Hugh!" She turned to kiss his strangely cold hand. He'd never been cool to the touch before, not even when he'd been a spirit trapped in a spell. "There's nothing to forgive!"

"Too…harsh. Forgive."

"I forgive you then!" she cried. "Oh, Hugh, I love you!" She burst into tears again, uncaring that the medic could see and hear everything. Her entire universe had narrowed down to the warrior lying broken and burned before her. She cared for nothing else.

Hugh swallowed again, and the movement seemed to require a lot of strength. His eyes quit rolling, and he appeared to sink into a quieter place. His arm suddenly went limp, dragging her hand down. Tara stared at him, desperately afraid that he was leaving her forever. She had to do something—make him hang on to his last flicker of life until they got to the hospital. She had to appeal to his undying sense of duty.

"Sir Hugh!" she exclaimed, as the medic positioned Hugh's arm along the cot and covered it with more damp gauze. "You are not released! Do you hear me?"

Hugh's handsome face remained impassive and stone-like, eerily similar to the effigies she had seen in the ancient Corbin chapel. She couldn't tell if he had heard her or not.

"Sir!" she commanded through her tears. "I have not released you! You are not released!"

Hugh was rolled into the hospital and whisked away to the intensive care unit before Tara could say her good-byes to him. She stood at the doors as they closed in front of her, shutting her out, and felt as if a limb had just been wrenched from her body.

Tara sank into a chair in the waiting room and called David, leaving a message for him about his uncle. Then, thinking his phone might have been burned in the fire, she called the police and reported the accident. Afterward, she filled out paperwork for Hugh, using her own information for his address and hoping she would hear word of his prognosis soon.

An hour passed. For the first time in a long time, Tara opened the Psalter without putting gloves on, and gazed down at the ancient pages, trying to concentrate on the verses instead of what might be happening to Hugh and what the next few hours might bring. But the verse that swam before her mind's eye was the one from his crypt.

On Michaelmas shalt thou rise anew,
A mortal man, again to face the fire.
Together we shall change our fates,
And thou shalt be mine heart's desire.

Hugh had faced the fire, and if he survived, he might transcend the spell at last. And that could mean he would be free to live life as a mortal man—and hopefully with her. But he would never be entirely free until he completed his quest. Tara looked down at the Psalter. One way or the other, Hugh's future hinged on the little book in her hands.

If he were meant to die of his wounds, Tara knew the knight would hang on as long as he could, extending his agony in his determination to finish his quest. And if he died a second time, he might never be released from the spell, and his spirit would be chained forever to the Corbin Estate.

If he were meant to survive, she wondered what would happen to him if he had not completed his vow by the time Michaelmas came to a close. Hugh could be trapped in his ghostly form again, but this time in a severely damaged state and without a witch to make him whole again.

She couldn't imagine the hellish existence that would be.

Tara's worried thoughts fanned out around in her a hot wave. Hugh's life might not depend on modern medicine but on carrying out the promise he'd made. She also feared that the magic required to restore Hugh might only be present on Michaelmas, the day of reckoning—a day that was swiftly passing. And it was her fault that he had failed to deliver the book.

Maybe she *was* his knight in shining armor, like he had said. Maybe it was possible that she could make a difference in someone's life, instead of waiting to be rescued from her loneliness and abandonment. Maybe Hugh's God *had* brought her to Scotland for a very special task, and that He had not abandoned his loyal knight after all.

Startled, Tara jumped to her feet, trying to outdistance the strange concepts birthed in her own mind.

She strode up to the desk at the waiting room. The attending clerk looked up. She didn't appear much older than a teenager.

"I'm waiting for news about the condition of Hugh Lachlan," Tara said as she wrote down her phone number. "Is there anything yet?"

"No. I know you are waiting, Miss Lewis. And I'll tell you as soon as I hear anything."

"I have to run an errand," Tara explained, holding out the paper. "Would it be possible for you to call me as soon as you find out anything?"

"Certainly." The clerk reached for the paper she held out.

"That would be great." Tara nodded at the cell phone number. "That's a U.S. number. I put the prefix on there for you."

"Okay."

"And if he comes to, would you please tell him that I've gone to Edinburgh and will be back as soon as I can?"

The clerk made a note under the phone number.

"And do you know how I can get to the Merristone chapel in Edinburgh?"

"Merristone?"

"It's probably a really old chapel. From the twelfth century."

"The only chapel that old would be St. Margaret's. On the grounds of Edinburgh castle."

Tara paused. She was sure she remembered Hugh saying he had to deliver the Psalter to Merristone Chapel. "What about outside of Edinburgh proper?" Tara inquired.

"Maybe." The clerk shrugged. "I'm not a history buff. You could ask someone in Edinburgh when you get there."

"Okay, thanks."

Tara turned to leave, just as Susan walked through the door of the waiting room.

"Tara!" she called, hurrying forward. "Are you all right?"

"I'm fine. What about you?"

"I lost my favorite pair of shoes in the fire, but I'll survive."

"What about everyone else? Mrs. MacMillan?"

"There were no casualties. Only Morag." Susan adjusted the strap of her purse. "Chris is pretty torn up, though, about losing his cameras. He did manage to save some footage."

Tara nodded.

Susan studied her. "What are you doing here, though? David said you went off in the ambulance with some guy."

"It's a long story, Susan, but it will have to wait. I have to get to Edinburgh."

"Why?"

"I have an errand to run for a very dear friend."

Susan's brown eyes clouded with confusion. "A Scottish friend? You know someone in Scotland?"

"Yes." Tara touched her arm. "Do you have a car, by any chance?"

"I borrowed one from Corbin Hall."

"Then drive me to Edinburgh, if you would," Tara said. "And I'll tell you a tale you simply won't believe."

By the time they rolled into Edinburgh, the October light was already fading. Tara used Susan's iPhone to search for the location of Merristone chapel, which was now part of a local park north of Princes Street. They parked near the gate and slipped out of the car. Only a few brave souls strolled the park grounds, as the temperature plummeted with the falling light. Tara glanced at the sign welded to the iron gates. They had only until dusk before the park closed. She hurried her pace, and Susan struggled to keep up.

The chapel lay in the northeast corner of the park. Tara nearly jogged in her haste to get there. They passed by a pond, black as ink, and a huge rose garden pruned back for winter, a statue of a war hero, and then another of Sir Walter Scott. The path grew more narrow and the vegetation more wild as they made their way to the oldest section of the park, where a rock face rose out of the soil like a slumbering stone beast.

At the foot of the rock lay the perimeter of a stone building, rising out of the blackberries and broom. Tara ground to a halt.

"Is this it?" Susan puffed.

"It can't be." Disappointed and worried, Tara scanned the tumble of stones. The building was in much worse shape than the chapel at Castle Corbin. How could she leave her precious Psalter in this ruin? It was obvious no one had been here for years, not even the gardeners.

"It's the chapel, all right." Susan pointed at a rusted metal sign near her shoe.

Tara glanced down.

Merristone Chapel, the sign read. 12th century.

"This just can't be right," she murmured. She strolled forward, carefully picking her way through the briars. Hugh had mentioned an altar, a place where men had knelt to receive their knighthoods, and a stone that could be lifted. She squinted, trying to see through the gathering darkness. There at the end of the long building, she thought she spotted the shape of a cross on the far wall.

"This place gives me the creeps," Susan muttered.

"Lots of places here give me the creeps," Tara countered. "It's a magical country, Scotland. Of that, I'm finally convinced."

"I feel like something is watching me."

"Something probably is." Tara no longer doubted that ghosts could linger long after a person died. And who knew how many spirits clung to the stones of a thousand year-old chapel? She stepped over a thick bramble and could now make out the lines of a crucifix carved into the wall. She tried to visualize where the old altar might have stood and where a knight would have knelt.

"It's got to be somewhere around here." Tara paced the stone pavers, which were nearly engulfed by weeds. "Somewhere in front of the cross." She squatted to inspect the ground at a closer vantage point. "Hugh said the stone would be loose."

"After all this time?" Susan snorted. "I kind of doubt it."

Tara sat back on her haunches and gazed at the stones around her. An unmortared stone would look different. The lack of mortar might allow for more vegetation to grow around it than around others. She let her eyes go out of focus and gazed at her surrounds. One patch of green grew darker than the rest, and it was in the dead center of the building.

"There!" Tara cried. She scurried forward on her hands and knees and reached for the stone. She couldn't budge it.

"Do you have anything in your purse?" Tara asked, pulling

desperately at the weeds around the stone. "Maybe we can wedge it up."

Susan dug into her bag and produced a sturdy metal nail file.

"How'd you get this through security?" Tara asked, as Susan handed it to her.

"I didn't. I bought it in Ayr."

"Lucky for us." Tara slipped it between the stones. She pushed on the file, but nothing happened. Pressing her lips together, she moved the file to the other side of the stone, and tried again. Nothing. Susan dug in her purse again and held out a ballpoint pen.

"Try this," she said.

Tara jabbed the pen into the seam at the top of the stone and the file at the bottom. Gritting her teeth, she pushed down, praying that the rock would move, enough to let her know she had guessed right. She felt something shift.

"That's it!" Susan squealed. She dropped to her knees beside Tara and helped her tip the stone upward, and back. It flopped to the ground, revealing a stone chamber beneath it.

"There's your secret chamber," Susan murmured.

Tara gazed down at the hole, which looked as if it had been constructed only days before. Each joint was straight and true, each corner clean and dry, without a single cobweb or dangling root from above. Her Psalter could rest here quite safely. And she could always come back and get it, should Hugh be wrong about his brethren still existing in modern day.

"What else do you have in there?" Tara glanced at Susan's purse. "Have anything I could wrap the Psalter in? I can't just leave it bare to the elements."

Susan bent to her purse once more. "I have a magazine," she ventured, holding it up. "That's the only thing I've got beside my wallet."

"What about a cosmetic bag."

"That would work." Susan unzipped her bag and dumped her lipsticks and accessories into her purse. She handed the empty pouch to her boss.

"Thanks." Carefully, Tara slipped the Psalter into the bag and zipped it. Then she placed the small book in the little chamber. For a moment, she gazed at the Psalter, knowing she might never see it again. It was like saying good-bye to an old and dear friend. But to save Hugh, she would surrender the book willingly now. Swallowing a hard lump that rose in her throat, Tara pulled the heavy paver over the chamber and settled it into place.

"We should go," Susan commented as she rose to her feet. "They're going to lock us in if we don't hurry."

"Wait." Though Tara knew she was about to do something totally unlike her, she felt compelled to sink to her knees, with her kneecaps nearly touching the edge of the altar stone. She clasped her hands together and lowered her head over them. She heard Susan suck in a breath of surprise at such unusual behavior by her boss.

"Dear God," she prayed, closing her eyes. "I have never prayed to You. I have never asked You for anything. But I beg of You now, to help Hugh Lachlan. He is a good man. He is Your devoted servant, and he deserves to live. I know I have often doubted Your existence. I have scoffed at others who have believed in You. But I beg You to forgive my ignorance. And to accept my deepest apology. I pray to You now for the soul of the best man I have ever met, and hope You will deliver him, Lord. I don't care if you smite me down right now, right here, for all the things I have said. But please, please, dear Lord, help Hugh. Amen."

She paused, allowing her words to filter down about the altar stones, and was suddenly too exhausted to move.

"Jesus, Tara," Susan whispered behind her.

Tara and Susan plowed through rush-hour traffic in the suburbs of Edinburgh and arrived back at the hospital at seven o'clock. Tara hurried to the desk in the ICU's waiting area, anxious to hear news of Hugh. No one had called her, and she had a horrible feeling in the pit of her stomach that told her things might be very bad.

The shift must have changed, for a different clerk glanced up at her, a man this time, in his early twenties.

"Hi, I'm Tara Lewis," she said, looking down at his desk blotter.

"Tara Lewis, of *Fact or Fiction*?" The clerk studied her, as if he doubted her claim.

Tara considered what she must look like. She had been up for two days straight, scratched by bushes and stained with dirt and garlic, shot, almost killed in a fire, and hadn't eaten for forty-eight hours. She was a trembling, dirty mess. But for once in her life, she didn't care what she looked like. Her thoughts were centered on Hugh.

"That's me," she replied briskly. "I'm looking for information about a man who was admitted earlier today, a good friend of mine. Hugh Lachlan?"

The clerk checked his computer screen. "Oh," he said. "Someone left a message for you."

"A message?"

The young man shuffled through some papers and pulled out a handwritten note.

"Mr. Lachlan has been transferred to a private clinic."

Surprised, Tara leaned over the counter. "What clinic?"

The clerk shrugged. "It doesn't say."

"By whom?"

"It doesn't say that either." He looked up. "Sorry, Miss Lewis."

"What does it say?"

"That should Mr. Lachlan survive and wish to contact you, you will be notified."

"What?" Tara exclaimed.

She felt Susan come up beside her and stroke her back in support.

"That's all it says, miss." The clerk held up the paper. "Read for yourself."

Tara scanned the handwriting, searching for clues, but the note was as brief as the clerk claimed.

"How could someone just waltz in here and take a patient away?" Tara hit the paper with the back of her fingers. "Without asking permission?"

"Asking permission of who?" the clerk asked. "Mr. Lachlan has no relatives, according to the information in his paperwork."

"What about the attending physician? Can I speak to him?"

The clerk swung around to consult his computer again. "Sorry, but that doctor went off shift about an hour ago. I could have him call you."

Tara stood up straight, outraged at being left powerless and unsure of Hugh's condition. "You're telling me that I have no way of finding out where Mr. Lachlan is? Or that no one can tell me *how* he is?"

"I'm sorry, Miss Lewis." The clerk rose from his chair. "I wish I could tell you more. There's just nothing here." He swept the air in front of his computer monitor.

"This is unheard of! I'm coming back here," Tara said through gritted teeth as she pointed at the clerk. "With a policeman!"

The clerk made a face of helplessness and shrugged.

"Come on, Tara," Susan wrapped her arm around her boss' shoulders. "You need some rest and something to eat. We can deal with this in the morning."

"But Hugh!" Tara couldn't hold back the tears of frustration that scalded her eyes. "What if he dies without me there? I have to be with him. Especially tonight!"

"He's probably in expert hands," Susan crooned, urging her toward the door. “If he was taken to a private clinic.”

“But who would take him away?” Tara countered. “I’ve got to find him!”

Susan dragged her into the chilly Scottish night. As the blast of cold air hit Tara, she suddenly realized who had secreted Hugh away. A secret society. *The brethren.*

Chapter 27

Ayr Estate – November 2009

"Mr. Beck."

Samuel turned at the window of the study, where he'd been staring out at the back lawn. The first snow of the season was falling. He knew he should enjoy the beautiful sight of the big white flakes floating down on his sculptured gardens, outbuildings and park, but all he could think about was how the weather would keep him indoors. Lately, he'd had less and less patience for lounging in the rooms of the manse. He'd spent far too much time here recuperating, and had a restless urge to break out and away.

But where would he go? He had no memory of the world, no inkling of what faces or places held any meaning for him. Even though the medical profession had claimed he'd cheated death, he felt a bit cheated himself. He had a life now, but no life story to go along with it. It was hard to describe how empty that left him.

People called him Samuel Beck, Lord Ayr, but he had no idea what sort of history he'd forged in his thirty-some years. Hell, he didn't even know how old he was for sure. He'd been told that he was a lucky bastard—by not only surviving near fatal injuries, but by qualifying as master of the Ayr estate, an inheritance that had hinged on his DNA matching that of the recently-deceased lord. His had been an astoundingly close match. But he'd inherited only property. No living relatives came with the Ayr Estate—no one to tell him how he mattered in the scheme of things. And that's what seemed to matter to the man they called Samuel Beck.

Samuel had money and prestige now, and servants to do his bidding. Yet he felt a growing restlessness—an urge to seek something out—to finish something left undone that lay far beyond the world he had come to know. If only he knew what that something was.

"Yes?" he finally answered, leveling his gaze on his middle-aged nurse, a man named Colin McKenzie. He was glad to be attended by men, as his restlessness included a great deal of sexual hunger. Lust had awakened within him the moment he had come out of his drug-induced coma. Had his present companions included females, he would have jumped one of them months ago and made a complete ass of himself.

"Time for your pills."

Samuel ambled to the tray Colin held out. Though he was mostly healed and getting stronger every day, he still had to take an array of medications, including anti-rejection pills. So far, however, his new skin was not causing him any trouble. There were still grafts to do on his legs, but only for cosmetic purposes. He popped the pill in his mouth and flushed it down with a long drink of water.

"Mind if I turn on that new television program everyone's talking about?" Colin asked.

"What program?" Samuel's secretary inquired, sweeping into the room. Pudgy Greg Alexander carried a sheaf of papers for him to peruse and sign. Even after six months since inheriting the Ayr property, there were still legal documents that needed attention. Running the household and looking after the land was no small job either. Samuel was grateful his benefactors had supplied Greg and Colin and a host of other household help. He couldn't have managed without them during his months of recuperation. And now that he was ready to take over the reins of the estate, he was reluctant to let any of them go. They were the only family he had.

Colin picked up the remote. "That American program, *Good News*."

"I've heard about it," Greg replied, motioning Samuel toward the desk. "Kind of an odd spin, though. Do people actually like it?"

"I do. I like hearing about the good things happening in the world." Colin cycled through the channels. "It's a refreshing change from all the gloom and doom."

Samuel sat down to look over the documents, and had to smile. Some lord he was. He hadn't given permission to Colin to turn on the television set, but the man had gone ahead anyway, and was now lounging on the sofa. He'd have to sharpen his managerial skills if he wanted to establish his place at the helm of the Ayr Estate.

The sound of an advert droned in the background as Samuel studied the papers before him. Restlessness set in again, and he shifted in the chair, trying to concentrate on his task. He didn't know much about himself, but he was fairly sure that paperwork had never been his strong suit.

A new voice cut short his resolve to concentrate and made him look up. Something in the tenor of the person's voice sliced through him like a sword, going straight to his chest. He knew that voice! It was the first time anything had struck him as even vaguely familiar. Samuel glanced at the television. A female was speaking. Apparently she was the host of the program, and was introducing the upcoming topics. She was an attractive brunette, with shining shoulder-length hair, greenish-brown eyes, and a sad smile that slammed him in the chest a second time.

Samuel rose to his feet, his heart pounding.

"Who is that?" he gasped.

"The news anchor?" Colin glanced over his shoulder.

"Aye."

"I believe her name is Lewis. Something Lewis."

"Tara Lewis?" the secretary inquired, sitting down in a chair beside Colin. He leaned forward. "Didn't she used to be on that other program, *Fact or Fiction*?"

"Yes, but she left it after they won an Emmy for that Scottish ghost segment. The show folded soon after."

"I always liked that show."

Their voices merged into the background as Samuel stared at the television, at the woman's face, and the way she moved her mouth. He knew her! His entire body flushed with joy and relief at the sight of her. He knew a human being in this world! Maybe she could help spark other memories. Maybe she would know what caused the sense of urgency and restlessness that plagued him.

"You should be on this program, sir," Colin commented, turning to look at his patient. "Talk about a stroke of luck—inheriting this place, inheriting millions. You take the cake, Mr. Beck, as far as good news goes."

Samuel nodded. He glanced at his secretary. "Could it be arranged?" It was his first official request as Lord Ayr.

Greg Alexander's eyebrows rose in surprise. "I suppose I could make a few calls."

"Do so, then." Samuel stood behind the sofa, his attention fixed upon the woman on the television. He watched the entire program without saying another word. And when it drew to a close, Colin held up his hand.

"Okay, listen, now, this is the curious part, when she signs off. No one can make sense of it, and she won't talk about it to the press."

Samuel waited for the last few seconds of the program and was sad to see it end. He must remember to ask Colin to record the program the next time, so he could watch it as many times as he liked and use it to jog his memory.

"Okay, here it comes," Colin commented, still holding up a finger.

The camera zoomed in on the news anchor's face.

"And that's it for *Good News* of the day. Good night everyone," she said. Her gaze stared out at the world. It seemed to Samuel that she looked directly at him. He felt the nerve endings of his new skin tingling, felt himself holding his breath. "And good night, Hugh."

Samuel felt goose pimples race down his back.

"How weird is that?" Colin asked. "She says it every time!"

"She obviously has a secret friend," Greg Alexander replied. "And to my mind, it's rather juvenile to do something like that." He rose from the chair. "Did you have a chance to look over those papers, Mr. Beck?"

Samuel dragged his consciousness back to the present. He glanced at his secretary, trying to recall what the man had just asked of him.

"No," he replied. "I was detained by—"

He broke off, unable to complete the sentence.

Detained. The word hung in the air like a signpost of a pub swaying in the breeze. There was something significant about that word. But what?

"Are you all right, sir?"

Samuel blinked and glanced down at his secretary. "I'm fine. Just— " He broke off again. "What was that woman's name again?"

"Tara Lewis."

Tara. Warmth burgeoned inside him at the sound of the name. He felt a new awareness settling around him. A subtle shift had just occurred. Tara Lewis' voice had sparked something deep within him and opened a gate to a part of him that had been closed since the coma. Samuel strode for the door.

"Mr. Beck?" the secretary sputtered, trailing after him.

"I'm goin' ridin'," Samuel barked over his shoulder. He had to be alone. He had to be out in the fresh air, in the snow, and under the same sky as that woman in America. He was going to remember her, he was sure of it. He was going to remember who he was.

December 15, 2009

Tara stood in the foyer of the Beck House as she took off her long wool coat and gave it to the butler. Susan echoed her movements, and handed over her shorter down-filled jacket with the faux fur collar. Outside, the crew unloaded their gear from their truck.

"Seems kind of like déjà vu, doesn't it?" Susan said near Tara's ear.

"Yes." Tara smiled at the butler but felt nowhere near as jaunty as the outward expression she conveyed. Being back in Scotland, back in Ayrshire especially, brought back many memories—most of them sad. It might have been better if Hugh had died in her arms, for then she would have known his fate for certain, instead of living a life of limbo, always part of her waiting to turn around and see him. Her mind told her that she was a fool to let her past haunt her again, but her heart refused to give up hope that Hugh might still be alive.

She glanced around the main hall of the house. Corbin Hall had been built in the Georgian era with light and airy rooms painted in pastel colors. This house was much older, probably built during the reign of Henry VIII, and was full of heavy wood paneling, huge oil paintings, bulky furniture and dark drapery. A man's house.

"This way, if you please," the butler said, turning for a side hall. "Lord Ayr will see you in the study."

They turned to follow the servant, but he held up his hand. "Excuse me, Miss Fritch, but Lord Ayr asked to speak to Miss Lewis privately for a moment. Please wait here, and I shall be right back."

Tara exchanged a puzzled look with her assistant, and then followed the butler. She wondered what kind of person Lord Ayr was. Because of the short notice she'd been given for the assignment, she hadn't been able to find out anything about the man himself, other than he was a victim of amnesia discovered to be connected to an ancient family.

Tara walked forward, not happy about going into the interview blind or being rushed into a job. The whole trip had been rushed, in fact. Lord Ayr seemed anxious to tell his tale to the world, and had paid premium prices to get her to Scotland before Christmas. She doubted his story would be interesting, not if the man couldn't remember his past. Half the story would be missing right there. No, this was likely going to be an essay in narcissism focused on a newly-minted millionaire who wanted to see himself on television. She would make quick work of it and get back to the States in time for the holidays.

But really, what was the rush? She had a few prospects for Christmas and New Years, but no functions she really cared to attend. Christmas had always been tough for her, knowing she had no family to share it with. If she were honest with herself—and she truly tried to be lately—there was no good reason to hurry back.

Tara was still thinking about her Christmas Eve options when the butler opened the study door and announced her. She took in the room before her and the two men who occupied it: a small pudgy man standing by the massive desk and another one sitting in the chair at the blotter. At her entrance, the man in the chair slowly rose. Tara was startled to see how tall he was and how achingly familiar his figure seemed. Then she looked at his face.

At that moment, all thoughts of Christmas vanished. Tara couldn't believe her eyes as she watched the man walk forward. She stood in the doorway, rooted to the parquet floor.

It was Hugh. But it was not Hugh. This Hugh didn't have a scar running up the side of his face and through his eyebrow. This Hugh didn't have shaggy black hair and old-fashioned suede boots. The man before her was a polished, well-groomed gentleman dressed in wool slacks, a crisp cotton shirt, and a navy blazer. He looked as if he were a charming spy who had just stepped out of an action adventure movie.

"Miss Lewis." Lord Ayr stopped a few paces from her and looked down. "Thank you for comin'."

He might have acquired the trappings of the modern world, but the deep Scottish burr lingered on his tongue, and the steady, serious look in his eye was achingly, gloriously familiar.

"Hugh!" she gasped. Her heart turned a cartwheel in her chest. She had reconciled herself to the fact that she would never see her knight in shining armor again, but here he was, still alive and still so handsome he made her heart flutter.

"Hugh?" the pudgy man asked, coming closer to stare at his companion.

"My name is Hugh." Lord Ayr repeated with a broad smile, as he rolled the name on his tongue. "Hugh."

"Not *the* Hugh!" the pudgy man glanced at Tara and then back at his master. "From your program?"

"Yes. Hugh! Hugh Lachlan!" She beamed, drinking in his face and figure. He appeared to be completely restored and thoroughly at ease in the modern world. Her heart burst with joy. "You're alive!"

"I am, thanks to my benefactors."

"I looked everywhere for you! For months!" She touched his chest, making sure that he was as solid as he looked. "Why didn't you contact me sooner?"

"I only just discovered that I knew you." He slipped his hand over hers. He was as warm as ever. Tara swayed toward him, longing for more.

"Oh, Hugh!" she cried, still not believing he was standing in front of her.

"One of my nurses likes your program," Hugh continued. "And had it on a few weeks ago. When I saw your face, I knew that I—"

She cut off his chatter by reaching up to his new cheek, unable to stand another moment without caressing him there. He broke off and smiled down at her. Just as before, the smile transformed him, making him seem younger and completely focused upon her. Tara felt herself melting.

"I thought I'd never see you again!" she exclaimed. "Oh, Hugh! Where have you been?"

"In a coma."

"But alive!" She flung her arms around his neck and stood on tiptoe to embrace him. "Alive!"

His arms came around her and pulled her close, nearly off the floor. He still smelled like the old Hugh, full of sun and spice. She took a deep breath of him as she hugged him with all her strength. Her heart soared with happiness.

After a moment, Hugh pulled back, smiling widely, but holding her elbows to keep her close. "Dinna take this wrong, lass, but I brought ye here on false pretenses."

She looked up at him. "Oh?"

"I will do your program, if ye wish. But I would like t' employ you for a time as well."

"Employ me?" she drew back, not sure what he intended.

"T' help me remember." His dancing expression sobered. "I have a feeling you are the key t' remembering my past."

Tara paused, and the joy in her heart clouded. "Sometimes our pasts are better left in the past, once they are fully realized."

Hugh's brows came together. "So 'tis not a happy tale?"

She shook her head and gazed up at him. "Only the part where you kissed me and told me that I tempted you."

The pudgy man rolled his eyes. "I believe this is where I excuse myself," he said, briskly walking out of the study.

Hugh chuckled and settled her comfortably against his frame by linking his hands around her waist. "So you tempted me, did you, Miss Lewis?"

"Yes. And you nearly cracked, I'll have you know."

"I can't imagine that I resisted. Was there some restriction on my affections?"

"Yes, but that's all over." Tara stroked his cheek again. "You earned this new life, Hugh. And that's all I'm going to tell you."

"Perhaps in time, I will recall these things for myself." He leaned down. "But until then, perhaps a kiss might jog my memory."

Tara grinned back at him, reveling in the heat flooding from his eyes. His warm, firm lips sank toward hers. She rose on tiptoes to meet his mouth, and the world fell away as he swept her up and kissed her. She'd never been happier than this moment, standing in the arms of the man she cherished—free at last to love him for the rest of her life. As he kissed her, the scars that had bound her heart slowly dissolved and the past faded into the mist where it belonged. Hugh stroked her with reverence, and then with gentle urgency and a long sigh of homecoming, as his body awakened to her memory.

When the kiss finally ended, Hugh gazed down at her, his eyes brimming with love. "Ah, Tara," he breathed. "I could never forget ye, love. Though Fate did her best to part us."

She ran a finger over his newly-healed eyebrow. "And I could never forget you, Hugh. Not one day went by that I didn't long to see you again."

"Perhaps we should continue the kiss, then." He brushed her lower lip with the pad of his thumb as his gaze lowered to her mouth. "Until I remember all."

"What about the interview?"

"It can wait. Now that I have ye, I dinna wish to release ye just yet." He urged her closer, and she gladly pressed into him.

"Fair enough." Tara's heart did another cartwheel. "Because I never released you, Sir Hugh. And I never will."

ACKNOWLEDGEMENTS

I would like to give my sincere thanks to those people who answered my research questions willingly and fully during the writing of this book. T. Robin Hirsh helped explain the ins and outs of filming onsite in an old castle. Thank you, Robin! And my friend, Donna Rydberg, MSN, RN, CWOCN, who teaches Wound and Ostomy Management courses at the University of Washington, suggested ways I could make the burn sequence better. Donna, keep up the great work you do.

I would also like to thank each and every one of the museum and park docents who cheerfully answered my questions about their castles and displays during my latest trip to the UK and Germany. My thanks to the Bavarian guard who insisted that I take the long tour in his museum ("Someone like you should never take the short tour!") And my gratitude to the crew of HGTV's My House is Worth What, who recently did a show at my home in California, and inspired me to write a book about a television host.

Printed in the United States
148162LV00001B/33/P

9 780982 344248